"It feels good in your arms..."

Gurth unwound her   l and buried his face and hands in the abundance of Gerlaine's hair. "Yes." She was tiny, only halfway up his chest, and her lips against his skin went through him like hot needles.

"You don't hate me? You said you'd never hate me."

"No. God, no."

His hands slid down her back, hesitated and stopped. Gerlaine felt him shaking. His fingers laced again in her hair, pulling her mouth up to his . . .

A MEMORY OF LIONS

PARKE GODWIN

BERKLEY BOOKS, NEW YORK

A MEMORY OF LIONS

A Berkley Book/published by arrangement with
the author

PRINTING HISTORY
Popular Library edition/November 1976
Revised Berkley edition/February 1983

ISBN: 0-425-05824-7

A BERKLEY BOOK ® TM 757, 375
Berkley Books are published by Berkley Publishing Corporation,
200 Madison Avenue, New York, New York 10016.
The name "BERKLEY" and the stylized "B" with design are trademarks
belonging to Berkley Publishing Corporation.
PRINTED IN THE UNITED STATES OF AMERICA

"Every man must have a lord."

This is the story of Gerlaine de Neuville and Gurth Brandson, Norman girl and Englishman. Love stories need no explanation, though a few facts may help the reader understand the mind of the eleventh century.

The Normans conquered England in 1066. They brought an iron feudalism backed by a military aristocracy to a country much more socially complex than their own, a people they understood not at all. When Gerlaine tells Gurth that "every man must have a lord," she voices a feudal belief as unquestioned as the Bill of Rights to Americans.

The English, more loosely organized and backward in many ways, still had the crude beginnings of a parliament, county courts, trial by jury of peers and a precise scale of rights and personal value (reckoned in cash) for every man. Their women could inherit property in their own right.

In Gurth's world a man could rise; in Gerlaine's, he or she was fixed by birth. This vast difference of mind is the background of *A Memory of Lions*.

Imagine the United States conquered by Communist China. Think of yourself, not rich but owning what you earned and knowing considerable liberty within a framework of law and duty. Suddenly you're told by a commissar (through an interpreter) to forget all that. The Party will take care of you. The Party is pledged to your welfare, but you own nothing. Your idea of personal property is corrupt and unrealistic. If you try to escape or even walk on the commissar's grass, they can by the new laws torture or kill you.

Most Americans wouldn't understand the alien system, but they'd have no choice. Conversely, the commissar would be exasperated by reactionary dolts who resisted the proven logic of communism. Too bad. They'd just have to learn.

On an autumn day in 1066, this is what happened to the English way of life. They were just as confused as you would be and just as resistant. And the commissars were equally exasperated and determined.

—P. G.

A MEMORY
OF LIONS

BOOK ONE:

Bound Loki

Northern England – A.D. 1073

I

"It is like a caught wolf, this north land," Père Vaudan said once. "You can teach it the house but it will always remember the forest."

That didn't bother Gerlaine de Neuville. What mattered to her Norman practicality was that it was *theirs*, won at Hastings by her father and her brother Hugh, and this new-created barony of Montford was their share of England. On the hillside now with big, mute Bête beside her, Gerlaine breathed the cool air of her first English summer.

She resembled her father more than anyone else: small, practical, faithful, durable as catgut and, by Parisian or Roman standards, not terribly civilized. She was country-bred and loved the gamble of their new life in a new land. It drew her from the first. Like Gurth Bastard it was *there* with a silent challenge that could not be ignored. The loneliness of the moor was unsettling as it rolled away on three sides in dusty yellow and black. On the other the black forest stretched to the horizon. The wind was never still, and the silence brooded under it as if no sound but that low, incessant keening had ever disturbed it. A sudden bird cry might rend earth and white sky like a knife through fabric.

They'd lazed long enough for her restless blood. Gerlaine rose and fastened her cloak by its silver brooch. Bête squatted

3

near the horses, wind-loosened strands of yellow hair hanging over gentle, vacant blue eyes, most of his brutish face overgrown with dull yellow beard. Gerlaine would have shaved him if he allowed it. Bête would tolerate an occasional bath at her hand—no other—but no one could touch him with a razor. He feared it.

Bête shifted his huge body as Gerlaine rose. He could never stand straight for very long. Both legs had been too badly broken. His habitual posture was that of a seated dog, knotty-muscled shoulders forward, weight resting on callused hands. Bête had a tongue but couldn't speak. Père Vaudan found him the winter her father marched north with King William, in the gutted Saxon church, ragged and frozen and too witless to build himself a fire. The priest had found dozens like Bête, reminders of the king's vengeance on Saxon rebellion.

Perhaps Bête should have died. It seemed too much misery; God had probably created him with less mind than other men, but the whitish furrow across his skull traced the sword stroke that had cut out the rest. But Bête lived, tough as blighted oak and mild as a housecat. He might have been younger or older than Gerlaine, there was no telling. He was simply her Bête. From the day she playfully wreathed his shaggy head with heather flowers, he was Gerlaine's shadow, mastiff and protector. He sensed her moods like a loyal pet, by the tone of voice, happy with little attentions or sulking if she neglected him too long. As his head lifted to her now, she smiled.

"*Hé, Bête. À cheval.* We ride."

For her it was a day to feel glorious and new, to ride as high as heaven and far as fancy with no one to chide her for leaving her veil at home or not riding like a lady. Like all her family, she was born in a saddle.

She pointed to the southwest: "*Suivez*, Bête!"

She knew where they would go today. She was curious; the week before, she and Bête had come upon Gurth Bastard sitting one of the manor horses at the top of a rise. Gerlaine knew him then only as her father's clerk and interpreter for the sparse local population. The young peasant was motionless in the saddle, looking at something far away, and barely acknowledged her. It was a puzzling slight; normally Gurth was more than attentive to her. Gerlaine was sure he sought her out many times on one pretext or another, and she rather liked it. There was a detached quality about him that piqued her curiosity.

She saw what he studied: the last hill before the forest, a crescent of oaks half circling a dark smudge on the earth. She'd seen others like it, remains of farmsteads like littered bones from York to the Roman Wall, a testament to her father's zeal. The ruin among the trees was very large.

"What was that place, *Maître* Gurth?"

Before answering, Gurth reined close to Bête and carefully brushed the thistles from the mute's dirty sheepskin vest, pushing the hair back from the brown face.

"You should keep him combed, *demoiselle*. He'd like that."

"Hard enough to wash him, let alone getting a comb in that hair."

Bête seemed pleased with Gurth's attention. His huge hand went out to brush at imaginary burrs in Gurth's dark hair and wool tunic. Gurth spoke softly.

"*Hoch*, Bête."

"Does he understand, *Maître* Gurth?"

"Who knows what he understands? He knows I'm a friend."

Gerlaine pointed. "What holding was that yonder?"

"What Montford is now." He spoke French well. The accent was Île-de-France, not Normandy. Tall and thick through the chest and shoulders, Gurth's Saxon blood was obvious but very likely mixed with Scot and Dane. Like Calla, his mother, he had the gray eyes and olive skin often found in these northern parts.

Gerlaine knew nothing of English language or customs. She regretted it around Gurth. There was something quietly superior about him, as if he were judging her. But she remembered a name mentioned often at Montford.

"Ulfson? Brand Ulfson. He was the *seigneur*?"

"He was thane," Gurth said. He wheeled his arm in a circle about the horizon. "For five hundred years, all you see was ruled from that hall. They fought the Scots, the Danes, even their own earls sometimes. When Paulinus brought Christ, they fought that too."

Gerlaine laughed. "How did they fare against God? Surely no better than Jericho."

"Not a conquest. More like a truce." Gurth inclined his head

to her respectfully and started his horse away toward Montford. "They called it Brandeshal. With the baron's permission,
I'll take you there sometime."

And now she and Bête sat their mounts in the shadow of one
of the circling oaks and looked in silence at what had been
Brandeshal.

You could see the trenched rectangle in the ground where
the stockade timbers had been pulled, and the ox trail leading
northwest to Montford. The timbers were seasoned and solid,
no reason to waste them. One by one, they were pulled like
teeth, carted, winched erect and sunk into place around the
new keep.

Gerlaine touched her heels to the mare's flank and began to
skirt the crescent of oaks. Almost every one of them had been
defaced with ax blades, but here and there, as on the salvaged
timbers, were partial remains of carvings. When he found
them on the logs, Père Vaudan had them seared out with hot
iron and sprinkled with holy water. They all seemed the same,
a crude figure holding a horn in one hand. From the remnants
here, she was sure these were identical.

Within the rectangular trench was a smaller rough square on
the earth formed by flat, broken stones and raised on earth-
work. The cracked rubble of several hearths remained as well
as a long stone step at what must have been the entrance to the
hall, and there were slivers of timber here and there, but
nothing had been left upright in the house. The place must
have been large, more spacious at its base than her father's new
keep.

The treetops moved heavily. Without actually thinking of it,
Gerlaine became aware of the silence under the wind. It was
cold, that wind. Even in summer it bore an edge. She
dismounted and drew her cloak around her. Bête slid spider-
fashion out of his saddle, squatted, and took the bridle reins
Gerlaine passed to him.

Smaller brown patches within the rectangle evidenced a
number of sheds: a stable, several outbuildings and a smithy.
The forge and bellows still looked workable.

There had been a chapel too, though its stone now lay under
the foundations of Montford. All that remained here was the
brown square of packed earth over which grass and gorse were

creeping again. At the north end of the bare patch stood the
only erect piece of masonry on the hill, a large cross of the
British kind, the points encircled. King William did not spare
churches in his march, but no Christian would deface a cross.
Further away, on a dark square so small it could only have
been a sort of shed, hulked a weathered dais of split timbers,
and beside it the sundered remains of four wooden figures.

The destruction of the hall had all the marks of methodical
thoroughness, but the ruin of this pagan altar was the work of
savage wrath. The figures were barely recognizable as such.
Here lay a wooden arm clutching a bronze horn, battered and
green with age, similar to the stockade carvings. Beyond that a
head, the face mangled into splinters. One of the most curious
fragments was a strangely elongated, only partly human trunk
wrapped about in a rusting iron chain. From the position of the
hacked bas-relief arms, held behind the back, the figure
appeared to represent a being in bondage.

Strangest of all, thrust through the chain and clasped to the
maimed trunk were two long bars of iron plaited in the manner
of a woman's hair. The chain was rusted and the carved figure
rotting, but the plaited iron was clean and black. It glistened
slightly. Gerlaine ran a finger over the twisted surface: it had
been greased carefully not too many days past.

Nearby lay a faceless hunk of woodwork that should be the
head, distorted as the trunk. With a shock Gerlaine saw that it
was horned.

The intake of her breath was sharp enough to reach Bête.
His head came up, questioning. Then there was another sound.

"The one bound is Loki."

The tall woman advanced without haste, a reed basket on
one arm, the wind parting her worn wool cloak in front to
reveal the rough deerhide smock beneath. Gerlaine had never
seen Gurth's mother at close quarters. Calla was shy of the
keep as were most of the other country people. She was a
striking dame, her black hair caught in a bronze ring at the
back of a graceful, unlined neck and winged with gray that
grew from the temples to the waist-length ends. She had, too,
that peculiar olive coloring that made her son a more disturbing
figure than Gerlaine was prepared to admit.

Calla's smock was belted with woven rawhide around a
waist and hips almost as slender as her own. *Fortunate*,

Gerlaine noted, *for a woman who's had children*. Calla was a handsome woman. As a young girl, she might have commanded the favor of a king.

"Good day, mistress."

Gerlaine shivered a little, not merely from the wind. The woman's eyes looking through her were merciless, calm and sure.

"Calla, isn't it? What brings you here?"

"The gathering of the herbs. Needfuls for the harvest."

Vaudan spoke against this woman frequently. Calla was never seen at mass or vespers, but Gurth said the harvesters would neither begin nor end the barley gathering without Calla, whom they called Corn-Woman.

Now Gerlaine felt those gray eyes fixed on her. It was by far the strongest face she'd ever looked on, strength tempered with a great deal of sadness and perhaps the remains of fire.

"Will you do me a kindness, mistress?" Her halting French, learned from Gurth, was thickened with a burr and difficult to understand. "Tell my son he's needed home. The sheepcote needs mending if he'd not feed our mutton to wolves this winter."

"I—I will tell him," Gerlaine stammered.

The stern mouth softened. "Gurth said you were fair." Calla touched the girl's red hair under the open gold-work headdress; the long brown fingers traced Gerlaine's cheek, feeling the wind-roughened skin. "The wind's been at you. That's tender skin for this place. You won't last the winter, girl."

Not the familiarity but the sudden, unreasoning fear of this dark woman made Gerlaine flinch away. Bête hunched closer. His vacant smile became a grimace of bared teeth.

Calla read her instinct. "No harm, mistress. But you've felt no real cold yet. When your cooks roast pig, do you take the grease and rub it into your face and lips."

Calla moved closer to the girl as if to say something else. Again Gerlaine stepped back involuntarily; as she did, a slight movement made Calla turn her head. Bête was poised, weight forward, ready to spring. His intent was clear. Bête sensed his mistress' fear like a dog and coiled ready to launch himself at its object. "Tell him I mean no harm."

"He wouldn't understand," said Gerlaine, trying to fathom her own feelings. She felt herself in the presence of something

—not necessarily evil, but strong enough to snap her soul like a dry twig at its will or pleasure. Her lips moved, forming the Ave Maria: Pray for us now in our time of need. . . .

A cloud sheathed the sun like dirty fleece.

"What do you call him, mistress?"

"My father's people call him Bête."

"What is that?"

"It means—" The word stuck in Gerlaine's throat. She'd said it a thousand times and never realized till now how wrong it was for him. Unable to speak, barely able to think, he was still much more than this word to her, and she loved him. "It means a beast—an animal."

"Aye," Calla returned Bête's dull stare calmly. "And a thousand like him under the ground. Poor bastard." She inclined her head to the ruined carvings. "You were looking at them. Do you ken who they are?"

"Our priest says they are devils."

A hint of humor played around the woman's mouth. "I know what the Christ-man says. These gods are not evil, girl, just . . . other. Older. There, what's left of him: Woden, the war god. He kept justice, wisdom: man-things. And there—Freyr to bring children and good crops. Him with the horn: Heimdall, the guarder of gates, the watcher who warns against evil."

"And that?" Gerlaine pointed to the chained trunk and horned head. "That is not evil, not Satan's image?"

Calla shook her head. "Only Loki, the Bound One. He betrayed the gods and was cast out in bondage. They buried him at the roots of the World Tree. Part evil, yes—and part good. Like most men. And beautiful, they tell."

"So was Satan," Gerlaine said. "Most fair in the sight of God before he fell."

Calla looked at the girl with something like tenderness mixed with pity. "You're still green, girl. You've not yet found anything in life—or lost it." She turned her back on the girl. "Do you not bleat like a lamb about evil until you know its face."

Gerlaine would have snapped back at the disrespect, but in an instant the cold edge was gone from Calla's voice. "Be still, child," she said as if soothing one of her own. "I've things to do."

She took a small leather pouch from her reed basket and

crouched beside the trunk of Loki. Thrusting two fingers into the pouch, she extracted a small gob of grease. Meticulously, taking care to cover every inch, Corn-Woman applied the ointment to the plaited black iron bars.

Whether all this was evil or not, she didn't know, but it frightened Gerlaine. She was young, eighteen and alive. She knew that air was good to breathe, food good to her hunger, sleep a pleasure to her hard, healthy body and all of these warm, known things lay in the hand of God, with the Church as His fingers. This place was *other.* Calla's word said it all. It was *other,* and in the middle of Christian land, Montford land.

"This is heathen, what you are doing." She tried to muster as much authority as possible against the Corn-Woman's strength. "My father will burn what is left here—"

"No!" Calla raised herself and came toward Gerlaine. "Your father has all of Tees. This is mine."

Gerlaine stepped back. "Witch, if you hurt me, Bête will kill you."

"Will he, now?" The low, soothing laughter rolled like music from her lips. "Watch."

With slow, deliberate movements, Calla knelt before Bête. "Poor creature," she crooned, "I'd do you no harm. See? I'll build you a house out of air, and no one, not even mistress, can find you. Watch me, Bête."

Slowly, Calla raised her long forefinger till it bisected their locked glances. Then the finger descended; Bête's vacant gaze followed it till it touched the earth. For the space of a heartbeat the finger was motionless, then Calla drew a straight line away from Bête toward herself. "A house out of air, and this is the only gate . . . be you Heimdall, and this . . . the Rainbow Bridge to Asgard. You must watch this line, Bête." Her voice rose and fell, lulled and caressed him. "Watch this line."

Again they were motionless. Gerlaine felt the hair rising on her arms. Bête remained with his head bent over the line in the dirt, barely breathing.

Calla took up a small stone. Unhurriedly, she began to trace a circle in the earth around Bête, speaking softly to him all the while. Gerlaine could not understand the words, but they seemed full of affection and security, like a mother whispering to a child at her breast. Now and then soft laughter rose like music under the words.

The circle was completed. Corn-Woman crouched again in front of Bête, whose eyes had not left the line.

"A house out of air, strong as a stone *broch*, and Bête's safe inside. Warm and safe. Room enough for Bête alone, and not even mistress can find you . . . safe." The last word was no more than a whisper.

Calla straightened herself, laying her brown hand on the shaggy head. "Call him, mistress."

The girl's throat was dry. Her tongue moved like a stranger against the roof of her mouth. "Bête . . . Bête?"

He did not move.

"Come, Bête: *home!*" Her own voice was unnaturally loud against the silence.

"I've not hurt him." Calla retrieved her bag of ointment and continued her work on the plaited iron as if there had been no interruption of any consequence. "Nor will he hurt me."

The pallid sun slid out of the clouds again. As she worked, Calla talked casually to the girl, a mother telling tales to her own over the making of soup.

"Do you ken the word 'witch' in my tongue, girl? It means only 'one who knows.' Just as the men who made laws under our kings were called the *Witan*."

Her fingers spread and poked the grease into the smallest crevices of the twisted bars.

"You're a baron's bairn, well brought up. I'd guess you've never known a man. A girl ignorant of good shouldn't prate of evil. I'll tell you what evil is: it's all good things gone sour. Evil is a woman who can't love, with ice and false pride like cold porridge in her veins instead of blood. Evil is a man locked in that cold till he goes brittle and breaks and still has to be a man."

Under the soft siren voice, Gerlaine's fear drained away. Bête had not stirred nor had she; the need to move, to run away was gone with her fear. No world existed beyond the lulling words and the low, incessant wind.

"Evil is what happens to a man when he finds warmth and has to deny it and live in the cold for man reasons like duty. Evil is . . . years made out of alone that might have been together. It's growing oak broken off and gone dry, good milk gone sour. All the good things that want to move, ride, run, laugh, bear children, rest—turned back on themselves to grow in the dark into something ugly. That's what evil is, mistress."

She wiped her hands on the hem of her smock. "This bit of grease is for a man, not a devil. They called him one; well"—her mind seemed to brush the edge of memory—"he was when he drank, he was *bear-sark*. But he was a man, and I remember him with this as you'd say Latin or leave flowers."

Calla rose and moved toward them. *She walks like Gurth*, the girl thought. *Straight as a lance and swaying from the shoulders. It must be their height that makes it so.*

"You should leave now," the Corn-Woman said. "Take the creature and go."

Gerlaine had never doubted the palpable existence of witches, though she'd never seen one. But it was strange. After the first few minutes, there was no fear of this captivating woman. Was she a witch, Gurth's mother? The things she spoke were sad, not evil, and of common concern and understanding to women. But behind this . . .

No; it was clear what she said. She spoke of the thane, and she must have been one of his pleasures. If she loved him once and still remembered, that was woman, not witchcraft. God knows, there must be little else for a woman without a husband and still young enough to need one.

She would not tell her father. But in the matter of Bête . . .

"What have you done to him?"

Calla held the stirrup for her. "Nothing. I gave him rest." She boosted Gerlaine into the saddle with ease and looked down at the still frozen Bête. "It must be dark where he is: all the candles blown out and him stumbling about in the black to find a door, something he knows. I gave him a little rest."

Calla approached Bête's horse—downwind, so the animal would not shy. She stroked the animal's ears and passed the hanging bridle over its head, then went to kneel once more before Bête. Her stern mouth moved silently and her whole face softened into tenderness. Her arms slid around his neck and she kissed him.

This woman, Gerlaine realized with a pang of envy, could enchant any man she wanted with no other sorcery than herself.

"You can call him now, mistress."

"He will hear me?"

"For sure; he only rested. Call him."

"Bête," the girl assayed. "*À cheval*, Bête."

He stirred; his whole frame heaved gently, breathing deep as in waking. He saw the Corn-Woman's face close to his, and his twilit mind remembered danger. His muscles bunched and he reared away from the unknown. Gerlaine thought he might attack the woman. Then, as quickly as he had recoiled, Bête relaxed. With a little shaking of his head, he appeared to have forgotten any sense of threat. Instinctively he searched now for what he knew and found it. Seeing Gerlaine mounted, he thrust up, grasped the saddle horn, then stopped in mid-motion, crouching half-erect like a baffled hound confronted by a sound or smell with no source. He looked at Calla. His lips moved tentatively under the dirty beard.

"All right, Bête," Gerlaine soothed. "It is all right. Up. Up, *ma Bête*."

The high, sweet voice was known safety. He vaulted the gelding's back and gathered up the reins.

"So this was Brandeshal." Gerlaine gazed around her. The ruin was ugly, cold. Even in its pride, it was impossible to conceive of love or warmth in this place.

"It *is* Brandeshal," said Calla. "This house is not dead, mistress. The Christ-men tried to kill it and failed, and wrote their curses in a silly book. A house is spirit, not stones. Old Anfric knew it and Father Vaudan, too. Do you tell him to read it to you one day," she directed, then added with pride and malicious humor: "Or Gurth, if the wee Norman's not up to the big words. My son's a scholar." She raised her hand in farewell. "Give you good day."

The alien dreariness of Brandeshal, the summer day that held no summer as she knew it, the cryptic, brooding strength of the Corn-Woman—all gathered in around Gerlaine. She ached for home and live things.

Damn—she seldom swore, even to herself, but it was unnerving to find all in one day things both stronger than herself and beyond her understanding, like feeling for a wall that should be there and wasn't, no step underfoot where one has been always. Some part of her boundaries were gone. *The place smells of hate.*

"Come, Bête—home!"

Gerlaine jerked the horse about with more than necessary force for the well-trained horse, and spurred the startled animal to a gallop. Bête plunged after her.

Corn-Woman watched them ride.

II

Against the ancient hills, Montford keep appeared presumptuous and temporary. Two hundred serfs had trudged north to gouge out the great circling trench and cart the fill dirt to build the central mound from which the raw oak tower rose four levels high, dwarfing the older outbuildings that housed the force, the horses, fowl, sheep, cattle, men-at-arms, the steward's low house—all the tight, organized bustle, surge and thrusting energy that had enabled a ragtag rabble of twenty thousand shirttail vavasors, many landless and most in debt, to conquer England in one pitched battle. Wherever they swarmed, the square towers rose on the mounds.

Gerlaine loved it all, the newness, the promise, the place found at last to match their drive. From the last rise before the gentle dip to the river plain, she rested her horse and drank in the scurrying, shouting life below her, hungry for it after the gloom of Brandeshal.

She squinted in the white glare, trying to discern those she knew. The moat would most like be finished today. The great wooden gate would open to let in the river like a great snake around Montford. Once the moat was filled, the water and the inner stockade would render the keep impregnable. Nor hell nor Saxons—about the same, the baron judged—would prevail against it.

Men filled the ditch, but they appeared to be idle and waiting. A few soldiers lounged on the moat banks. Others passed back and forth, busy at the forge, the stables, or coming and going at the entrance to the keep. On the inner bank of the moat ditch, below the stockade gate, a covered pavilion had been set up. The figures beneath were tiny but she made out Eustace and her mother Élène and next to them, a bright yellow bliaut belted over his dun tunic and trousers, the slim figure of her older brother, Hugh.

"Look, Bête: it must be almost ready. Father has a pavilion. They've come out to see."

Her eyes roved now along the trench filled with ant-workers until they found Gurth. There he was near the sluice gate, his long body lounging easily against a stack of logs. Beside him, naked to the waist, was Godric the master carpenter. As usual Godric looked angry, marking his speech with wide, vehement motions of his arm, and though she couldn't bear, Gerlaine knew he was cursing. The man was a hothead, respectful to Gurth but few others. Until Godric came to shore up the moat sides and build the sluice gate, she had never heard the Deity's name so often or so artfully linked with what, by the sheer, thumping virulence of its sound could only be the most incredible profanity this side Aquitaine. As a lady—and especially in Gurth's presence—she now and then found her ignorance of the language delicately convenient.

Now she perceived the small figure in rusty black that bustled out to Gurth from the pavilion. Père Vaudan pointed emphatically at the sluice gate and wagged his head furiously in denial of something. Whatever, it brought another violent reaction from Godric. The hairy giant whirled away from Vaudan in disgust, pounded out three or four heavy strides, turned, and wheeled his arms in exasperation. Gerlaine saw Gurth move to the priest, his shoulders heaving with mirth, while at the perimeter of the melee, like minnows around fighting trout, two boys in short red tunics wheeled their horses in gleeful excitement. Now one of them looked up toward the spot where she and Bête stood their mounts, shouted something to his companion, and the two of them plunged into the dry moat ditch, bolted across and up the near side toward her.

Her brothers rode like centaurs, part of the horse, taught from toddling to control the animal with their legs toward the day when lance and shield would occupy their hands. Often their coltish energy drove Gerlaine to distraction, but not today. She watched them come, anticipating the warmth of their endless esthusiasm: her baby brothers: Guy the older, and Robert—Robin he was to them— only fifteen and already able to break anything on four legs without a saddle. *We may not grow tall, Gurth, but no one rides like the Normandy men*.

They charged up the rise, shouting welcome, whirling about her with their news.

"Sister—"

"Gerlaine—"

"Eh, Bête!"

"Almost done! Father has a pavilion and there's wine from home."

"—and *Maman* will give the signal!"

"*Pardi*, you should hear the master carpenter—"

"Spitting nails!"

"Wait!" Gerlaine hugged them from the saddle, ruffling their short-clipped hair. "I saw, I saw, you monsters. What's the matter?"

"Well," Guy began, "everything was ready—"

"And sure enough," Robin bubbled over, "Vaudan finds another of those devil signs on one of the gate timbers they took from the old place."

"But Gurth Bastard says it's not the devil, just something called Loki—"

"And Vaudan says back they're the same thing," Robin took it up, laughingly short of breath. "And Godric starts to boil because a gate's a gate, he doesn't give a damn if it sprouts *lilies*!"

"And *then*—" Guy pounded Bête's wide back in rough greeting: "Eh, Bête—*ça va!*—and then Vaudan says it's got to be purified before they open the gate." Guy slapped his thigh. "Did the carpenter lose his temper, Robin?"

"Not much, not much. Gurth said he told Vaudan—"

"No, no. Stop." Guy held up a mock-formal protesting hand. "Our sister's a lady. In truth, we cannot."

"Oh, stuff! What did he say?"

"Well," said Robin, "it was marvelous inventive. If old Vaudan *could*, it would be more fun than he's had in years."

Guy stood up in the saddle and waved to someone below. "Father's waiting. Come on."

When they open that gate, Élène thought, *Eustace will be —at last, thank God—a seigneur.*

No more trotting the king's heel like a hound, no more living in the saddle. He was forty-six; he was old. Now at the end, a full barony. And for her at last, God forgive the selfishness—a little rest.

Life had never been easy for them. She and Eustace were both younger children of second sons from families where patrimonies ran thin even for the firstborn. She and Gerlaine knew the backache of the grinding stone and milking stool, the sweating dawn-to-vespers toil of harvest, and the boys' hands hardened on plows and axes before they ever curved around the pommel of a sword. They had cut and shared the hard bread that followed a year of ruined crops. But now—Montford, and her son Hugh knighted at Hastings by the king himself.

Like all things, there was a price.

I love this house because he made it, but I will never love this gray country. It has stolen something that was mine, and I can never have it back. Since Hastings . . .

They never spoke of Hastings, Eustace and Hugh. Once, only, after too much wine had her husband muttered the few words that said it all.

"They called it *Sangue-lac*," he said. "The Lake of Blood."

Hugh rode into that lake with him, a quiet, earnest youth of eighteen—in autumn it was; the leaves were turning at Neuville, Robin was down with fever—and he died there. The Hugh that followed Eustace on the king's march north in '69 was a different man—cold, taciturn, drinking too silently for a young man with life before him.

What they did was hard but necessary. The north was too distant for the king's easy control. He trusted the Saxon earls. They rebelled, were pardoned and rebelled again. It had to be done, but—children, too? Infants, women?

I will not believe what they said. Not my husband, not Hugh. Not murder.

The thane's lady, Algive nailed to her own altar while she prayed. A heathen altar, some said, but still—

Élène sipped her wine as the children led their horses to the

pavilion, all three chattering at once and none listening. God
bless them, the world was theirs. The boys were dark like their
father, but Gerlaine had taken her own auburn hair and fair
skin. Her stomach, too; there was strength in the girl. There'd
be a good marriage—south, Élène hoped, where the men and
the land were richer—if the dear bobbin could ever keep her
hair bound decently.

It was good to rest. Costly but good.

"The more I see," Vaudan despaired, "the more I dislike."

The little priest worried up and down in front of Eustace.
The baron listened gravely. If he felt impatience, it was well
concealed.

"The estuary tide is high, Vaudan. I think no harm will come
if we postponed your rites for a few hours."

"My lord," said Vaudan. "I am not, I think, unnaturally
superstitious, but I am acquainted with the most modern
Roman writ, and these things have been *defined*. To begin
with, the woman Calla is an abomination—"

"Damn the woman," Hugh yawned. "I'm sick of her name.
She's a peasant who makes dolls out of cornstalks, no more."

Vaudan turned to him. "And the carvings on your stockade,
messire?"

"Are just that," said Hugh. "Not a bit more." He put down
his goblet and lounged back in his chair. Even in relaxation his
body instinctively prepared itself for attack. Hugh always
looked to Gerlaine as if he were about to spring at something.
"We'll miss the tide. I say let's get on with it."

Eustace would not indulge the momentary irritation with his
priest. He controlled it as he easily controlled everything of
which he was the acknowledged master. His eyes swerved
once more to the gate and the lounging workmen. It would be a
shame to miss the tide, and years of command had taught him
what dissension would breed in the minds of the watching
Saxon workmen. However, Vaudan was a sober priest, not a
hysterical heresy-hunter. His malaise over the Saxon carvings
was beginning to disturb Eustace.

"From the church of Anfric," said Vaudan, "I acquired a
book."

Enjoying the sight of Gurth some distance away, Gerlaine

gave her attention to the priest. They wrote their curses in a book, Calla said.

"Much is unreadable Saxon, but as I translated the Latin," Vaudan looked quickly at Élène and lowered his voice. "A word privately, Eustace."

They walked a few yards toward the ditch. The priest's features were screwed in a mask of concern. "Of that place, Brandeshal: were there any survivors?"

The memory was cruelly clear to Eustace. "None."

"You are sure? His son Leofwine?"

"I saw him die."

"The Saxon monks at Sockburn had no love for that house," Vaudan said, "but the thane's wife was a Christian. Ulfson himself was not. It is also said that he had a large number of children by various women, but only one baptized son. One, my lord, and so it has gone here since—" Vaudan broke off; his voice had risen. He softened it again. "In Anfric's rolls, there are baptismal records for every one of your serfs save Calla and her son." His glance drifted to the tall young man near the sluice gate. "One cannot say for sure, but sheepherders with the manners and education of Paris are rare on Tees, *n'est-ce pas, mon seigneur?*"

Eustace frowned. "What are you saying?"

"This book is a storehouse of dark things, blasphemous things that could not be allowed or even conceived of at home. What these Angles call ancient custom has in recent years been unmasked as the work of Satan. The Cross was not the only altar we found at Brandeshal. There may have been survivors—"

"Damn you, Vaudan," the baron hissed. "There were *none.*"

"—And those signs on the timbers of the gate and wherever else we find them must be burned out *now* with the weapons of the Church."

Eustace made to answer, but instinct and the long habit of alertness lifted his head toward the south. Even as he looked, the first of ten riders topped the low rise and started down toward the bailey bridge. As quickly as Eustace counted them, Hugh was at his elbow.

"King's men from York."

Eustace grimaced. *And here I stand splitting hairs with my priest.* The riders decided him. They'd see that moat filled with ten feet of water, by God's eyes, and take the message back to de Mowbray at York that Montford was already a working fortress. To bolster the decision, Gurth waited respectfully at his side.

"All's ready, sir."

"Your purification can wait, Vaudan," Eustace dismissed him. "No more argument. Tomorrow. Gurth, they can open the gate anytime after those men clear the bridge. Ask the Lady Élène to join me there."

It will cost me a confession, Gerlaine turned the delicious thought in her mind, *but I will watch that man walk.*

He moved with the ease of complete relaxation, not tense like Hugh but erect and graceful. He intrigued her, this Gurth: the son of a moor peasant sent to Paris to study for holy orders? His father, she observed, must have had a large purse.

"A larger conscience," Gurth replied.

And if his father were a priest as Gurth casually guessed, the motivations were clear. Still, Gurth irritated her sometimes with his air of equality. More like superiority it was. To read and write was not the responsibility of well-bred folk. There were clerks for that, but Gurth could do both as well and better than Père Vaudan. On the day when all available men had reported for work on the keep, she got her first close look at the shire bucks. Pitiful few they were and most past their prime except for a surly blond giant named Godric and his friend in surprisingly clean French-cut linen, whose appreciative study of her own person was just short of impertinent and so absorbed that Vaudan had to call him twice.

"Name . . . you there: what is your name?"

"Gurth."

"Condition?"

"Free."

Vaudan's quill speared the inkwell and hovered. "Formerly free," he corrected. "Holding?"

"One croft, one quarter hide of plowland. Sheepcote and twenty sheep, eight hens, one cock."

"Persons?"

"Myself and my mother. She is called Calla."

"Father?"

Gurth merely shrugged. "I think he was a priest."

Vaudan remarked aside to the baron on the morals of the Saxon clergy and dipped the quill again. "I see. Bastard."

To Gerlaine Gurth had seemed rather amused at the ordinary term. Half the serfs in any village in Normandy were so; but she noted the smile did not quite reach his gray eyes. He canted his head to read Vaudan's writing. "*Excusez-moi, mon prêtre,*" he said in rather good French. Vaudan's head bobbed up, startled.

"*Qu'est-ce que c'est?*"

"A small thing, but isn't *bâtard* spelled with an *a*?" He pointed to Vaudan's incorrect *e*. "To be misborn is sad enough, but to be misspelled in the bargain . . ."

Thus they learned he was clerkly, and this strange, preoccupied man became her father's interpreter. Gerlaine reckoned his age near Hugh's. She was glad he shaved himself clean in the French fashion. It was too fine a face to hide behind a beard. Part of her attraction arose from the feminine divination that he wanted her. *Bien,* there were not many women left on Tees. *No,* she decided; *not that. He wants me.*

As Gurth strode toward the pavilion, she schemed: *I'll tell him there's a message from Calla but I can't remember, let me see . . .*

And he would linger.

Gurth bowed to her mother. "Baroness, the seigneur wishes you attend the visitors with him."

"Oh, no," said Robin. "She's to give the signal for the gate."

"Oh, it doesn't matter." Élène rose and accepted Gurth's arm in stepping down from the pavilion. "There's probably news from York. One of you can do it." She turned away and moved toward her husband where he awaited the horsemen clattering across the bridge.

Gurth stroked Bête's head fondly. It was one of the myriad little things that made him dear to Gerlaine. He had the gentleness of strength that needs no show of proof; gentle with men as well as women. With her father or the lowest serf laboring in the ditch, Gurth's manner was the same. He treated men as if they were worthy of the name.

"*Demoiselle,* the men and myself will be honored if you would give the signal."

"Of course." She rose to take his arm with an alacrity that did not escape her brothers' notice.

"Oh, Master Gurth," Guy said falsetto, "may I come, too?"

"The hell with you, *bébé*." Gurth pulled him up by one arm, tussling the boy good-naturedly.

With a whoop of pure high spirits, Robin swooped down on the wrestling pair and fastened himself to Gurth's broad back. Strong, lean and agile, the boys were still like puppies worrying at a grown mastiff. Deftly, Gurth rolled Robin off his back as Guy dove for his legs. Gurth caught and deflected their clumsy holds surely, without exerting real pressure, laughing all the time. The boys fought with the half-jest, wholly-in-earnest spirit of their untried blood, but in a matter of moments both were off their feet and locked in Gurth's arms, arms and legs churning helplessly. Guy's face was crimson with effort and humiliation.

"Put me down, Bastard."

"We'll put Bête on you," Robin panted, "I swear we will."

"No, enough," Gerlaine scolded at them with a glance toward her parents. "King's men here to see Father and the lot of you acting like yokels. Enough, now."

Robin made one more futile effort to free himself. "*Bête!*"

From the beginning of the mock fight, Bête hovered around its edges, weaving back and forth a little in sympathetic excitement. Dimly he felt there was no danger, since he heard no sound of fear or anger, but he quivered to be part of it.

The sound of his name freed him. He shot forward; at the same instant, Gurth released the boys and squared on him. Gerlaine moved to call the mute back but Guy stopped her.

"No. Let's see who's stronger."

Gerlaine saw them poise for an instant, one erect, the other half crouched. Then Gurth moved in. Grasping Bête about his thick body, he locked his arms across the small of the back, ready to throw him. But the mute reached back and took the man's wrists, pulling them apart as easily as parchment. Gently, inexorably, Gurth's arms were forced out and up. Then Bête stooped, changing his hold, and lifted Gurth clean off his feet, helpless as he had held the boys. Slowly the heavy legs straightened until Bête stood erect. A moment only, then the imperfectly knit limbs buckled under the strain and he bowed with Gurth's weight.

"His legs," Gerlaine breathed. "Guy, his legs are healing. Down, Bête. Down."

He smiled as if to assure her that there was no harm done and lowered Gurth to the ground.

"Good, Bête." Gurth gripped the huge shoulder. "Good."

"He did not hurt you, Master Gurth?"

"No." Gurth rose, dusting himself off. "There was no anger."

"*Hé*, look, Robin!" Guy pointed to the knot of men around Eustace at the bridge. "Ring mail, every one of them. And new, too. Come on, I want to see the style."

With something new to interest them, the boys loped off.

Again Gurth offered his arm, and they walked toward the waiting Godric where he slouched against the gate with a poor attempt at patience.

"I saw your mother today."

"Where?"

"At the old thane's hall. There was a message for you."

"What was that?"

"*Là*, but I've forgot," she said in the tone she'd rehearsed, as if there were more important things to think about. "But it will come back. There is something you may do for me."

"Of course, *demoiselle*."

"There is a manuscript at Père Vaudan's church. I want you to aid with those passages I can't read."

Which would be all of them, she admitted honestly to herself. And he knew it.

"It would be my pleasure," Gurth offered. "What book is it?"

"One," she remembered, "that was taken from the old priest's church."

"The Deira Book," Gurth nodded. "I've heard of it."

They walked a little way in silence, Bête slouching contentedly behind them.

"You learned your French in Paris?"

"Yes," he said. "To become a priest."

"But you did not take orders."

"I thought I wanted it at first. But, Gerlaine—"

It was the first time Gurth had addressed her familiarly. She felt a rush of warmth at the sound of her name.

"Gerlaine, there are new things being taught there. Men from all over: England, Denmark, Germany, all of them have come to Paris. There are new ideas. Rome calls them foolish, maybe even heretic. But they are good men. They can't all be evil or mad."

His intensity unbalanced her somewhat; she tried to regain familiar ground. "And the women? I hear they are very beautiful."

"And becoming more so. They lace themselves now. It's a new style."

"Lace? How is it done?"

"Like this." His hand circled her waist to touch lightly against her back. "The kirtle is laced tightly up the back—so, from the waist, and not nearly as full as they used to be."

Gerlaine considered the aesthetic consequences. "It seems immodest," she judged. *But about high time.*

Gurth caught the hint in her smile and grinned. "In a commoner it would be immodest. In the Queen of France, it becomes fashionable."

"You've learned more than Latin in Paris."

"Yes." He seemed to consider the statement. "They taught me how to think."

"You're a strange one, Gurth." She allowed herself the familiar address, liking it. "Not sullen like the others. You do not hate us?"

"Hate?" He echoed the word. "I hated a man once, I wanted to kill him. I prayed he'd die. He did. It didn't help."

They began to walk again. Gurth waved to Godric. "Yes, we're coming!" He swung his arms, flexing the shoulders, man-fashion. "Maybe if I were like Godric there, if this were all I knew, if I'd fought for it like him—perhaps then."

He stopped and scooped up a handful of dirt. "Here is what I love, this. It isn't Norman or Saxon. It speaks one language: life. It says one simple word over and over to the seed: *live*. Kings and earls and barons come and go. This stays. And *we* stay, my people here. We believe in that life so much that we gave it a shape and a name. It is the Freya-spirit. In the old religion she was Freyr's sister. The Greeks called her Ceres, some here call her *cailleach,* but it's the same word whispered to the seed, making it grow."

Gurth worked the soil in his fingers. "I can hate. It's there like a sickness, like Bound Loki inside me. Some times when I have too much to drink, I can feel him stir and wake. . . ."

The image of that twisted wood flashed through her memory

again. She was glad he stopped. His hand had crushed the earth into a tight clod.

"So I don't drink. Anyway—"

"What, Gurth?"

"How could a man with eyes hate you, Gerlaine?"

She forgot to breathe for a short moment, hearing him say it at last. *Would he think me immodest if I laced myself?* No, he would not, not Gurth. She opened her mouth to answer, to say —something. It would have been happily foolish, but the chance never came. Godric was thumping toward them.

"What's the word, God damn it? Do we open the gate or miss the tide?"

Gurth pounded him on the back affectionately. "We *open* it! *Demoiselle* will give the signal for the baron. Come, lady."

"Gerlaine! Sister."

Robin was sprinting toward them, even more excited than usual. "News! You're got to hear."

"In the name of *Christ!*" Godric roared, wheeling his great arms in a frustration that was almost comic. "What now?"

"Sister, *attend*," Robin hugged her. "We're to hold a court, a real manor court for the king's officer from York. He's on his way to meet Edgar Atheling and take him to ship. They'll stop here before Durham. A banquet, soldiers, High Mass— everything."

"Wait, Robin—*wait*, idiot." Gurth broke in. "What of the Atheling?"

"They say he's asked pardon and renounced the throne."

"That means no more war," said Gerlaine, "doesn't it, Gurth?"

"Yes." Gurth looked at his feet. "And no more England."

The way he said it took the flush from the happy moment they had just shared.

The last Saxon claimant to the crown of England had renounced his title in favor of peace with William. It was truly a conquest now. *I won't care,* Gurth told himself. *Nothing changes, the land is still here. Only the lords are different. I will—not—care.*

Godric pricked up his ears at the word "Atheling" in Robin's tumbling French. "What's he saying, Gurth? What of Edgar? Damn, man, what of the prince? Does he raid south again?"

"He comes in peace to be pardoned," Gurth told him in a dead voice. "He calls William king."

The big carpenter seemed to crumple where he stood. Gurth said something to him that Gerlaine could not understand. They were close, these two men. There was love and pain between them. She felt for both of them now. She wanted to hold Gurth, wanted many things still only half comprehended. *If it were later. If we were closer, I would say, This is us, Gurth, not kings or princes or Winchester. This is Montford. We're not part of them.*

Godric croaked thickly. "It's a lie."

"It's true," Gurth said. "I've known it would come. Now it has."

So many times Gerlaine had seen her own brothers hurt in their pride, wanting to cry and fighting back the tears. It was like this with Godric now. His face worked. His eyes reddened with the hot pressure behind them, but he choked it down, turned on his heel and lumbered blindly away toward the sluice gate.

Gurth made to follow him. "Stay here."

"Gurth?"

"No, this is a"—he fought for the word—"a man thing. And *that's* a man, if God ever made one. Robin, stay with your sister. We open the gate."

He caught up with Godric in a few long strides. "Brother, it had to happen."

Godric plunged on, the tears rolling freely down his cheeks now that he was away from the woman. "No . . . no."

"There was no hope, no place for him. He's a man. He got tired of living for a dead dream."

They had reached the gate. Godric pressed his head against a beam, beating slow anger into the wood with his fist. "You weren't there, you don't know how it was. I fought them, Gurth: *me*. I was to Ely with Hereward. God damn good men left to rot in that fen because they wouldn't give up."

The hard, hurting knot of it rose and burst out of Godric in a dry sob. The shame of tears, of baring his hurt, rounded him on Gurth like a wounded boy who understands nothing but his pain.

"*I* was with Brand, not you, not his little favorite. I fought them while you sat on your ass in Paris learning to be a

Frenchman. How would you know how I feel?" Godric
dragged the back of one dirty hand across his eyes. "The little
Atheling has gotten tired, has he?" He ground the words out
heavily. "Weak-spined, mealy-mouthed, *niddering* son of a
bitch!"

With sudden fury he sprang onto the gate beams and grabbed
the large ax ready by the counterweight ropes. Gurth saw what
he intended and whirled on the workmen.

"Out of the ditch," he roared. "Out. The gate's going up!"

The loungers in the ditch were jolted into frantic action.
They heard Gurth's warning but it was the dooms day sight of
Godric with the ax that sent them scattering up the sides of the
moat to safety as the blade swung high.

"*Here's* your bloody moat!" Godric sobbed. "Take it. Take
it all."

The ax bit through the thick rope and deep into the beam
beneath with a *crack* heard as far as the church and the bailey
bridge. The counterweights rumbled down, the sluice gate rose
and the river spilled into the trench with a deepening roar.

Godric crouched over the ax, both hands trembling on the
haft.

Gurth sickened at the shame of feeling no shame.

At the door of his church, Père Vaudan heard the deep
thunder of the river and crossed himself.

III

"Bless me, Father, for I have sinned."

"In what way, child?"

Vaudan hardly needed to ask. He had confessed Gerlaine from the time she had to be lifted to horse. On any given occasion he could have dictated her transgressions from memory.

"My mind wandered at matins. I didn't pray as I should."

"Do you pray before bed?"

"Always."

"Then I add five Ave Marias and one rosary to your prayers tonight as penance, and you will dip five new candles for the altar. Our supply is low and the king's sheriff will want High Mass. Is there anything else?"

"I have lately taken the Lord's name in vain. I have cursed at everything, myself, my brothers, even my horse."

The priest was not surprised. The girl had spirit and a temper. "Do you know why you have done this?"

She paused, kneeling beside and slightly behind his chair. Out of the corner of his averted eye, Vaudan caught the physical nuances of hesitation.

"This is a strange place," Gerlaine began with difficulty. "I cannot think as I did at home."

"We are Christ's own wherever we are," he said. "This is

29

more serious than omitted prayers. For penance I bid you think on the consequences of blasphemy and on the cunning of Satan who makes it easier and less like sin each time we do it. Will you do this, my child?"

"Yes, Father."

"I absolve you with that condition. What else?"

She was silent for so long that Vaudan's thought was confirmed. Years at the confessional had taught him, beyond the import of words, the language of silence.

"What else?" He canted slightly toward her. The preoccupation of her fingers with the edge of her mantle spoke before she did.

"I feel that I should be instructed in marriage."

Vaudan waited.

"I feel," her clear young voice tiptoed across the words, "that there are duties of a wife that—" Then her back straightened. "No. This is only half true. I have had thoughts of men."

"Carnal thoughts?"

Her hesitation was gone. "I have sinned in my mind. It does no good to keep busy. When I was making this kirtle, working the embroidery, I thought how it would please . . . a man. And from that thought came the others."

Vaudan's poised hand came down decisively on the arm of his chair. "What else?"

Gerlaine raised her head. "Nothing."

He gave her five more Ave Marias, more because she expected them than anything else. It was a situation that could not be neatly expiated in prayer.

"Listen, child: what you have honestly confessed means that your soul is ready to act now as a vessel for either God or Satan. Both want you. You have a choice and a responsibility. There is a way in which you may have these things. Only one way and for one purpose. Do you understand?"

"*Oui*, Père Vaudan."

"Your desire for instruction is wise, but it is your mother's place. I absolve you with these penances. Go now, and pray for me."

They were alone to one side of the altar in the empty church. Vaudan studied the girl as she genuflected and crossed herself with a graceful smoothness that never quite became perfunctory. Her kirtle was new, the embroidery carefully done. Gerlaine had cut the linen well but had obviously misjudged the size as the bodice seemed much tighter than usual. The womanliness of her slim body, sharply defined by the confining material, told the priest that marriage was not only wise but urgent. The girl was ripe as June.

There was a movement in the doorway where Bête squatted, waiting for Gerlaine. He shifted outward as someone laughed and called to him. At the sound, Gerlaine rose from the altar with a hint of eagerness. Her hand went up in an instinctively feminine gesture to adjust her veil. The small action confessed more to Vaudan than Gerlaine ever could. He frowned.

"It's Gurth, *mon prêtre*," she told him. "I've bid him come. That book you told my father about. I want him to read it."

He'd been working in the fields, she noticed. He never wore his good French clothes now, only the rough woolen trousers tucked into leggings, a short tunic and a worn sheepskin tabard, belted and adorned with a crescent-headed ax.

Vaudan indicated the weapon. "There will be no ax in my church, Master Gurth."

Gurth laid the ax outside the door, genuflected and strode down the nave. "Good day, Father. Gerlaine."

She skipped up to him. "Gurth's come to read. He's a scholar. He can read his own language and Latin and Frank." The proprietary tone was not lost on Vaudan. "He was almost in orders."

"Almost is not a priest," Vaudan noted gravely. "What turned you from it, Master Gurth?"

"I lack the calling," the young man replied simply.

"Honestly put. Yet scholarship is the responsibility of that calling. In the hands of the laity—" he shrugged. "I question the wisdom of allowing you this book."

Nevertheless, he reflected, there were long passages locked from him that should be opened for the understanding of the subtle evil of this place.

"You did say my father should know of it," Gerlaine cajoled.

"Come then," Vaudan led the way. "You will translate for me."

Vaudan's timber church lay on the outer bank of the moat just beyond the bailey bridge, a small, squat rectangle thrown up by Eustace with the promise of stone later on. Behind it a hut, one of the outbuildings of the old steading, served as Vaudan's living cell. His habits were timeworn and simple. A large crucifix dominated one clay-daubed wall. There was a cot, a reading stand, a stool and a plank table. The reading stand was by far the most elegant object at hand; Vaudan's one forgivable pride brought from Normandy, dark and smooth from generations of devout hands and soutained bellies. As he drafted many of the baron's letters to York, the stand was equipped with a dusty jar of quills, an inkpot and parchment.

The cell was dark. On inspection Vaudan decided another candle was needed and left them alone while he returned to the church for a spare.

"How has it gone, Gurth?"

"It goes well. You are wearing a veil."

"I hate it but *Maman* says."

"It was prettier with just the gold wire. Do you have it that way underneath?"

"Indeed, it's a *ruin*, my hair!" Gerlaine laughed—musically, she hoped, and with just the right mixture of carelessness and modesty. "There was so little I could do before confession that I gave up and just tied it back. But look!"

With supreme nonchalance—arduously practiced in private—Gerlaine undid the dun cloak, swirling it aside to display her handiwork.

"My new kirtle," she informed him, parading casually to the reading stand. "Just for the warm days. It is a poor effort . . . do you like it?"

She writhed under his inspection, her confidence evaporating. She had not made a kirtle but a clumsy turnip sack, and had the temerity to present it to the most beautiful man in the world for comment. As his eyes went over her, Gerlaine saw herself ill compared to the wilting, sensuous women of Paris. *You will hate it, but be kind.*

"It is exquisite," he said finally. "So becoming to you. And the bodice—"

"Oh well," she noted hastily, "there was not material to make it fuller. I'm lucky there was just enough."

Gurth nodded, smiling. "So am I."

He was laughing with, not at her, and he knew. Gerlaine flushed with pleasure. His reaction had been far from critical;

so far, in fact, that she felt a little flustered. There was so much
to know about the mystery of him. She dipped a quill in ink
and held it out to him.

"Here, Gurth: write your name for me in Saxon. You all
have names like earth and stones and trees. Brand, Godric,
Gurth. *Goo-oors*. How is it written?"

He took the pen and formed the letters.

gyrð

Gerlaine frowned over the result. "What's that at the end?"

"How we write *th*."

She took the pen and dipped it in the pot. "Now I'll write
mine for you." Laboriously she pressed out the characters of
her one literary accomplishment.

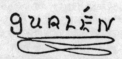

"So!" She wove a triumphant flourish beneath the letters.
"That, Master Gurth, is my name in Normandy Frank, and as
good as any Île-de-France scholar could ever do."

"True." Gurth's tall bulk moved close to her by the stand.
She inhaled the man smell of him—the sweat, the rough
clothes, the oil from the sheepskin. "Would you like to see
how they'd write your name in Paris?"

"Oh, show! Show."

"Then take the quill—" His hand closed over hers, guiding it
unnecessarily to the inkpot again, then down to the paper.
"You see, they're an idle lot in Paris with nothing to do but
write prettily, and so—"

I love him, Maman. I don't care who he is I love him.

"No, now comes the *L*—"

*She burns me. Like her hair under that veil. I know this
gentle dance. It's going to happen.*

"*Voilà!*"

GERLAINE

"Ooooh!" Gerlaine delighted. "So many beautiful letters. It's gorgeous! Which do you like best?"

"Your way."

"Why?"

"Because it's short and strong and honest like you."

"Look!" Gerlaine snatched up the paper and shoved it under Vaudan's nose as he returned with the candles. "My name! As they write it in Paris."

"*Très belle,*" Vaudan nodded. He noticed that she had discarded her cloak. The kirtle was much too revealing. "It is chill, *demoiselle,*" he observed tactfully. "You must put on your mantle."

Bête dozed by the church door. In the noonday warmth, his great bulk slumped against the wall, mouth open. Sleep for him was a time when he was not, but more and more in the night when he lay by the fire in the hall, not far from Little Red's door, pictures came and the pain and cold again, till he woke shivering and shifted himself closer to the fire.

He had the picture again: cold. He moved his shattered legs as much as he could to keep them from freezing. The blood had dried stiff on his trousers, black and crusted all over his face where it ran from the trench in his skull.

And then the dream changed. For the first time, it was different.

He was riding.

What Vaudan produced was not a bound book but a loose folio of parchment pages wrapped in canvas, not very ancient, much of it in Latin of varying erudition, with a good portion in Saxon. Written at Sockburn Abbey on the southwestern boundaries of Tees Riding, it was evidently begun as a letter-chronicle to King Edward the Confessor, incorporating the standard entries for earlier years from older manuscripts.

Gerlaine flanked the pages with lighted candles and moved in beside Gurth. Vaudan sat apart at the table, listening and watching the baron's daughter. Every move she made was toward the Saxon, to draw closer, make contact.

He is the one, Vaudan decided. *He is the temptation.* The girl, absorbed in the nearness of the young man, did not catch Vaudan's softened glance. *It is a beautiful thing to love for the first time. The first outpouring before we learn to reserve, to parcel our hearts by the measure of what must be. But this man—c'est impossible. And dangerous. I will speak to the baron.*

Gurth arranged the loose pages, moved the candles closer and began to read.

TO THE GRACIOUS AND MOST CHRISTIAN
EDWARD
KING OF THE ENGLISH, JUSTLY CALLED
CONFESSOR,
AS HE HAS LATELY REQUESTED A HISTORY
OF NORTHUMBERLAND
AND INQUIRED INTO THE STATE OF
HOLY MOTHER CHURCH, FOR WHICH
HIS LOVE IS EXEMPLARY AND MUNIFICENT—

The prostrate prose ran on and on. The writer, it seemed, could not find adjectives enough to praise his king, though Gerlaine sighed that it was not for want of effort. Gurth caught her mew of impatience and skipped over several flowery cadenzas.

"It just means," he winked at her, " 'don't forget us come Christmas.' "

IN THE TENTH YEAR OF HIS INSPIRED REIGN:
BRITWOLD, ABBOT OF SOCKBURN, LOWEST OF
THE SERVANTS OF GOD, SENDS GREETING.

There followed older pages in a different hand, the factual history of Northumbria. As Gurth translated, a new world opened to Gerlaine. She had never heard history as such before. Oh, there were the *jongleurs* with their ballads and tales, but here were accounts written out of men's witness, their courage, their anger—told with poignance or prejudice according to the writer, but always as he saw the truth. And the names *were* like trees and hard earth, looming like giant shadows in mist.

"Here it is." Gurth pointed to the page. "The beginning of Brandeshal."

> *Anno 547* In this year, Ida was crowned king of Berenicia and built Bamburh. He sent his picked war companions into Deira to waste the land if it would not submit. When they returned with victory, Ida called the chief companions to feast with him and asked each what treasure of armor or rings they desired as gifts. And Ida Ring-Giver kept his word to each companion, as was necessary, since they fought for his glory and not their own.
>
> Then Brand said: Give me no rings but the land I won, and I will hold it for you as your thane till Ragnarok, till the end of earth. And so he claimed Tees Riding.
>
> *Anno 548* In this year, the king's reeve reckoned Brand at 25 hides of land on Tees and a thane's wergild.

Both Gerlaine and Vaudan found the word *wergild* and the concept behind it totally incomprehensible even with Gurth's patient but inadequate explanation.

"It means man-price, what you have to pay if you kill a man. Unless you choose to fight his family."

"Never mind," Vaudan gave it up as inscrutable. "Read."

The years paced by with Gurth's voice rising and falling with the fortunes of the north and the house of Brandeshal. Backward and forward shifts of power, betrayals, loyalties. The treaties, the marriages, the bloody deaths, the sacrifices —the gritty survival of that grim, stockaded hall from the dim, legendary years to the more fully documented Christian times. The coming of Augustine, of Paulinus and the cross, the heartwarming baptism of young King Edwin and all his chief men, the enthusiastic march of the newly converted to tear down the altars of Woden . . .

> When they came rejoicing to Brandeshal, Thane Wulf would not deny Woden nor pull down the altar, saying he would feast them as friends or bury them as enemies, the choice was theirs and the supper ready. And so they

feasted. Then, in honest debate, Wulf accepted Christ, but gave him only equal place with Woden. Nay, since Woden had brought good fortune, as much was owed to him as might be to Christ, and Wulf would not deny him.

"It grows much worse," Vaudan brought wine to Gerlaine. "We must tell your father what we've heard."

"I will," she promised. She sipped the wine and passed the cup to Gurth. They were not, at the moment, overly concerned with heresy. Each watched the tiny candles dancing in the other's eyes.

IV

Anno 866 In this year, the Danes sailed up Tees in great numbers, led by Ivar. They looked for an easy victory on Tees, for everywhere else men had made terms of tribute, the peace of sheep with wolves. But there was no victory at Brandeshal, and what they saw on the battlefield no Christian man would believe and even the Danes sickened at it.

This entry was followed by a brief I-told-you-so by the tattling, servile Britwold who then appended part of a report by a Roman bishop to the Vatican on the state of the Church in the north.

As nuncius among the English to correct the errors of the Northumbrian Church, I find their minds a puzzle and their hearts a mystery. The events at Brandeshal on Tees in the Year of Our Lord 866, a tale much chronicled and wondered at here, will illustrate my point.

Thane Cynric of Brandeshal had a daughter Sigrid, called the Plain. It should have been the Mad. She hated all men but her father whom she loved in that curious manner described by certain Greeks.

When the Danes came to Tees, the English were so

outnumbered there was little doubt of the issue. Cynric sacrificed for victory to Woden (an ancient local deity) but was slain in the first encounter.

Among the northern English there is a tradition called *bear-sark,* difficult to translate, but nothing more than a tendency toward that madness of which Sigrid was the open confession. Before their father's body, she and her two brothers defected even from the crude battle god they had worshiped, and prayed instead to a demon called Loki (merely Satan disguised) for victory and vengeance for their father. For this favor his image would be carved next to Woden's and one son in every generation would serve him in gratitude.

Satan, it appears, favored them, and the children of Cynric looked out on the field where the retreating Danes had left their wounded. Her brothers cast lots for the right to dispatch the marauders, but Sigrid begged to tend them, and from their boats on the river, the Danes saw her mercy.

Stripped naked but for a mail shirt, spattered with blood to her shoulders, Sigrid went with her knife from man to man. Those that would die she gutted with the detached efficiency of a cook; they were fortunate. Those that might have lived she cut with such calculated and diabolical skill that, blind, tongueless and unmanned, they were still alive when the crows found them.

But for Bjorn, that kinsman of Ivar who slew her father, Sigrid reserved the genius of her barbarism. To a post driven into the ground, she tied the ends of his living entrails, then flayed the murderer until he rose and ran and could run no more—

The narrator stepped prosaically from horror to horror, reporting without comment. Gurth glanced up at Gerlaine. She was half turned away, her head shaking slightly in disbelief.

"I sickened when I read this," Vaudan muttered. "It is madness. Animal."

In the following year Sigrid bore a son, though she never had a husband. The more superstitious claim it was an incubus in the shape of her brother. Let him believe who will; an incubus perhaps, but her brother for sure. When this son was near grown, Sigrid had the blacksmith plait iron which she placed at Loki's altar so that the demon would recognize his own when the boy claimed and finished his sword.

This custom has continued on Tees to the present day even where idols have largely given way to the Church. Its preservation is doubtless due to the ascendency of the Danes with whom these people intermarried. One child in every generation, usually male, is dedicated to Loki, the demon who was cast out by the gods and who will rise again to destroy them. Forgetting the horror that spawned it, they keep the custom and insist, as with the household gods of Caesar's time, that their luck comes from the ugly figure of this chained monster.

The Latin deteriorated now as the busy Abbot Britwold continued his breathless condemnation.

Royal Edward, I now bring this chronicle into the sphere of present memory. You will recall the recent events in which the Earl of Wessex was justly exiled. Siward our earl came at your call for men, and I with him as witness to the following.

Thane Ulf of Brandeshal, who came tardily and in poor grace, was against your Royal will, saying that Wessex opposed you rightly in defending his own man who killed your Norman friend. He said the Norman had tried to enter the man's house unwelcomed, and that Wessex only upheld hearth-right.

Earl Siward held that Wessex was a danger, that he owned more of England than Yourself the King, and hungered for more. And thus they debated as seasoned chiefs before tried men.

But the thane's young son Brand was not seasoned except with drink. He leaped upon a wagon and shouted to all the men that *he* would not fight men of his own blood for a half-Norman monk of a king better suited to a habit than a crown. Shameful words, but I write as I heard.

The earl chided him for a drunken boy, wherefore Brand answered scornfully that as the half-king, so the half-earl; for this insult to the good old Siward, Brand's father struck him to the ground.

Then it was that Satan claimed his own. Brand drew his dagger and would have killed his own father, but the thane laid him out with good proper blows until the *niddering* scut could not rise.

In his own blood, in his own shame they chained him like his demon Loki and sent him home that true men might not have to look upon him.

"For the rest of it," Vaudan said when Gurth paused, "I can't read it at all. It's Saxon and so clumsily penned I think the man could barely write."

He moved away from the desk, musing. "You are a scholar, Gurth. The Church could have used you." He turned to face the man. "Obviously the rest of this deals with Brand Ulfson. I recognized the name and"—he hesitated delicately—"that of your mother."

"I see." Gurth's tone was flat.

"I did not think it would surprise you."

Let me tell you about evil, child . . .

I should have known, Gerlaine thought. *Oh, God, I should have guessed. It's for Gurth she tends that graveyard ruin, for what he is.*

"The baron must know," Vaudan concluded firmly. "You will read, please."

The script was agonizingly labored, the style plain to the point of monotony. It had no life but the monk's narrow hate. It began with a poem in an older style obviously copied from a more literate source.

> In Loki's twisted fetters
> Brand Ulfson found the iron.
> Plaited it was, and waiting
> For the day when he was thane.
> He drew it forth in anger
> And hammered out the blade,
> (*Bear-sark* as his fathers before him)
> In the darkness that blinds the heart.

He cooled the blade in water
And hung it on his side;
No relic set in the handle
But the end of a raven's claw,
And at the gate of Brandeshal
Like Heimdall at the bridge,
He waited for Ulf his father
And love was at an end.

On the thane's men fell a stillness;
                 Death-still, Brand Ulfson said:
I have taken my sword from Loki;
Now, father, strike again.
Still and cold it was then;
Father and son were still.
Father and son looked cold
And nothing heard but the wind.

Gerlaine had never heard poetry before, at least not without music or rhyme. The insistent repetition of words like *cold* and *still* in the last lines were like the day at Brandeshal a moment before Calla came, when the world was deserted but for herself and the wind.

The laboring monk struggled on:

Anno 1055 In this year died the good Abbot Britwold, and he was a good man, much abused. Yea, if men mock God, he repays them in kind, and it has come to pass, thus: on the moors of Tees, there lives even now a mongrel girl, the whore of Brand Ulfson and a proven witch. And on this whore named Calla—

Gurth broke off. His whole frame stiffened. Gerlaine felt that tension in her own flesh. It was wrong, cruel. One could find many names for Calla—rock, tree, earth, darkness. But not that word.

"That busy little man," Gurth murmured. "That busy, vindictive little man." He took a breath, glanced at the impassive Vaudan and went on:

on this whore named Calla had Brand Ulfson already got a
bastard as on other common women of Tees.

He fell silent again. Vaudan coughed behind his hand.

"Pardon, Master Gurth: it comes as no surprise. Country
priests are not so rich that they can send their off-spring to be
educated at Paris."

"No."

"You are the child referred to?"

Gerlaine saw his dark head, bowed over the manuscript,
move in a slight assertion. "Half Tees could say the same."

"He never claimed you?"

"No. And as a matter of taste, I never claimed him. I hated
his selfish, arrogant guts."

He snapped himself erect and tapped the pages. "Do you
want to know why all this? Why these crawling little men have
dipped and scribbled for twenty years? Because of a forest,
Vaudan. What King Edward didn't give away to his Norman
prelates, he couldn't wait to give to the native Church: any
dispensation, any exemption, any privilege. The hell with the
English, he couldn't even speak our language. Britwold
wanted all of Tees forest land south of the river for his own
hunting preserve, so good Edward handed it to him with a pat
on his tonsured head. Which neatly ignored not only Brand's
rights but those of every freeman with hunting rights that
they'd earned and depended on for a hundred years and more.
Well, for *once* Brand did something by law. He took it to the
earl, who took it to Edward's witan, and they shoved it up his
—throat. Britwold never forgave it, and so"—Gurth held up
the page as if it were dirty—"this. Forgive me," he clipped off
the words. "They've told no lies, but they've been most agile
with the truth."

Now Earl Siward counseled young Brand when he
became thane that it was time to marry since one true wife
produces many heirs while a hundred whores do none.
And all Brand's kinsmen counseled the same. The earl
urged on him Algive, a pious lady of the house of Mercia,
whom he married not for her excellence but for her rich
dowry. But she would not be wife to him unless he put

away the moor witch and her bastard, for the truth was
Algive wanted to give herself to no man but would have
taken up the novitiate save for the marriage. She spent
much time with Book and rosary, and the sight of the
witch was hateful to her Christian soul.

Then Brand put away the whore Calla, and it is said
that she wept at the parting, a feat thought impossible for
witches. But many times afterward, Brand broke faith
with his lady and came to her.

But now he hears the harsh laughter of God and feels
His judgment on his sins and those of his idolatrous
fathers. Aye, he is thane, and in cold duty has his lady
borne him children. But where he looks to be warmed, he
finds no warmth. In the midst of feast is he starven, in the
midst of men he walks alone and must slake his thirst, like
the wolf, on the moor.

> *Dies Irae, Dies Illa,*
> *Solvet saeclum in favilla . . .*

"Day of wrath, day of sorrow," the candle flame shuddered
slightly with Gurth's breath. "What trembling lies before us
when the Judge cometh cannot be told."

Gurth laid aside the last page. "I'd say the winter of
sixty-nine was suitable wrath. The baron rules a graveyard. Do
you think it was evil, Gerlaine?"

"I—cannot say. It is not like home. *C'est sauvage*, Gurth."

Vaudan rose, rubbing his hands on the front of his soutane.
"The baron must know all."

"Yes, tell him," Gurth nodded wearily, "that his clerk is
Ulfson's bastard. Tell him another one, a better man than I'll
ever be, built his sluice gate to make him master of Tees."

"And the other children," Vaudan pressed. "The legitimate
heirs. Leofwine? Brand Brandson. And a daughter, was there
not?"

"Maud, yes," Gurth drained the last of the wine. He looked
at Vaudan with an expression Gerlaine could not penetrate, and
his voice was acid. "I hear someone found a piece of her
afterward. Gone, Vaudan. All gone. Dead, down the wind
with last year's leaves." He turned to Gerlaine. "Pity that man,
Gerlaine, because he was born too late. The old days were

gone long before you came, but my father couldn't change. And with Calla, it was not like that ignorant little man wrote."

"I believe that, Gurth," she murmured.

"He came to my mother because he could talk to her. Because they knew the same things without speaking, and he watched over her all his life. I hated him but I won't take that away from him."

Gurth wrapped the canvas around the parchment and handed it to the priest. "Pity, Vaudan. He was alone."

V

Eustace de Neuville was a direct, competent man. He was aware, among the world's realities, of the tendencies of seigneurs toward the comelier women of their fiefs. He was not unduly surprised to learn that the two best serfs of his thinly populated demesne had been sired by the former lord. Nor did the intelligence ruffle his wife beyond an ironic sigh: "It appears"—one brow elevated at Eustace—"they are not entirely alien to us after all."

It did not bother Eustace overmuch. Neither Gurth nor Godric had any claim even under the old laws. Legitimate sons, on the other hand, would have bothered him tremendously. Proper sons could raise loyal if ragged resistance under their names and disrupt the efficiency of his holding, possibly even destroy it. If Gurth or Godric had been suspected for one minute of that status, they would be imprisoned or dead.

For days Montford had seethed with a hundred preparatory details for the coming of the Lord High Sheriff of York: the slaughter of beef, the salting of fish, plans for quartering a hundred men where there wasn't room. It was decided quickly that some of the soldiers would billet on the larger farmsteads.

Everyone was occupied. Even Gerlaine, customarily in charge of the sewing women, had found time to dip an inordinate number of candles for Père Vaudan. Eustace did not delude himself that this was entirely charitable, recalling the priest's few discreet words concerning his daughter. The situation clearly called for Élène. As for Bastard, the baron took his opportunity when Gurth reported to him in the hall that his barley was in and the men would be turning to their own grain if that pleased his lordship.

It did; however, certain peasants were husbanding swine for him. He might have sent Gurth or Ralph, his steward, to report on their welfare, but he called for horse and rode himself, summoning Gurth as interpreter. Casually, he mentioned his plan to quarter the sheriff's men wherever possible. It was an offhand remark; he was not prepared for the reaction.

"Seigneur, you can't," Gurth stated flatly. "You must ask first."

Eustace turned in astonishment. "Ask?"

Gurth was deadly serious. "They won't have it. That's hearth-right, Baron. You must ask."

The notion was absurd. Eustace shrugged it off, his mind already on a more important matter. *"Eh bien, Maître* Gurth, I will take note. Tell me," he remarked as they jogged along, "in need, how many men with spear and shield could we raise for defense?"

"Not many," Gurth reckoned. "Less than twenty, I'd say."

"Landworkers did not carry weapons at home. But you say it was a custom here?"

"A duty, sir."

"Not without value," Eustace admitted. "I fought your father."

Gurth kept his eyes on the ox track ahead. "My father by chance. We weren't close."

"But he made you free."

"Aye."

"That," said the baron, "is another odd distinction here. Some of you were free—"

Gurth caught the slight emphasis on the past tense.

"—and even women, I understand, could inherit and own property in their own right. Our women, while we honor them, have no such latitude." His lean, compact body turned toward the Englishman. "They are not free, for example, to choose their company among men."

The horses clopped softly over the trail for a space of seconds.

"I think my lord has something to say."

"I mean my daughter, Bastard."

They stared at each other, then Eustace went on. "I think your nearness to Brand Ulfson, your time in Paris have distorted your view of reality and certain differences. Because of your qualities, you are valuable. You have the privilege of my hall." He paused to give it significance. "But so have my dogs, Bastard. You are no longer free, and this is not Paris. Don't presume."

They paced on. Gurth betrayed no emotion, but his knuckles were white on the reins.

"There are lords who'd flay the hide off you at the mere thought of it. That would not be economical. We're so few, I'd train crows if I could."

The baron brought his horse up short and wheeled it around to face the big Saxon. "You are silent. You don't deny what I've said?"

He was answered with an unfathomable coldness. "No."

"Then listen, boy: I'll use that whip if I have to. It is *no*. Never."

Abruptly he turned and rode on, waving Gurth to ride at his knee. "You'll be traveling in any case. I want to know how many men we can kick into shape for some kind of defense come spring." Then he dismissed the subject casually. "I hope they've fed those sows decently."

According to his values, he had faced the situation and disposed of it with efficiency and a good deal of tolerance. The world he knew was ordained and immutable, a balanced triangle with God at its apex and beneath Him the Church. Next came the king (when he was as strong as William) flanked by his peers, the *noblesse*. Beneath them a great bar was drawn. Under this line, almost in outer darkness, lay the villeins and serfs necessary to the ballast of the whole. This was the order of things; it had always been so. God willed it.

The baron had—tragically—not the haziest concept of the mind of his English clerk, which was neither static nor tidily triangular.

* * *

"The child is the center of its own world. To himself the child is God and his wishes divine right until he learns his natural place. Are you yet a child, *Maître* Gurth?"

So said his theology master in Paris sensing Gurth's inability to accept his lot. Such perversity was weakness where a priest needed strength. He might be a scholar; of that dangerous Pelagian breed who saw man's world as improvable by man, but a priest needed surer vision. He was young but not that blind. Some day the men of learning would change things, within the Church or without it. The world had to improve. It couldn't get worse.

So Gurth hunched on the hillside while his manor horse cropped at grass, and glared at the distant brown smudge that had been Brandeshal. He was not sure where to aim the boiling emotions, at his own father or Gerlaine's. They were much the same. He couldn't part one from the other.

The baron made himself very clear about Gerlaine. Where Gurth sought her out before, he avoided her now, held himself in tight rein while he wrestled with a knot of confused rages. It was hard to be bound in a narrow space and defined by a narrow word like "serf," but there it was. He was kenneled like the baron's hounds, they all were. John Plowwright accepted it, wise Calla largely ignored it, Godric seethed but managed, he'd tried himself. No, not so. He'd simply ignored it all, taken as an easy gift the freedom his brother fought for, and like a child expected it to endure forever. He almost succeeded in the self-deception till Gerlaine came. He reached for her naturally. Why not? There wasn't that much difference of birth. De Neuville was of less *wergild* than Godric before Hastings and of no better blood. This was England—had been once—where anyone but a bought slave could point to his own and say, "this is mine." His own father gave him a chance for advancement, but—and that was the rub of it all—no clear idea of what was his to begin with. Brand's world was gone, but Eustace couldn't take what was left without giving him something of value in return.

There, that's brave. We're all slaves now. You're beaten cold like the Atheling. Swallow it as he did and go on living. Forget her.

"Gurth!"

He started out of his brooding. Gerlaine cantered toward him with Bête at her knee. The day was warm. He saw the new laced kirtle tight at her small waist and open at the throat. She did burn him. He felt the energy of that spare body and knew what it could be to his. She was all the more desirable now for being denied him. Gurth filled his lungs with air and saw with a young man's passionate despair the sun on the heath, purple and yellow with heather and ragwort. His patch of the world could be a beautiful place, but without her only dirt.

Forget it, fool.

Bête squatted by his horse as Gerlaine skipped forward to Gurth. "*Ça va,* Gurth?"

"Well, thank you."

"One sees you have been busy. I greeted you in the bailey this morning. You were too preoccupied to answer."

He saw how the sun had freckled the fair skin in the hollow of her throat. "Yes. Excuse me. Where do you ride?"

"Oh." Gurth read the answer in her hesitation. She'd followed him from the keep. She had sought him out. Her closeness was a physical pang, and he turned away from it.

"It is a good day to ride," Gerlaine said lamely. "You are on father's business?"

"Yes." His tone was hard as the truth under it. "Learning my place, *demoiselle.*"

"What? Gurth, what is it?"

"Nothing at all. What's a sensible man to do when he's beaten but learn his place? God knows I've tutors enough. Your steward has told me where I may not harvest for myself. Your brother tells me where I may not hunt. Now your father tells me where I may not look."

Gerlaine understood some of it, what was in his eyes, but not all. "You are unjust."

"*I* am unjust?"

"You harvest for my father only what we need, not a grain more. The forest has always been the lord's preserve, and every man must have a lord. My father answers to the high sheriff and he to the king."

"And I to your father, world without end, amen." He busied himself with his saddle cinch.

"Father talked to you about me?"

"Right enough. I am to remember my condition and yours and the distance between them."

He heard the rustle of her skirts behind him, then felt her hand on his arm. Her voice was small with the lie. "You are my friend, Gurth."

"You're too honest for that, Gerlaine. You don't lie well."

"I've never done that in my life," she lied.

"It was never just friendship but *us*. You knew it that day in Vaudan's cell. You must have known."

"Wait." Gerlaine struggled for the right words; it was all happening too fast, she was losing it before ever winning. "I am stupid beside you, I know. There are things I don't understand. All my life there has been work, hard work to keep my father's house. Now I try to learn what is mine."

"So do I."

"You're the scholar, Gurth. Must I know everything at once? Must I?"

But he wasn't listening, looking past her to Bête with an old man's sadness.

"Dead. God, I know it now. Dead and gone. At least he'll never know how beaten we are. Be kind to him."

"Don't you know what I am saying? Tell me how to understand!"

"I can't."

"Please, Gurth." Gerlaine snatched at his hand and clung to it. The touch of her went into the pit of his stomach.

"You shouldn't be here, lady."

Her grip tightened. "Look at me. I don't care what Father said. Look at me!"

"But I have to care, for the best of reasons. He could flay me or geld me like the rest of his pork. He could kill me and take what Calla has left, and you Normans don't leave very much. That's what your father gave me to understand. If he asks, tell him I do. Goodbye, Gerlaine."

He trotted the horse down the hill then kicked it into a dead run. He tried not to look back at her, but he had to. Gerlaine was still watching him from the hilltop. Help her to understand? Christ, who understood anything but that he'd hurt her and felt both ashamed and satisfied.

* * *

Gerlaine's closet was on the third level of the keep proper, less than a fourth of the area the rest of which constituted the main hall or court where everyone from the family to servants ate and her father received visitors, issued business and orders. The tower was a drab wooden block, no less comfortable than the stone towers at home and certainly no more. It was not the farmhouse at Neuville, worn smooth with time and love and a hundred sweet-sour smells. They rattled loose in this place.

The ground level was for storage and the drafty jakes they all used in common, a damp, musty place with the inevitable adventurous rats. Gerlaine decided that she would rather suffer of nights or avail herself of a chamber pot rather than barefoot down, candle shuddering in the draft, to stumble across one of them.

Above this was the main scullery smelling of lentils and sweat, burned wood and food, straw, salt and flour, and leading by narrow wooden stairs up to the main hall and her room. Beyond that, on the next level was the armory, closets for Hugh on one side, Guy and Robin on the other, and the stairs leading to the open platform above with its catapults.

Her mother and father had chosen a small bower near the smithy, one of the buildings from the old Saxon steading, not far from the entrance to the keep though much more inviting. Its carefully wattled walls and thatched roof remembered Neuville.

Gerlaine's closet was more than twice the space she'd had at home. There was a well-carved bed with a straw mattress and good linen sheets under the blankets (an extravagance she reveled in), a worktable for sewing and those discreet few cosmetics allowed by propriety, *two* chests, mind you, one for linen and one for the heavier garments, a little votive altar for her private prayers, and a loom.

She did not revel in the loom. It made cloth, which was a chore like the candles and the hundred other tasks Élène set for the women and which she had to supervise. Gerlaine hated the hours with the women. They wove, chattered, insinuated, their tongues unraveling reputations with the same narrow peasant sureness of their nimble fingers. In their company Gerlaine pretended a gravity and devotion to the loom her results could barely support. She was not a good weaver. Her one venture into the higher art of the implement, a gloomy, brownish Pietà brooding over her-votive altar, depicted a Jesus so lumpy and unbalanced that His woolen mind seemed bent more on shifting his position than the rigors of purgatory.

But to *ride,* or bending over the wheat at harvest, the wind cool on the sweat between her breasts—the clean, purgative feel of work that used all of her. And the resting afterward with warm, simple food. To love, she thought often, must be like that: to grapple and sweat, with a delicious quiet at the end. To love, yes, or to carry a child.

And I'm a lady with a new hawk on my gauntlet, and when I loft my bird—God, I wish it were me. I want to climb, soar, attack, pierce . . . you. I love you.

From Gurth she rode home to the keep, snapped at her brothers and went to her own altar to pray vehemently. After a few moments Gerlaine realized she wasn't praying but complaining. What Gurth said disturbed her most because it was true.

The paneled shutter of her casement stood open. She leaned there gazing out over the fields to the west where the tiny harvesters scythed their way through the grain. The pestle, moving through pumice in her mortar cup, ground more and more slowly.

"Gerlaine?" Élène stood in the entrance from the hall.

"Oui, Maman?"

"Père Vaudan thanks you for the candles."

"It was nothing."

"I've been looking over the linen, counting ells," Élène moved casually into the room. "You have enough?"

"I think so."

"That's curious," Élène riffled the folded cloth on the worktable. She studied the definitely contoured bodice of her daughter's kirtle. "I thought from your new gown you might have skimped."

"No, I was careless. I misjudged."

"Of course. But then it can only be used as a chemise. You will wear one of your supertunics. The fitted sleeve looks fine, but I really don't think—no. Even if it is the fashion in Paris."

"Oh, did you hear?"

Élène sighed. "Master Gurth is a bottomless well of information," she said in a preparatory manner. Gerlaine knew what was coming.

"Shut the casement, *ma fille*."

They sat together on the bed.

"The women of the French court," her mother began, "have to be nothing but amusing and beautiful. They are not at the center of things. But you will rule a fief with your husband someday, and you will command in every place he cannot. As I do. Without respect that is not possible."

She traced the embroidery at Gerlaine's throat. "Lovely, such care." She spoke gently but with a firmness allowing no denial. "Modesty in dress is only part of that obligation. You should measure your linen more carefully."

"Yes." But she hadn't fooled the earth wisdom wrinkled about those steady blue eyes.

"Then, too," Élène's fingers toyed with the neck of her veil. "Being women, let's name the card as it falls. What must be guessed at has more intrigue than what becomes a common sight."

The unspoken thing passed between them, became a mischievous smile, then Élène hugged her daughter, and while Gerlaine giggled on her breast, she murmured into the thick hair. "You little hellion. *Je t'aime, tu sais?*"

"I love you, too, *Maman*."

"Here, rub my back. I haven't been off my feet today till now. Thank God it's only a sheriff and not the King. We'd never survive."

She moved gratefully with the soothing pressure of Gerlaine's fingers, sighed, then broached her main topic as if they had already spoken of it for some time.

"Master Gurth is a man of many colors—rub harder, *chérie*—so. I don't understand him any more than Hugh. They go away, they change. And Gurth? *Bien,* he is attractive if you like them a mile high and smelling of sheep, which I do not. The men in this country are louts, even the nobles. Which," she observed pointedly, "*he* is not."

"He is half."

"So was Neuville," Élène retorted flatly out of an old bitterness that no longer pained. "Little Jehanne and Gar: they look like your brothers, don't they?"

"I'm not blind, Mama."

"Half of Neuville, half France, half the world, sweet. But there are distinctions. You should not be so free with your time."

When Gerlaine made no comment, Élène probed: "Has he been familiar?"

The girl's fingers continued to knead. She looked tenderly at the back of her mother's head, hidden by the veil. *Is this how it goes with women, Maman? A moment when, without lying, I begin to tell you less than the truth; when I must hug myself to some other breast than yours for succor? If so, it's lonely.*

"He has been kind."

"Undoubtedly. And interesting. Paris is full of the like. They go to study and stay to drink. *Goliards,* too lazy to work for the Church. They spend their time rhyming Latin and with the sort of woman we may well imagine. So our sheepherder goes there and comes back filled with all sorts of new ideas, thinking the equality of the tavern will do at home. Now *attend,* Gerlaine: when the sheriff is here, your father will discuss possibilities among the younger men, perhaps those around the king."

She turned to regard her daughter levelly. "I said possibilities, those things which you may have. If you were older, if you were light as those titled harlots around the king of France in their tight gowns, laced within an inch of their lives and gasping for breath—then you could put him here"—she patted the bed—"and put him out in the morning; it's been done before. For anything else, he comes with the land like his sheep. Your father owns him. He can use him or throw him away." She rose and moved to the door. "Do you understand?"

"Very clearly, *Maman.*"

Something in the voice made Élène turn. She saw the girl's straight back and level eyes. *No, you are not a child anymore, I was carrying Hugh two years younger. You will be hurt.*

"There is enough pain for women, *ma chère.*" She opened the door. "We need not reach beneath us for more."

Alone, Gerlaine rose heavily from the bed and stood in the middle of the room. She looked to the altar, then to the Pietà. Thoughtfully, she went to the casement again, opened the shutter and leaned out, gazing beyond the stockade to the barley fields where the men swung rhythmically through the grain.

* * *

They moved like slow dancers through the barley, naked except for hempen trousers and running with sweat. They had worked like this for hours, Gurth and his brother, well beyond second wind, till their pulses, caught up in the rhythm, felt tireless, able to move all day. Behind, Godric's wife Hulda and his six-year-old son shocked the cut grain into bundles. Beyond them, other men and other wives swung and bundled in the same earth-caressing dance.

They all knew it would be today, and it would be Gurth. All the rest had a head start on their own strips, but Bastard, with all the time he spent at Montford, would be last even with Godric helping. It was well Gurth would have the Maiden, there'd be beer and mutton and Calla's house would burst with the noisy lot of them swilling half the night with the Maiden in the center of the full table, a promise kept in an age-old bargain. The circle is closed. Old Wife dies, Maiden is born. The year turns and turns again, grows green, grows old, dies and is reborn. The primal promise, the faith beyond Faith, is kept.

It would be today, and so Calla was here. Today her hair was not bound. She wore a simple white smock and her feet were bare in the stirrups as she paced Gurth's manor horse from group to group, greeting this farmer, joking with another. They answered with a deference in their greeting. Today she was Corn-Woman.

"Let's have some beer, Hulda." Godric leaned on his scythe, looking gratefully at the unclouded white sky. "Good thing the weather's held." He jerked his head toward the keep. "Bloody generous of him to let us get our own in finally."

Hulda brought the warm, thick beer in a leathern bag. She was like her husband—rawboned, blond, moon-faced, joyously profane and durable. Godric drank noisily, passed it to Gurth, then swept his grubby namesake up into his hairy arms, making the boy squeal with the tickling of his beard. "How you like it, boy? Huh? How you like helping your da?"

"He's been good," Hulda patted the boy's tiny rump. "Not a whimper the whole day."

"First time in the fields, Gurth. There's a farmer for you."

Hulda studied her brother-in-law. "What's the matter, Gurth?"

"Nothing."

"Nothing hell!" she hooted. "Look at him, Godric: all day a face as long as a sermon."

"Not used to work anymore, that's all," Godric picked up his scythe. "Sitting in Paris. Come on, let's finish."

Their blades bit into the remaining stand.

"Look what's coming," said Hulda.

Riders had crossed the bailey bridge and were heading along the edge of the fields: Baron Eustace, a few men and his four children.

She rode behind with her brother, the hawk poised elegantly on her wrist. Godric cleared his throat and spat.

"Know how to tell a Norman from his hawk?" he chuckled. "The bird looks smarter." He flicked an appraising eye at the baron's daughter. "You get a taste for French girls over there?"

"Like good wine," his brother grunted over his work. "Warm and delicate."

"Delicate don't last," Godric judged. "Get a *woman* like Hulda that'll stand up and spit back. Smart at the oven, hard out here and soft in bed."

Their scythes *swushed*.

Someone called to him. Robin it was, proud of his new bird, holding it aloft for Gurth to see. He waved back and hailed the boy. His eyes found her now, she was coming abreast of him, glancing at him once, then riding on.

He felt heavy and old.

"Now, *that* skinny chicken," Godric observed. "Probably split in two the first time you rammed her."

"I don't think so." All morning the booming obscenities of his brother had been enjoyable. Now Gurth wished he'd shut up.

"You think too much."

"And you talk too much." *Swush!*

"She's cold like the rest of them. That brother of hers, *Sire* Hugh, no less. You see the eyes on that snake? Cold: freeze the balls off a stone saint!" *Swush!* "They say 'twas him killed Brand." *Swush!* "In the back, I'll bet."

"Lords are lords," Gurth muttered. "They kill each other, we stay. *So*." The blade swooped.

"It's not the same. They're not us."

"Neither was Brand."

"The hell he wasn't."

"The hell he was. You call him what you want. He left us like spit on two doorsteps, your mother's and mine. Of course, he freed us; there's that." *Swush!* "When he was too tired to come as he always had." The blade swooped viciously. "Taking and taking and *taking.*"

Gurth threw down the scythe and wiped the sweat from his browned face. "They take. But this is mine." He pointed to the barley in front of them. "And Maiden's mine, today is mine, so the hell with it. What do you say, big brother? Let's get drunk tonight. Let's get good and drunk. Bugger 'em all. *Mother! Everyone!*"

They all watched him bend to touch the barley. "Send for the Old Wife. I've found the Maid!"

As Calla rode toward her son, the shout went up across the fields:

"Barley-Maid! Barley-Maid is here."

She had not seen him for a week and then only as he passed down the stairs from the hall with her father.

Today it was unbearable.

They were to hawk with the new birds today. Halfheartedly Gerlaine tried to interest Bête; for some reason he would not be coaxed but squatted in the mud near the stable, disinterested and remote. She couldn't blame him. It was a day for sulking, for being alone and hating virulently everything in sight.

God damn it!

She tried to remember Vaudan's caution on blasphemy, but the English words came back, the way big Godric said them, and nothing else so precisely translated her mood. No, she did not want to hunt or even ride with this ridiculous bird on her gauntleted wrist. Her younger brothers caught the brunt of it.

"Pardi," Guy made a face at her, ducking his head between his shoulders. "Gerlaine's in a fine mood."

"Let's ride by the fields." Robin pranced his horse about. "I want to show Bastard my new bird."

So he was in the fields today.

The baron and Hugh rode out of the stable and joined them.

"Hé, Hugh," Guy said, "as a man of responsibility, give our sister a boot in the butt."

"Oh, shut up, you tire me." Gerlaine wheeled her horse away from them and took her chosen place at Hugh's side.

"Ah, she'll spoil the day, she's been at us since breakfast."

"You are well, Daughter?"

"Aye, Father. Perhaps there is a cold coming on."

"Women have their mysteries." Hugh appraised her with satiric eyes that were, in their own way, remote as Bête's. "Come ride, Sister."

The baron led with the falconers, Guy and Robin trailing close behind. Gerlaine and Hugh brought up the rear. Hugh rode with absent command. He might have slept in the saddle and still guided the horse. He seemed to take no more overt pleasure in horse than in anything else, she thought. A good knight, a professional soldier, yet performing each act perfunctorily and without joy. *He's gone gray all through like a dead tree.*

Of nights he sat drinking alone before the dying fire in the hall, oblivious to the snoring servants about him. Lying awake, her own conflicts denying sleep, she would hear him pacing about till he stumbled unsurely up the stairs to his bed.

His silence grew uncomfortable for her; it was a presence.

"I didn't want to hunt today," she said.

"It will pass the time," Hugh answered distantly.

In her boiling heart boredom was not the problem. His retort irritated her. "Till what, pray tell?"

"Twixt now and dying."

"Oh, Hugh! You're not serious."

"No. Nothing is serious."

Gerlaine started to reply that he was wrong. Perversely she would have welcomed an argument, but they were approaching the harvesters, and he was there, half naked and brown.

Do you know it is you claws me hollow this way? Will you look up, look at me? Will you give me something to hold through this horrible day; a thought, a smile? Look up, damn you!

Then her blessed Robin sang out: "*Hé, Gurth—regardez!* Look at my bird!"

She saw him wave to Robin, say something and turn back to his work. For a moment, his glance was on her, opaque, invulnerable, then it passed her by. She felt it physically and slumped with the disappointment, then forced herself erect, concentrating her hatred on the hooded goshawk.

You silly bird. I hope you break your neck.

The tercel hawk was a miserable haggard. It took a tedious long time to lure her back after the first loft. The second time the falconer whirled the lure in vain.

Gerlaine seethed. "Give me a dog any day. A hound at least has some brains. We waste time." She snatched the lure from the falconer. "Father, go on. I'll bring her down."

She spurred back across the heath, keeping a malevolent eye on the errant hawk. Insufferable as she was, the hawk did her a favor. Gerlaine saw she was winging straight back to the familiar environs of the keep, directly over the barley fields. Time enough later for wandering birds.

They appeared to be waiting for something, most of them drifting in twos and threes toward Gurth and Godric. As Gerlaine approached, an elderly farmer ran over the fields toward the others, waving above his head a crude doll made out of plaited straw. He plunged into the group and threw the doll onto the stubbled ground. A flint was struck, the spark nursed in the straw till smoke wisped out followed by a tongue of bright flame, and the burning doll was handed up to Calla.

"Old Wife is dying," she cried. "Old Wife is dying!"

Her calloused heels raked the mare's flanks. Swinging the doll round and round her head, Calla rode in a wide circuit about the borders of Gurth's strip. After one complete circle, she threw the black remnant to the ground. There was a rush: ten, a dozen farmers stamping as if afflicted, pounding the burnt straw into the ground, shouting words Gerlaine couldn't understand.

Gurth had not joined in the stamping but remained alone by the small shock of barley still uncut. It was as if he were oblivious to her presence; his attention was fixed on the men and his mother.

"Who found Barley-Maid?"

"I have!"

Gurth moved now, taking the horse's halter and leading his mother to the little stand of barley. Calla had never looked so young to Gerlaine or so womanly beautiful.

"Where is Barley-Maid?" she asked, loud enough for all of them to hear.

"Here, Mother."

Calla held out her hand. Proudly, Gurth helped her dismount. Calla produced an ancient bronze knife, gathered the stalks into a tight sheaf and cut them.

"Aye!" they applauded. "The Maid is here."

Calla's deft fingers wove and plaited quickly as the others circled about her, the women stroking Gurth. One of them kissed him, and Gerlaine raged behind her eyes when he responded lustily. They paid her no heed. The lord's daughter might have been a scarecrow for all they noticed her.

He knows I'm here, damn him.

Then Calla mounted again, the new doll thrust aloft. "The Maid is born!"

There was a huge shout from every throat in the field; it rose as one then splintered into a cacophony of cries, everyone bellowing at Gurth while little Godric, not understanding a bit of it, hopped about the fringes shrieking for the pure noise and fun.

The women jostled in on Gurth, vying for kisses, hugging him, jabbering, while he attempted to kiss every one of them, torn from one to the other with raucous joy.

"Gurth will be married this year!"

"Who? . . . . who?"

"Me!" Hulda screeched, diving at Gurth's legs, rolling him on the ground. "I swear I'll leave this useless husband of mine and marry you."

"Feast!" Godric commanded. "Feast!" It was a signal; the cry went up from everyone. "Feast! Feast at Gurth's house."

They were all pummeling him now. Only half understanding what she saw, Gerlaine moved in closer. When they let Gurth up, Calla tossed the doll to him. "Take the Maid, boy."

But Godric intercepted it with a whoop, tossed it to Hulda, and a darting game of keep-away swirled suddenly around Gerlaine's shying horse. She longed to be part of it, to be noticed by Gurth, who was roaring and swearing louder even than Godric now, releasing a terrible, beautiful energy. They dodged him nimbly, one man passing the doll to another just as Gurth reached him, and the fat, screaming blond who had knocked him down still hanging on, fondling and hindering him at the same time.

Suddenly Gurth twisted in Hulda's arms, kissed her hard and slapped her rump sharply. Hulda shrieked with surprise and swung wide at him as he ducked away and plunged after Godric holding the doll.

"Hey JohnheyJohn—*catch!*"

The doll sailed high over Gurth's fingertips toward Gerlaine. Something joyous and savage welled and burst inside her, moved her arms and heels to its bidding, thrust out her arm and caught the doll.

They paused. The laughter became uncertain, weakened and died.

Gurth held out his hand. "The Maid is mine, *demoiselle*."

"No." A tight, nervous laugh came out of the blackness in her. "It's mine."

His look told her nothing, admitted no opening or familiarity. He reached to take the doll from her. Gerlaine eluded him effortlessly, backing, rearing away, then trotting in circles around and away from him while the others watched. The girl was a marvel; the horse responded to her thoughts with barely a touch or word. She kept Gurth away as easily as a clumsy child.

Then the other voice, low but stern. "Give it back. It's his."

But she would not be warned, not today. Dimly she knew it was wrong, but the reason was faint, drowned under the more urgent thing. The smile set hard on her lips. She drew him further apart, now backing, now making him jump aside from cleverly feigned charges, never taking her eyes from his in the cold dance.

"Come get it . . . *hé* . . . *hé* . . . *va t'en . . . va!*"

Then Calla was beside her, hedging her in toward Gurth, grasping at her arm. "Give it to me. You don't belong here."

Calla saw through her. She was naked to this strong woman's will, read the brusque contempt in Calla's command. The black thing screamed deep, twisted her arm free with cruel force, coiled and slammed the heavy gauntlet across Calla's cheek.

For a hot, shame-ridden eternity, Gerlaine faced them —him. She wanted to curse them and beg Calla's forgiveness at the same impossible time. *All day I have needed to cry, to touch you.*

They confronted each other, the wall between them like a positive force on her fingers, twisting the reins, turning her away, flogging her with invisible whips toward the forest, still clutching her pitiful prize.

Calla dismounted and regarded her son. "It begins, doesn't it? Are you still a fool?"

He couldn't face her or any of them. They all knew. The lord's little bitch had played with him, courted him, then kicked him aside and insulted his mother.

Like Brand—

—having to wait outside, allowed to care for the big man's horse while he was in the hut with Mother. Thrust outside, away, alone. And she crying aloud sometimes not out of pain but something else they would not share with him. Outside in the dark, small and deserted.

"There's so little," Hulda pulled her son close to her. "Now they take even that."

They moved now; the group around Calla began to break up and move silently away.

"No." Gurth shook his head doggedly. "No, wait. Not this they don't."

He swung himself onto the mare. "Feast!" He threw the word like a stone. "Feast at my house—everybody. You hear? Everybody! And the Maid will be at the table. Feast!"

He kicked the horse to a gallop after Gerlaine.

VI

It didn't matter if she rode into hell or her father's lap, he would follow. For a doll. For more than a doll. For one slap too many, jolting him to reality as it slammed across his mother's cheek.

Paris had been a dream—the wine, the wit, the illusion of mind against chaos, the easy equality. The generous, unde-manding love of women like Solange—all a dream.

And yet I came back to this because I belong here. Nothing is changed. I'm still waiting outside while that son of a bitch takes his pleasure, and where am I, where can I turn? What is mine?

It was much more than Barley-Maid.

Don't tell me to understand him, Mother.

I'm not your son. You hurt Calla. You made her cry, and still she goes to you.

She rode straight as an arrow, giving the horse its head. The mare was tired from the morning's hawking; Gurth gained steadily as she drew toward the small neck of woods. There was no more purpose to her flight than the taking of the doll, but it would all come to a head now. He wouldn't speak; if he did, the whole mess of it would boil over, the anger, the wanting her, the baron's insult he had to swallow. Gurth kicked viciously at the flanks of the mare as Gerlaine plunged into the trees.

There was a futile, aimless quality to her flight now. She wasn't trying to escape; the horse slowed almost to a canter, weaving in and out of the trees until Gerlaine found herself in a cul-de-sac of high brambles and reared hopelessly about to face him.

The trembling began again as he slid from the saddle and approached her.

"Barley-Maid is mine."

He saw the torture in her eyes before she collapsed sobbing over the horse's neck. "God . . . oh, God . . ."

It wasn't fair that she should take his anger away like this; not fair to pity her, to want to hold her. Gurth forced the harshness. "Your father was quite clear. I would have left you alone." *God, I want to despise you.* "You . . . you're all alike!" He tore the doll from her unresisting fingers. "You take."

He turned his back on her.

"Listen to me!"

It tore out of her, the shame and the hopeless defeat. They faced each other at last, painfully. The wall was down.

"They have been at me too. But I came to you, and you would not look at me. You pawed at that fat blond pig in front of *me* . . . when I came to you." Her throat tightened, quavered with shame and a depth of fury she had not guessed in herself till now. "*I* have been told, too. What I may have and what I may not."

Gurth moved closer. The thing was shaking Gerlaine apart.

"I have lain awake because of you, eaten food and not tasted it because of you; seen the servants turn aside with whispers when we passed, heard them gossip and titter: *la petite demoiselle* wants to sow for the Bastard. Oh, yes, Gurth, and I have endured it. One does not answer dirt like that."

He knew the cruel habit of life that straightened her wracked body even more, forcing it into the mold of her breeding; broken, committed and beautiful in one breath.

"—Because you . . . you were so fine. I knew what my father commanded, and still *I* came to *you* like—like one of those bitches in the field!" She tore the gauntlet from her hand. "And the Bastard would not even *look at me!*"

The last word wrenched out in an agonized sob as she struck at him. Gurth didn't move. The blow released her anger, and she struck again and again, flailing blindly at him. One of the gauntlet studs tore a thin red line across his cheek, but he made no attempt to avoid it. Gerlaine bowed over the pommel, exhausted by her own passion. With infinite tenderness Gurth reached out to her. Gerlaine slid down into his arms like a weary child and he held her.

"Sweet Christ, help me."

"Both of us," he whispered.

"I am so ashamed," Gerlaine choked against his chest. "It was so wrong. I will do anything. I will sew clothes for Calla, send gifts—anything, but she must forgive me."

"Calla has been hurt by masters," he said softly. "She'll forgive you."

"It feels good in your arms. I am so tired."

"Yes." He unwound her veil and buried his face and hands in the abundance of her hair. "Yes." She was tiny, only halfway up his chest, and her lips against his skin went through him like hot needles.

"You don't hate me? You said you'd never hate me."

"No. God, no."

His hands slid down her back, hesitated and stopped. Gerlaine felt him shaking. His fingers laced again in her hair, pulling her mouth up to his.

"Gurth, I—what do I do? There has never been a man. I have never felt like this before."

He was kissing her and—impossible delight—she wanted to touch his lips with hers, taste them and trace them with her fingers all at the same time.

"It is wonderful," she whispered. "So wonderful. You are crying? Oh, you are crying, too!"

It was not like anyone else, not like anything but Gurth and me: what we need and what we are. I wish I knew writing. I would remember all of it, how he moved, how I answered him, and that there was no pain. None, Maman. Only a sweetness and a hunger for more, and more to feed the hunger. I ache now, but even that is delicious. I will not confess this; it's mine and a joy. I cannot repent what I will never regret.

I love you.

To hear you say that to me and know in my heart you mean it. You love me. I have known wonders.

Even kneeling before her little altar was a fresh experience, her body a languorous new gift, hardly known till now.

"Blessed Mary, Mother of God, intercede with your grace for all those in purgatory that they may the sooner see the Kingdom—."

"You're not abed, child?"

Élène surveyed the room with old habit. She poked the fire and turned down the coverlet. "Such a country: only August and already the nights are November. You'll take cold in your bare feet. Come to bed."

"Oui, Maman."

"I should be in bed myself," Élène sighed, "but there is always something."

"Oh, Mama, you should trust the people now. They know what to do."

"Aye, aye; still." Élène canted her head toward the casement. "Listen. You hear it?"

"What?"

"The wind. It never stops."

"I like it sometimes. It puts me to sleep." Gerlaine kissed her mother and slid luxuriously down between the linen sheets. "Oh, I feel good."

"Well, this is an improvement. Guy said you looked like Black Friday when you rode after your haggard."

"Silly bird," Gerlaine yawned. "I could fly better myself."

"Whatever happens under that veil of yours? Your hair is all tangles." Élène brought the brush from the table.

Gerlaine sat up. "Brush me, like you used to."

It doesn't stop me from loving you as much; it helps.

"Such a head of hair." Élène brushed through and through the auburn river. "Lazy, you don't plait it enough; just catch it up under your veil, don't you? That is, when milady condescends to wear one."

"Don't scold." *I want to tell you and I can't. Already I miss you.*

"Is that nightgown warm enough?" Élène bent closer. "You ought to close the throat these cold nights. Perhaps a catch in front—"

The loose gown was open and fell to one side of Gerlaine's

throat. At the juncture of the shoulder and the delicate neck, Élène saw the bluish-red, unmistakable imprint of teeth. As she touched it, Gerlaine's telltale hands moved to close the gown, her eyes widening suddenly.

Élène rose. "Get up."

She threw back the blankets and took Gerlaine by the wrist. "Get up!"

Her mother was a cold stranger. "Take off your nightgown."

Numbly she obeyed, slipping the gown over her head. She shivered now before her mother's mute, horrified judgment —nude, the gown trailing from her tight-knuckled fist. Élène's glance swept over her, reading every mark and bruise. They had not thought to be careful. Her mother spun her roughly about. Gerlaine held the gown in front of her. She tried to read the pale, tight-lipped silence—hurt, loss, outrage. And pity? Was pity there, too?

"You little fool."

It was too late for pity.

"Who? Was it him? *Was it?*"

The girl said nothing, dry-eyed, not defiant but now cowed. Élène moved stiffly toward the fire. She took a wooden goblet from the hearth, poured the warm wine into it and drank deep, refilling the cup. When she spoke, the words splintered around Gerlaine like cold metal—jagged, cutting. And under it, she felt the deep wound she had made and could never heal.

"We sit here in this dirty wooden box," Élène began. "It is not much, it is the end of the earth, but we are seigneurs. Possibly you might think on what that cost your father." She came back to Gerlaine. "The years, the scars. Not all of them showing. Like Hugh. Your father has raised all of us—and you —out of nothing, to give us something beside pride and an empty belly to back up our name, to take us just a *little* way from the pigsty, my sweet daughter. Years it took, because that other bastard who now sits on the throne, that tanner's grandson, was never known for generosity. Years. And in one afternoon you have brought that pigsty back to us. Your health —Daughter!"

Her hand darted out with the cup. The wine dripped from Gerlaine's face, but she barely blinked.

It is done. I can't plead. You would not have me beg for mercy.

Élène groped for the door latch. "Pray God forgive you. You've hanged that man."

"He didn't rape me!"

"I know," Élène nodded with cold disgust. "*We* know that, woman. But he'll hang the same." She opened the door. "I am your mother; I can never deny you. But I don't want to think on the lesson you will learn tonight."

The door closed like a sentence. Beyond, Élène's voice knifed up the stairs. "Guard!"

Gerlaine crept back into the bed, pulling the covers around her. She felt cold.

No, she could not hide in bed. She must dress. Her hands shook. She must remember to stand straight and answer clearly and not beg.

Mais, j'ai peur. Dear God, please, I am afraid.

The fat lamps had been filled twice, and the open hearth in the middle of the floor no longer flamed but glowed with a steady heat deep in its blackened stones, a golden warmth, cozy and smelling of mutton, soup, beer and contentment. They had wrestled, sung, eaten, drunk, shouted, cursed and wassailed each other to exhaustion. The plowwright's son belted another man in the mouth and was suitably laid out and peace restored with no hard feelings. Someone's son and someone's daughter discovered Calla's hide-partitioned bower and proceeded to enjoy it in noisy secret and no one gave a damn. The feast had risen, crested, roared with life and fallen back, unbuckled and mellow.

The table was a battlefield after the fact, a ravaged panorama of thick bread trenchers, pots of beer, bowls long emptied of vegetables, a middling fall of bread crumbs like first snow from the loaves sliced and smeared generously with thick, sweet pork fat, the clean-picked bones of a young ewe and various smaller ruins; and in the center of the long table, triumphant in a sanctuary of flowers, lay the Barley-Maid.

It was late, the talk had died to contented murmurs. Beyond the open door, a few farmers talked tomorrow's weather. Little Godric, with a stomach tight and round as an apple, lay collapsed and oblivious in his mother's ample lap on Gurth's cot as she nuzzled her husband with drowsy affection. Two diehards still munched at the lower end of the table arguing seed, while at the head, in a heavy oak chair used only for such feasts, Calla reigned in her white smock under a crown of flowers. Her hair was still unbound, but she had brushed and arranged it to fall behind and over her breasts, framing the bronze gorget at her throat.

At her right, Gurth leaned on the table sipping the last of his beer. He hadn't gotten drunk after all; there was no need. The happiness was deep in him as the heat of the hearthstones.

He buried his face in his palms. For all the savory odors in the cottage, he hoarded this fading secret scent in his hands, along his arms, all over him. Strange—a hundred details about Solange could still spring to mind at any time, clear as this morning, yet of today he had no more graspable memory than sunlight dancing through leaves. There was a blurred, changing picture of thick, scented hair against his face, a mouth finding his again and again. Of tomorrow and the day after, there was no clear thought but he had to see her.

"So quiet you are," Calla remarked subtly. "Was it a battle bringing home the Maid?"

"No."

"I thought not." Calla toyed with her cup. "The bairn was sick with shame." She studied her son. "It does begin, doesn't it?"

"What, Mother?"

Her laugh was rich, earthy and knowing. "I'm an old woman —well, getting there, for sure—"

"Och," he denied, "you're still beautiful."

Gurth enjoyed her pleased little preening. "Well, I've kept my looks longer than I've a right to. But I'm no fool. My son returns one day from riding with his wee lordship, answers me short and goes about all week tight as a drumhead. Then does he ride off after a girl ready to kill her and comes home peaceful as morning"—she took his hands and kissed them —"smelling of rosewater and woman. Am I wrong?"

"No."

"Well, I'll grant you this: when you're a fool, you be not a small one."

"I love her, Calla."

"Indeed," she answered with a deep irony. "Then do you rise up tomorrow, ride to the keep and ask her da for the *demoiselle's* rosewatered hand."

"Mother, listen—"

"No," she cut him off. "You listen. I'm not blind, I've seen it coming. That's a fair girl. Her back's straight and her hands aren't soft. But she goes with the keep. No, listen! Your father loved me. I never wanted before the Normans came. But in all those years, I was never allowed inside Brandeshal gate, never in the house. First his parents, then Algive. Bloodless bitch." She brushed at crumbs with vigorous contempt. "I don't know why she grudged him *my* bed; there was enough of that in her own. When I met his sons, it was here. Leofwine and little Brand were taught to respect me and my house. But not once could I walk on his arm in York or grace his table. And out of the million times I wanted to share some little thing with him, only a few of them was he with me." She drank and wiped her lips. "The girl will be married and gone in a year or less. Where will you be then?"

He folded his arms and stared at the table. "It's not just a woman, Calla. She's something I must have. She's strong, proud. I don't know what will happen, but she's mine."

They heard a murmur of sound beyond the door that was not part of the guests. John Plowwright stepped into the doorway.

"Gurth, it's the lord. In iron with his men."

"The wee baron here?" Calla got up. "He knows it's barley harvest. We got the steward's permission to stay alight past curfew."

Instinctively Godric nudged his wife aside and rose with Gurth. They moved to the door, but it was blocked by a man-at-arms in mail, holding a torch.

"Gurth Bastard?"

"That's me."

"Outside."

The guests near the door grouped silently to one side of the torch-lit ring of twenty men, every second man holding a crossbow at the ready. In the center, formal as death, were Eustace de Neuville and his three sons.

The soldier shoved Gurth into the ring to confront Eustace. They were all in mail except Guy and Robin, who wore only helmets. The iron cones with their nose guards robbed the young faces of any expression save the aversion clear in every line of their carriage. They would rather be anywhere than here.

Gurth went cold. They knew. There could be no other reason for this, the nocked bows, the chains in Eustace's hands. Godric moved forward to join him; immediately the way was blocked by two soldiers.

Gurth's throat was dry. "Don't move," he said. "Any of you. They'll murder you."

The baron handed the manacles to Robin and dismounted, drawing a small truncheon from his saddle.

"I warned you, Bastard."

The truncheon whirled and the world exploded. When he could see again, he was on his knees, trying to shake his ears clear of the blurred echoes. But one voice came through, low, taut as a bent bow.

"Say the word, little brother."

It was hard to talk or even think, but he couldn't endanger them for this, not on his account. "They'll kill you, Godric," he mumbled. "This is my affair."

Robin stepped in front of him, agonized under the helmet, holding the manacles like something dirty. Eustace ordered him sternly: "Do what you must."

Robin twisted toward his father in mute supplication.

"Strike!"

The boy stiffened. He closed his eyes; blindly, with more desperation than force, he flayed the iron across Gurth's shoulder, then bound his arms behind him in the manacles.

"Put him up."

A ready horse was led into the circle. They threw him across it on his stomach and passed the rope under.

"Baron!"

Eustace opened his mouth to warn her back but something in the woman's bearing silenced him.

"I'd say goodbye to my son."

"Be quick," he grunted.

Against Gurth's cheek, she whispered, "Boy, boy, listen to me."

"It's all right, Mother."

"No, hear me. It's their law and their right. Your da might have done the same." She kissed him. "But do you remember this when the pain starts. I cut an arrow from his leg once, and when the knife was furthest in and him white with it, he said"

—her voice broke slightly—"he said, 'When you're done playing, what's for supper.' Remember."

Then the horse was moving, and they pulled Calla away.

She dressed carefully in a brown kirtle under a red tunic with a heavy cloak closed with two round bronze brooches. Meticulously, she plaited her hair with precise concentration on each strand and bound it tight under the white veil. When this was done, she selected a ring for each finger, knelt by the altar and prayed.

Hooves thundered hollowly on the bailey bridge. Beyond her closed shutter, someone shouted a command. Her father had returned.

"You are dressed—good."

Élène looked gray, old, as if some huge phantom leech had sucked all the love and life out of her, leaving this dry stick.

"Come."

She followed Élène out into the dim hall. Bête hunched, oblivious by the fire. She wanted insanely to run to him for protection, to any one of the few mute servitors standing in hushed groups here and there. They all knew something was wrong, but not its nature. No word had gone beyond the family except that the clever Gurth had overstepped himself in some monstrous way; if rumors coursed, they traveled in cautious whispers.

Élène led the way up the stairs through the armory guardroom to the open platform roof. The wind snatched at Gerlaine's cloak. She wrapped it closer, throwing one end over her shoulder as her mother pointed to a spot on the parapet. "There."

It all lay below her, the south loop of the moat, the black silhouettes of the barracks and stable, the moors pied by moon and scudding clouds. There were torches set in a circle in the space between the stable and keep. And in the center, chained to a stake, was Gurth.

The scream was soundless inside her.

"Where there is no lord, there is no law," Élène said. "And where no line is drawn, there is no lord. You tore a rift in that line. Your father must seal it. And you will watch."

* * *

The waiting was worse than the cold, though that was sharp enough. Gurth shivered, trying to work his arms as much as possible in the chains. The men who ringed him stood so still they might have been acting trees in a miracle play, holding leaves instead of torches. The thought was oddly humorous; he giggled nervously.

Now and then a shadow moved beyond the torches, or a smothered word traveled to him on the cold air. They had all turned out of the barracks, the stable, the cookhouse to watch. It would be soon.

A graceful figure came out of the dark and pushed through the circle, holding a leathern water bag.

"They'll be coming," Hugh told him. "Get ready." He tore Gurth's shirt open down the back.

They'd never had much to say, he and Hugh. The young Norman was an unreadable book, though sometimes Gurth sensed a curious bafflement under the cold bearing when the knight looked at him. More than once he felt that Hugh was probing him silently for the answer to some immense question. He gave the impression not so much of strength as ascetic intensity like certain masters of theology at Paris who lived, breathed, thought and wrestled loftily on a rarefied plateau remote from men and with a concomitant contempt for them.

"Do you know poetry, Bastard?"

Gurth shivered. The question seemed inane at the moment. "Books of it, why?"

"It helps, they say, when the pain is worst, to screw your mind to a line of Latin, to concentrate on nothing else." Hugh unstoppered the flagon. "As I don't read, I couldn't say. Water?"

"Please."

It was not water, his dry palate discovered greedily, but harsh turnip gin, clawing at his throat but warming all the way down. He gasped with it.

"That helps, too," the mask commented. "Drink."

Gurth took another long pull.

"I won't join you," Hugh noted with punctilious courtesy. "They'd know what it was. Swallow easily. Don't make a face, you fool."

The liquor began to work in his stomach immediately.

Horrible stuff, fit to eat the rust off a plow, but he was grateful. "Kind of you to think of it."

"I rarely think." There was a sadness, a defeat behind the careful boredom. "You puzzle me, Bastard. How long were you in Paris?"

"Five, six years."

"With an ample living beyond your studies, I heard."

Gurth had no desire to chat. "Aye, my da was very generous. Give me some more, please."

"Here," Hugh held it up to his mouth. "All that. And yet you came back here. Why?"

He saw the torches issuing from the keep and felt the trembling start again. The baron walked ahead with Bardeau, his smith, Guy and Robin behind.

"Why, Gurth?"

His gaze was riveted to the whip in Eustace's hand; it had four or five strands. In the wavering light, Gurth caught the glint of metal barbs at the ends. *I will remember, Calla. I'll try.*

"Because I belong here."

Again that baffled, searching glance: "Are you afraid?"

"Yes."

"Good," said Hugh. "You are not completely mad."

They stopped in front of Gurth. Eustace ran the strands of the whip through his fingers. "Bardeau, how much of this can a man take short of death?"

The smith did not relish his job. Simple and strong, he loved horses and good men. Gurth always had a cheery word for him.

"It depends on the man, seigneur," he mumbled. "When he faints it is dangerous to go much further. But *this* whip—"

"Aye, man, what is it?"

"This is for flaying. It may kill him."

Eustace appeared not to have heard. He grasped Gurth's hair and jerked his head up. "All within hearing! This man broke the law of his liege lord. The whip, the rope or the iron are not what I would use to hold the king's peace, but that law will hold for Saxon or Norman alike."

His grip tightened on Gurth's hair. "The baroness wanted a rope," he said under his breath. *"Pardi,* I wish I could afford to please her."

Eustace stepped back and handed the whip to the smith. "Short of death, Bardeau," he said tightly. "Break him."

The barbs sang their nasty prelude and struck.

They cannot take what is ours, but the marks of their hands are on its birth. The thing is done. We are changed, we can't go back. You have wisdom, I have a faith. In that faith, you are my husband, Gurth, and we have borne something both bloodied and beautiful.

VII

The fire on the hearth was no more than embers and the smoky torches sputtering in their sconces when Eustace, followed by Hugh and his pale younger brothers, ascended the stairs to the hall. Élène stood midway down on the steps to the armory above. Ralph the steward hovered about the fire with a clump of servants, those who usually slept in the hall. Kept up by the unknown crisis, they had already dragged out their mattresses and hoped to go to bed.

"Ralph," Eustace commanded, "Send the others away. Tonight they sleep below."

Ralph cast his wizened glance at the hulking shadow by the fire. "And *demoiselle's* Bête?"

"Put him below as well. Clear out! *Vitement. Vite.*"

Ralph transmitted the orders. They obeyed in hushed whispers, hurrying down the stairs with their mattresses. When Ralph followed with the unprotesting Bête, Eustace turned to his wife.

"Where is she?"

"Above," Élène said tonelessly. "She has not moved."

"She saw?"

"All of it." Élène was white beneath her composure. "She would not turn away."

"Tell the men above to send her down."

He took his place on the dais just as Vaudan puffed up the stairs. The priest had come in a good deal of haste; his soutane was only half hooked under his cloak.

"Lord Eustace, pardon the delay. I was asleep. *Nom de Dieu,* what has happened! Madame Élène, Sire Hugh, good evening. The Bastard's brother carting him away half dead. What happened?"

"What you warned me of," Eustace replied. "Keep your voice down. You're here as our priest. You will hear a confession and prescribe penances."

To Vaudan, his lifelong friend seemed to be suppressing a great pain. His voice and every movement of his body were controlled and tight.

"You will observe the secrecy of that sacrament and anything else you may hear."

Vaudan bridled. "You need not tell me—"

"Do you *understand,* priest?"

"Oui—mon seigneur."

Élène sat rigid in her chair of state. "My father would have hanged him."

Eustace leaned across to her, suppressing a savage desire to strike the woman, strike them all. He spoke so gently that the boys and Vaudan might have thought it a quiet, husbandly reassurance.

"Élène, what I've done I did for the best. What we do now is to save what can be saved, and if you open your mouth once more, I'll put you below to sleep with your cooks."

She flinched. "You think this is easy for me?"

"I know it is not."

Gerlaine descended the stairs alone, the cloak still wrapped about her. Her small face was almost as white as the framing veil, but if there was fear or weariness, they did not show. She took a few steps toward the hearth and paused. With precise care she undraped the cloak and let it hang from her shoulders. Then, satisfied that she was prepared, she came forward to within a few paces of her family.

"My lord summoned me?"

Robin looked away at the walls, at Guy trying to be as stern as his father and not sure why. In the unnatural silence, a fire-eaten log collapsed in a loud shower of sparks.

"Gerlaine, my daughter, *attend.* Your mother, your brothers and I are not here to revile or cast stones. What you have done is unthinkable. Because of it I have taken a valuable man and made him either useless or an enemy. I cannot afford either. But more than that, it is impossible to keep within the family. There are rumors already."

He leaned forward to her. "In a week the Sheriff of York will be here with a hundred men and servants. Lackeys who will hear stories from ours and carry them up the stairs, good cart horses that they are, whinnying for sweets from their masters in return. I could imprison or kill anyone I heard carrying such a tale. Rest assured it will never be said in my hearing. I'll be frank, Gerlaine. You're not the first *fille du manoir* to indulge herself this way. But you have placed yourself among those *demoiselles de noblesse* for whom really good marriages somehow cannot be found. Because of a truth everyone knows and no one speaks aloud. Your mother and I have decided."

Élène picked nervously at the folds of her kirtle. *It is pain. It hurts me, my baby.*

"—When the king's men are gone, we will send you to Winchester to court. This climate is not good for your health. There, as speedy and as advantageous a marriage—"

"*Did you kill him?*"

"No. Godric—" Robin blurted. He shot a guilty look at his father, then mumbled quickly, "Godric Carpenter took him home."

The girl's shoulders slumped; she squared them again. "Thank God for that."

Élène had a small handkerchief in her hands. She pulled at the damp, crumpled square. "If we are deeply shamed it is because we deeply love you, all of us." She looked up at Guy and Robin. "Sons?"

"God be with you, Gerlaine," said Guy. "And my blessing."

"Aye, Sister." Robin managed her a faint, sick smile. "I—I bless you."

"The first stone could never be mine, Gerlaine," Hugh confessed with a sardonic grace. "I've been a whore for years."

Eustace rounded on him with a long-withheld frustration. "What kind of language—what kind of blessing is that? What's the matter with you?"

"Forgive me, Father," Hugh lifted his brows in placation.

"But I have been thinking. I'm not used to it, so it's confused me. Sister, I have no strength and very little love. But I wish them both to you. Go with God."

The parents exchanged a quietly despairing shrug. Sire Hugh was more than usually drunk tonight. It wasn't good for a man to talk that way. Not in front of younger brothers, certainly not before women. The baron cut him short.

"Gerlaine?" he prompted.

The girl seemed remote, apart from them all in a dark closet of her own mind. She might have been carved there by a sculptor.

"Can you accept our decision? Do you not think it just?"

She moved slightly. "One kindness. May I have my Bête to go with me?"

The dim-minded giant would protect her. "Of course."

"Thank you."

"Then we're done." Her father settled back in his chair with a distinct air of relief. "Before you sleep, Père Vaudan will confess you in your closet. I leave it to him to prescribe—"

"No."

Vaudan needed a moment to believe it. "What?"

It was frightening but the surest thing she had ever uttered. "I will go to Winchester or wherever you say. I will marry when it pleases them there, or wait on the Lady of England, or sew, or whatever is given me to do. But I will not repent."

"My child," Vaudan went to her urgently. "Not censure, but caution. You stand in mortal sin. These are unsettled times, and if you should die on your journey, if you go to God unshriven—"

"I know," her voice quavered slightly. "And yet I have only one repentance to make; to Gurth for the pain I have brought him. Of what use to me or God a false confession?"

"False confession!" Eustace rose slowly. "After what I had to do, you have not the grace—you stand there *proud* of what you have done? Who taught you this kind of disobedience?"

"You did."

"I?"

Gerlaine could not fight the incredible weariness any longer. She sagged with the weight of it. Every word was an effort.

"When we were little, you taught me that, poor or not, we held what was ours. And I baked your bread and worked in the barn . . . to hold what was yours. I sewed, I cooked, I stood with *Maman* at the door giving alms to beggars not much poorer than us to hold what was yours. I have worked in your house always to hold what is yours, and never grudged it, because I love you."

She swayed weakly, then caught herself. Vaudan moved to support her, but she waved him away.

"Now there is something given to me . . . that is not yours. God pardon me for what I've done to you, but it frightens me, *Maman*—" Her shaking hands clenched into fists, with the intensity of the emotion. "I don't understand it, but it—is —MINE!"

Élène shot to her feet. "Gerlaine, this is your father!"

A numb shaking of her head: "I don't care, I don't care."

For the first time in his life, Eustace was confused as to what to do and totally without an answer. He wanted to thrash her, but suspected dimly that would do no good. The girl was hysterical.

The shriek of *mine* loosed everything. Every muscle in her body became uncontrollable; she convulsed like a slaughtered chicken, bent double, her empty stomach retching with painful, ugly sounds.

"He-help me . . ."

Guy broke first, then Robin. They knelt beside her.

"Sister, do as he says. Go with Vaudan."

"No, I can't, Guy. I can't." Her nails dug into his arms.

"She's sick," Élène fluttered. "She is exhausted. To bed, child."

"No!" Eustace sent his doubled fist into the back of the chair with blind fury, bowling it over twice. Small, he still had a strength of body and will that frightened them all sometimes. "No, she is not sick, she is spoiled. I had to half-kill a man to preserve an honor she does not even respect. She goes to no bed unshriven of her part in it."

He pulled the girl roughly to her feet. "Go with Vaudan."

"N-no, please . . ."

"Go!"

Vaudan restrained him: "It can be in the morn—"

"Now."

"No, I won't, I won't." She twisted in his arms, then the last white fury spent itself. Her nails raked his forearms viciously. "Let me go, *God damn you!*"

"What . . ." Élène gasped, what was that?"

"That, my dear," her husband replied with a deceptive stillness, "is the sweet sound of the English gutter," he took a breath, "to which *la Neuville* is so attracted."

His open hand whipped across Gerlaine's cheek, knocking her sideways into Guy's arms; in the same motion, Eustace rounded on them all, murderous.

"Not a word." He challenged each of them, his eyes already filling with tears of rage and self-hatred. He could cut off the hand that had done it. "Not one word. I'm still master here. Tonight I am not proud of it. Robin—you, boy, I speak to you!"

"S-sir?"

"Fetch a candle. *Move.*"

The boy obeyed, a miserable automaton.

Eustace passed the lighted taper to Guy. "Take her below to the cellar. Since she chooses dirt, by God, she'll sleep in it. Don't look pained, any of you. Because this has never happened before, did you think we are above the rules we make? Up, girl."

She needed Guy to help her stand.

"Confession," said Eustace "is between you and your God. But when you curse me, it's my province, not His. *Allez!*"

The bower was dark except for the firelight. Élène tried to sleep, though it was always impossible until he lay next to her, quiet and at peace. So long as he brooded into the fire, sleep eluded her.

"Eustace, please come to bed." He didn't answer. "I heard the watch change, it's gone three. Please."

When he still refused to answer, she sat up peevishly. "You did right, man; what you had to. Leave it."

"It isn't that."

"Then what?"

He got up heavily out of the chair and sat down on the bed. "This place."

She knew it, had felt the *apartness* of this moor from the first day.

"I don't understand these people. You hear? A lord must

know his men. I don't know them or their God-forsaken country."

He lay down beside her. "And we are changed."

He felt for her hand. They listened to the wind.

The little sleep she had was far from rest. The bright hell of the past hours still rampaged across her mind—Gurth's body, that whip, her father; even in this shallow sleep, Gerlaine had an awareness of shivering.

How long she slept it was impossible to say. The candle was low, flickering in the draft, and the first thing she heard when she opened her eyes against the rough material of the sacks was the wind. She felt desolate and ravaged, still shuddering uncontrollably. It was not over within her, though that morning seemed years ago. She felt old.

It is not real. There are devils in me.

She turned on her back; small chitterings and scurryings followed. The rats. They'd stay their distance so long as the candle lasted. When it was gone they might come closer. There was no real alarm, the cellar fed them well, they merely revolted her. There would be no more sleep tonight, even though her Judas body would sell all her courage, sell Gurth himself for food, wine and her own bed.

Aye, it is real. It is not devils, but me. I have dreamed of it. I've seen the stallion mount the mare, and wondered and wished. If there are devils, they were born with me. I am so lost in him.

Iron clanked on iron. The cellar door was thrown open, light flooding down the stairs.

"Who's there?"

"Me, Sister."

Hugh descended a little too carefully. From long knowledge Gerlaine knew how much he must have drunk. He set his candle down by hers and placed a small cloth sack beside it.

She rubbed her aching eyes. "What hour, Hugh?"

"Almost four," he mumbled. "Be light soon. I thought you might be hungry."

From the sack, he took a small wrapped parcel and passed it to her: cold pork, generous slices of it. She snatched and tore at it.

"Slowly, Gerlaine. You'll be sick again."

"No . . . no," she gasped, her mouth full. "It is so good —no, don't take it away."

But he made her chew slowly and swallow each bite before stuffing more. When the meat was gone, she wiped her mouth on the cloth and settled back gratefully. "*Zut,* that was good."

Hugh dipped into the sack again and brought out a flagon, opened and passed it to her. She felt near to tears.

"Wine—oh, *tu es gentil, mon frère.* Give . . . give me."

"Drink slowly."

It was not wine but harsh turnip gin, bitter, hot and strong. She coughed and gagged, but would not give up the flagon, swallowing avidly, spilling it in her need. It was vile, but the best thing in the world. It warmed through her. The shuddering muscles began to relax. Hugh took the flagon and swigged.

"It numbs me," Gerlaine lay back, staring up into the gloom. "I felt like an animal."

"Yes, it does that," he said, his usual clipped speech blurred with hours of drinking. "I gave some to Gurth before they started. It helped, I suppose. He fainted after a time."

Gerlaine raised up on one elbow. The gin was working already, hanging weights on her eyelids. "I'd forgotten you could be so good."

He smiled distantly. "I admire courage. I envy it."

"Courage? I'm not sure I know what I've done."

"You did it, though, without knowing why." Hugh drank again, swaying back against the piled sacks. He was very drunk, she could tell, with enough of the potent gin in him to lay out three ordinary men.

"—and *he* came back without knowing why. Because he belonged here. I don't understand him. To be given all that: Paris, the finest masters, the door to the Church opened wide for him. How I envy that man."

"But you are knighted," she wondered. "The highest honors. Not even our father has that."

He took another drink. "When I was sixteen, remember I went to Bayeux with Uncle Ranulf? He had business with the bishop; while they talked, I wandered into the *scriptorium* just to see and touch the books. A monk was reading aloud to another—words, feelings that might have been my own; about a man battling not with giants or heroes or armies, but with that horrible enemy, himself. I begged the monk to read more. He was reading my soul, my own battle. He told me the book was the *Confessions of Augustine*. I promised God that day in the church that I too would fight that battle for Him."

He lolled back against the sacks with a hiccup.

"But dear Father needed me—*pour l'honneur de Neuville* —for the somewhat more secular crusade of William and to grab our share of Eden." Hugh stared into the candle flame. "There was a moment when I could have said no. No, I will not. I have my own, splendid combat to fight for my own lord. I could have said that. But Father would have called me a coward. I couldn't face it, and so I picked up the sword—it is lighter than the cross—and I have been running ever since."

Gerlaine stretched a sleepy hand to touch his. "You are my good brother Hugh."

"It is easy to be a knight," he sighed. "Matter of . . . a certain efficiency. Don't be home when anyone calls, that's the secret. That's how I got through Hastings . . . Brandeshal" —the flagon tilted and sloshed—"and all those places in between. Your arm rises and falls and kills, and you don't feel it because you're not there. You're dead, you see, and your eye —unclouded with anything like anger or life—can measure, parry and thrust much more quickly than someone else."

Hugh looked at her. "Then every so often, God comes with that old promise like an overdue bill. And I have to run again."

A drowsy warmth enveloped Gerlaine. The shuddering had left her exhausted body and it was going to sleep. She closed her eyes and began to drift on the soft tide of his voice.

"You saw his father?" she murmured.

"Whose?"

"Gurth's."

"Oh, yes. Briefly." Hugh drank again. "Big, angry devil with a huge ax bellowing at me by a pile of bodies. One of them was his son. He might have killed me, but his foot slipped. God was not home that day either. The king's orders were explicit. No mercy, but Father would have made it quick. We found some of our men had . . . crucified the lady. Singing hymns while they hammered. We couldn't hang them for following orders. God knows, we wanted to."

There were remembered horrors in the gloom beyond the candles.

"They are as cruel, the Saxons, cruel because it is part of

them. They find you down on the field, it can take a week to die. . . . 'Kill me, Hugh, don' let those women get me.' "

She heard him distantly. Just this side of sleep, something in a red-spattered mail shirt moved with a knife.

"Father couldn't eat that night. He's still alive. Slaughter makes him feel something. Being dead I ate like a pig."

He took another sip to loosen his dry tongue. The mask of ennui had dropped. Hugh looked younger, gentler and with a remembered glimmer of eagerness. "To read Augustine," he slurred, "to have . . . all that and throw it away for this. Because he belonged here. That is puzzling, *n'est-ce-pas?* I mean, he belongs to *us,* doesn't he?"

Once more he raised the flagon. It was empty. With a sigh of finality, he stoppered it and glanced across at Gerlaine. Her eyes were closed, the strong young face battered by the fatigue of her ordeal. He pressed her hand and received the tiniest squeeze in response.

"Sometimes I believe that God in shame at what He made goes away inside Himself while that practiced arm rises and falls, rises and falls."

Silence. He leaned to her. "Gerlaine?"

She was deeply, blissfully asleep.

Hugh got to his feet, reeling with the liquor in him. He was drunk enough to sleep now. This place was cold. Gerlaine's cloak was not enough. He spread his own over her.

Sweet Sister, good night.

He lurched toward the stairs.

VIII

"He knew his business, that smith." Godric inspected Gurth's back with rueful respect. "Hardly hit you twice in the same place, you can count the strokes. I make it fifteen."

Gurth clutched at the frame of the cot as Calla smeared the herb poultice over his back. "It was more."

For days he had lain on his stomach, sleeping when the pain would let him. When Calla was sure there would be no festering, they had to be closed with salt while Gurth bit on a knotted rag until his jaws ached. It was almost as bad as the whip while it lasted. The pain was less now. The taut lines around his eyes and unshaven jaw began to relax a little.

"Ease up, now." Godric lifted his brother's torso gently as Calla passed the bandages under and around.

"Are you hungry?" she said.

"No."

"Not even soup? You've hardly eaten."

"No."

"Your beard must scratch." She spoke gruffly to him as she had from the moment Godric brought him home. All the pity was in her hands. "Shall I shave you?"

"No. Leave it."

"It's time he had a beard," Godric scratched the stubble. "Makes him look more like his da."

87

That's true, Calla thought. Strain, lack of sleep and food had hollowed out the gentleness, leaving hard planes familiar in their hinted cruelty.

"Fifteen strokes," Godric admired, "and not a sound out of him."

Calla knotted off the bandages. "Did you think to hear any?"

"No . . . no. But tell me—now it's over, was she any good?"

"She should have been, by what it cost him." Calla said.

Godric hulked to his full six foot, stretching the muscles cramped in squatting by the bed. "Well, maybe the wee baron had a right—maybe. The other way around; well, that's different." He lounged in the doorway, looking out over the moor. "Peter Fletcherson said over in Normandy they even have the right—the *right,* mind you—to take their farmers' wives on the first night. Is that true?"

Gurth nodded absently. "It's happened."

"Like to see him try that with Hulda. She'd have his skin for a God-damned tablecloth." Godric vented a short bark of laughter. "Almost had mine first time I grabbed her."

His eyes narrowed at the moor. "Speak of the devil: there's old Peter now. Running like his ass was on fire. *Hoch!* Peter!"

Someone shouted a long way away.

"What?" Godric bawled back.

The voice came again, thin with distance, urgent.

"*Och,* he wants me," Godric swung out the door. "I'll be back."

Gurth watched his mother stir the pot of thick broth hung from a crossbeam over the fire pit. True, he hadn't cried out, but only part of that was will; the rest was Hugh's strong turnip gin numbing him. After the fifth stroke, that didn't help anymore. He tried to think of Gerlaine then, but she was unreal. Even now it was hard to picture her. When he did catch the image of her white body under him, the whip curled about them both and brought him back. By the fifteenth stroke, Bardeau must have been hard pressed to find a clean landing for the whip. It began to flay over open wounds, and then came the blow that broke him, took away his courage and will. He opened his mouth to scream, to beg *for Christ's sake, mercy . . . stop, please,* ready to crawl before de Neuville even if she was watching. But as the words formed, the whip cut them off. What would have been a plea was only a gasp, then he was hanging from the chains in a dim red twilight. If they hit him again, he never felt it.

I had no courage like Brand. I only fainted. And I sneered at him once, not knowing that he held this whole place together. If life paid him back for his selfishness, he grew into a man and made the best of it. I sat in Paris, wasting the money he sent me, refusing the Church like a petulant child because he wanted it for me. I know why I came back, Hugh: shame. I couldn't live with myself any longer. Christ, my father loved me and I didn't have the guts to take his hand . . . old bear-sark, forgive, forgive. I thought that any lord was better than you, and so I courted them. They're not our lords; they don't own the land. Their blood isn't half a thousand years into it. They're not even human—maggots with titles. And she—

"Gurth!"

Godric burst in the doorway like a storm, red and stammering with baffled rage. "Peter says the Sheriff of York is at the keep, and—and he's quartering men in our houses."

A cold presentiment chilled Gurth. He saw his brother's face and knew what could happen.

"Doesn't he know that's hearth-right? He can't *do* that, Gurth. Didn't you tell him?"

Gurth tried to raise himself. "I told him. I thought he understood. Mother, help me up."

But she restrained him. "What can you do, and your back torn open?"

"I can't just lie here. Maybe I can talk to him, I don't know."

Godric moved to the door. "I'll be taking your horse. Never you fret, I'll handle this."

"Will you lie *down!*" Calla pushed Gurth back onto the bed. "Down, fool."

"They can't do this," Godric asserted stubbornly, never seeing that they could. He was standing on a right so old, so deep that not even kings had dared violate it: the hearth-right, the absolute, unquestioned right of a man to the privacy of his own house. He turned in the doorway, choked with it. There were years of it to spit out. He was twenty-seven; he'd seen his world die in pieces, the world of Brandeshal and Tees Riding.

He'd been free, the word "serf" meant nothing to him. You owed certain duties to your lord. He could yammer from now until hell sprouted barley that you were bound to the land and the land was his, but that didn't make it so. And he didn't open your door without permission.

"They can't do this, Gurth. Not my *house*."

The doorway was empty. A moment later, they heard the hooves drum away westward.

Godric's mother, Emma Lightfoot, was bound to the land but her family had been virtually free for years. Their men were the backbone of Brandeshal's fighting fyrd and their land service had come to be no more than a token porker delivered to Brandeshal each year at the Yule feast. Emma was allowed to inherit the family holding as a gift from Brand Ulfson on Godric's birth. On her death in 1065, Godric became master of his own land, a free man with a wergild that Eustace de Neuville would have envied had he understood the concept. Godric's steading was a smaller Brandeshal, built on the site of an older tun more ancient than Caesar. The raised stone that marked his northeast boundary bore Pictish carvings.

In practice Godric had been free all his life. Open and uncomplicated, he was happily free of those conflicts of spirit that divided his half brother. Gurth's subtle mind awed him a little, but he had never grudged Brand's gruff favoring of the stubborn boy who spat on his attentions. Close to his father from the start, Godric was Brand's shield bearer at fifteen. When the ousted Earl Tostig raided the north with Hardrada, the Raven of Brandeshal was the first flag planted at Stamford Bridge beside Harold's. Godric was twenty that year and Hulda heavy with child. Gurth was six months gone in Paris, learning French, salting his letters with Latin phrases. As the priest Anfric read them, Brand would listen with eager pride, making him repeat certain studiedly erudite passages.

You hear, Calla? You hear how the boy writes? Go on, read more.

They had been warriors from the time of Hengist and damned good farmers, too. But Gurth would be the first scholar.

Little Godric was born the day William landed at Pevensey.

They waited, baffled, while Earl Morcar deliberated which side was the more profitable. He decided too late for Harold.

Life went on. Godric waited and plowed. The seasons passed. The false Morcar went, a Norman duke came with impossible taxes. The curfew fell and the curtailment of every small liberty once taken for granted. Sometimes Godric wished himself in Paris with Gurth for just one day to be free again. He didn't understand these sharp-eyed little Normans who organized everything down to the last pig and chicken. The ignorance was mutual; in fact the new duke died of it when the North rose up in '69 to puke the Normans out of its gut. Brandeshal gathered for the last battle they knew was coming. And King William marched north against them.

Go to Ely, Godric. There's good men there. Hereward is holding out and laughing at them.

Will you come, Father?

His father looked as if he barely understood the question. *Leave? Leave Brandeshal? Boy, don't you remember? I own this place.*

They took ship at the estuary, carrying only necessities. His father was there, and Leofwine and young Brand already growing into a mountain like the rest of them. There were gifts: a warm cloak each of the finest wool for Hulda and the boy, and for Godric a new war ax and a shield painted with the Raven of Brandeshal. They sailed south to find a man called Hereward.

For two years in that swamp, there was a dream. They froze and starved, Hulda lost the new child, almost dying herself, and William's fist tightened about the dream, strangling it day by day until the end, the death of the last hope, and what few of them could escaped with Hereward. *Poor old man,* Godric mourned. *Old sword with a blunted edge. You'd have been happier dead.*

News came at Ely how the north was broken, but it had to be seen. At first they traveled warily, hiding during the day. But there was no need to hide. Nothing was left. They traveled then during the day without sighting more than a few ragged crofters, most of them old. William had wiped out a whole generation. At Brandeshal there were not even the stockade timbers left. His own farm was no more than charred beams and the old Pictish stone.

Down the wind, Gurth said. Down the wind like leaves.

At the old earth house in the hill fort at Eston Nab, they found others like themselves, coming home because there was no place else to go. Calla was back, and John Plowwright and old Peter. Peter was the poorest man in Tees Riding. He shared his hut with his pigs, but he'd saved Godric's life at Stamford Bridge. No one talked of fighting anymore. The women's faces were pinched; the men's eyes lowered with a shame the women could never wholly understand.

There was a new lord, de Neuville, and any law was better than none. Holdings needed to be plowed, sheep husbanded, life started again. They looked to Brand's son for answers.

Hulda, what can I tell them? I'm a farmer, not God.

Then be a farmer. The boy is hungry.

Aye, the boy was hungry. What more to say?

He set them an example, the first to place his hands between those of de Neuville at the fealty swearing. He became a foreigner's man because his son was hungry. Yet for days afterward, clearing the ground and building a new house on the ground they said was no longer his, Godric could feel the Norman's hands over his. He hid the ax and battered shield under the roof beams and they lay there gathering dust, haunted by something never voiced, never quite dead.

You can put a free man in a cage, but it is dangerous to taunt him with it and doubly dangerous to enter the cage yourself.

Large consequences spiral out of small choices. Gurth's hut was too small for efficient quartering of troops, with no outbuildings but the sheepcote. Godric's rebuilt steading was much larger. For this reason four men-at-arms were sent to one house and not the other, and one thing happened while another did not.

They were hard-bitten men, not terribly kind or excessively cruel, living in the saddle since Hastings, honed to a fine edge by constant war. Used to sensing trouble before it materialized, they were instantly alert when they sighted the steading. The tall man stood by his low gate, his right hand resting on the handle-butt of a large war ax. Drawing closer, they saw the smaller Danish ax in his belt. His woman stood in the doorway of the hut with a small boy clutching at her skirts. Orders were to be firm but to avoid anything like hostility. The idea of open resistance was not even considered.

Their sergeant noted with satisfaction the good-sized barn not far from the house. The farmer and his family could bed down there. They would take the house. Two or three nights, no interference with their lives and hands off the woman by the baron's express order. All pretty reasonable and a hell of a lot better treatment than some would give them.

The sergeant spoke no English, Godric Carpenter no French.

"Stay up," he told his men. "I'll talk."

He dismounted and walked toward the tall man. At five bowlengths or so, the man shifted his stance slightly, almost casually, but the sergeant halted.

"*Par l'ordre du seigneur—*" he gave his instructions. They produced no result. The big Saxon remained silent and calm, even a hint of cold enjoyment beginning to curl around his bearded lips. By signs, the sergeant indicated their purpose. He pointed to the farmer, then the woman and boy, and made a clear gesture toward the barn. Indicating himself and the others, he signified their intention to take over the house.

Godric's cold smile widened, like a wolf about to break his fast among lambs. Insolently his eyes went over the sergeant from helmet to shoes. With elaborate nonchalance he spat and wiped his mouth. Imitating the sergeant, he pointed at each of the Normans in turn and then, emphatically, toward the east and Montford keep.

"*Ut!*"

The demands were semaphored again, more peremptorily this time. The men shifted in their saddles. But with that damnable smile, the farmer shook his head.

"Out," he said again.

The waiting men watched the slow mime of the encounter. They saw their sergeant draw his sword; it looked to be all right then. As he drew, the farmer sensibly laid the war ax against the gatepost and stood empty-handed. Feeling some relief, the sergeant turned back to his men.

"He understands now. Put up the hors—"

The ax caught him at the base of his skull just below the line of the helmet. There wasn't any time to warn him. In a motion so smooth it belied its speed, the small, throwing ax was free of the Saxon's belt, aimed and thrown. Even as the man fell

Godric scooped up the larger weapon and charged them, keening a high wail of battle joy.

"*Yuk-hey sa-saa-aa—*"

The nearest man urged his horse forward, drawing his sword. The first scything sweep of the ax missed him by inches and broke the horse's neck. The animal went down convulsed and kicking; instinctively, the soldier cleared the stirrup and brought up his shield as the mount collapsed, landing on his feet over the dead horse. He caught the ax cleanly center-shield, but the incredible force of the blow bowled him over backward. With no break in his forward momentum, Godric took the heavy ax into a backswing and brought it down, neatly severing the helmeted head and plowing into the ground.

But they were too many. He roared his cry again, yanking the ax from the dirt as the horses trampled over him, knocking him aside, and even as he scrambled up, the truncheon crushed his shoulder. With one last surge of power, Godric raised the ax left-handed as the next blow struck him behind the ear. Even falling, he clawed at the man, trying to drag him from the saddle as the woman left her child and came shrieking down on them. She reached Godric's ax, lifted it—

"You whoresons, let him go—"

They knocked her aside with a blow in the stomach. Even doubled on the ground and helpless, Hulda cursed them.

They tied Godric over the sergeant's saddle. His long war was ended.

IX

The hard riding opened his back again. Soaked through with the pelting rain, Gurth could feel the warmer, sticky wetness seeping outward from the bandages. His mare was lathered with exhaustion, punished by Hulda with the boy, rested just long enough for her to blurt out the tale and Gurth to take the saddle painfully and gallop to Montford.

There was no plan in his mind, only half hope that to speak for Godric in their own language might mitigate the sentence, at least make them understand, to remind Eustace of his warning. He owed it to Godric.

The trial must have been summary and the sentence immediate. They hanged Godric from the keep wall. He was hanging still. Gurth sat motionless a long time below the bedraggled figure wind-buffeted out and back, out and back against the wall of the keep. Ralph the steward had to call him three times.

He rode home oblivious to the rain, an odd stillness falling like night over his soul. In some inexplicable way, he felt light and free, possessed of a terrible clarity of reason. Lucidly, with icy thoroughness, he placed the thoughts each on each like bricks in a wall.

He led the tired horse into the cote, pushing aside the milling sheep, unsaddled and rubbed the animal down, his thoughts beating in rhythm with his arm. At length the mare was dry and rubbed to a fare-ye-well. He trudged out into the downpour and opened the hut door. Hulda and his mother sat at the long table.

"Is the boy asleep?" he said.

"In my bed." Calla helped him off with the cloak and laid it near the fire pit to dry. "You've seen Godric?"

When Gurth didn't answer, Hulda said, "They've done, haven't they?"

"Before I got there."

There was nothing else to say. In the silence Hulda traced a crack in the table. Little Godric stirred and turned over fretfully in the bower beyond.

"Is the broth hot?" she asked vaguely. "I've got to feed the boy."

To save her life, Hulda found she could not think for the moment beyond that necessity. Her large red hands insisted on their practical habits of life, brushed lint from her smock, dallied pointlessly with the braid ends of her hair in small denials of death.

Gurth stood over the fire, his back to them. Calla winced at the darker stains on the rain-soaked cloth.

"Vaudan will be bringing him," he said.

"And me and my son?"

"Godric's house and livestock are forfeit. You're to go to Montford, to the scullery."

Hulda seemed to be digesting the news word by single word. Then her head moved back and forth in negation. "I'll burn it first," she said thickly, "kill the sheep, wring the chickens' necks, the oxen, I'll kill them all myself."

Her nail dug into the crack in the plank. "I'll burn it all. My baby lost and me too weak to keep her alive. *Two . . . years* dying in that fen, starving, Godric worked to death to build us something again—and for *you*, too—"

Her voice razored to a high-pitched accusation. "He built this place again for you, Calla, while the sulky scholar there lorded it in Paris—"

Gently, the mother said, "That's my son, Hulda."

"Aye, and Godric's brother!" She threw it at his back. "Look at me! You're the man now, what are you going to do about it?"

"What *can* he do, woman?"

"Nothing! Nothing, the same as all his life. Poor thing, his back's all sore. Should I feel sorry they spanked him for spreading the baron's brat?"

"Shut—up."

When he turned on her, Hulda knew he meant it. "I know what I've been. I'm not proud."

Gurth loomed across the table and grabbed her hand. "If I didn't know what I was going to do, I couldn't have come home tonight."

She tried to pull away; he held on relentlessly, all the warmth frozen out of his eyes.

"Kill and burn if you will, but first count it all: every sheep, fowl, pig, ox, every pot and pan, the house, the land —everything. Give me a reckoning in silver pence. Quickly, before he's buried and they come for you."

"Why?"

"For Godric's *wergild*," he said.

Hulda's mouth dropped open. "Are you ma—"

"You said I was the man," his fingers tightened cruelly, hurting her. "The man has decided they'll pay his price. I loved him too. Now shut your bloody mouth and listen, because there's not much time. Mother, hot up the broth. The boy wants feeding and so do I."

They buried Godric next day when the rain let up, on his own land near the Pictish stone. Godric had been baptized by Anfric and was entitled to the priest's office. Nevertheless, to Vaudan it was a Christian burial only for his presence, and curiously dry-eyed. The husky wife was a sullen statue with a war ax in her arms. At her side, half hidden by his task, the tow-headed boy balanced a shield between his feet.

Gurth, Peter Fletcherson and two others lowered Godric with his head to the west. As Vaudan took up the handful of wet earth, Gurth stopped him.

"We're not finished."

He took the raven shield from the boy and carefully placed it over Godric's shrouded breast. Now Calla came forward carrying a brightly colored jug and a large drinking glass mounted in silver. With unhurried care, each was placed by the body. Vaudan was speechless at the profanation. In the midst of preparations for Judgment, they were supplying him for Valhalla.

"Master Gurth!" he whispered vehemently. "This is not Christian."

Gurth didn't look up. "Neither was the way he died."

Last of all he laid the ax on Godric's right, the haft ready to his hand.

"Say your words, Vaudan, and sprinkle your dirt. We're done."

When the priest was gone and the women inside with Hulda, Gurth and Peter Fletcherson remained to fill the grave.

"Not much time, Peter," Gurth grunted as he worked. "It has to be today."

The tight-knit little man worked as a lifelong farmer, without apparent exertion. An archer in Brand Ulfson's fyrd, grizzled and spare, Peter was approaching middle years as tough wood ages, weather-darkened, strong as ever.

"For sure," he agreed.

"You'll still go?"

"Aye, didn't I say?"

"You're a friend, Peter."

The little swineherd hawked and spat. "Well—'twasn't much of a house, the old woman gone and myself sick of pigs."

"Let Calla guide. She knows the earth houses this side of the Roman wall. And you'll need two more horses."

Peter lifted a spadeful and dropped it into the grave. "There's two quartered on John Plowwright."

Earth clumped softly into the grave. "And the riders?"

"Well, that'll be a shame."

"They'll be missed."

Peter snorted with pleasure. "Won't we all!" He rested his arms on the spade and studied his dirty-bearded friend. "And you? You know what you're doing?"

Gurth jammed his spade into the dirt. "Dig."

Eustace had done what he had to do and if his stomach turned at it, no one but Élène would ever know.

"He pushed me to it, Élène. I couldn't pardon him."

"If you heeded me," she said against his shoulder as they lay in the bed, "the brother would be buried, too."

"It may come to that." Eustace stared bitterly into the

darkness. "We have been tolerant. No more. By Christ, they'll learn if I have to hang half of them and flay the rest."

For traveling Calla chose her old deerhide smock, stained with cooking and the fields, but ample proof against the wind. Dun with blackish streaks, some from age and others cleverly painted to blend in, covered by a cloak of the same patternless scheme, she could melt into moor or forest by simply freezing still. Hulda had dressed the same on Calla's shrewd advice. There was more than a streak of Pict in Corn-Woman: what magic she knew came from them, including their tricks of protective coloring.

They waited in the fading daylight, two women and the boy, by Calla's door. Two small bundles, needfuls for the journey, rested on the ground before them.

"What's keeping Peter?" Hulda fretted.

"Does he come with us, Mum?" Godric asked.

"Aye, he's your da's best friend."

"Look!" Calla pointed suddenly. "There."

Over the western rise of the moor, the distant smoke rose sluggishly against the last of the light. Hulda's lips moved. Gurth came out of the sheepcote, wiping blood-spattered hands on his tunic.

"All of them, Son?"

"Yes."

"*Och*, the dears," Calla murmured tenderly. "I'll miss them."

Gurth looked off toward the western hill. "Good Peter," he smiled with satisfaction. "He's on time."

A rider galloped down the near slope, leading an extra mount. It was time. Calla eased close to Gurth's saddled horse. The mare smelled blood and shied nervously, its eyes showing white.

"There," she crooned, "there, now. No fear, you great fool."

"Goodbye, Mother."

She pretended to fuss with the bridle. "I've laid out your needfuls. And a few trifles beside."

"Mother." He turned her face in his hand, then her lips were against the rough new beard, no longer trying to hide what she felt. Her eyelids squeezed tight against the tears.

"Oh, I have had such men!"

Then Peter trotted into the yard, hailing them, a man transcended. Over his ragged tunic and trousers he wore a Norman mail shirt, torn at the breast and somewhat stained. But Peter himself looked marvelous, ten years younger, almost debonair with the longbow and full quiver proud on his back, and the satisfied grin of a boy who's stolen a whole meat pie and made off neat as a fox.

"Done, Peter?"

"Done," he laughed. "The house, the stock. And a few pigs that belonged to his unfortunate lordship."

Gurth nodded at the fresh mounts. "Any trouble?"

Peter touched the bowstring. "A little off the mark," he judged professionally, "but close enough. By the time someone finds them, nobody'll want to. Hey, Godric! By God, here's the man!"

He swung down and caught the boy in his arms, tousling the blond hair with a dirty hand. "It's me: old Peter, remember?"

"Petapeta!" Godric squealed. "Where d'we go?"

"North, boy. *Up* now." He lifted Godric to horse, tied Hulda's bundle securely to the saddle, then held the stirrup while she mounted.

"Take my promise, Hulda," Gurth said.

She spoke the ritual words. "Where do you go?"

"To claim the *wergild* of my brother."

"It belongs to me. Do you swear it now?"

"On my life."

She laid her hand on his head. "Do not greet me again without it."

Gurth helped Calla mount. "Be careful, Mother."

"Haven't I ridden north before and come back?"

"And still beautiful to boot!"

"By God," she draped the cloak over her breast. "So I am."

"Peter, when you reach the river, ride the shallows as far as you can. They'll be two days picking up your tracks."

"If they're lucky." Peter held out his hand. *"Hoch,* Gurth Brandson."

"Goodbye, Peter." The grip tightened. They searched for a way around the moment. Then Gurth punched the wiry arm. "Come Yuletide I'll drink you out of your silly mind."

"You'll be the first." Peter clucked to the horse and moved off.

He watched them clear over the hill until they disappeared. His mother did not look back.

His needfuls lay on the plank table: one of his father's swords in its fleece-lined scabbard, a gift to Brand on his accession to Brandeshal—fine-tempered, beautifully balanced, cleaned this day and the edge reset. Next to it rested the ax. Gurth hefted it absently, knowing the balance as well as his own stride. It was not the crescent Danish ax his father had worn as a badge of rank, which Gurth had carried for reasons rather muddied till now. This was a light, vicious weapon designed for close quarters and throwing.

Still, he found it hard to think of the weapons beside what else Calla left him.

Draped regally over her great oak chair were trousers of white carded wool, a green knee-length tunic trimmed at the neck with cloth of gold, the hem generously lapped in fur. There was a broad leather belt cunningly set with blue and red enamel and beaten bronze. Calla had polished the buckle till it was a flashing oval of gold emblazoned with a *B* only half recognizable letter and the rest curving, fantastic, fire-tongued dragon. More sumptuous than all the rest was the heavy bronze-clasped red cloak, lined throughout with marten.

Wrinkled from long incarceration, smelling of their chest, left behind by a man perhaps on the day his world ended, these were the trifles Calla bequeathed her son.

He dropped his bloody clothes on the dirt floor, washed and dressed himself in his father's garments. The tunic was a hair loose; it would have better fitted Godric. Gurth shoved the long-headed ax into the belt just left of the buckle, and slung the scabbard over his right shoulder.

"Well," he said aloud. "Let's be about it."

He tore the bloodied tunic to strips, doused them in drippings from a fat lamp and wrapped the soaked rags around a stick of kindling, thrusting it into the fire. When it burned steadily, he applied the brand methodically to all four corners where the roof thatching sloped down, and toppled the plank table over the fire pit. Quickly, as the crackling whisper rose from the roof, he doused the cots with lamp drippings, tossed the brand into the kindling pile and stepped outside.

The flames spread rapidly across the thatching, drying the rain-soaked top from beneath before consuming it, crept down across the roof of the sheepcote. Presently a black, greasy smoke mingled with the lighter issue from wood and thatching. In a million roaring sparks, Calla's roof collapsed inward.

Gurth turned away and walked eastward over the darkening moor toward Montford.

For Guy and Robin it was a feast to their popping, delirious eyes. Never at Neuville had there been anything like this; father and mother resplendent in their best, the place bursting with people, being deferred to by soldiers as sons of rank, hobnobbing at close quarters with the men-at-arms, even allowed to try their swords and harness, suppers fit for a king. Jugglers there were, attached to the sheriff's train, and all through the feast rainbows of brightly colored balls lobbed high, fire was swallowed, acrobats tumbled, each trick followed by more applause than the last. Never so many torches burned; the hall rattled with lusty life, a hundred shouted conversations flew up, down and across the two long, lower tables where the men-at-arms and servants mingled below the salt.

For all of this, it was still less than a joy. Their father spoke to Gerlaine only when necessary; callow as they were, they knew how she hurt. Then the hanging of Godric, from which they thanked God to be excused. Even the weather was against them. The hawks brooded in their pens, and Guy and Robin had to spend hours in attendance on Sire Guillaume de Mowbray, the Sheriff of York.

First, he was almost as high as King William and personally appointed by him, with all kinds of family behind him and already a name in the north. But he accepted de Neuville hospitality coldly, as something due his loftier rank, looking down on Father and condescending to their mother. He'd lost an arm at Hastings, a good soldier but totally without the graces that made him welcome at one's table, especially after so much preparation. All of them—Father, too, they bet —were glad he was off tomorrow.

The strained courtesy was not warmed by de Mowbray's

summary handling of Godric or rather the manner in which Eustace was himself forced to deal with it. The situation was a vise. Godric was his man, therefore his responsibility as to justice. The men killed were de Mowbray's. He could and did demand immediate hanging after a hearing that lasted five minutes in which Godric said nothing, bleeding and defiant as a cornered boar just as the hounds took him.

A trained lifetime saw Eustace through the visit, but he was grateful for Élène's flawless handling of every detail, especially thankful right now for Hugh's ease of manner. Seated on the other side of the sheriff, politely drunk though not showing it, Hugh drew off the necessity of conversation with aristocratic ease. King William had new Arabians, and Hugh displayed an inordinate desire to hear of them in detail from hooves to hindquarters. It was his sardonic gift to his father.

Amid the noise and movement, Eustace fiddled with his jeweled goblet, pricked again and again by a niggling memory of Bastard's queerly urgent warning the day they rode together. He'd hardly listened; it was a passing note not worth elaborating. You always quartered troops on peasants. And his mind had been on his daughter. The uncomfortable sensation was not remorse or even the suspicion of a too hasty judgment; he merely wondered in his practical fashion what hindrance this might be to the efficiency of his charge. Not an hour since, the platform guard reported the dull glow of fires to the west. Half the duty watch was quickly dispatched to investigate. It might be burning refuse, but curfew was long past. He hoped it was nothing. He had no wish to exhibit further disturbance before the sheriff.

Under it all was Vaudan's old warning and the picture of the determined little priest trudging with brand, brazier and holy water from post to post along the stockade wall, searing out the crude carvings wherever he found them.

"Wine, *mon père?*"

Gerlaine held out the flagon. Eustace signaled yes without meeting her eyes. The girl was pale, a little distracted, but served the high table with dispatch. It was her job, as long as de Mowbray blessed them with his company, to serve rather than sit at table, supervise the cooks and serving girls and keep the courses coming as needed. The sheriff's filled goblet was her personal charge. She did not sit at all but moved continually from the high table to the scullery, cookhouse and back, and retired exhausted only when the tables were put away.

The present course seemed about through, she noted with a careful eye. "Shall I call for the partridge, Father?"

"Yes, bring it."

"The wine is all right?"

"Yes." Why did she hover over him so?

"It is the Provençal that you like. I broached it specially."

"See to the partridge, Gerlaine."

"Yes, Father."

As she stepped from the dais, hurrying footsteps thudded up the stairs from the scullery. Three of the watch, mailed and armed, strode up the hall toward the high table. Their leader was apparently trying to be as confidential as possible. Pointedly he crossed around to address Eustace on Élène's side, emphatic and flabbergasted at the same time. He'd seen what he'd seen, his gesturing hands conveyed, but damned if he could explain it. Gerlaine continued on her errand, passing a stubble-bearded knight just ascending into the hall, richly dressed in a style somewhat out of date and very tall for a Norman. As her foot touched the first step, the realization sank home.

"Gurth!"

She threw a glance toward Eustace and pulled Gurth into the shadows behind the stairs leading above. He seemed not to care whether he was seen with her or not. And he was so changed.

"I didn't know you, Gurth." When he said nothing, she came close to him. "I saw. They made me watch."

"I'm sorry for that."

"No . . . no, I'm not sorry for anything that day. I've prayed for you every night." Gerlaine searched his eyes for some warmth or remembrance, but there was none; only an odd preoccupation. His pupils were huge and black in the gloom, the set of the eyes peculiarly intense.

"They—they wanted me to confess. I wouldn't," she said with pathetic pride. "Gurth, say something. Is it Godric? Father had to do it, don't you understand? Everything that's happened, he *had* to do."

He started to turn away. She caught at his sleeve. "They're sending me away to Winchester, to court. I'll never see you."

"They'll be sending me away too."

"Where? I have to hurry, they'll miss me. *Where*, Gurth? I can follow you. I have Bête, no one can hurt me."

"No."

"*Why!*" It was a wail of despair. All through the horrible week, one thing kept her balance and her sanity: the thought of him, and now he was brushing it aside. She was on quicksand with no hold. An unaccountable terror seized her. "Gurth, I love you, I've been your wife, I—"

But he was laughing—dry, bitter catching sounds from the rim of hysteria. After a moment, he stroked her cheek with roughened fingers.

"You are life and air and yes to everything I need, Gerlaine. But my brother's dead because he couldn't learn to be a dog, and I've learned too late to be a man. And if we ever touched across your father's kennel, who in the rutting world will ever care?"

She would rather he'd slapped her. "You don't mean that."

"Gerlaine, they've made me mean it."

He strode away into the lighted hall. Gerlaine slumped back against the wall, fists to her mouth. *Why did you come, then? You are cruel, so cruel. I did nothing but love you.*

Then something rode over the hurt, another bright shock of fear. Why *had* he come, dressed so and armed? A gray premonition began to grow in her. She hurried down to the scullery, gave her directions to the sweating cooks, then hurried back to the hall. He was mingling with the crowd watching the jugglers. Gerlaine paused, looking for Bête, snatched a flagon and goblet from the nearest board and went to him. Nearby, the riders who had lately reported to Eustace were drinking with some of the sheriff's men. She caught part of their talk as she passed.

"—burned right down to the ground, the sheep fried nice as you please."

"Both places?"

"Same thing, and the old swineherd's, too, what's-his-name. Blood? The horses smelled it a mile off."

Oh, God, what are they doing? Gurth was part of it, he must be.

Bête hunched alone, munching at half a chicken, a contented digestive mechanism surrounded by bones, fragments of bread and other bits of the fare. Seeing Gerlaine, he swallowed enormously, belched and wiped the larger fragments from his mouth.

"Here, Bête," Gerlaine offered him the cup. "Drink."

The vessel dwarfed in his ham fist. He drank noisily, dribbling in his beard. Gerlaine bent to him.

"Look, Bête. Look who's come."

He followed her point toward the red cloak.

Pipe and tabor ceased amid hoots and whistles, the bright balls were caught and stowed away, and the jugglers drifted down to the lower end of the hall to grab what they could from the tables. The knot of spectators clustered between the tables broke and dribbled away, leaving one man alone in the center of the hall.

Eustace and Élène saw him at the same time, the cloak making him seem even bigger, a green and scarlet mountain. It was impossible *not* to notice him; already heads were turning.

"My lord!"

Clear, strong, the Latin-trained diction penetrating like a February wind, his voice reached every ear in the hall.

"I have news."

X

Effortlessly, without the loss of the smallest syllable, the words carried even to the scullery below. The French was impeccable and courtly, Gurth's manner almost touching in his apparent eagerness to conciliate.

"My lord, I've looked into the cause of the fires and have come to report."

"Fires?" de Mowbray puzzled. "What is he talking about?"

"It is nothing," Eustace answered. "I sent men to investigate. Bastard, what have you to tell me?"

"Sir, three persons have forsworn their fealty and left Montford. While I have promised to represent their cause to you, I would not have you think their decision has swayed others. The rest of us stand behind you; we are our lord's men." He paused, then added innocently, "All twenty-five of us."

A nervous snicker rippled over the lower table. Gurth advanced to the dais. "Sir, I have also to report on the loss of sheep."

He made a courtly leg to Élène, meeting her venom with Parisian grace: "Baroness, Sire Hugh, *votre serviteur*. Guy, Robin, *ça va*."

She hated his insides virulently, but at this moment Élène could somewhat understand her daughter's problem.

'Baron," de Mowbray surveyed Gurth's elegant dress, "this is one of your knights?"

Gurth replied for himself, bowing to the sheriff. "Guillaume de Mowbray, Lord High Sheriff of York? Gurth Brandson."

"Gert—?"

"*Gurth*, sir; difficult for Normans, I realize. The lips and teeth must be used."

"I have been admiring your mantle. Is it by Baldwin?"

"No, by the Lady Algive of Brandeshal and her maids. However, my lord's taste is commendable. I will not trouble you overmuch. I merely—" He fumbled in his belt and brought out a folded square of vellum, presenting it respectfully to the sheriff. "I merely carry bills. This is for you, Sire de Mowbray."

The hall had grown still. Those at the board were curious and unable to quite understand what they saw. Riveted at Bête's side, Gerlaine waited, her premonition growing with every second to a horrible certainty.

Eustace searched the man for the smallest insincerity. Beyond that he was amazed that Bastard, who had been carted home scarce a week ago with his back laid open, could walk so blithely now, without the slightest sign of discomfort. It wasn't human. His instinct distrusted, but Gurth displayed only a courtesy bordering on servility.

"Bastard, houses are burned, stock slaughtered and serfs gone. If you are part of it—"

"But, my lord, if I were involved, wouldn't I be with the departed? Would I be here, so soon after my just punishment for poaching?"

There was an audible hiss of intaken breath here and there. Gerlaine could hear her heart pounding. *Stop . . . please, stop.*

"Who has gone?" Eustace said in a low voice. "Where?"

"Aye, sir. It's all related to the sorry matter of the demised sheep and several of your lordship's swine."

"*My* swine?"

"Which, in haste, I had forgotten to mention." Gurth produced another slip of parchment from his belt. "Those gone—"

"Gone?" Eustace thundered. "Gone where?"

"Well, that is a point which must be clarified," Gurth began in the bookish manner of a scholar. "You see, under Northumbrian law, never rescinded in writ by King William, any person of a free status may choose his or her own lord or leave him as they please. As my father was baron before you, I can vouch for this law as extant on the rolls at Sockburn."

Hugh wiped the grease from his knife with a slight, sad smile. Gurth was climbing the scaffold step by step, undoubtedly mad. But by God's blood, he had style.

"Which," Gurth continued with clerkly precision, "brings me back to your lordship's late sheep."

De Mowbray was laboring over the careful French he could barely read. The missive and its bearer were beyond his comprehension. "Baron, what's this talk of law? Is this one of your men?"

"Who has gone, Bastard?" Eustace said carefully. "Where?"

"Well, sir, the sheep—"

"Damn the sheep, you miserable liar! Where are they gone?"

Unruffled, Gurth read from the parchment. "Those gone: Hulda, the widow of Godric Carpenter. Her son, Godric, minor. Calla, the hand-fast widow of Brand Ulfson, late thane of Brandeshal. Peter Fletcherson, swineherd. All were of free status except Peter who was churl, which points up a fascinating comparison in French and Saxon law. You see—"

"Attend, you law-spouting ass," de Mowbray held up the paper. "What am I to make of this?"

"That, sir, is an accounting of charges. The widow feels Godric was unjustly executed in the defense of hearth-right —Sire Eustace, I spoke of it; I did advise you with all urgency —and, therefore, as his heir, may claim full recompense from you as master of the men he killed in said defense. The amount is two hundred silver pence."

"Two *hundred*—" the sheriff's gasp was caught up and whispered through the hall.

"Approximately one third the value of a thane, or"—Gurth searched the ceiling for his figures—"for your easier understanding, twice that of a minor Norman baron . . . roughly. As Godric's brother, I may collect the debt for his wife. My Lord Eustace—"

He was flashing from one to the other, giving them no chance to regain mental balance. Imperceptibly, the tempo of his speech had increased. He unclasped the red mantle and dropped it on the dais. Gerlaine, unable to take her eyes from him, saw the new dark stains on the rich material of his tunic.

"My lord, I don't know where they've gone." He paused. "It pains me to report it. I have been whipped once this week. They said north or south or east or west, it made no difference, for in any direction they would find a better lord. And now, sir," Gurth plunged on with convincing urgency, "I *must* get to the matter of the sheep."

It was mad, not happening at all. The monumental absurdity welled up in Hugh de Neuville, dammed behind his clamped mouth, though his shoulders trembled with it. Through the telling, a few chuckles rose here and there, smothered quickly behind embarrassed hands. Eustace, on the point of calling the guards, heard that fatal titter. Gurth's subtly comic insistence, throughout greater calamities, on the importance of the sheep had built below the salt a reservoir of expectant laughter. "Sheep" was the trip word; when he pulled it, the laughter could no longer be politely hidden. It dribbled, spilled and rolled irreverently through the air.

Had Gurth betrayed one moment of insolence or knowledge of the effect he was producing, he would be dead. But he looked around at the laughter, puzzled at the interruption. And, sickly, Eustace knew the way in which he was beaten. He could torture the man, tear out his tongue and hang the writhing remnant, but Bastard had dropped the insult with such innocent, unassailable irony that none of them, from de Mowbray to the scullions, would ever forget the Day of the Sheep. But a man who stood before his lord reporting plain facts with lamb-white honesty, the fresh blood seeping through his clothes, could not be called a liar.

"My lord Sheriff, the widow Hulda requests you pay promptly, if possible, as she is quite poor."

"Pay?" de Mowbray laughed. "Pay what? This?" he wadded up the reckoning and tossed it at Gurth. "You are droll."

Gurth's smile was as full of enjoyment as it was devoid of malice: "Good."

He hooked a thumb in the broad belt and addressed the baron. "My lord, the demised sheep—"

Again the scattered ripple of mirth. Élène had not taken her eyes from him. He was hateful and yet with a negative fascination; like Gerlaine she now sensed the demonic energy

masked by his clowning, the distended black pupils, the slight
twitching of his fingers.

"—have always thought of themselves as English—"

A healthy, vulgar roar of laughter ripped out from the high
table itself. Hugh could no longer conceal his insane enjoyment of the irony. His break was license for all the held-in
lunatic laughter of the lower tables. It rolled back and forth like
a wave as Hugh lurched to his feet.

"You . . . you magnificent horse's ass!" he sputtered. "I
may kill you myself."

"—and when their masters left, I fear that, in desperation,
they took their own lives."

It was impossible, beyond all reason. The man was hanging
himself while they screamed with hysterical glee. Eustace
threw one swift glance at his gasping son, and made his
decision. Bastard knew what he was doing. He was not only
going to hang, he would beg to die. He lifted his head to call
the guards, but they were part of the thundering insanity. In
that split, unbalanced second, with the highest tide of laughter
lapping about him, Gurth spun like a dancer; his arm whirled
viciously and buried the ax in de Mowbray's brain.

Before the body slumped forward, Gurth's sword was
drawn, spinning in a bright arc, descending on the baron.
Reflex alone saved Eustace. He dove flat among the plates and
flagons as the blade chopped deep into the back of his chair,
but already Hugh was over the table, yanking the sword from a
startled man-at-arms and plunging at Gurth.

"My game!" he warned them all. "Stay out."

"Take him alive!"

"Bête," Gerlaine pulled at him. "Now."

They moved forward toward the ring of men already circling
Hugh and the Saxon, whose sword darted everywhere like the
tongue of a snake, keeping them at bay. Incredibly, he was
laughing. It seemed to release even more of that savage energy
Gerlaine remembered from the day of Barley-Maid.

Hugh feinted and struck. As the swords met, Gurth's foot
whipped out with murderous force into the Norman's stomach.
Hugh gasped and doubled over, and as Gurth stepped in to
finish him, Gerlaine shot through the ring of men and hurled
herself on him.

"Gurth, don't. *Don't!*"

She had a glimpse of the cold madness in his eyes and lips drawn back in a cruel grin. Then he caught her backhanded across the shoulder and shoved her roughly aside. Gerlaine flailed, off-balance, and fell against one of the tables. She had intended Bête to save him, to put the huge block between Gurth and the men, but it was too late. At last Bête understood. Unbelievably, Friend had hurt Little Red. He was already moving, a lumbering juggernaut bearing down on Gurth.

Someone called: "Let *la bête* take him."

"I want him alive," said Eustace hoarsely.

Gurth paused. He could have taken Bête's head with one swipe of the blade, but he faltered, the fury blurred with bafflement.

The mute was inexorable purpose. He reached clumsily. Gurth dodged away. As Bête came at him again, he flipped the sword to his left hand and drove his fist into Bête's jaw. The sound of the blow cracked through the hall; in anyone else it would have shattered bone, but the hulking Bête merely rocked on his heels, blinking stupidly. Gurth closed, tripped the unstable legs, and Bête fell like a landslide. In his fury and momentum, unthinking, Gurth raised the sword.

"NO . . ."

The sound didn't end. It stretched out and up into a scream of terror, pouring from a dark reservoir of remembered fear as Bête writhed, covering his head from the bright dream-sword still falling.

The sword froze in the air. In that instant they were on Gurth, but the maniacal strength was still not spent. Four of them were needed to claw and batter him to the ground. Eustace crouched over him trembling with hate.

"Tell Bardeau: in the morning, before we hang this thing, he will prepare irons and a fire."

Spread like a hawk with a broken wing, Gurth's bruised mouth cracked in a grin. Blood frothed over his lips.

"They know what you are now," he rasped. "You've nothing left, wee man. And she was worth it."

They carried him away.

Near the still writhing Bête, Gerlaine slumped on a bench, ignored by the milling servants, staring numbly at the awkwardly crumpled Sheriff of York. She could not feel anything.

His head, propped crazily on the imbedded ax, was a vaguely distasteful absurdity.

Bête was curled in a fetal ball, shuddering. His legs kicked feebly. He looked like a dying horse. Gerlaine slid forward to him on her knees. At her touch, his eyes opened.

"Ma pauvre Bête," she whispered. *"C'est fini."*

His thick fingers spread like crab's legs, his weight gathering over them. Bête heaved up onto his haunches, then half erect, befuddled. She remembered distractedly that he had spoken. He made something like a word.

He swayed dizzily, looking down at her with a caricature of human expression. Then it faded into his accustomed vacuity, blank as a tired hound waiting to be petted.

Dear God, Gerlaine thought, *what is this place? What are we? Was there ever a moment when any of us were not mad?*

Eustace stepped out into the first gray light, drawing his cloak against the chill. Ralph had roused him at the first cock and then gone to the smithy where Bastard was chained. The morning air bit sharply for early September, and the familiar outlines of the bailey were dim with fog off the river. He could barely make out the far guard tower along the west stockade wall.

When he reappeared, the steward looked pale. His mouth opened and shut in the manner of a beached fish.

"The Bastard is gone."

"What—?" Eustace started for the smithy.

Ralph caught at his arm. "Baron, for the love of sanity, don't go in there."

"The guard?"

Ralph looked away, nodding. "He is there . . . with Bardeau."

Eustace shook him off and covered the ground with quick strides.

He stayed motionless in the doorway for a long time, till Ralph stirred behind him.

"I have seen men cruel in their madness," the steward murmured feebly. "But *this* . . ."

"Bring the priest and three men. Have them buried quickly. And keep the women away from here."

The steward scurried off. Grimly Eustace studied the scene

until his search rested on the thick timbers where they had chained Bastard. Harder than his steward, he was not sick with what he saw but it was hard to believe.

I will kill you if you can be killed, and my priest will do what must be done. You will be buried face down in unsanctified ground that you look to Satan for your deliverance, because you are his, Bastard. You are not human.

The chain was gone, leaving a splintered hole where the four-inch bolt had been torn with incredible force out of the solid oak.

Loki—

I claim the sword you have held for me, and I vow to you everyone who carries their name.

I will take from the Norman everything, as he and his kind have taken all from us. And he will live to see it.

The wife first, that he may wait for death in a cold bed.

The sons, one by one, that he may see the branches drop from his rotted tree.

I will take him only when he has died once for each of them, as we have died in ours.

The daughter, too. All, Loki. Take my promise. Give me the power now.

BOOK TWO:

And Early Comes

the Dark

I

The earth house was gloomy but warm, the entrance hidden behind the height of a crag. It was proof against discovery so long as no fires were lighted during the day to send their smoke through the small ceiling hole.

Dirty, exhausted but full of mutton and oatmeal porridge, little Godric sprawled inert against a saddle. He was cranky before they ate, child-weary and fighting sleep till he collapsed mid-wriggle like a spent puppy, and Hulda laid him against the saddle where he'd be quiet until morning. She and Peter sat nearby on a blanket, away from Calla.

"No one can see our smoke?"

Peter's hands moved with absent patience, working the mutton grease into the longbow. "Black as pitch out there."

"How far have we come?"

"That water we saw west today, that was Solway. Another day," he reckoned, "we'll be in Malcolm's land."

"Couldn't we rest a day?"

It was a temptation; Peter resisted it. "Still smells of Norman. That farmer who sold us the sheep, he just might sell us too."

By the glow from the fire pit, Calla sat cross-legged and absorbed, scraping the last fragments of flesh from the shoulder blades of the sheep. She used her bronze knife. Peter's blade would have been more efficient, but it was iron and would kill the magic.

The bronze knife hovered over each bone in turn as Calla spoke the ancient charm. She touched them, took them up, laid them down again. Peter and Hulda remained silent out of respect and more than a little awe. Though baptized Christians, they would no more have questioned her power than Christ's.

Now Calla's voice rose a half tone in the crooning sounds.

"It's the magic," Hulda whispered. "It's come."

Calla raised the bronze knife and drove it deep into the dirt between the bones. Her rich voice was exultant with faith.

"Gurth is alive!"

"*Och,* don't hope for it," Peter said. "There was no chance."

"He's alive!"

"Corn-Woman, he knew where he was going. He knew what—"

Her glance was a hand over his mouth. Peter argued no further. Calla was always frightening to him. That power of hers could put a man in fairyland at its will, make him howl like a wolf, anything.

"I've cleaned the bones without iron and said the words three times. Gurth is alive. Peter"—she threw the bones into the fire pit—"when we're safe from the Normans, do you go back and find my son."

"Go back? I'm as good as hanged if I do."

Calla gazed into the fire, serene and sure, the flames highlighting her cheekbones and the sheen of grease rubbed into her skin. "I saw more than Gurth. There was the baron. He hasn't the winter left on Tees."

Hulda crept closer to the fire, squatting across from the Corn-Woman. "What death has he?"

"It was dark. There was snow. He was in shadow."

"Brother," Hugh remarked as they rode, "do you appreciate the small ironies of life?"

"No," Guy grunted in disgust. "I don't even know what it means."

"It just struck me how droll of de Mowbray to die of a brain injury. One thought it his least vulnerable point."

They trotted doggedly through the cold rain leading five equally weary and disspirited soldiers. For two and a half days

out and back, they'd ridden the serfs' trail, slept in clammy
clothes, eaten only twice and that mere thin gruel commandeered from crofts along the way—dark, reeking hovels that
killed the appetite before you could bolt the miserable stuff
down.

The runaways had to go north. Without a boat the east was
closed. South and west meant more Normans, but northwest
beyond the wall lay Strathclyde and hundreds of displaced
Saxons. The track led to the river where they lost more than an
hour before Guy picked up the readable marks of three horses,
one of them ridden double. Sometimes the trail vanished
completely where it absolutely could not without the use of
sorcery, a fact attested darkly by Hugh's sergeant, Aimeré.

"There, sire. All clear ground. You could read a bird track
across it. They vanished."

Then Guy would pick them up again, skirting the soft
ground and doubling back before moving on into the higher,
rocky places. Again and again the trail disappeared and Guy
would ferret it out while the soldiers mumbled of witchcraft.
He was no skeptic, merely a natural hunter. What could be
found he would find.

"The black-haired woman," Aimeré muttered. "I know what
I know, and the priest, too."

At length Hugh had to reckon on a twenty-hour lead for the
runaways. The ground rose higher, the track grew impossible
even for Guy. It was time to use the lessons of experience.
They were far beyond Tees in a driving rain with horses as
weary as themselves. To go on might bring them up against
armed Scots or the mailed brigands of some freebooting
Norman lord out to pick up a ransom or two with the king
safely far away. Hugh had his brother and five men to answer
for. Four serfs weren't worth it. Gratefully the others heard his
order to turn for home.

Guy's first mail shirt had been a novelty until the rain came.
In seventeen active years, he couldn't recall a misery to
compare. His clothes were wet through and the iron rings acted
to hold in the damp chill. His teeth chattered until he clamped
them tight, his shoulders ached from the weight. Still there
were proprieties and pride. He didn't mention it until Montford
keep was in sight.

"Think of the poor sheriff," Hugh said as he lifted his eyes heavenward, "packed in salt, rest his soul."

Supper would wait for some time yet. Five of Gerlaine's women—the worst gossips, she noted grimly—worked their looms for the new woolens she would need at Winchester. In poor grace, the men from York had agreed to stop on the return from Durham. She'd have a good escort to York. Beyond that she must wait for another cortege going south to Peterborough, weeks of cold riding, nights of makeshift beds from keep to keep, nights of strangers where all her life there had been family, and only Bête for friend. Days of looking back, wondering if Gurth followed.

You are light and air and yes . . .

She remembered that, hoarded it and brought it out like a secret treasure to relish behind her eyes as she plied her loom.

"They're sending me away, too."

She guessed now he'd meant to die that night, and wondered would he follow her to Winchester. Her mind spun out its own logic as the material lengthened under her hands. Her place was nearest the fire where Élène was heating wine for Hugh and Guy, sighted half an hour ago from the parapet. They trooped heavily up the stairs now, Eustace and her three brothers. Hugh smiled gravely at her, touched her cheek and kissed Élène.

"You're wet." Élène hugged him. "Off with that cloak. Guy, you too! You'll take chill."

Bedraggled and lurching with fatigue, Guy still managed to look forlornly debonair in his mail, his mouth full of cheese pie snatched from the scullery.

"Save you, Sister," he mumbled, chewing. Hugh motioned him to the fire. Guy straddled it, leaning his back against the lovely warmth of the stone. *"Mon Dieu,* that feels good."

"They're past the wall," Hugh reported. "Those toads you sent with us couldn't find a nun in a convent. It was Guy here kept us on the track."

His brother smiled wearily at the grace. "They kept doubling back, Father." He was almost too weary to feel important. "Witch or genius, one of them knows how to cover a trail."

"So does Bastard," Eustace acknowledged. "Robin and I have been over both sides of the river for ten miles."

"Every inch of Tees," Robin was anxious for his share of
glory. "Your shoulders hurt, Guy?"

"Of course not," Guy wiped his mouth casually on the back
of a dirty hand. "After ten minutes, it was nothing."

"He's been at Brandeshal," Eustace said. "We're sure of
that. The forge has been used."

Gerlaine's hands froze on the loom. She listened closely,
knowing with what effort the other women strained to hear
news of Gurth, sure that fat Audrée flicked an eye toward the
other women at the mention of his name. It was one of
Gerlaine's bad days, beginning with a dull headache and the
inevitable cramps, at once a relief and a vague sadness this
time; worse perhaps for the changes in her, but like all the
other times in her minute tolerance to irritation. She contem-
plated Audrée, cold murder festering in her heart. *One word,
Cow-face.*

"We've been to every holding," Eustace went on. "They
know what it means to help him. If he's still here, he's
starving."

Élène shot a quick glance at her daughter bent over the
loom. "Why in God's name would he stay here?"

"I don't know." The truth was not easy to grasp let alone
speak. In the past month, Eustace had learned the frustration of
things impossible to fathom. Now he sensed the beginnings of
something he could not control. "That man would do nothing
in God's name."

Élène sensed her daughter's silent reaction to the whole
conversation. And the women were listening too. "I must see
Hugo about supper. Guy, out of those wet clothes, you'll be
feverish. Hugh, *aussi;* you're not so big but I can tell you're
worn out. Gerlaine, have your women put up the looms. We
must take candles to the mill."

The women packed up their workboxes and pushed the
looms against the wall. Audrée, plump to shapelessness, was
not much older than Gerlaine, a cook's wife and already burst
at the hips from childbearing. *The great ball of blubber,*
Gerlaine thought. *She spits them out like apple seeds.*

"*Dm'selle,*" Audrée simpered with feigned innocence, "is it
true, as they say, that Gurth is a devil and eats girls?"

She was answered with lethal calm and an eye to match.
"Only those above a certain weight. Fat ones, *chère* Audrée."

Gerlaine's courtesy was distilled vitriol. "For the grease, one thinks."

Audrée reddened. "Oh, *dm'selle,* that is cruel of you."

Cruel but justified. It was Audrée who led the other women in "Fair Yolande" as they worked, with its painful and tactless double meanings.

> *It is not for sewing nor for cutting,*
> *Nor for spinning nor for brushing;*
> *Nor is it for too much sleeping,*
> *But for speaking too much to the knight.*
>   *I chide you for it,*
>   *Fair Yolande.*

"Would Père Vaudan lie? There were men, too. Fat men. *Alors,* Bardeau was a substantial fellow. We were not allowed to see, of course, but—"

"By your leave, *dm'selle.*" The girl retreated, huge buttocks jouncing urgently under her smock. Maliciously victorious, Gerlaine snatched up a mantle from her closet and met Élène on the stairs burdened with four heavy tapers. She handed half to Gerlaine.

"Whatever's taken Audrée? She's on her knees babbling Ave's by the soup."

"She improves," said Gerlaine inscrutably. "More time on her knees and less on her back might end that stream of brats she presents every year like Christmas gifts."

They passed out into the raw air of the bailey, down the steps dug from the smaller promontory of the keep proper, and trudged toward the mill. Élène bent against the wind. Its dampness never left her, settling into fingers and joints with a continual ache.

"Audrée is fat and stupid," she admitted. "But at least she is married."

"Not today, Mother. Please."

"For all that, we don't know that you have seen the last of this."

"Yes, we do," the girl sighed. "With everything else, there is this, too."

Élène halted, instantly full of relief and concern. "You are sure? Oh, *ma pauvre,* there is pain?"

"It is the first day; what else? *N'importe.*"

They walked on toward the mill, a squat, clay-walled cylinder isolated near the north stockade wall.

"I am glad," Élène confessed a little awkwardly. "You said nothing. One didn't know."

"There is no child."

The mill was deserted; Eustace's grain already threshed and ground, the only visitors now were odd serfs milling their own. The interior was dark and cold enough with the help of salt to keep the late Sheriff of York presentable for his journey home. Gerlaine closed the door behind them.

Élène looked away. "I'm glad. The child would have to be exorcised before baptism. Even then we couldn't be sure."

"Mother, Gurth is not evil. He may hate us, he may hate me. But that's a man, not a devil."

"Indeed? Your father, *Dieu me pardonne,* is not the most pious man alive, but even he has begun to believe. You are infatuated."

Gerlaine massaged her dull headache with cold fingers. "Devils are not—so." *They are old and wise in pleasure. They do not discover you like a child finding bright gold in the plain earth. And yet he is there in my sleep, as the incubus came to Sigrid in the shape of her brother. Is it Gurth I hold then, is it Gurth in me or something else?*

She dismissed it with a weak gesture. *"Je ne sais pas.* Come, the candles. Mind the step there."

The stairs were wet and gritted underfoot as they descended to the excavated cellar below the mill where, illuminated by the one unexpired candle, a heavy wooden case held de Mowbray's remains. The cellar was clammy and oppressive, colder than the outside air. They lighted the new tapers and framed them about the casket. As the light threw their shadows hugely against the earthen walls, Élène bowed over her clasped hands in the prayer for the dead. They signed the cross; as she kissed her fingers in culmination, Gerlaine noticed the white crystals spread in a trail from the casket to the steps. She took up a pinch.

"Mother, look." Salt. The floor was sprayed with it. "Where was the casket sealed?"

"In the cookhouse, where the salt is. Why?"

"Regarde."

The leaden seals were broken.

Élène spoke, low and tight. "Come—quickly, the priest."

In the bailey, she snapped commands at the first soldier she saw: "You, soldier! Off your rump. Fetch the baron. Gerlaine, cry the bridge tower. Tell them to bring Vaudan."

They gathered within minutes by the mill door. Eustace leading the descent to the cellar. The priest's voice sounded flat in the heavy air.

"The shroud was sewn tight with the salt inside. It did not leak."

"It is for you to say," Élène moved back from the casket. "What must we do?"

The harassed cleric had hoped this afternoon for a quiet hour over wine and a book of hours. He allowed himself the small irony. "It appears, *ma maîtresse,* we must open it and look."

His distaste ruled by duty, Vaudan grasped the lid and pushed it up.

What greeted them was not immediately comprehensible. The heavily packed salt blurred the human outlines to a lumpy and curiously foreshortened oblong. Gerlaine and her mother stood well away as Vaudan pried through the torn folds. He mumbled something to her father; she heard the answering hiss of disbelief. Eustace turned away from the casket, white in the gloom.

"Devil . . ." He looked helplessly up at the dark earth walls as if Bastard were there to condemn. "Devil—*devil!*"

"What, Husband?"

His fists clenched by his sides. "What does he *want,* that man!"

Vaudan closed the lid. Firmly he shepherded the two women toward the stairs. When the mill door slammed after them, Eustace placed his hands on the casket lid.

"Vaudan—my friend—we're caught in the middle. The Bishop of York will expect his body, and the bishop is de Mowbray's cousin. There are enough harmful stories to go south as it is. What can we do?"

Vaudan pondered, heartsick and bewildered at the descration. At length he sighed and tapped the lid decisively. "There is only one course. We can say that the salt was not effective, that the humors of his constitution would not allow preservation and burial was imperative. The bishop will have him removed later to York, but the casket will not be opened. This may suffice."

"It must have been last night," Eustace mused. "Impossible: in past the guards, over the wall, back out again. A man I thought to have broken, who should have been abed two weeks with no skin on his back, walks into my hall to mock me —bleeding but *there*—rips an iron bolt out of a wall without a whisper of sound, leaves two strong men hard to recognize—" Eustace ran distraught fingers through his short, graying hair. "I've never been religious, Vaudan. I've dealt with men—*men* —made out of blood and muscle and guts and mistakes. Now I'm dealing with something else. I should have listened to you earlier. Vaudan, how much of Bastard is human?"

"It is hard to say. His mother—they wrote of her as a mongrel—has blood that was old here before the Britons came. One has only to see their idols to measure the distortion of belief. Obviously he does not feel pain deeply. Satan has done that for him."

"Can he be killed?"

"Oh, yes," Vaudan assured him. "It might be difficult; one must remember he is more than earthly wise, like the mother, but there are certain times when he is less powerful. All Hallows—the day itself, not the night before. Christmas, Easter." He beckoned the baron to the stairs. "We must be practical. We'll bury him now, before vespers." He sighed as they mounted toward the door. "Related to the bishop, and myself a poor priest. I have no wish to explain to *him* why his cousin is sent home without a head."

II

The weather grew noticeably colder, the wind off the estuary keening to an even sharper edge on the few clear days. More often the fog rolled so thickly over Tees, borne in from the North Sea, that from the parapet Gerlaine could barely make out the watchtowers.

The dark came earlier now and with it something as pervasive as the fog, always present but surfacing with the hasty interment of de Mowbray. In the long nights by the fire and the fat lamps, creeping through the scullery and barracks, fearful imaginings began to shape. Crosses appeared about the necks of women, cooks, ostlers, even hard-as-oak soldiers who hadn't prayed since Hastings. Attendance at Vaudan's mass rose sharply. Charms that the priest would have denounced out of hand—amulets old as Loki—nestled against breastbones under wool tunics and smocks. More torches were consumed within the keep, but the gloom was hard to rout. They lived in a world without color, a drab cosmos of shadow and dull gray in which it was hard to believe any cheerful hue had ever existed.

Gerlaine had fallen asleep to the familiar sounds of the keep settling for the night, timbers creaking, footsteps passing from

126

guardroom to scullery as some soldier from the watch went to
warm himself with cheese and beer. Hugh pacing the hall on
his own restless journey and climbing unsurely to his closet
well past midnight. The sighing and popping of the fire on the
hearth, and the wind rising and falling in its eternal lament,
lulling her to sleep.

She dreamed of Gurth sometimes and firmly did not mention
it in confession despite Vaudan's pressing queries. Besides,
the dreams of possession were mostly before that day in the
forest. There was still a hunger, a wanting, but when she
dreamed of him now, it was usually the warmer, gentler
things. She loved the way he spoke French with no telltale
gutturals and even more when in his excitement or irritation the
Northumberland rhythms with their oddly softened vowels and
queer glottal stops broke through the years at Paris. It was a
ringing voice, most beautiful when he laughed. She treasured
that.

Nothing was very clear in her dream, no time or place
remembered, but there was a happiness to it. He was laughing
at something she said, as when she shaped her tongue
fruitlessly with its throated *r*'s and liquid *l*'s to the splintering
jumble of his language.

No, again. "My home is in Northumberland."

My 'ome ees en—

Is in—

Ee . . . is in Nort'umbehlon—oh, nom de chien, Gurth,
c'est trop difficile! *I'd starve to death before I could ask for my
supper.*

The rich laughter again. She smiled in her sleep, turning on
her back under the fur coverlet. As the dream faded, the
laughter echoed again. Gerlaine opened her eyes to the dull
glow of the dying fire against the ceiling. She stretched,
yawned and pulled sleepily at the coverlet.

And heard it again.

Gerlaine jerked upright, listening. Not a dream, it was there,
somewhere in the bailey or even closer. She slipped from the
bed, throwing the coverlet about her shoulders, and padded
across the cold floor to open the shutter.

A world of dark gray wool lay beyond her casement. She
waited, listening, until the cold floor numbed her feet. There

was no unusual sound, nothing but the acrid smell of the fog in her nostrils. It might have been a soldier who laughed, but— *Gurth?* . . .

"We didn't even know their names."

When Guy didn't answer, Robin concluded pointlessly, "For the grave markers."

His cloak thrown across his chest and shoulder, Guy rested against the catapult, glad for the fresh air. Beside him, Robin breathed deep with the same silent gratitude.

The fog had cleared; there was even a weak dash of sun. The river valley spread out before them, clear but drab, the dun sea rolling away for miles, unrelieved and dreary as clouds.

The morning had been grisly.

They were growing up this summer and autumn. More and more responsibility fell on them, and if it galled, both boys shouldered it uncomplainingly as the wearing of mail, once a coveted honor but now a monotonous necessity. They accepted it, learned their fence from Hugh and Aimeré, rode Tees with the daily patrols, visited steadings, trotted the cold beaches on continual watch for the low shapes of Danish raiders off the inviting coast. Even hunting, once a joy, was now a necessity. Their first year was far from fat; while the baron planned for more cultivated land next year, riding ceaselessly to assess and map every inch of arable land, his sons kept the board supplied with venison.

Today the forest yielded something less appetizing. The two bodies were still recognizable after a fashion, though scavengers had taken their revenue. The two were arrow-shot, the missile economically retrieved from one corpse. The other still retained the arrowhead and part of the shaft where it had been snapped to strip off the mail shirt. De Mowbray's missing men, rather far gone to throw over a horse. Canvas and a wagon were needed. It was not a pleasant task.

Now they gulped the fresh air, the wind whipping their short hair about their foreheads, ignoring the stolid soldier pacing the north end of the parapet.

"You think it was Gurth?" Robin asked.

"Like everything else," Guy answered absently. His attention was on the low hilltop to the south. A moment ago there was a tiny flare of color near the summit. Distant but not missed by those mercilessly sharp young eyes.

"It's hard to know what to think," Robin attempted shyly. Harder even to express it. His esteem for Gurth had amounted to hero worship. "He was a friend, almost—*eh bien,* you know it is hard to talk to Hugh sometimes."

"Aye."

The terseness was not affected. Since de Mowbray's death the boyhood was being squeezed out of Guy with each day, and, Christ, if his own father couldn't understand all of it, how could he? Aye, they were lords, but de Neuville was no longer a world. This place dwarfed it, shriveled it back on its roots.

"I mean," Robin groped awkwardly, "Gerlaine is miserable. *Zut,* I can't remember the last time she smiled. I mean, she and Gurth—"

"She and Gurth *what.*" Guy didn't want to talk about it.

Robin tried very hard to put into words what he had never felt himself. It was too difficult. "God's blood, who knows?"

"He's a pig," Guy spat it vehemently. "A dirty Saxon pig. He tried to kill Father; he'd do the same to you or me or Gerlaine. Grow up, *bébé.* They're animals. You see the way they live: no heart, no brain—"

He broke off suddenly, lunging to the parapet. "Rob!"

"What?"

"There," his arm thrust out, "on the hill. Thought I saw it before."

Eyes shaded, Robin searched the southern hilltop, a good two bowshots distant. "Can't see. What is it?"

"Wait," said Guy. "Just this side of the top. Bastard."

"Point me."

"Straight ahead—so? Now bear right—*there,* look! He's running!"

"Got him!"

The tiny figure was visible for a few seconds, then gone. Running east, Guy calculated. And yet there was nothing east of the keep, no one ever went there. It might be a chance farmer, but that green tunic was a vivid memory.

"Hallo, stable—*hé,* down there! Look alive! Who's saddled?"

In the absence of Eustace and Hugh, Guy made his own decision as he and Robin took the stairs three at a time and bolted across the bailey. To take more than a couple of men would waste precious minutes. In the time it took to mount a proper patrol, Bastard could be two miles away. They recruited two soldiers lounging near the stable door, saddled hastily and clattered across the bridge.

With no time to arm properly, Guy and Robin had snatched up two boar spears. Their escort had nothing but daggers. Still, if it were Bastard this was sufficient. Time was all-important. They charged to the rise and reined in, Guy searching the moor to the east.

"There!"

The green tunic. Bastard loped easily, long legs eating the ground, barely breaking stride as he started up another rise hundreds of yards ahead of them.

"Take him alive!" Guy spurred forward.

The next rise was steep with loose soil that slowed the horses, but they'd narrowed his lead. Beyond, the moor stretched away toward the barren hill called Eston Nab with no place for him to hide. He couldn't get away. Bastard was running straight up the last slope. When he reached the top, Guy was only two hundred yards behind and closing. He unsocketed the spear and couched it, never taking his eyes from Gurth. Nearer now, he saw the rabbit dangling from the running man's left hand. *Last hunt, Bastard.*

As they closed in, Robin couched his own lance. They drew abreast then veered apart for the final run, bodies low and braced forward in the saddle.

Gurth appeared to stumble and fall. One moment he was churning through the heather, the next he fell forward into a slight declivity, out of sight.

"Gone to earth!" Robin cried. "We've got him."

"Spread out! Circle—"

The archer rose out of the heather, a man where there had been only grass. Guy had barely time for a rush of sick horror in the pit of his stomach as the longbow bent on Robin.

"*Garde-toi,* Rob—"

His brother jerked sideways and then slumped as his mare plunged past the man. Already the bow was bending again. The second arrow claimed the man behind Guy. Inexperienced, paralyzed by the quickness of it, Guy's hands stiffened on the reins. He lost a vital fraction of time before his instinct brought the horse to a ground-gouging halt and wheelabout in the same stride. In that lost moment, his one remaining man fell backward out of the saddle, pierced through the throat.

Guy's scream was half rage, half fear. He recognized the man as he charged. He'd kill the swineherd, spit him like one of his pigs before he could ready that last arrow, but the man's arm moved with a mechanical, deadly life of its own, able to loose four arrows to a crossbowman's single bolt. At the last possible moment, Guy hurled the spear and with the same momentum slipped forward to the offside, shielding himself with the horse's neck and shoulders.

The ruse saved his life. To dodge the spear, the swineherd lost his aim, and the arrow meant for Guy thudded deep into the horse's shoulder where it joined the neck, sinking into the windpipe. At gallop speed the horse dropped like a stone. Guy saw the ground come up, felt a blow that bludgeoned the will from his body, then nothing.

Instinct screamed through him: *Get up or you're dead.* Barely conscious, he lurched blindly to his feet, fumbling for his dagger.

The man was gone.

It was over as quickly as it came. Guy swayed on his feet, still stunned from his fall, in the middle of a hilltop with two dead men and his own horse bleeding its life away from the mouth and throat. The other two mounts were scattered and running aimlessly. Robin's roan mare walked slowly toward him bearing the slumped form of his brother.

I'll answer to Father for this. I should be beaten. He brushed the dirt from his raw-scraped cheek, sick with shame and his own stupidity. Green fool, he'd run them right into it, lost two men they couldn't spare and perhaps—

He caught the mare's bridle and looked into his brother's white face. The arrow had completely pierced Robin's side, pointing crazily at the sky. Blessed Christ, it struck his leather belt. One of the bronze studs had deflected it outward. With shaking hands Guy sliced away the belt and Robin's tunic, forcing himself to look. Luck. So much was luck. The wounds were barely deep enough to hold the shaft in.

"Guy . . ."

"Shut up, shut up. It's not deep."

"I'm sorry. It was so quick."

"Be still, damn you. It's almost through. Hold tight, now."

He pulled at the arrow, almost retching. Robin's hands splayed stiffly, quivered, clenched; then the missile was free, red-wet in Guy's hand. He splintered it with vicious force.

"Merde!"

Robin tried to right himself in the saddle, tallow-white and covered with sudden perspiration. "I'm going to be sick."

He fainted instead.

For the slightness of his wound, Robin was treated as if he had personally won England with slight assistance from William. All Montford indulged him deliciously. It was a marvelous break in the monotonous round of fog-bound patrols and the feeling that every minute of the day must be put to profitable use. Kitchen women dropped in with bits of pastry at odd moments to assuage his unceasing appetite, and meals proper were served with hovering solicitude by Gerlaine and his mother who apparently never tired hearing of his adventure or were gracious enough not to say so.

But there was a puzzle none could answer without endorsing an ungodly explanation. Bastard and Fletcherson were sighted in the middle of a field and then simply vanished. Subsequent search revealed nothing, no hold or crevice anywhere near the spot where they could have hidden. It reinforced Vaudan's theory of supernatural forces.

"They just weren't there," Robin swore, slurping noisily at the steaming soup.

Gerlaine held the bowl for him while Élène adjusted his pillow. Close by the bed, Bête turned over in his hands the arrowhead on its two inches of shaft that Guy had retrieved for a souvenir.

"Hé, Bête," Robin demonstrated. *"That* long it was. Three foot, I swear by any saint you've got."

He felt painfully good and very important, much better than Guy. Eustace gave Guy a more thorough lesson than a beating. When the cauterizing iron was heated white, Eustace handed it to him.

"Close the wounds, Guy. Lay it on and count to three."

Then he took his son's sweating hands in his own and gripped tight. "Hold on, man."

Man. Father called him man—sweet Jesu, he would have

held on forever. Now he was scarred. It imparted a trace of
condescension toward his mother and sister who were outside
the fraternity of shed blood.

"What stops me," he mused, "is how Bastard could just
vanish like that."

"He is part devil as the priest says," Élène said matter-of-
factly. "That's why you'll wear your cross even when you
sleep. Finish your soup; I must be at church sometime before
vespers."

"Why?" Gerlaine asked.

"Oh, no reason but those soldiers who weren't so lucky as
Robin. Perhaps none have prayed for them."

"But you're so busy."

"I know," Élène sighed. "These things must be done. They
were good men."

Robin sniffed: "What stinks so?"

"It's Bête," Gerlaine appraised her pet distastefully. "I
should wash him before we travel. It's such a chore."

"Nevertheless," Élène insisted, "wash him today. I've
noticed it myself. How do you tolerate it?"

"I love him," Gerlaine smoothed the tangled hair. "He is
good." He engulfed her small hand in his, stroking it. "See
how he takes my hand? He understands some things. You saw:
he wouldn't let even Gurth hurt me."

"Neither would a smart dog," Robin grimaced, "and *pardi,*
he'd smell better. Take him out, Sister. I'm a sick man and I
need fresh air."

With Clothilde and Thérèse, she dragged a huge laundry tub
to one corner of the busy scullery and filled it with warm
water. Bathing him was the only bother connected with Bête.
She managed it every month or so, whenever he could be
cajoled. Once a week like respectable folk would have been
more pleasant. But today Bête seemed actually to enjoy it, not
fidgeting while she scrubbed across the huge shoulders and
furred chest, humming an old Normandy tune.

There was no question of modesty with Bête. She was a
farm girl, neither prudish nor naïve, aware of his body as she
might have been of that of a horse or a baby. But now there
was something in her hands beside absent thoroughness. She
did not desire his body, but it evoked a rich memory of darker
skin and a more graceful line.

His stomach was flat; it's flatter now. He must be hungry.

Bête was easily as tall as Gurth and much heavier, the fair skin weather-tanned, the hair on his chest and arms gold in summer but darker now. The strength of him moved like a river current, the power always there, never needing to be tested.

Thérèse, a dark little cat of a scullion, leaned on the tub rim, appreciating the vast continent of Bête. "That's a bundle of man, if I weren't married."

"You think so?"

"*Demoiselle*"—Thérèse went over Bête with the unhurried appreciation of a true connoisseur—"cut the hair, shave that goat beard, show him what a woman's for and—*zut!*" She cocked her dark head quizzically. "How old is he, do you think?"

Gerlaine shrugged. "Who knows? Twenty, twenty-one; one can't tell with these English and all that forest on his face." Gerlaine shook the water from her hands. "Bring me a razor. I want to shave him. He's quiet lately; perhaps it won't frighten him."

She took up a small fish knife and stood well away from the tub where he could see her. "Look, Bête."

She pantomimed shaving her face and throat while he watched with vacuous disinterest. She came closer, repeating the motions, but still he evinced no fear of the blade. Then Gerlaine laid the blunt edge against his cheek and made scraping movements.

"See? No fear, *ma Bête.*"

She had made him new clothes for Winchester. Thérèse laid them out while Gerlaine worked delicately with the razor, a little excited at the prospect of unveiling him. The beard floated in wet clumps around his hips as his face gradually appeared, lighter in hue where the beard had long covered it.

"*Très beau,*" Thérèse murmured.

Aye, it was true. In a heavy, brutal way, Bête was handsome, the jaw ponderous and the mouth cruel like certain Norse traders seen at Bayeux, the brutality of the expression oddly offset by a kind of open innocence. A face she'd seen hundreds of times between Wight and Montford, bent over plows or peering from the edge of the forest. Much too coarse a look for her liking. Even were Bête not dulled a-mind, he would not have intrigued her. Her memory held something more complex. And yet the huge-muscled body was magnificent.

My God, I've become a lustful bitch.

"Thérèse, the towels. Up, Bête!"

"Yes, yes, *yes,*" Thérèse rubbed him down with gusty vigor. "God help the maid he lays an eye to."

"Oh, stuff, woman; you're ten years married."

"You do not find him so?"

"He's a big ox. Even with brains, English have no grace to them."—*And a hypocrite as well.*

"*Bien,*" Thérèse passed it off with subtle tact, "they are not all like him." She avoided her mistress' glance. "For myself, if I kicked this ox out of bed—hold still, lout—I'd certainly watch where he rolled. There. *Finis.*"

"It's always so dark now," Élène said. "Even at midday."

She lit the candles from the hearth and set them on the table. "Miserable fog, I've never seen it so thick."

The gloom in the bower receded grudgingly as the candles burned brighter. This was a rare time for Élène and Eustace nowadays, a quiet moment together before a hundred duties called them separate ways, not to meet before vespers.

Élène touched his shoulder. "You look worried. What is it?"

"What is it not?" He sat back from the pile of maps in front of him. "Provender, seed, not enough men."

"Gerlaine?"

"I don't think of that."

"She's never gone to Vaudan about him," she said. "That creature has possessed her. He still wants her; that is why he stays."

"I don't want to speak of it. How is Robin?"

"Tough as leather. Eats for three. I think he wishes the scars were bigger." Élène threw the fur mantle about her shoulder.

"Where do you go?"

"To the church, then to Hugo. I promised Robin a treat for supper."

"The boy got creased," he chuckled. "He's not dying in your arms."

"I know, I know," she nuzzled his rough cheek as she passed

to the door. "But he feels like a vavasor. Don't growl, old man."

"If you go to the church, take a soldier with you. It's outside the stockade."

"Of course, of course." Élène was already halfway out the door. "The handsomest I can find."

As the gray fog darkened outside, Eustace nodded in at Robin's closet, paused at the smithy for a look at a broken plowshare, then entered the cookhouse where Ralph, Hugo the master chef and Vaudan small-talked by the bubbling pots, the priest nibbling at a morsel of partridge and onion on a skewer.

"Lady Élène is at the church still?"

"She desired to pray for the soldiers," Vaudan greeted him. "I had confessions to hear. I used my house and left her in the sanctuary."

"Pardon, seigneur," Hugo hovered respectfully. *"La maîtresse* wanted something set aside for Master Robert, but hasn't said what."

"She's not been here?"

"No, seigneur. Perhaps the baroness is still at church."

Hardly, with all she had to do, Eustace thought. "Ralph, try the scullery. Tell her Hugo is waiting."

The chef offered him venison spitted with spiced apple, one of his favorite snacks. He sampled it, grinning at the moist-eyed priest.

Vaudan snuffled wetly with the beginnings of a cold. "Miserable country."

"Not like home, eh? Never saw weather this thick. Danger-ous, too," the baron reflected. "An army could walk up to your gate before you saw them."

They snacked in quiet for a time, enjoying the warmth and the busy kitchen life as Hugo and cheerful, quick-handed Jehan prepared the evening meal. Thin as his wife Audrée was gross, Jehan moved at a breakneck but expert pace through his duties. Gerlaine often wished for a trace of the same vigor in his slattern wife.

"Odd," Vaudan pondered. "How long have I been a priest? Twenty-five years, almost twenty-six. In all that time, I've never felt lonely till we came here."

It was not the sort of reflection Eustace would have expected from Vaudan. "It does that, this place."

"I mean," the priest went on, "no family, no woman for all that time, none close except de Neuville." It was evidently something he had mulled over. "You wouldn't think it, would you?"

"Ah, the cold's got you," Eustace brushed it aside. "Gerlaine will fix you a draft of wormwood and horehound after supper. *Hé*, Ralph," he greeted the returning steward, "what's the lady's word? What does my son eat tonight that I couldn't get with a royal order?"

"She wasn't there, sir," said Ralph, perplexed. "Nor with the sewing women. *Dm'selle* hasn't seen her."

The inefficiency exasperated Eustace. "She can't still be at church. She could've prayed them to paradise by now, and she knows better than to keep a soldier standing around when he has other duties."

"Madame was alone," Vaudan asserted. He meant it to ease the baron's pique, but it produced the opposite effect.

Eustace put aside the plate and rose. "I told her to take a man."

"Such a short while," Vaudan recollected. "She felt it wasn't necessary."

A twinge of worry nipped at the corner of Eustace's mind. Élène usually found some pretext for puttering around the sanctuary; this or that, a new cloth for the altar. It was her only time to be alone. Still the church was outside the wall; he'd given her explicit orders and *damn*, when was she going to listen! He was already striding toward the entrance, the priest and steward hurrying in his wake. They crossed the bailey toward the dim shape of the bridge tower.

"Hallo, the tower!"

Only thirty feet above, the soldier was a mere phantom in the fog, peering over the rail. "Who's there. Baron?"

"Yes. Did Lady Élène pass back over the bridge while you've been there?"

"Only the priest, sir. I challenged. The lady must be working in the church."

"Working? Does she have men in there?"

"I don't know, my lord. There was hammering a while back."

The small gray apprehension dissolved into relief as Eustace turned to Vaudan. "Dithering around as usual. Was there work to be done?"

"There were some loose boards near the altar," Vaudan remembered as they crossed the bridge and walked toward the church. "I think Lady Élène would rather fix it herself than trust a mere joiner. It is a wonder she allows me in to say mass."

Eustace threw open the door and stepped into the semi-darkened nave. A single tall candle burned on the altar, its feeble corona barely illuminating the large crucifix above where a carven Christ dominated the small chancel. Below it, half in darkness, Élène crouched in front of the altar.

"Élène, we've been looking—"

His body knew it before his mind. Her position before the altar was *wrong*, somehow. Then he screamed and kept on screaming her name and hoarse animal sounds out of a terrible memory.

"*Élène—*"

He would have run to her, but Ralph and Vaudan held him back. He was still shrieking as they dragged him in rough mercy from the church and slammed the door on the obscenity within. The candle flickered in the draft, dancing light and shadow over the wooden agonies of Christ and the newer crucifixion, nailed with two daggers to the altar beneath.

III

Half a Roman mile from the ring of standing stones, the croft lay so low off the ground that anyone might miss it at fifty yards. The interior had been dug down rather than the roof built up, to give standing room. Abandoned for years, crusted with the filth of decades, it stood nevertheless on Malcolm's land. They were in Scotland. Whoever challenged them from here on would do it in Gaelic.

"It's dark enough," Hulda peered at the sky from the small doorway. "I'll light the fire."

"Keep it small," Calla warned.

Godric tugged at his mother's dirty sleeve. "Finish the story."

"Anon." She struck a flint spark into the prepared tinder and nursed the tiny flame into struggling life, feeding it twigs and leaves, then larger sticks until there was a small bed of embers. When the fire burned steadily, Hulda brought Godric close to sit by it.

Her small treasury of tales was almost exhausted, as was the sack of oats. Storytelling to some extent took their minds off their empty stomachs and the dreary cold.

"Well, now: Earl Tostig was the brother of King Harold and as bad as the king was good. So your father and Grandfather Brand—and a few others," Hulda amended generously, "they

said, *'Look here! We won't have this!'* And they took his
houses, his treasures and weapons and brought in a new earl,
Morcar, who turned out *nithing* as Tostig, but that's another
tale. Anyway—"

"Tell about the battle," Godric hunched closer to the small
fire. "What Da did to the Norwegians."

"I'm coming to it—mind your foot, it's half in the fire.
Well, devil that he was, Tostig went to Norway where he told
old Hardrada that your da and Grandpa Brand wouldn't be hard
to beat with a big enough army. And back they came to a place
called Stamford Bridge to steal England away from King
Harold, if you please!"

"Where was I then?"

"That was just a few days before you were born," Hulda told
him. "Your da was worried I'd be all right, but the king needed
him, so I sent him off. *Och*, boy, you never saw such a battle."
She tossed the heavy blond hair over her shoulder, painting the
scene with her hands. "King Harold killing his own brother and
the Norse falling here and there like grain on the mill floor, and
your father laying about with his ax like the Black Angel, when
he looked around and found he was alone and the Norwegians
thick as fleas on him."

Godric jiggled with excitement. "Did he get mad?"

"For sure, but he was hurt too. Down, in fact, and there they
were over him, and himself without even time to pray. Your da
knew he was like to die."

Hulda drifted a little, stirring absently at the fire with a stick.
Like to die. How many times had they both been like to die and
lived? A song with so much sadness, so much ending, could
never be put to harp by a skald. He should have died at Ely, not
gone on to see the whimpering end of it, or have to put his
hands between the French baron's and swear with his mouth
what his guts couldn't believe. And here was his son with the
same golden hair dull-dirty and snarled, trousers tattered and
out at the seat, the fine birthday tunic of carded wool too filthy
now to rub a horse with.

Husband—

The loneliness was not yet habit; she ached for him.
Foolishly, she twisted her head suddenly toward the entrance
as if the great whole of him might suddenly fill it as before
with a dish-rattling curse and a kiss for her.

"Mum?"

"Ah," she came back to the moment, the stick blazing in her hand. "The smoke's got me. Well, there was your da about to be finished. But guess what happened *then*?"

"What, what?"

She bent close. "You know the song the arrow sings as it flies to the clout? Well, he began to hear it. Again and again. ZZizz . . . ZZZizz, and the Norse began to fall, one, two, three; so fast there wasn't a stop between 'em. And by God, not a one could lay a hand to your da."

Round-eyed, Godric said, "Was it Grandfather Brand?"

"No," she teased.

"The king?"

"No," said Hulda. "It was Peter."

"Our Peter?"

"No one else."

"Oh." Godric felt vaguely disappointed. Peter was too close and familiar to be a hero. Heroes didn't keep pigs.

"Oh," his mother caught him up. " *'Oh'* indeed! Why such an *oh,* and your dirty face fallen like an ill-made loaf of bread?"

"He's just our pigman."

"True," she said, "he kept our pigs and he could hang for what his bow has fed you since, so don't sniff."

"Listen!" Calla poised like a listening bird.

"What?" Hulda heard nothing but the wind.

"Shod hoof scraping a rock." Calla uncoiled from the dirt floor, drawing the bronze knife from her belt, and moved quickly to one side of the low entrance, warning Hulda and Godric back into the shadows. Hulda held her breath. She heard footsteps approaching the entrance.

Calla raised the knife. "If it's Peter, he'll call."

Then the voice after a seeming eternity. "Calla? Hulda?"

They relaxed; first he was a vague mass in the shadowed entrance, then edging sideways through the door, a young doe sprawled over his shoulders. Heaving the carcass to the dirt floor, he looked around at them, dulled with weariness, then flopped down beside the fire. *"Hoch,* Godric," he beckoned the boy to him. "I've a gift for you."

Calla remained at the entrance expectantly.

"He didn't come," Peter said. "But the bones said true. He's alive."

She went to kneel by him in the firelight. "Free or a prisoner?"

"Free."

She searched his face for more meaning, saw nothing but fatigue. "And he stays there?"

"He stays," Peter's tongue slurred with exhaustion. He dropped back on his elbow, pulling a fine sheathed dagger from his belt. "This is for you, Godric."

The boy gasped. It was a soldier's weapon, the sheath two fitted pieces of ivory and the blade not mere beaten iron but fine-tempered with a straight gutter.

"*Och,* Peter, where'd you *get* it?"

"In a rabbit's ear," Peter chucked him in the ribs. "He won't need it more. Hulda, I could use some food." He tossed her his knife. "The doe's dressed out. Wake me when it's ready."

"And when did they reckon you for a thane, giving orders so?"

Peter was tired enough to sound drunk. He lay back, closing his eyes. "I've ridden five days, seen and heard wonders and come back to tell of them, but not on an empty stomach."

An insistent shadow, Calla bent over him. "Peter?"

". . . uh?"

"How is he?"

Peter was already started down the soft road to sleep. "Don't worry about him, Calla. He'll be there when they're gone." He opened one red-rimmed eye. "He's paid his promise. But the devil's loose on Tees, Corn-Woman."

When it was late, when they'd eaten and Peter set the boy to sleep with another rattling tale of Stamford Bridge, he fetched the sack he'd left by his horse and set it before Hulda.

"Gurth's promise," he said with a measure of pride. "The *wergild.*"

"Let me see."

He loosed the drawstrings and drew out the heavy, salt-flecked prize by its short-cropped hair. Hulda's cold blue eyes did not flinch away; rather she bathed the head in a long, pleasurable inspection.

Calla pointed to the deep wound in the skull. "Gurth did this?"

"Aye," Peter affirmed, "and 'twas him got over the wall to get this for Hulda. For the bloody rest of it," he shook his head, "it's hard to believe."

"You hear, Hulda," Corn-Woman put her long fingers to the prize. "You have the proof. Is my son quit of his debt?"

"I quit him," Hulda nodded slightly without taking her steady gaze from the sightless, half-lidded eyes. "Thank you, Peter Fletcherson."

She would sleep better now.

Élène had been the heart of Montford. When that heart stopped beating, the whole body lay dead for a time, the smooth flow of routine faltered and ground to a halt. Restless as a wasp, rarely off her feet between sun and dark, a hundred details balanced on her mind's unerring slate, she was the workhorse of the keep. From the plucking of pullets and the proper recipe for *lèche lombard* to the firing of the catapults on the parapet, there was no quarter turn of the tiniest wheel in the machinery of Montford that Élène had not known. Now, suddenly, there were at once a score of questions for Eustace and Gerlaine on things taken for granted for years. *What shall we do about . . . where did la maîtresse leave . . . we have not had instructions . . . it was always the baroness who . . . my lord, can you tell us?*

He could tell them nothing, unable to conceive her death. Under the numbness grew the dull but ponderous realization that there had never been a time without Élène. He was a blind man accustomed to a wall, a guiding rail, a known path that suddenly was not there anymore.

Gerlaine and her brothers passed down the steps from the keep and across the bailey toward their father's bower. The night was unusually clear. There were even stars here and there and a cold sliver of dead-white moon.

"Be clear tomorrow," Guy reckoned. "Another damned patrol." There was more stolidness to his gait now. He laughed less, moved with more economy. "Good view from the towers. It'll be hard for—" He glanced at Gerlaine and broke off the sentence.

"—for anyone to get in," she finished it for him. He couldn't tell from her tone how she felt; no one could these days.

Hugh knocked respectfully at the bower entrance and waited for the muffled answer before they entered. Eustace sat before the fire. His back, usually straight, never compromising with the curve of any chair, now seemed wilted against the wood. He barely turned to acknowledge them.

"Guy, how soon can your brother ride?"

"I don't know, sir."

Guy was not prepared for the reaction. Eustace whipped around, lashing at him. "*Why* don't you? In the middle of nowhere, in the middle of—I have to depend on scuts like you? Robin's a soldier, part of the keep defense, and he rides with you. When I ask again, you'll know. *Tu comprends?*"

"Yes, Father."

"Coast patrol tomorrow," Eustace grunted, turning back to the fire. "Take five men, start at first light. Hugh?"

"Sir?"

"Hugo says we're short of fresh meat again. God, those sculls couldn't go to the jakes without Élène to—" He trailed off into fretful silence.

"I'll start early," Hugh volunteered with unaccustomed gentleness. "Was there anything else, *mon père?*"

The baron threw his answer to the fire. "*Rien.* I won't detain you, Sire Hugh. You were undoubtedly occupied in the hall."

Hugh caught the sarcasm. He inclined his head civilly. "Good night, sir."

"Guy, go with him. I want to speak with your sister."

Gerlaine waited in silence after they were gone, while Eustace dropped a split log onto the fire, pokered the embers and sat down again. "You are tired, Daughter?"

She nodded. "It's chaos. They all depended on Mother."

He paused, not looking at her. "They will turn to you now."

Gerlaine dared not hope for it. "What?"

"You will learn her place. Learn it quickly," her father clipped off the words. "You will not go to Winchester. I—you are needed here."

She was glad his back was turned, glad of the semi-darkness that hid her, gratitude welling in her heart. Out of the insane *waste* of it, the unspeakable loss and the nightmare of logical conclusions, one desperate hope had been born: *they will need me*.

"Thank you, *mon père*."

She waited again, the unspoken things heavy between them. Tentatively she opened the door. *"Á demain."*

"Gerlaine." The words were deeply felt, heavy with his incomprehension. "Why have you never confessed that . . . creature?"

Eustace turned when she didn't answer. Her black mourning swaddled her in the deeper black of the open doorway; only the white face could be seen dimly.

"That was mine."

"It is on your soul."

"And I will account for it. Give you good night, papa."

He stayed up until sleep could be denied no longer, not wanting to go near the bed. At last he undressed sluggishly, dropping the clothes carelessly over a chair and slid listlessly under the covers. Sleep still eluded him; he lay awake listening to the wind. She'd always hated it. It hurt her joints and chapped the fine lips . . .

Tower to tower, a watchman's voice rode on the wind.

With a soft shock, Eustace realized that even now he lay on the right side of the bed, leaving room for her.

Baron Eustace was not at breakfast in the hall next morning, only the first of his erratic departures from a lifetime of discipline. Gerlaine saw to Robin's breakfast and told him of their father's decision, warmed by his joyous hoot as he threw his arms around her.

"I'm so glad, Gerlaine, really."

"All right, all right," she gasped as he squeezed her. "You'll squash me. *Dieu,* you're getting big!"

"I hated the thought of you going away."

She tucked stray wisps of hair under her veil. "So did I."

"You lean on us, Guy and me. We'll handle Bastard."

She kissed him, feeling more like a mother than anything else. "You are brave."

Ralph the steward pushed in the open door. "You summoned me, *dm'selle?*"

"Call the women," she directed, "the servants, everyone

who answered to my mother for their tasks. I will speak to them in the hall. Till later, Rob."

"Have Bête with you," he laughed after her. "They don't mind, he'll break them in half."

She waited in her own closet while they gathered, inspecting her toilet in the bronze mirror. She felt unsure; there were women under her already, had been for years, but the direction of the whole keep in whatever her father did not personally command was a different and frightening kettle of eels. Élène had been a baroness, a *châtelaine* worthy of every letter of the title. For a moment she quailed with doubt. They must respect her, yet some like Audrée already knew or guessed at her and Gurth. Selecting a ring from her jewel box, she remembered Robin's joke: *Have Bête with you.*

The idea was more astute than comic. The sullen, brute presence of him might help while she grew to Élène's authority.

Gerlaine slipped the ring on her finger, hearing the babble of voices and footsteps as Ralph herded them into the hall. *I'll push them so hard, they won't have time to know if I'm wrong.*

The knock at her door would be Ralph. She straightened her back before the mirror, trying to look as much as possible like her mother. "Enter."

He stuck his head around the corner of the door. "Ready, *demoiselle.*"

We begin now, this minute. "I am *maîtresse,*" she corrected him quietly. "You will all address me so. Come."

He stood aside to let her precede him. She paused only to summon Bête from the hearthside with a wave. He hulked behind her as she proceeded to the dais through the crowd of men and women making respectful way for her—scullions, laundresses, chamberwomen, seamstresses, Hugo's cooks. Ralph, she noted, was more prepared for this moment than herself. He carried his staff of office and had set Élène's chair of state precisely at the center of the dais, a detail she would not have remembered but would not forget again.

"Sit, Bête." She ran her fingers through his hair, taking in the waiting, upturned faces. Then she assumed the chair as Ralph rapped with his staff for attention.

"Give ear! Give ear. *La maîtresse du château* will speak to you."

Gerlaine waited for absolute silence, using the time to gather herself before the curious, tentative eyes. Norman faces—suet pudding like Audrée or lean-tough like Thérèse—they were Normandy, an island in this bleak place, lives to be commanded and cared for.

"The grief in this house is not for blood alone," she began. "No man or woman here who did not love my mother. We cannot replace her; yet it is the desire of the baron, my father, that I carry on. Where she was kind, I will be like unto her. Where she was firm, I must be firm as well. I ask your prayers and your good work."

They waited for her to go on. The little figure in black seemed too small for the chair. Suddenly, as if it sapped the energy of that wiry form, she thrust herself out of the chair and stood at the edge of the dais, hands on her hips.

"Now to work. Things have gone slack for a day or two; they'll be put right. Hugo!"

"*Maîtresse?*"

"I shall be in your cookhouse at nine to supervise supper, note your shortages and acquaint myself with your stock and schedule. And Hugo, have Jehan sweep the place out, it's dirty. Thérèse!"

The woman stepped forward, curtsying.

"You and Clothilde will cook today. The others will scrub the scullery down."

"But *maî—*"

"Ratcatcher!" Gerlaine rode over any protest. "*You*, Bodo. *Lève-toi!* Are you the ratcatcher?"

"Aye, *maît—*"

"You are to kill them, Bodo, not breed them. The cellar's overrun. The dirty beasts eat better than we. Be about it, I'll be down to see. Audrée!"

The fat girl made clumsy obeisance, confused and uncertain at the sudden, rapid-fire manner of her mistress whom she had envied as a spoiled pet.

"These rushes are moldy; you've not changed them. The baron's hounds wouldn't root for scraps in dirt like this. Sweep them out and gather fresh ones from the river today. *Now*, you . . . you, and you," a finger jabbed at three hardy male servitors. "At ten, I shall be here in the hall. I want fresh firewood brought up and the cellar supply replenished if necessary. For my women, I shall at least see to the beginning of your work this afternoon. For the rest, conduct yourselves by duty and habit as if my mother were still here. Do this and I'll be happy. Fail to do it and I'll be at your elbow—as she was—finding out the reason. Go now and give me your help."

As they dispersed, a little stunned by the force of her orders, she seated herself again, one hand on Bête's shoulder. "You must always be with me, big Bête. I am alone."

She trudged through a fierce day without pause, everywhere at once, answering questions and only half sure she was right most times. She would learn very quickly who could be counted on to work without supervision. There were the inevitable mistakes: Guy clumped into the hall cold and curt from a bleak day on patrol, and there was no hot wine or snack waiting, and supper was a catastrophe. Because of the scrubbing detail in the scullery, not enough chickens had been plucked, but at least the machinery was staggering forward again. When she retired at last, she mumbled the mere form of her customary prayers and promised more the next day.

She heard the watch change at midnight. Most of Montford was long asleep, but her mind still revolved about tomorrow and the order of tasks to be overseen. There was a blessing to the labor. It dulled with fatigue any bewildered personal longings. Gurth existed, he was a fact, but distant and less painful because of the work. She dare not bring him closer to the light, because there would be that one, terrible question—

Over the muffled snores and night sounds of servants sprawled about the hall, she heard Hugh's pacing. The flagon on her hearth was empty. Hugh would have something stronger, and not since that purgatorial night in the cellar had she needed it more.

The firelight made an island in the dark hall. He sat in the center of it, toying idly with his dagger. Bête slumbered mountainously nearby.

"Save you, Sister."

Gerlaine sensed about him something of the old Hugh from Neuville. His eyes were clear; they held some of the old warmth, not sodden or masked with his habitual indifference.

"Hugh, have you any gin?"

"No, but there's wine on the fire."

No cup stood by his chair. For the first time in months, Hugh was not drinking at all. Gerlaine measured a wooden cup of the spiced wine, drained it in one pull and poured another.

"You drink like a peasant," he said with gruff affection.

"I work like one." She settled on the clean new rushes by his feet, her head against his knee. "Is Father feeling better?"

"One can't tell," Hugh flipped the knife. "He's always contained his joy in my presence."

Bête stirred and turned over. From his lips came a sigh with a hint of voiced sound.

"Dear Bête," she drowsed. "He doesn't sulk anymore. He followed me about all day. I'd rather have him out here anights than the whole cohort upstairs."

She drank in silence as something occurred to her. "Most queer, Hugh: I've seen dull ones at home; they babbled all the time. There's no reason why he can't speak. When Gurth was going to kill him, he made a sound. Remember?"

"I was busy at the time," he recalled wryly. "Aside from Master Gurth's unsporting foot in my gut, he damn near broke my arm when I parried him."

"Yes, he is strong."

"More than strength," he mused. "Like some I saw at Hastings, beyond fear or even anger. A kind of cold madness. It's said they don't even feel pain then."

"*Bear-sark.*"

"What?"

"Nothing." She lifted the cup to him. "Wine?"

Hugh declined, vaguely preoccupied.

"Not even wine? Doing penance?"

"Hardly." He held the knife between two fingers with the concentration of a man working large mental sums. "Thinking."

"What in the world about?" she lazed softly against his firm leg. Her unbound hair fell about her throat and over her breasts. She was too tired to plait it now. Tomorrow.

"A problem," he answered with a note of relish. "Suppose there are black and white. And white can change to black. Question—does white really have the power to become black, or does it merely seem?"

She hadn't the faintest notion and cared less. "Oh, Hugh, don't. I'm tired."

She turned her face up to him. He was truly involved in

whatever nonsense the foolish words came out of. Gerlaine yawned and kissed his knee. "Good night, Hugh."

She woke once before morning to hear him still pacing among the sleepers, the tread measured and firm.

From his chosen spot on the hill, Gurth watched the mounted contingent pass over the bridge and climb the southern rise, bound for York. Gerlaine was not with them; he was sure of that. He watched every day—the coming and going of patrols, hunting parties, the funeral processions to Vaudan's small churchyard. Yesterday he had gotten a glimpse of her. The whole keep, by the look of it, followed Vaudan over the bailey bridge. She walked in black just behind her father and Hugh. The procession made a complete circuit of the keep to the riverbank and back.

The reason for it escaped him. Vaudan had blessed the bloody place in the beginning. Watching the priest figure, he tried to interpret the tiny pantomime, awkward and senseless with distance. After a time, he guessed at it.

Exorcism.

The censer swinging in Vaudan's hand was the clue. The good priest with the arsenal of God at his beck was weaving a girdle of sanctity around Montford keep.

He grinned tightly and scratched at the thick black beard, feeling hungry. The rabbits could not be cooked till dark, but he still had some oats. With clean expertise, he cut the head from one of the fresh kills and held the carcass up by the hind legs. The warm blood ran in a thin trickle over the dry oats in his other palm. When they were well soaked and swelling, he chewed and swallowed slowly, studying the sky. Neither its color nor the smell of the air indicated snow for any predictable time. When it came, he must move out of the earth house. His tracks would be too easy to follow.

Carefully, he memorized the ground between himself and the keep, every possible point for cover on a moonless night from where he squatted to a certain point of the east wall . . .

IV

"*What* tales, Père Vaudan?"

With Hugh holding the candle close, the priest continued to root among the chest's contents, placing an occasional sheet of vellum on the reading stand.

"Not tales," he modified, "rather suggestion, a glance, even silence. These things are eloquent in themselves."

"Which of these pigs has talked about my sister?"

Vaudan raised a conciliating hand. "None, Sir Hugh, but they cannot help what they have been taught. *Regarde*: a daughter of the Church who has heard two masses a day and made confession twice a week since childhood becomes suddenly enamored of a man for whom I can find no record of baptism among Anfric's books and whose mother is a known sorceress. They see her follow after him, court his company with unseemly eagerness—"

"Oh rot, he's the first man to catch her fancy, that's all!" Hugh shuffled the piled letters. "He was baptized in Paris. He said his mother neglected it."

"And," Vaudan bore on, "who will not make confession of her intimacy with him even though his malignance has touched her mother."

"And they feel Gerlaine is responsible?" Hugh, as always, found the thinking of peasants a contradiction in terms.

151

Vaudan spread his hands. "We have done what we could. As long as she will not confess, she is, unwittingly perhaps, an instrument of Satan."

"Rot," Hugh said again, brushing the lengthening dark brown hair away from his forehead. He'd always worn it short, but increasing cold and lack of leisure made barbering impractical.

"When I look at Gurth Bastard," he said, "I see no devil but a very subtle mind—rooms within rooms, shadows, hiding places. Not an ordinary mind, Père Vaudan, perhaps not driven by ordinary wishes, but human all the same. The maze of that man was a fascinating puzzle to Gerlaine. Until this year she spent her life in the barn, in the fields. What were her prospects of an advantageous match, *hé?* Some country vavasor like Father or me—*c'est ça. Bien,* she meets a man who is both attractive and beyond her understanding; well made, charming and a mystery at the same time. She's drawn to him—a thane's bastard at once privileged and denied. With a woman's sentiment, she takes his part. And just when her curiosity itches the most, she's told she can't have him." *What else?* his gestured signified.

The reasoning was a little too facile for Vaudan, a dangerous indulgence in the light of Holy Writ. "You are saying?"

"That I am no heretic, *bon prêtre,* but for like reasons more than one woman has fallen very determinedly in love."

"You doubt his alliance with Satan?"

Hugh bent over the lectern, head cocked at the stubborn little cleric. He had come directly from the beach patrol, still in mail and armed, but the idea germinating for days now had a definite shape and a starting place.

"That's the simple explanation. I'd be happy to believe it if I could."

A discussion of dualism—was that what the scholars called it?—was not pertinent now. He simply had no trust in hysteria as a basis of faith; it reeked too much of peasants and those leprous grovelers writhing toward roadside shrines as they babbled incessantly the same *ave,* grown meaningless with repetition.

Beyond that night in the cellar with Gerlaine, Hugh had never attempted to define his beliefs for anyone, even if he could. Voraciously intelligent, his mind was at once powerful and helpless, like a muscled giant with paralyzed hands. What learning he had was at Vaudan's tutelage, imperfectly gleaned from an imperfect source, a pitiful smattering of Latin, enough French and numbers to reckon simple manor accounts, and his name. What others like Bastard or the men at Paris could absorb and accept at a glance had to be threshed arduously through his quick but untrained awareness a symbol at a time and ground fine on its stone. God was, and Satan was—or so he was told—and yet the God he sensed and reached for blazed far above the muck of witches, charms, pattered prayers and the pathetic fallibility of flesh. Beyond this encumbering dirt, pure and imperative, lay the true battlefield of the spirit. But if it groped unsurely on Olympus, that mind could still close like a vise on deducible fact.

"Read the letters to me."

They were communications to Eustace from his cousin Hubert Fitz-Osborn, priest, a favorite of Edward in the years when the half-Norman king was surrounding himself with the French accents he loved and filling every church and secular office possible with them. The letters glittered with keen observation, contempt and sometimes bewilderment at English ways. Eustace had scanned them for personal and political news, then buried them without further reading.

Riding the coast that morning, the embryo of a suspicion already gestating in his mind, Hugh remembered vaguely Uncle Hubert who had come to York.

"I'd forgotten these were here," Vaudan confessed. "Before my ordainment, I think. Yes. I just packed them in with everything else." He riffled through the letters. "Ah! Here."

Heathenism is rife and ignored by the slothful English clerics who themselves are so sunk in ignorance, they can barely say the Latin of the mass.

. . . In battle they are like unto nothing I have known, for the common people fight here as well as nobles, not brave but cunning as wolves and aided by most evil magic . . .

The letter rambled on, describing a skirmish near Durham in 1047.

. . . for they rose up, it seemed, out of nowhere, most fantastical in appearance, and in no wise visible until the earl's men were hard upon them. And when they had made great slaughter, they vanished away into the earth, and though men followed close, they could not be found as the sorcery had made the ground to swallow them up. And this was told to me by a man known for his veracity.

Vaudan made to put aside the letter. Hugh put his hand on it. "That last part. Read it again."

He straggled about the small hut while Vaudan read, one hand in his sword belt, the other clawing at the back of his neck in concentration.

"How, Vaudan. How could they do it?"

Vaudan discarded the letter. "It is a clear statement. They had the devil's aid."

"*But*—" The young man whirled on him, impatient with his half-born idea. "Suppose they didn't. Suppose it could be done without sorcery."

"Impossible."

"*Suppose*. For a moment imagine *not* magic but cunning method. And if method . . . how?"

"Holy Writ is clear on this point," Vaudan reminded him, "and that quite recently written. Surely you do not question what is spoken *ex cathedra?*"

"Of course not," Hugh neither felt nor sounded convinced. "But you have taught me that Rome itself deliberates for years before affirming a miracle. Surely we can spare a moment to the same end." He riffled through the brittle, yellowing pages. "If Bastard's a devil, I'll pray with the best of you. But if he's a man, he has methods like an animal has tracks. Read on, please. Slowly."

The problem beckoned like the thought of a woman after long celibacy. His mind had never lain fallow, the pose of ennui always a mask behind the outer defense of drink. Inside, that mind had worked cruelly, a fierce engine without a stopping lever, churning out the pathetic ghost of the higher battle Hugh yearned for.

Alone in the hall the night his mother died, he cried a little secretly and prayed for her, but even as his hand signed the cross, the realization flared bright as a thousand sudden candles in a dark room. Élène was not killed by a demon or any agent of one. The skepticism was unforced. He simply could not accept the idea that night or the next day or the next.

The engine stirred restlessly and came to life. *Then*, it purred, *if not a demon . . . what?*

And the gin remained untouched before him.

Robin shivered. The mist was not thick enough to be called rain but just as uncomfortable. He licked chapped lips and huddled smaller inside his cloak behind the fallen tree trunk, next to Hugh. Not far off but barely seen in the mist, the grooms waited with their horses, gentling them to an occasional soft neigh. The huntsmen squatted among the hounds ready to bring the stag to bay when the flushers deep in the forest should drive one toward them. Ten yards away their father coiled on his haunches, a profile in tension.

"I can remember," Robin muttered, "when hunting used to be sport."

He glanced at his older brother for reaction. There was a subtle difference in Hugh of late. His eyes were clear and sharp, and he seemed to take more notice of the world around him. He still paced the hall of nights, but Robin passing late to the jakes or the scullery for cold leftovers would be greeted soberly. If Gerlaine hadn't sworn to the truth of it, Robin might have scoffed, but damn if his brother had touched a drop in days.

"Fantastical in appearance." Hugh's fingers drummed lightly on the log.

"What?"

Hunt-wise, Hugh kept his voice to a whisper. "Robin, the day you saw Bastard, how much do you remember?"

"Not much. It was all too quick."

"You were riding after Gurth, then what?"

Robin made an effort. "He was running, then fell down into a dip. Out of sight."

"Aye, so Guy says. We've been over the ground too," Hugh confirmed to himself. "What then?"

"I got hit."

"Think: everything that happened. You said Guy yelled."

"He did, but I was watching where Bastard went down."

"Did you see the archer?"

"No."

"Not at all?"

"Zut, Hugh!" Robin felt at his side where the new scar tissue

twinged with dampness. "That's all I know. Guy yelled, I got
hit. By the time I turned around, they were gone."

"Where were you looking?"

"What?" The whole inquiry mystified Robin. Damn it, how
should he know these things, badly hurt, half blind with fear
and pain.

"Nowhere," he admitted.

"Yes . . . so." The answer seemed to corroborate something for his brother. "And Guy said he blacked out for a
moment when he fell. Yes . . . yes." He seemed pleased,
satisfied with something in his mind. "Maybe more than just a
moment, so that possibly—"

"Ssh!" Robin craned back over the log, hearing footsteps.
Four men at least, thrashing through the underbrush, taking no
care to be quiet.

As the men came nearer out of the misty forest, Eustace rose
expectantly to meet them. One man carried a Saxon longbow
and full quiver while two others shouldered the buck on a pole,
the stump of an arrow shaft visible just behind the left
shoulder. Another prodded a thick-set, middle-aged peasant at
spear point, the man's arms hobbled around a stout length of
deadwood.

"He found it for us, seigneur," one of the huntsmen reported
dryly. "Just prancing off when we caught him."

"I know this one," the baron's mouth compressed to a cruel
slit. "Tie him to a tree and bring the whip." He turned to his
sons, oddly triumphant. "His name's Swegen. I've seen him
with Bastard."

By inflexible rule the forest was Montford's preserve. In
some places the king had exclusive rights, though this far north
he could not enforce the claim hence the privilege belonged to
the manor lord. Serfs could hunt the open land, but to poach
the forest meant punishment up the scale from a beating to loss
of an eye, even death under some lords. The gentlest Norman
—Élène or even Gerlaine on the most tolerant day of their lives
—would dictate the whip out of hand for such a breach of law.
It did no good; the bowstring *thumped* daily and the goose-
feathered arrows sang constantly through the gray forest.

They readied Swegen and brought the whip.

"When are you going to learn?" Eustace grated. "Yes, he
knows what I'm saying, they all know. *Where is Gurth?"*

Swegen turned his head away, but Eustace wrenched him
cruelly back. *"Bastard! Where?"*

Swegen stared back at him, shifting his thick body on powerful legs. He was filthy, clad in dirty wool with a hide tunic over it, his skin clear and unchapped but dark with grime and the grease they wore against the cold. He stank even in the open.

"Give him twenty."

The huntsman used a light whip, nothing like that wielded on Gurth. He wound back his arm and struck. Swegen hunched, biting his lips against the pain. After five strokes, Eustace stepped in again.

"Now," he repeated, "where is Bastard?"

Nothing came from the bitten lips but a slurred mumble.

"More," said Eustace.

Under the relentless rhythm of the lash, the Saxon swayed, whimpering softly, till he hung against the tree. Again the baron stopped it.

"Where is Gurth? Tell me."

"He doesn't understand you." Hugh let the breath out between his teeth. It was senseless. If the pig knew French, he'd have screamed it out by now—anything, even a lie.

The answer was sodden with contempt. "I'll decide what he can understand. Again."

The last strokes whistled out. "Twenty, seigneur."

"Twenty more."

The Saxon hung like a side of beef now, the sounds he made barely human. Hugh glanced at Robin beginning to fidget with a queer malaise, and read his mood: distaste. The Saxon was dirt. Kill or cripple him, it was not very important beyond the waste of a worker, but his father had somehow crossed the bar in a manner more foolish than Gerlaine. A lord meted punishment when it was necessary. He did not involve himself like this, with something in his expression a man didn't want to watch.

"Thank God for one buck at least," Robin shifted awkwardly, suddenly conscious of his hands. "The others are in Scotland by now."

The men around him shuffled and looked away, trying to make their faces into blank masks, avoiding their master's frenzied glare, the hands clenching with the strokes.

"Twenty, seigneur." The huntsman was breathing hard now.

"More," his master croaked. "Faster."

It's twisted him, Hugh realized sickly. *He's enjoying it and letting them see.*

The huntsman paused, hesitant and uncertain. "Seigneur, he's uncon—"

"I—said—*more.*" Eustace sprang forward, tearing the lash from his hand, pushing the man aside. A red mist blinded him. He flailed at the inert form, half-words wrenched like sobs from his throat.

"Where—is—Bastard! Where! Where!" No longer whipping now, but reaching for her, for Élène, for anything to hold or strike, to find where he was. It was Bastard, all of it, just beyond his grasp as he reached, too high, too far. His arm slowed with sheer fatigue, slowed, slowed, until the lash dangled then dropped from shaking fingers and the scarlet mist cleared and he saw them around him.

Why did they gape at him? Why was it so quiet?

One by one the men broke from the appalled tableau around their master, their movements small and tentative at first, then moved away in embarrassed silence. Two of them took up the trussed buck, but the others walked apart. Even the boy, his Robin, turned away to hide a sick shame.

What's the matter with him, Élène? I did right.

Only the other one remained, full of revulsion and pity; the Judas, the lost hope. The deep hurt.

"Lost your belly for discipline, Hugh? Or did you ever have one?"

Hugh stepped past him as if he hadn't heard. With the distaste of a fastidious man disposing of fetid garbage, he drew his dagger, cut Swegen loose and walked away to the waiting grooms.

"You hear me?"

Hugh took his bridle from the groom, mounted and rode for home without looking back.

V

The wind veered and blew for a time from the south, bringing night sounds from the forest. The moon wore a halo, drifting through small clouds as the cries piped from tower to tower:

"Bridge tower: all quiet!"

"East tower: all quiet."

Then faint, fighting the wind that blew it out to sea: "North tower . . . all . . . quiet."

"West tower: all quiet."

The soldier cupped his hands and bent far out over the battlement. "Main watch: all-ll quiet!"

And quiet it was. The moon stood ghostly sentinel over scudding clouds like a shepherd counting home-drifting sheep, and the dark and the loneliness became a dead weight on the soldier's restive soul.

Fitz hated this watch. Tough and mauled as an alley tom, he was Hugh's age but looked older, and afraid of very little, though like the rest of them he wore his cross anights, fortified with the sliver of saint's thumbnail which he considered far more effective against the demons loose on this hellish night of nights. All Hallows Eve. He had prayed all day, heard matins and vespers and made confession to Père Vaudan of everything —or nearly everything—on his soul. Peering out over the moor now, Fitz wished he'd confessed the cook's fat wife. That would be one hell of a thing to go to Christ with, were he taken this night. But Audrée was his kind, plenty of meat on her, and they met by chance alone in the mill. It had been a long time for him.

He thought something moved on the moor and strained to see it again. Nothing. Always nothing beyond nothing beyond nothing, emptiness that smothered prayers on the lips, made men small and pitifully alone, and God at once inaccessible and a desperate necessity. He wished for wine and someone to talk to. More to shake the crawling fear than from cautious duty, Fitz made another slow inspection of the moor, starting with the closest ground and moving gradually back. His eyes stared till they watered.

Anything out there tonight we'll never see.

He braced himself against the battlement, watching the little snakes of mist twine like mistletoe around the other towers, hungry for movement on the platforms. Anything alive.

"Good evening."

Fitz whirled—"Who's there!"—dagger ready, to see the motionless figure at the top of the stairs. "Who is it?"

"Robert de Neuville."

Fitz let out his breath. "God's eyes, never call a night guard behind his back."

The boy laughed with easy grace. "Forgive me. I should have known. Who's there? Fitz?"

"Aye, sir. Not abed? I thought Sire Hugh was the late watcher."

"He's not in the hall," said Robin. "I couldn't sleep myself."

"That's a wonder," Fitz rejoined, "the way the seigneur's working you and your brother. You'll make better soldiers for it, trust me. Glad to have company tonight," he added. "It gets lonely up here."

They leaned out over the parapet for a time, speaking elliptically in the manner of nightbound men of the things they held in common, how they both hated the sudden fogs, the inevitable saddle talk. Robin had to ride about the steadings tomorrow, ordering boon work and keeping an eye out for any sign of Bastard. Fitz's mount threw a shoe returning from the coast, and the new smith had damned well better have it reshod in the morning. The conversation struggled in the dark like fire in wet wood, flaring up, faltering then smothered again in silence. The wind blew steadily from the south over the forest, and then they heard it: faint at first, rising again stronger than before. Robin's hair rose on the back of his neck.

"What in God's name is *that?*"

"Wolf," Fitz murmured. "We hear them now and then. I hate the sound worse than the sight of them."

The wolf cry sounded like many things. A lost soul chained to the wind, Satan howling for mercy from hell, a woman mourning. It was a deep, mournful hunger prowling the rim of the night world, forever alone and apart, touching each man who heard it in the deep places of his soul where the sun rarely shone. To Robin it was all the things that made this place Other, made him more and more wakeful like Hugh, driving him from bed even on this unholy night to talk, to touch someone. He was still sick and bewildered at his father's conduct in the forest. One did not physically touch a serf. You didn't wield the whip yourself. Father crossed the line even more than Gerlaine, and it was this *place* that made them so, took away their boundaries, left them nothing familiar to hang on to. The wolf howl rode the wind once more like a tortured ghost then died away. Unconsciously they edged closer together on the parapet. The silence was a thing they could feel.

"I need a drink," said Fitz with deep conviction. Robin was surprised to find himself holding his breath.

"So do I."

"Would be good of you to send down a man from the guardroom, sir."

But Robin was already striding toward the steps. *"De rien. I'm hungry anyway."*

He descended the stairs, careful not to wake the men on their straw pallets, down through the dark hall murmurous with sleepers, into the dimly lit scullery, stepping delicately among the few servants for whom there was no sleeping room above the barn or in the hall above; older ones, mostly, for whom privacy would have been a needless waste.

Leftovers of fowl and cheese lay on one of the tables covered with cloth. Robin helped himself to both ravenously, licking his fingers and wiping them on the cloth. As an afterthought he placed two fat joints of partridge and a generous chunk of cheese in a cloth for Fitz, found a wine pouch and looked about for a broached cask with a pull or two

left from supper. There seemed none. He'd have to root about
the cellar, kicking a few foraging rats out of the way. Not too
many now; with Gerlaine snapping at his heels, Bodo made life
difficult for them.

A blast of chill, dank air struck his skin when he unbolted
the cellar door. He descended the ten steps into the darkness,
set the torch upright in the earthen floor and began to search
among the casks. Not Father's Provençal. Christ knows, his
temper was bad enough already. Nor the Breton, which wasn't
fit for washing out the mouth. No, something with warmth to it
to make him sleep.

The door above groaned slightly on its hinges. He looked
up, half expecting to see someone. Nothing. The draft, most
like. The place was a regular chorus of nuns at night with its
groaning. He remembered a hearty Angevin red somewhere
about; yes, there it was. He filled the pouch and took a long
pull, resting against the large cask. It warmed him, admirable
company for the partridge and cheese. Fitz would want some
too. He took one last long nip and bent to the bung stop again.

Something scurried away on small, frightened feet in the
darkness behind him. The rats; they were venturing out again.
Bodo would have to

Shouting in her dreams, footsteps drumming upstairs and
down. One ragged, querulous demand edged with hysteria.
Who was there? Who saw him?

She came awake when someone jostled clumsily against her
door, hearing the jumbled voices from the hall and bailey,
realizing instantly that something was terribly wrong. She
pushed the hair away from her face, writhed into her overrobe
and stumbled to the door.

New torches burned in the hall. Her father was there, and
Vaudan, Guy, a dozen soldiers and servants in a tight circle.
Bête hovered on the edge of the closed ring of men through
whose legs Gerlaine glimpsed a slight form stretched out on the
rushes.

She commanded the first frightened eyes that darted to her.
"Thérèse, what has happened?"

"Please, *maîtresse*, do not—"

But her father was on his knees, face buried in his hands.

"Get out of my way." She shoved Thérèse aside only to be

blocked by Guy, looking as if he'd been slapped hard for no reason. "Sister, don't."

"Let me *go!*" She wrenched herself away from him and tore through the circle. "Father, what is—"

Robin lay too still at their feet. From the queer angle of his lolling head, there could be no question of how he died. The dark bruise on the side of his neck suggested one quick, powerful blow.

Gerlaine slid to her knees, reaching blindly to hold him.

More feet thundered up the stairs, and Hugh strode into the ring. "I've got men everywhere, even the church. There's a good, bright moon. If he's still inside, they won't miss him."

Vaudan reared at him, sharp with desperation. "Man, what good are soldiers against Satan?"

"Who saw him last?" Eustace trembled. "Who was with him?" He searched wildly the stricken faces above him. *"Are you dumb?* Has that devil bewitched you all? Who was with him?"

"I, seigneur," Fitz stepped forward uncertainly. "He came to join me on the parapet just after midnight."

"What happened?"

"He went to the scullery, my lord, to get some food and wine."

"That's true," Hugh reflected. "There was a bundle by him."

"He was bringing it to me," Fitz faltered. "Forgive me, my lord. It was lonely on the parapet. I thought a bit of food, a sip of wine—the boy was good enough to go for it himself. It's my fault."

The man might have broken with it then without the surprisingly strong hand on his shoulder.

"Stop moaning," Hugh commanded. "Stop! Robin always ate at night. He always went to the scullery. Gerlaine, come."

She only wanted to be left alone with her Robin, but Hugh pulled her away with gentle insistence. She clung to his shoulder, only gradually aware of her father and Vaudan. The way they looked at her.

"Now do you see?" Eustace said tightly.

"See what?" She looked from one to the other, finding only rejection. "Père Vaudan, what?"

The others, too; wherever she met a glance, it fell, avoiding her.

"In Christ's name, *what?*"

Then Hugh was pulling her away from them. He dragged her into her closet, slamming the door behind. "Put on a warm cloak, we're going outside. I wanted to get you away from them. They're hysterical. They can't think anymore."

Dazed, Gerlaine pulled a thick cloak from her chest and managed to get it fastened about her as Hugh extended his hand.

"Come."

As they passed down through the scullery, Hugh noted how the knot of servants abruptly ceased their gabbling. He led Gerlaine out into the predawn darkness of the bailey. She had to hurry to keep up with his stride. Her mind had gone riot, refusing even to register the simplest thoughts. For the moment, she concentrated on keeping pace with him.

"What is it, Hugh?"

"Something to think on," he pulled her on. "I hope you, at least, can still think. Christ, they've all gone mad."

He halted by the east wall and pointed up. "There. I've been the circuit of the wall. Every timber sharpened to a point and resharpened again when we brought them from Brandeshal. Except here. *Regarde.*"

Gerlaine peered up into the darkness, saw the top of one paling more blunted than the rest. "I see it."

"A wall with four towers," Hugh mused, "manned on All Hallows by ignorant soldiers so quiveringly alert for evil spirits they might easily miss one agile man with a hook wrapped in rags to muffle the sound. That's how I'd do it."

She knew she must think. Blessed Hugh was giving her reasons, ways, possibilities like bright candles where everything she had ever been taught was pulling her back into darkness and fearful belief.

"Once inside, a man walking near the barracks is not uncommon, especially one who speaks French better than the king. How difficult, then, to walk to the keep entrance, which opens into—" Hugh paused, inviting her to make the connection.

"The scullery."

"*Vraiment,*" he nodded, "where the servants usually swill themselves to sleep with the dregs of supper wine and couldn't be roused by Gabriel's trumpet. And what opens off the scullery?"

"I don't know," she moaned, unable to see anything but Robin. Her voice cracked with sudden, rising hysteria. "I don't know, I don't know—"

"Who's there! By the wall, who's there!" The challenge ripped from the east tower, high-pitched with fear.

"Hugh de Neuville. Carry on."

"Startled me, sir," the watchman rejoined in an easier tone. "Not good to be out this night."

"We are advised, God save you." Hugh drew Gerlaine around to him. "Look at me. If there's a demon loose tonight, it's fear; fear that freezes the mind. That's Gurth's weapon. Fear is growing in this place like a disease. Don't let it take you too. Think! What opens off the scullery?"

She hadn't been able to remember a moment ago. "The . . . the stairs to the cellar."

"Where," he caught her up dryly, "nature being a constant nuisance, sooner or later one of us will come alone during the night. I think there's a pattern in all of this. Why didn't he take Father? He sleeps alone, apart from the keep. He would have been the easiest."

The moon slid behind a cloud as Hugh took her arm and guided her back across the bailey. "I told you these people are cruel. He wants Father but he wants him a piece at a time. And we, *ma chère,* are the pieces."

Gerlaine recoiled from the thought. "No!"

"Gerlaine, there's a logic to it—twisted, but it leads somewhere. He's had a hundred chances at Father in the forest, on the moor, but that's too quick. First our mother to start him cracking."

"Hugh, stop!"

"Then the adored youngest. The rest of us one by one."

She said it evenly, with more conviction in the sound than in the honest feeling behind it. "You think Gurth would kill me?"

"Easily." He took a small wine pouch from his belt and passed it to her. "Here. I got it from one of the soldiers. Drink."

The draft warmed her. She gulped half the flask before she returned it to him. He stopped it and tucked it in the belt.

"You have stopped drinking, haven't you?"

"I have a new pastime," Hugh said lightly. "Bastard wants to kill me. My part: find out how before he can. It amuses me —who's there?"

The three figures jerked to a halt, pikes leveled. "*Hé,* who's that? Speak!"

"Sir Hugh de Neuville."

"Aimeré, sir." They relaxed, materializing out of the stable shadows.

"Seen anything, sergeant?"

Aimeré nodded formally to Gerlaine. "Give you good morning, *maîtresse.* No, sir. Not a sign. Went over the sluice gate till our torches went out. If he were *mortal* man, sir" —Aimeré's emphasis indicated his basic belief—"there'd be mud or tracks. There's no human foot mark about the walls, and if he swam that moat he'd be half ice."

"Then get to bed," said Hugh. "Nothing more can be done tonight."

Still they hesitated, whispering among themselves.

"Pardon, sir," Aimeré began, "we wanted to say the young sir was a fine lad to ride with. A good soldier."

"You are kind to say so." Gerlaine reached to touch his arm and felt it tense oddly. The sergeant did not look directly at her.

"And myself, Rolf and Berald here, we would be honored to carry him. When it's time."

It would have pleased Robin, Hugh thought. He loved being a soldier, loved his first scars. God, he should have been born first.

"I'll tell the baron. Good night."

"Save you, sir, *maîtresse.*" They faded away toward the dark barracks.

"They blame me for this, don't they?"

Hugh studied the dim outline of his sister. Already there was a new set to her shoulders. She carried herself with more authority, duty and pain pressing the last of the girl into woman.

"Because of my being with Gurth. My fornication: that's the word. Say it, Hugh."

"Yes."

They had reached the steps of the keep. "Well, you're the priest would-be. What say you?"

"Shall I be honest?"

"Please."

Hugh sighed. "Père Vaudan is a simple man with simple beliefs. Of the subtleties of spirit, of God, he would be terrified. Father is no more complex than he. For the rest, they're animals with an animal's vague fear—fear, Sister, not love—of something higher than themselves which Holy Church teaches them to call God. If Rome made a saint out of this Loki, they'd worship him without question. They learn prayers, they genuflect efficiently, they sin with a dog's helpless incontinence and are forgiven as one pets a dog after having to whip him. We have one thing in common with them, the Church. You are *maîtresse,* but they won't obey one second longer than it takes that Church to frown on you. Be wise."

"And make false confession?"

"Oh, *damn,* girl!" he broke out. "Is it false? You can't still think he cares about you! Is it false?"

He threw it at her retreating back as she swept hurriedly up the steps away from him.

"Is it?"

The scullery was packed with servants bedding down at last. No one would sleep where the body had been laid out, especially on this night. A few still talked in low, tense half phrases under the flickering torches. As before, the murmurs ceased when Gerlaine entered. There could be no doubt now that they all knew or how they felt. She could probably thank Audrée for that.

They made way for her, mumbling bare courtesy. Gerlaine dragged wearily to the stairs, knowing that in the morning she'd have to rouse them again, bully and coax, reprimand, lead—when, dear God, she wanted only to crawl off and cry, to rest, to find a green tree under warm sun in a distant place for an hour's peace. Such things existed once.

She read their dull, upturned faces, wanting to reach and tell them about her Robin.

He was growing so fast, so full of energy and fun. Don't you remember how I cooked for him and made hot wormwood drafts when he had the fever at home, how I sat the night by his bed, cooling his face with a cold cloth. How could I hurt him?

But Hugh was right. They were animals to be moved to a

purpose, petted or punished. She could never reach them or
make them understand. The frustration chilled her anguish into
a cruel mold.

"Get you to bed. The cock will crow All Souls' soon. You'll
be safe."

She pushed in the half-open door to her closet. Her father
and Vaudan knelt before the little votive altar, the priest rising
as she entered.

"The funeral will be early, *maîtresse*. Pardon us, your altar
was convenient."

"Gerlaine," Eustace rose—not with his accustomed spring,
she noted. "Can you doubt we are accursed now? Or how? We
ask one thing."

"Why not?" She was incredibly tired. She wanted only to
fall across the bed and lose consciousness. "Everyone but Him
has heard of my folly." She crossed to the altar. "But not
now."

"When, damn you!" he knifed at her. "When he has taken all
of us?"

He was haggard, the strength drained out of him. If Hugh
were right, if this subtle, unspeakable cruelty were Gurth's
design, it was successful. Without surprise or disillusionment
she realized her father had never been really strong. Ready and
efficient, understanding with soldier's instinct the boundaries
of a small, unchanging world, but capable only so long as he
was not parted from it. In this place Eustace was lost.

Gerlaine genuflected before the altar. When she closed her
eyes to pray, she found only a darkness. She rested her head
against the cold wood.

"Your confession is most urgent," Vaudan pressed. "It must
be soon."

"Père Vaudan," the girl whispered against the wood. "If I
am Satan's servant, the wages are damned poor. Please," she
implored out of the dead weight of exhaustion pressing on her
shoulders, "I can't even think now. There is work in the
morning. Messieurs, I beg you leave me."

When they were gone, Gerlaine remained slumped against
the altar.

*You could never have loved me and do this, not to Robin.
There was a time when he even tried to walk like you. Laugh at*

that, but I will remember it. If you are innocent, go away. I
will confess and forget you and be done. Go away, Gurth.

With an effort she wrenched her mind to practicalities. She
had to function. For that she had to be safe. She pushed herself
up from the floor and out into the gloom of the hall.

At her touch, Bête turned over soundlessly and sat up.

"Come."

She placed his pallet in front of her door where it would lie
from this night on. Bête would kill anyone who tried her door
unwelcomed, even Bastard.

Still she lingered, needing his warmth, the mute iron of him.
He stood very close. She pressed herself to him. She breathed
harder and harder. Again and again the dry, rasping sobs
pumped out of her, reaching down into all she couldn't
understand and bringing out the deepest hurt.

"Bête, I'm afraid. Hold me. Hold me tight."

His huge arms went around her, gentle in their strength,
holding her as if she were just born.

VI

Fitz drifted aimlessly back and forth in the stable entrance, watching the grooms saddle Sir Hugh's mount. He felt uneasy, not knowing what to do with himself. The restiveness had persisted since Père Vaudan sprinkled the last dirt over young Robert's grave.

There were no orders given for the day. It unbalanced Fitz. The place always had a motion and thrust, a purpose to each minute of every life. Of course, *maîtresse* kept things going now, everywhere at once about the keep and bailey, black-kirtled in mourning and her big Bête in tow. "The black bitch," Audrée called her. He wondered was it true about her and the Saxon.

And the baron's conduct grew more and more disturbing. After the funeral, he stalked away to his bower, ready to break in two, with no instructions for patrol or the hunt. It made Fitz nervous not to know, and for sure the others felt the same way.

Eh bien, there were compensations; the cool close of the mill and Audrée's promise to meet him when it grew dark.

"Fitz."

He started out of the reverie. Guy stood in the stable entrance, mailed and belted with a sword. The lad had lost weight over the last few weeks, work and worry carving the baby fat of his cheeks to planes. Thin in his armor, the boy'd been crying.

"Find Aimeré," Guy directed curtly. "The baron bids him mount coast patrol to leave as soon as possible."

Fitz saluted, glad to be moving again. "On my way, sir," and he strode off toward the barracks.

"No hunt, Hugh?"

"Father gave no order," Hugh said with laconic significance. "Mount with crossbows," he told the grooms. "Meet me at the bridge."

Guy hauled his own saddle from the rack. He decided to take Rob's roan mare. She wasn't any faster than his gelding but steadier, though he'd denied it through a dozen arguments. The day Robin was wounded, she might have bolted and thrown him badly, but she held to her training.

Ah, merde! He threw the blanket and saddle over her back and began to cinch. Hugh watched him, saw how the recent tears had tightened his featured to red, awkward stiffness.

"Father never sends a coast patrol without one of us," he said.

"He does today," Guy went on with his task. "He's drunk. He was drunk at the funeral."

"You blame him?"

Guy gave the cinch a final, angry jerk. "I don't know, I don't know anything anymore. Christ, what's happening to us?"

"Steady, Guy."

"Is that all you can say!"

"You want pity? I've never had much, not even for myself." Then more gently: "Keep your head, vavasor. You'll end up talking to the wall like Father."

His brother relaxed a little. "You said you were going to that east hill again. I ride with you."

There was no denying him, not today. "As you will."

They led the horses out into the stable yard. "One boon, Hugh. If we find Bastard today, he's mine."

Infinitely tactful, Hugh didn't argue, though equal combat between Guy and Bastard was a gallant absurdity. Tempered to battle and danger, Hugh prepared for the ride with an efficient absence of anger. The grooms, Bertin and Remy, were tried campaigners. They had orders to kill Gurth on sight, a fact he carefully did not mention to his brother. They joined the waiting grooms at the bailey bridge and rode east.

Hubert's letters kept rising in memory, as he had described the peculiarities of the north. There was a link somewhere, a single loop of logic to bind together the hundred legends and the few shreds of fact. Hugh revolved on it as they approached the base of the round, queerly scalloped rise.

"At the top of this hill, wasn't it?"

"The flat ground at the summit." Guy sniffed several times. "Air smells queer today. Different than usual."

But Hugh's attention was on the slope ahead of them. He reined in suddenly, eyes traveling slowly over the curiously regular ridges running along the hillside. He'd never before noticed their odd uniformity,

"Stay here with the grooms," he ordered Guy. "I'll be back."

Before Guy could protest, Hugh spurred away, following the curving base of the hill. They waited in a perplexed attempt at patience until he reappeared on their right a few minutes later.

It irked Guy to be left out. "Have a pleasant canter?"

"Marvelous!" Hugh flashed him a broad smile of enthusiasm and fresh energy. "Instructive, too. *Allons!* Bertin, Remy —flank out. Keep a distance."

They urged the horses up the rise.

"You know what this is?" Hugh gestured ahead. "A fort, the whole damned hill, no telling how old. These ridges go all the way round. We never noticed because we hardly ever ride this way." After a moment, he added thoughtfully, "Or *think* this way."

Guy was totally mystified. "What way?"

"The ridges are old earthworks. Hubert said something about hill forts, how they once used them for defense."

They had reached the summit and began moving slowly toward the center of the plateau.

"And something else," Hugh went on. "It occurred to me just now. When we started to build, there wasn't a Saxon to be found anywhere. I was on the parapet the day they finally appeared, all in a bunch, following Godric from the *east*." He looked to Guy for comprehension. "Curious, no? Not even a pigpen out this way. This hill can tell us a great deal."

Stimulated and eager, Hugh pressed forward ahead of the grooms. It worried Guy; his brother was too far in advance. The swineherd had come so quickly out of nowhere.

"Hugh, they can't cover you so far ahead!"

The sudden blur of motion and sound tripped his tight nerves. Instinctively Guy dove forward along the horse's neck, seeing Robin and remembering death. *"Garde-toi,* Hugh!"

Flushed by the horses, the pheasant whirred into the air and drummed away, struggling for altitude. Bertin sighted on it without haste, led the bird a length and released his bolt. The pheasant jerked with the impact of the missile, flailed in a last spasm of unpurposed energy and plummeted to the ground. Closest to it, Hugh retrieved the bird, politely ignoring his brother's embarrassment.

"Sorry, Hugh. I thought—"

"I know," Hugh brushed it aside gracefully. *"Rien."* He traced a pensive finger through the brown-and-black-ringed plumage. " 'The valor that cares naught for death'—asinine phrase—is largely the invention of troubadours, Guy. There was one at Hastings: Tail . . . Taillefer, yes: insisted on charging the English ranks all by himself. It follows," one brow lifted in exquisite comment, "We missed him at supper. Not much, though. Fellow never would shut up."

He handed the bird to his groom. "Your game, Bertin. Good shot."

"Well brought down," Guy admired. "We were right on him; didn't see him myself."

The hand of insight laid itself across Hugh's mind, the loophole of logic he sought. "By God's eyes," he whispered, *"that's* what Hubert meant. *Look,* Guy. The plumage! You didn't see him because he looks just like the heath itself."

He paced up and down in front of them, excited, his mind racing to connect the crowding thoughts. "That old saying, something . . . something . . . 'see without knowing, know without seeing.' We've hunted all our lives; we've known *this* so long—" he pointed at the pheasant— "we've forgotten it. 'Fantastical in appearance.' And like the swineherd, you didn't see him until it was too late. Of course," his head bobbed energetically in confirmation. "Of course! It was the word, Guy, the *word* threw me off. Clowns are fantastical, mummers, *jongleurs.* You can see them a mile away, but these people have learned from every animal and bird on the moor. Hubert said they once painted themselves blue. How big a step to painting themselves *not* to be seen?"

It wasn't done. One didn't hide from an enemy. The concept was totally alien to Guy. He would never think of it, but . . .

"Wait." The picture flashed in clear recall now. "Hugh, I remember. The swineherd was in skins, all streaky brown and black. I wouldn't swear, but it looked like his face was streaked, too."

And Swegen in the forest, Hugh remembered. *It wasn't just grime caked into those clothes. They were painted that way.*

"Yes, *Pictis* . . . pixies . . . the Painted Ones. That's how they did it, *mon frère;* that's why folk called them weird. And they've remembered. Not magic, not sorcery or Satan. Just a shrewd brain and a little paint."

"Bastard was in bright green."

"And, sir," Remy spoke up, uneasy. It was as dangerous to mock Satan as God, and he was more vindictive. "We've seen the ground where he vanished. Without sorcery, how is that possible?"

But Hugh wouldn't listen anymore. "Guy, you said he looked like he fell."

"Into a dip of ground," Guy pointed, "up there."

Hugh turned to the grooms again. "Spread out, keep abreast, keep ready."

Between the mounted guards, they led the horses onward at a walk. "Now stop where you were when the pig-man broke cover."

Guy stalked ahead, reading the ground, then halted. "About here."

"You were at a run when he pinned Rob. You wheeled and came at him."

"Yes." Not wanting to, Guy struggled to reconstruct the confusion of those horrible seconds.

"You went down when he got your mount, blacked out. How long?"

There'd been no sense of time—seconds, perhaps half a minute or less, surely no more.

"And Robin was too busy bleeding to see anything. *Enfin,*" Hugh summarized, "they had a good half minute to get away."

"Where, Hugh? It's all open ground. I would have seen them."

"Then obviously they didn't run away." Hugh's satisfaction was positively insufferable. "What's left?"

It was hopeless: "Down, out, up—they vanished!"

" 'Vanished into the earth,' as Hubert wrote."

"Name of a saint!" Guy spread his arms in exasperation. "They couldn't, not mortal men. Where's the God damned hole?"

It's there, it has to be there. It's a hunter's pride to be able to think like the wolf or fox or deer we track, but somehow it's beneath us to think like English.

They had reached the rim of the bowl depression. Hugh squatted, gazing thoughtfully down into the center. "Not the Romans, not even the Britons knew much about these north folk, except that they were suddenly there and gone, stealing whatever they could. Hundreds, thousands of years. And the best protection they had was for people to believe in their magic. Well, I *don't* believe it!" Hugh pulled hard on a stalk of grass. "I'm a Christian, God save me, but I can't tell my brain or my eyes that they lie. And I won't go another day watching Father and the rest of them torture Gerlaine."

Guy understood Hugh more in this moment than ever before, understood and loved him for his own unique kind of courage. He'd felt that anger himself, able merely to look on helplessly while his father diminished in stature day after day, defeated by this place, turning in his madness on one of the dearest women in the world. And the others too, not fit to kiss her feet.

"Yes." Guy was convinced at last. "You're right."

Hugh brushed the grass from his hands and stood up. "Very near here," he stated precisely, "there is a hole in the earth. We will now find it."

They descended slowly into the natural basin, ten feet deep at the center and fifteen bowlengths across, cropped out here and there with small rocks and thick with wind-bent grass. On their knees at opposite edges, the high bracken and gorse scraping against the scales of their armor, Guy and Hugh inched around its circumference, working toward the center, feeling for any unnatural contour.

They worked silently; the time stretched out. Behind them

one of the mounts snorted nervously, shying about. Bertin soothed it, searching the moor on all sides. The horse shied again.

"Smells something," Remy muttered. He touched the cross about his neck.

Delicately as any fox parting the grass, Guy moved his hand forward, bringing it down to support his weight. His hunter's eye registered every inch in front of him. Nothing there, move up an inch, two inches, a foot. Look. Feel.

He froze to attention, concentrating on the vegetation before him. Something new and odd. The grass all around was bowed toward the west by the prevailing sea wind.

Except this small patch.

The angle of growth wasn't markedly different from the rest, but noticeable if one was really looking. He marked the place where it angled queerly to windward and parted the brown growth to note the crack in the earth that rounded into a circle more than three feet across.

Guy swallowed hard; his heart beat a little faster. "Hugh."

By sign, Guy traced the crack for him, indicating its circumference. Signaling the grooms to stand ready with their weapons, Guy inserted his sword into the schism and pushed. The blade sank without resistance to the depth of eight inches and scraped against stone. More probing determined the stone rim to follow the crack around, though the inner edge was of softer substance. With Hugh's sword assisting, they pried tentatively and then levered down.

A three-foot disc of the moor moved heavily and tilted up.

Hugh motioned Bertin to move in as Guy pushed back on the intact circle of earth.

"It's a wheel, Hugh!"

A wooden wheel, a boxlike-contrivance eight inches deep in which earth, loam and manure fed the gorse that looked so much like that around it, resting on a flat rim of dry stone. The passage continued downward for several yards, easily big enough for a man. Dimly they could see the opening that angled off parallel to the ground.

"So much for magic," said Hugh.

"Prenez garde," Bertin warned. "He might be in there."

"Who?" Guy felt elated. "Man or devil? He'd be a fool if he was still in there. You ever see a fox leave himself just one way out? There'll be another escape somewhere. And we'll find it."

A tiny point of coldness touched his nose. He brushed at it absently; another landed on his wrist.

"I thought the air was different. I've smelled it all day. Look."

The snowflake lay melting on Guy's skin.

Hugh thought quickly; as they stood there, the snowfall increased. "Bertin, leave Remy here and ride home. Tell the baron—" *No,* he thought, *leave Father out of it, he's not fit today.* "Tell Ralph to send torches, picks, shovels and all the men they can spare. Quickly. I'm going to gut this rathole by nightfall."

Dig it out, stuff it up. Bastard would never use it again. And with this gift from the sky, wherever he moved his track would be an arrow pointing.

The powdery snow whispered to the earth.

VII

At four the light outside the hut was already failing. Swegen gingerly slipped the loose smock from his shoulders and shivered half naked by the small peat fire. Outside the snow whipped about the hut flinging itself with a rattling whisper against the wattle walls. Across the low barrier dividing the dwelling into unequal halves, the aging ox lumbered about her straw, making ready to bed down like her masters.

Gunhild, plain and brown as her husband, brought out the grease strained from their last hoarded salt pork and mixed with hyssop poultice for Swegen's lacerated back.

"It pains?"

"Some."

After thirty years there wasn't much need for talk between them. Seasons changed, the world grew green or brown, they slept and rose and worked the fields. Now and then over a pot of beer they might recall the boy gone to Stamford Bridge and not come home, though that was rarer now, or the old days when Swegen hunted for Brandeshal. He had no close loyalty to the thane as Godric had, but he'd never been beaten or shamed nor could he understand the mad little baron who screamed strange words and flayed him senseless for doing as he'd done all his life.

His back was a torture; he barely winced, but Gunhild's

hands knew his body like her own and moved more gently over the ruined skin. "Easy." Her voice was like leaves rustling. "Easy now."

The sharp knock startled them both. Painfully Swegen lifted the spear from its sockets over the door.

"What man is it? Who's there on All Soul's Night?"

The wind rattled with snow in the silence, then they heard the voice, heavy with cold and fatigue.

"Let me in, Swegen. It's Gurth Brandson."

Swegen threw open the door. The tall figure stepped over the threshold, huge in the dim light, a heavy sack over his shoulder.

"Am I welcome in your house, Swegen?"

The old hunter held out his hand. "Fill him a bowl, 'Hild. He looks hungry."

Without the thick mantle, they saw he'd gone lean as a ferret, his green tunic dark with dirt under the painted buckskins. He was grimy and wild-haired and seemed strangely out of place under a roof, but fit enough as wild things went, wolfing at the bowl and heavy bread Gunhild set out for him by the fire.

"God," he mumbled fervently. "Cooked soup!"

"Welcome to it," she allowed shortly. "Calla's a friend, though I never held with some of her ways and herself not a Christian. Be she well?"

"All of them, the last Peter said."

He ate rapidly as he could churn the spoon from the bowl to his mouth, dipping the bread and tearing at it ravenously. When the bowl was twice emptied, he scraped the last barley from the bottom, sighed with incredible pleasure and lay back on the filthy cloak, scratching at his overgrown hair with black nails.

"It's dangerous for you to be here," Gunhild said. "The light's just gone. The curfew men will be coming."

"Not likely," Gurth answered. "They're digging out the weem at Eston. They found it today. I watched; the horses almost gave me away." He leaned over and appraised Swegen's back. "John Plowwright said they caught you with a fat buck."

"Prime," Swegen sat down painfully across the fire from him. "Could eat two weeks from it."

Gurth handed the sack across to him. "This will help. It's owed you."

"Well now," Swegen held up the generous chunk of venison, "isn't that a sweet sight."

Gunhild hid the prize in a dark corner under the eaves and returned to tend the fire, watching Gurth. Settled and no longer hungry, there was a disconcerting fixedness to his glance now, a concentration of purpose that reminded her of the Corn-Woman.

"John said de Neuville wanted me more than the buck."

Swegen managed a grin. "Your name came up. It was the only word I understood." He hunched closer to the fire. "He thinks you be a devil."

"The hungriest I ever saw," Gunhild poked nervously at the fire. "You've gone to gristle and bone."

She took up the grease and began to work on Swegen's back again, ill at ease with Gurth in the hut. "Why do you stay at all? There's nothing here for you, nothing but hurt for those of us who help you." She touched her husband's raw shoulder. "This is because of you, not the buck. He'll be scarred now."

"So am I," the gray eyes rested on her. "They still owe me what's mine."

"What's that?"

"Gerlaine."

They didn't understand at first; it was almost beyond them. "The girl?" Swegen gaped. "The *lord's* girl?"

Gurth nodded, rising. He took up the cloak and fastened it about his shoulders. "You should be putting out the fire now. They might not come, but you'd best be safe. My thanks for the welcome."

Gunhild eased the smock over Swegen's head, took up a bucket and doused the small fire to darkness and hissing peat. "That girl wouldn't spit on you now after what you've done."

They moved without fumbling in the dark, from a lifetime of rising with the light and bedding down when it was gone. They crawled onto their pallet, pulling up the worn blankets; Gunhild laid the tattered edge over Swegen's shoulder.

"Go now," she said to Gurth. "Swegen could hang do they catch you here. We only want to live."

She heard him move toward the door, heard the iron stubbornness. "De Mowbray's head belonged to Hulda."

"Fool!" The folly of it rubbed her raw. It was a danger to all of them while he stayed. "And the baron's wife? And young Robert they put in the ground this day? The blacksmith they had to bury in a sack? Where do you *stop?*"

"The old ways are dead," Swegen murmured against the straw. "Go away from Tees."

"When I have what's mine," said Gurth.

The door closed behind him.

They tore furiously at the earth with mattocks and shovels until darkness and snow made further work impossible, but Hugh's purpose was accomplished. The whole earth house lay bare.

For a construction wholly without mortar, the weem was a marvel, dry stones selected and fitted together so cunningly that the cracks between were less than finger-wide. The tunnel angling off from the entrance pit ran twenty or thirty feet before it widened into the circular main chamber. Halfway along, a large boulder partially blocked the narrow passage. They puzzled at its purpose, since the passage itself was barely wide enough for single-file movement.

"That's why," Hugh guessed finally. "Any man brave enough or fool enough to go in after them could be speared from behind it."

When the light began to fail, they worked by torches, stripping away the timber-shored earthen cover foot by foot, baring the main chamber with its delicate animal carvings pocked into upright stone slabs, the awl punctures joined into flowing lines not devoid of grace or humor—birds, foxes, the long-gone bog elk, incredible in their sense of life and movement.

"Devils," Bertin peered at them in the flickering light.

"Men." Hugh licked at a new blister on his aching hands. "Don't you ever learn?"

They found rags, picked bones and the remains of a recent fire. Guy's eyes gleamed with satisfaction as he sifted the ash through his own raw fingers. "Let's fill it in."

He wasn't used to digging anymore, but he and his brother had joined the labors—dragged the others behind them in their energy—to gut the place before dark. When at last the men banged the clotted earth and snow from their tools, they formed a rough line of twos behind the horses, and Guy bent one last, fiercely victorious look on the ruin, taking a deep breath. "Done!"

Hugh leaned from the saddle, clapping him on the shoulder with a raw hand. "You look happy."

"I am," Guy shook his head passionately. "I—I feel better, Hugh. It was something I could *do*." He flipped the reins; the roan moved forward. "Freeze or starve, how long has Bastard got?"

The trouble began innocently enough when Jehan left the cookhouse with a task for his wife, Audrée. She was not gabbling with the sewing women in the hall nor in the scullery. The errand was minor; Jehan would have postponed it, but one of Aimeré's cohort remembered seeing her going to the mill. The ambiguous snickers behind his back as he turned away were like lead on his stomach as he trudged across the darkening, snow-blown bailey. Like all the other times. But Audrée promised, and she'd been good. He believed her.

So he found them, Audrée and Fitz.

At the first cry, Eustace wrenched open the bower door and lurched out into the snow.

"North tower, where's the noise?"

"The mill!"

The cry levered instinctive response in Eustace. He scooped up snow, rubbing it clumsily into his face, and ran toward the mill, throwing open the door.

The last of the pale light fell on Audrée gibbering in fright against a post. Beyond, dagger at guard, Fitz circled the fear-crouched little Jehan with his cook's knife. The cook's mouth was drawn tight with hopeless rage and dark stains widened on his smock. He was no match for Fitz and knew it, but the mean little absurdity could not be stopped.

Eustace read and understood it all at a glance: the way of his men, the stupid, sow-to-the-world ways of Jehan's fat wife. Hot blood squeezed in his chest, imploded and flung itself outward at his brain. This was something he could understand, deal with; a definite thing to grasp, for all those he could not. He hesitated only a half heartbeat longer as Fitz shifted his weight, one foot slightly forward, coiled for the rush that would end it. Even as Fitz willed it, the lethal arm was caught

in an iron vise. He was flung with vicious force against the wall
with a dagger point pressing into his own throat.

"Drop it."

"Audrée, you bitch!" Jehan fell to his knees, sobbing. "You
filthy liar. Seigneur, please. The priest."

"For what?" Eustace grated coldly. "Vespers? I know the
look of deep blood; you'll live. And *you*, pig—" he pressed the
knife further into Fitz's skin, pinning him as well with a
murderous glare—"you move and I'll clean you like a pullet."

Now Aimeré lunged through the door followed by two of the
watch. "Seigneur?"

"Take this dirt to the hall," the baron shoved Fitz toward
them. "And the woman, too."

Gerlaine had no time to reflect that it was vicious Audrée
hoisted at last by her own petard. En route from Hugo's
cookhouse, she was snared by Vaudan, a worried wraith
against the darkness with the clipped news, hearing it even as
the bailey filled with people hurrying to the hall, kicking dogs
aside, warning back children on pain of paddling, by God, to
stay at home. The priest was short: the mill, a fight, Jehan
bleeding badly. She must bring the smith with a brazier and
iron quickly. He scurried off. She picked up her skirts and ran
to the smithy, gave her orders and was returning with Bête and
the smith lumbering in her wake when the familiar figures
trotted their tired horses into the bailey at the head of the small
column.

Guy picked out the familiar figure in black from the rest of
the scurrying populace, urged his horse forward. "Gerlaine!"
He swung down and embraced her. "You've got to hear. Hugh
and I— what we've found."

"Please," she kissed him hurriedly. "No time now; they need
me."

"What's happened?" Hugh stared at the running servants
swept toward the keep. "Where are they going?"

"To the hall," Gerlaine threw over her shoulder. "Bête,
come!" And she disappeared into the snowy darkness.

"What in hell—? *Hé*, soldier!" Guy commanded a passerby,
"What is it?"

The fellow blurted out the story, eager to be gone. Audrée
and Fitz, a knifing. Seigneur had called a court, justice to be
done. And like Gerlaine, he disappeared.

They led the horses to the deserted stable. Unsaddling, Guy nudged Hugh, indicating Bertin, Remy and the others hurrying through their tasks. "They can't wait to be in on the fun. It's a poor rub those mounts will get tonight."

"Human mercy," said Hugh, hoisting his saddle to the rack. "Such as it is. You will not go?"

Guy shook his head as he curried the mare carefully. "She's a good one, this roan. Worked hard, stood in the cold. You're tired, *n'est-ce pas, bébé?*" He kissed and patted her neck. Hugh could see the love in his hands, the deliberate care of each movement sharply contrasting the quick, slapdash work by Bertin and the others. He might order them to be more thorough; exhausted himself, he decided this once to let it go. He couldn't care less at the moment. The barnyard adultery of a servant was small fish beside what they'd found.

"Aye, we found it," Guy muttered as he worked. "We dug him out. *Pardi,* Hugh, I wish—I wish Rob could have been there."

They laid Jehan on a trestle table to wait the iron, the gaping, eager knot of them venturing as close as possible to see and darting repeated glances toward the door of Gerlaine's closet.

"Get away from him!" The baron hunched in his chair on the dais like a malevolent falcon, his speech slurred and thick. The agony fermenting through the horrible day burst and poured its acid through him, releasing the vavasor cruelty. He would not spare either Fitz or the woman. He'd teach them a lesson never to be forgotten. Life itself was falling apart. This was needed. If all round him were mocking, unreachable demons, this one mortal thing at least he could deal with.

"You want to see justice done!" he roared at them. "By God, you will and you'll remember it."

With a snarl of impatience, he hurled his bantam-cock body off the dais and across the hall, kicked open the door to Gerlaine's closet, where Fitz and Audrée huddled by the altar under the hand of Vaudan while Aimeré stood guard.

"Have these two been shriven?"

Vaudan murmured the last of his absolution over the cringing Audrée: "They are confessed, my lord."

Eustace signaled Aimeré: "Take them out."

In the scullery Gerlaine hurriedly tore bandages from clean tow linen while Bête hovered by, an island of placid unconcern in a surging sea of activity, and the smith blew his brazier to red heat. Hugh came in from the bailey as she worked furiously, swearing at the stubborn cloth. Hugh took a morsel of cheese from a bowl and leaned against the table.

"Poor Jehan deserves better," he observed, rubbing wearily at his eyes.

"Better than her," Gerlaine agreed, passing the bandages to him. "Hold these."

And yet it could be me up there, and they know it. She tore faster at the cloth. "Where's Guy?"

"In the stable," said Hugh. "He rode Rob's mare today. He prefers her company to *that.*" He elevated his glance to the ceiling. "You'll need someone to hold Jehan; I'll come."

"Thanks. Ready with the iron there? *Allons, vite!*" Gerlaine hurried toward the stairs with Hugh and the blacksmith following. They plowed through the milling servants to the table. Jehan lay gasping with pain and frustration, comforted nominally by Vaudan.

Observing the eager throng of watchers, Hugh knew Guy had been right; they could hardly wait. The cold disgust softened when he bent over the shuddering little cook.

"Ça va, Jehan?"

Jehan took the hand offered him. "I've never had the iron before, messire." He tried to hold back the unmanly tears but they rolled down his ashen cheeks. Gerlaine wiped his face.

"Is there much pain?"

"No . . . no," Jehan choked. "It's not that, I swear it's not."

More than the dozen infidelities, the broken promises, he had listened openmouthed to her pursed-lipped recounting of *la maîtresse's* indiscretion. He should have cut out her tongue.

"Sh . . . she lied."

At Gerlaine's signal the smith passed the iron to her. "Hold him tight, Hugh. Forgive me, Jehan. I must."

He swallowed hard. "Bless you, *maîtresse.*"

The hiss of the iron, the shriek; the huddled watchers surged forward, not individuals now but one organism shuffling closer to the table, and on that body Hugh turned his acid contempt.

"Get back," he snarled through his teeth. "Back! I can smell you!"

I know you to the core. You are all the things I would pare like festered flesh from my own soul. What is so fascinating about the pain of others? Death is ending and pain a soul-picker that takes nobility in clumsy claws and scrapes it raw to the animal center.

You babble the incessant, cowardly prayer: keep Me safe, let Me live, but you run toward death and pain like a forbidden lover. Spare my pain, but let me see the others', for it's all I can see of what must come.

So the serpent charms the rat that is its dinner, and the rat knows what is happening but cannot turn from its death.

And these are what will be divided at Judgment into sheep and goats. One might expect a Son of God to have better taste.

"It's done, Jehan," Gerlaine spread the poultice over the wound. "Nothing but to butter and wrap you like a pudding." She tried to be light, hating the nauseous smell of burned flesh, never used to it for all the times she'd aided Élène at this miserable duty. "There, now, *mon brave,* there'll be strong wine and lavender to help you sleep tonight."

"Is he ready?" Eustace roared down the hall. "Then get him up here."

"Up, man," Hugh helped him off the table. *"N'aie pas peur,* Jehan. You're in the right."

They led him between them to the dais to face Audrée and Fitz.

"In the name of God the Father, and of the Son," Vaudan opened the trial, "now let the truth be told."

Cold iron and wet clothes no longer bothered Guy. He drew out the mare's rub to a luxury she'd known only on Robin's best days. He talked softly to her as she dipped her head to the oat bin.

"You'll be mine now. Rob would like that."

Her water trough was near dry. He took the bucket from its peg and filled it from the nearby barrel, careful not to allow too much after the generous measure of oats. The weariness was seeping through him now. He replaced the bucket and rested with his arms over the roan's stallboards, having no wish to join the others at the hall. He preferred the clean smell of horses to the stink of the crowd. His soul was tired as his body under the mail coat.

I can remember waiting for the day I could put on this miserable iron. Iron collar for a slave, iron coat for me. What's the difference?

Ah, that was morbid. The dark did it, living day after day in gray and shadow. *No wonder the Saxons look bleak.* He splashed his face energetically at the icy water barrel.

God, I'd like to see color again! Cheery lights and green trees like there were at home—and red, red, red! A world of red and blue and yellow.

Something rustled beyond the flickering fat lamp. Tired, Guy was aware of it for some seconds before he raised his head.

"Hugh?"

Even as he said the name, he knew it wasn't Hugh, knew it from the neck down with a cold chill; not his brother, nor a groom. They wouldn't remain silent. Guy's hand edged along his belt toward the sword hilt.

"Who's there?"

He made out the large form now, a mere suggestion in the feeble light, darkness moving across darkness, assured and purposeful, between himself and the door. Guy drew his sword, trembling.

"Damn you, who's there?"

"Your turn, Guy," the deep, clear voice came out of the shadows. Guy heard something unintelligible, a phrase in English.

"Gurth Bastard?" Guy's mouth went dry with fear and hate. He set his weight in preparation, his legs slightly bent. "I've prayed for this," he said in a tight voice. He was frightened but glad at the same time. The game was here, and he asked no more. "God sent you to me this day. You're mine."

He had time to raise the sword in guard against the flashing blade as it descended, time to see the face rushing at him out of the dark, but beyond one shout of baffled rage, none at all to understand.

VIII

The trial was brief, the sentence predictable. Fitz would be marked on his left cheek for all men to see. Aimeré mourned as he secured the man's hands to the table trestles.

"You're one of my best, I always said it, but curse me if I don't sew your pants up proper after this." He gave the cords one last tug. "Stupid horse, everybody but the priest's had her. You had to get caught."

Spread-eagled on the table, Fitz grimaced up at him. "Oh, now, and here she told me she was a virgin."

Hugh and the soldiers held back the crowd as Eustace stationed himself by the fiery brazier. "Bring the woman," he ordered. "She'll watch."

Vaudan started to lead Audrée forward but she broke away, near hysteria, retreating to the farthest corner and collapsing in a pathetic ball.

Warning Vaudan away, Gerlaine went after Audrée herself. The hard justice of the thing was many things in a moment —sweet, trivial, ultimately worthless to her. She didn't want Audrée's pain; it fed no hunger, relieved no agony of her own, but the stupid girl would never understand.

"Audrée, you can, you must." She pleaded to the sodden parody of a face: "I didn't want this, but I know what you think. It is God, not me. Be brave."

She urged the woman to her feet, but Audrée twisted away.
"No," her teeth chattered with her fear and hate. "I'll speak it
out to them. If this is right, then *you* should be on that table."

"You'll watch," said Gerlaine grimly, feeling the control
slip away; she fought to retain it. "*That* is just. I did, they made
me, remember? You saw the whip they used. You watched
then, didn't you." Her hand shot out, grabbing Audrée by the
hair under her loose veil, twisting her about and hurling her
across the floor to Vaudan and the waiting soldiers. "Go!"

Till the last moment, Fitz watched the coming of the white
iron, then Aimeré pushed his head to one side and the sentence
was carried out. Fitz willed himself not to scream as the cook
had done; there was only a deep groan through clenched teeth
to release the tension of his body. Vaudan bent to inspect the
sear.

"It is deep enough," he pronounced. "He will carry it
always."

They untied him and Hugh helped him up. His vision
blurred with shock, Fitz tried to focus on the gaping crowd.

"Jesus." His hands were feeble on Hugh's arms. "You'd
think they'd better to look on than this."

Hugh shrugged. "What in hell made you think that?"

Eustace led Jehan forward to confront his wife. "Now, what
will it be for her?"

Jehan hesitated. Gentle, unequal to this, a dozen times
forgiving and thirteen deceived, he found he could only stare at
his feet.

"Speak up," the baron urged, louder this time. "The whip or
the iron?"

The others riveted to the cook and his wife. Only Hugh
noticed his father, sensing the unknown forces that drove the
man, knowing Eustace would override whatever leniency the
mild little Jehan might wish. Gerlaine edged close to him.

"Take my hand, Hugh. Please."

Gerlaine shivered as if the punishment were meant for her.
She despised Audrée to the core, but the woman's snarling
outburst shook her. It could be her and it would be just, and
who among them didn't know it? Every moment of the trial
and punishment brought it closer to the surface. The more
cruelly Eustace dealt with Audrée, the clearer the reflection of
her own guilt.

No, she fought it, *not guilt. I had all of myself to give. I betrayed no oath, hid nothing. Hugh understands; he knows how proud I am.*

Pride? Her honest soul roared its contempt for the hypocrisy. What she called her pride was no more than folly gone sour and hard. *He had me and kicked me aside, damn him.* God knows she could have bent weeping before her father, wronged and helpless—but what she knew of her own core was not soft; part of her moved naked and strong like Sigrid, claiming its own and answering the tremulous doubts with an equal savagery. If hell had fire, so had she to match it. *No . . . no. Sweet Mary, help me. I will confess. I will end this.*

Jehan must have stammered out something like a choice. One of the grooms placed the braided handle in his hand.

"It is for unruly colts," he was told. "To sting and leave a lesson, not a scar."

The groom went to Audrée, held between two soldiers, and tore the smock loose halfway down her broad back. Gerlaine's heart went out to Jehan holding the incongruous whip. He couldn't do it; she would have wagered a horse, were there one to spare.

A word dropped sibilantly from pursed lips caught her ear. She couldn't identify the speaker but read the expressions of the women around her: they were the true gauge—quick as wolves to turn on each other at a time like this, ready to condemn where most men might soften to compassion. *We are crueler than they.* But she could see none of this in them now. Their glances shifted uncertainly between themselves, sometimes to her. A few passed cautious whispers.

She put it out of her mind and stood straighter.

"Please," Audrée sounded pitiful. "Please, Jehan, you can't."

"I—" The whip twitched in his hand. Every word had to be cut from the hot ball of anguish inside him. "You p-promised and promised," he stammered. "I've always forgiven. They made jokes on me in the cookhouse. Hugo called me reindeer and made a do about looking for my *horns.*" The new tears started to flow. *"What'd you mean by that, Hugo—hé?* You think I'm stupid?"

He pointed to the table, shaking. "You lied all the time, not just about the men. You have b-borne false witness. You have lied about—"

"Shut up!" Audrée strained viciously at him. "You shut up."

"No! I'll say it. For that as well as the other, I will beat you. You lied about *la maîtresse*."

"I never—"

"You did. You women, isn't it true? Thérèse, isn't it so, the stories she's told?"

"Thérèse." The name lashed out over the voice of the quavering cook. "Come here. *Here*, damn you!"

Oh, God, Hugh realized sickly. *He looks like he did that day in the forest with Swegen. I think he's been waiting for this.*

He sensed now a change in the mood around him, a subtle shift from the morbid curiosity of the trial toward a quality less easily defined, with the beginnings of hostility in it.

"Thérèse," said the baron, "has this woman spoken against her mistress?"

Thérèse met the numb animal fear in Audrée's eyes, turned away from it. She nodded helplessly. "She has, but . . ."

"But what?"

The scullion writhed under his waiting stillness. She appealed to Vaudan, started to speak, then lost her courage. *"Rien, seigneur."*

"Nothing?" Eustace persisted. There was no mistaking now that odd look of triumph Hugh had seen in the forest. "I think it is more, and I think you will tell me."

Thérèse swallowed hard. She had an affection for Gerlaine and little use for Audrée, but the lord was pushing her into a corner with nothing but her rigid conscience for company. Audrée's tales might be stupid and malicious, but they were not lies. It would be a mark against her own salvation to say so.

"She—she should not be punished for that, seigneur."

Hugh read the charged silence around him and felt Gerlaine's fingers go limp in his. And Vaudan, with the courage of his deep convictions, stepped forward. His comment was clear and unequivocal.

"Amen."

The word echoed furtively through the crowd, given license by the priest: "Amen . . . amen."

Eustace turned a bloodshot eye on them. "I'll give you amen," he muttered. "Smith, put that iron back in the fire."

"NO!" Audrée collapsed to her knees only to be hauled erect by the guards. "Jesus, *maîtresse,* if I was wrong, I cry you mercy, but don't let them burn me!"

"Indeed," Eustace turned on Gerlaine with a veneer of patient justice. "Then it is for you to say, Daughter. Are you wronged?"

Hugh felt his stomach turn over. *This is what he wants. Gerlaine, not the fat one.* He felt helpless. There wasn't even the alternative of combat to aid her, not against the court itself, not against his own father, much as he wanted to.

"Remy," Hugh whispered urgently. "Get to the stable, fetch my brother. We must tell them what we've found. Quickly."

Remy ducked hurriedly down the stairs.

He would do this to me, Gerlaine ached. The loyalty in her cried for the last time to Eustace and then died. She felt the chill of its death pass over her with cold wings, and the deep, cold anger that stirred over the corpse, rising to the surface with a cruelty equal to his own. *To me?*

"It is no longer your province, Jehan," the baron stepped close to the brazier. "She will bear the same punishment as Fitz. And *la maîtresse* will administer the iron."

"Eustace," Vaudan was at his elbow, urgent, keeping his voice low as possible for what must be said. "I have known you all your life. I don't presume on that now, but this is wrong." He spread his hands in frustration. "Have the woman whipped for adultery, but not this. Stupid and spiteful she may be, but she has only said too loudly what we have known in silence."

Eustace turned to the brazier, inspecting its color. "This is a secular matter, Vaudan."

"You're drunk," his friend said bluntly. "You've been drunk all day, and *yes,* I understand, but what do you want, Eustace? You asked that once of Bastard. I say it to you: what do you *want?*"

"You dare stop me, priest?"

"Holy Church stops you. You compound the sin, Eustace. Gerlaine cannot punish this woman. She is not in a state of grace herself and will not be until she is confessed. You know it, and"—his head jerked at the others—"*they* know it."

Eustace pulled the ready iron from the fire. "Put her on the table."

Audrée struggled savagely as they forced her toward the table. "Mercy . . . no . . ."

And then Gerlaine's father was holding the iron out to her. "The judgment is yours if you are innocent."

Her hand cowered toward it, grasped it. She was moving toward the table. Far off she heard Jehan's pitiful supplication, please, not the iron, he would make her be good. Audrée's eyes bulged at the coming iron.

Now she poised by the table, and Aimeré was forcing the protesting head to one side. Gerlaine raised the iron, a scale-balance in her hand. For one endless moment she fought the cowardice and then, broken herself, defeated it. She looked once more to her father and dropped the brand back onto the coals.

"I will not."

The words came choked out of her. She closed her eyes against them all, blotting them out. It was equal to an admission of guilt, a confession without the blessing of the sacrament, and he had forced it from her in front of servants.

"I can't."

"Praise God," said Vaudan gratefully.

"I can't," Gerlaine said again, feeling the dark thing rise in her, blind and murderous. Her father had stripped her before lackeys and dirt. Her eyes raked over them, hot with pride.

You dare censure me, you sit in judgment on me when you have lived and eaten at my hand? You grin at my pain when the smallest part of it would snap you like tinder?

The formless phantom made her arms its own, wheeled, striking blindly at the air about her, at nothing.

"Get away from me!"

"Hold that pig down."

In three rapid strides, Eustace seized the brand, bent over Audrée and pressed it into her flesh. Her wail of fear rose into a shriek, then broke into hysterical sobs.

"Whatever has been said," Eustace dropped the iron, "a servant does not speak against her mistress." He weaved away from the table unsteadily. "Christ's eyes, what has happened? *I* am the law, have you forgotten? We hold this place for the king. There is a duty." He thundered it at them. "Duty! What has happened to you?"

"Satan!"

The sound was barely a human word as Audrée struggled up from the table, pain-maddened beyond fear. "Satan has happened," she screeched. Her arm shot out at Gerlaine. "She has lain with the devil!"

"Aye . . . amen . . . Jesu defend . . ." They twittered like frightened birds in a rattled cage. Hugh stepped forward to Gerlaine's side.

"You're mad, all of you. There's enough evil here not to need Satan. Vaudan, Gurth Bastard is a man. A mortal man. Wait till Guy comes if you don't believe me. Bertin, Remy, they'll tell you. We've found his hiding place. He's a mortal man!"

"She's lain with Satan!" Audrée screamed. "If I'm burned for a man, what punishment for her?"

"Amen . . . amen . . ." The chorus swelled. No longer afraid, their deep fear ignited by Audrée, the held-in judgment broke in a hot wave around Gerlaine's ears. She raised her hands to cover them.

"Stop!"

"She goes free with his seed in her! It's her lover killed the lady and Robert, and still he comes to her at night. He'll kill us all!"

An ugly snarl rose over her screeching, the savage death song out of Gerlaine's throat. Red and dim behind her eyes, Sigrid drew the small knife from Gerlaine's girdle with Gerlaine's hand, spun on Gerlaine's swift feet, raised her arm over the fat, flailing thing to be slaughtered. It was caught as it came down; she was whirled about with a glimpse of someone vaguely remembered as a father, and thrust brutally away from the table, falling on the rushes in a forest of legs, still screaming.

"My lord! Sir Hugh."

It was Remy, pale at the head of the stairs. "In the stable. We . . . Master Guy."

She raised herself on her elbows, saw the two soldiers appear over the edge of the stairwell, the mailed body limp between them, wide stains already clotting on the torn metal plates.

Guy . . .

And Audrée's last, vindictive triumph. "See! He is here now! Satan is here, *and she's his doorway!"*

Gerlaine staggered to her feet, a dull roaring in her ears with the name and the flesh to be torn—

Bastard.

—down the stairs, her own voice ripping him out of the fabric of her soul—

Bastard—

—out into the cold bailey with no roof between herself and the God to whom she must confess before she tore that throat.

"Bastard!" she screamed, pounding her fear and fury into the snow with tight-balled fists. *"Gurth Bastard, where are you!"*

Then they were around her, faces, torches, and Hugh holding her. *Why is he crying? Hugh never cries.*

"Get back," he challenged them all. "Let my sister alone. I'll kill you. Don't touch her!"

But she twisted in his arms, searching the shadowed circle of them, finding what she sought. Gerlaine wrenched away from Hugh and clutched at the old priest's legs.

"I confess. Père Vaudan, I confess. Bless me, Father, for I have sinned."

"At last," he touched her head. "To the church, someone. Quickly. The relics and holy water."

"I have fornicated with a servant of Satan. But I love my mother and my brothers. I swear before heaven I would do them no harm." *God damn you, Gurth.* "I have given myself to him and taken pleasure in it."

"Abjure him," said the priest over her.

"I do, I do." *I loved you and you took me like any mare, and you have killed what I love. In a thousand centuries God may forgive you, but I never. I'll burn myself to see you suffer beside me.*

"He has come to me in a pleasing shape at night, and I have welcomed him."

"Abjure and cast out the incubus."

"I do, I hate and repent of it. I have opened my body to him" —*Why is Hugh crying?*—"and let my lust and pride harden me against repentance." She clutched spasmodically at his thin old legs. "Forgive me my fault . . . my most grievous fault."

"Do you truly despise your sin?"

"I despise it heartily," she sobbed.

"Amen." Vaudan knelt beside her, gentle and radiant in his tragic victory.

"Because it has offended Thee, my Savior."

She huddled in Hugh's arms, hardly feeling the holy water that Vaudan applied to her lips and forehead or the relic pressed to her bosom, barely hearing the mumble of purgative Latin. In her heart, below the level of confession, she felt cold and free, walking with Sigrid, knowing her at last for sister.

I will go into you as you entered me, cut out your life as you destroyed mine, and red my hands with your blood as you took mine in pleasure. And God can have all vengeance since time began, save this, save you who are mine, Gurth Bastard.

BOOK THREE:

Twilight in Asgard

I

Half a day's ride from the ancient ring of stones at Holywood, Thane Wulfnoth the exile rebuilt the old hill fort of Duniskell, adding to the earthen walls an inner defense of dry stone laced with timber, and a circle of wicker outbuildings centered about a thatched hall. In the name of his new lord, but in practice for himself, Wulfnoth held sway over hills bleak and sparsely peopled as those he remembered, ransoming the occasional incautious Norman knight who strayed too close to his roving horsemen, or selling the less affluent travelers to the Danish slave-traders who nosed up Solway. It was not England, he didn't hold much with the new lord, but it was a life and the only one he knew. The faces at his board were English faces, the tongue Northumbrian, and the old skald, years past the power and skill that had charmed better boards, nevertheless still sang of Beowulf and Hengest.

The hall was hardly spacious. Brand Ulfson might have used it for a barn after a vigorous cleaning. A fire pit in the middle of the earthen floor blackened the rough-hewn rafters with continual soot. Two rows of trestle tables ran the length of the hall on either side of a center aisle filled now with lackeys vying for busy passage with the hungry dogs drawn to the smell of meat turning on the spit. Women served and poured rapidly as they could fetch from the outside kitchen, hurrying

their trips to keep from the bitter cold. The hall flickered in the
light of a dozen large torches that lit the round war shields
formed in a colorful frame about the four walls. The men
waiting for their master at the board were as rainbowed as the
shields in tunics of red, yellow, blue or green, here and there a
full-length robe trimmed with fur, though a sharp eye might
notice in the human tapestry a stitch, a clumsy patch or an
unmended rip. Old stains darkened many of the garments.
Their magnificence survived only in the benevolence of the
shadowed hall. Daylight would reveal wear and age in the
wool, the battered faces of the shields, the seediness and dirt
that pervaded the hall, fetid and slippery underfoot with
trodden garbage, scum-darkened mead horns, the one drinking
glass in its tarnished silver stand at Wulfnoth's place cracked at
the lip.

Wulfnoth's seat and those of his chief companions were
raised on a low dais in the center of the north wall. These were
empty now but the rest of the hall was crowded as they waited
for Wulfnoth to enter, the dogs snarling and snapping
halfheartedly about the edge of the savory spits, the men
sipping at mead, the old skald tuning his harp near the fire.
Then the doors opened inward.

"Hoch!"

Wulfnoth entered, followed by his chief *gesiths,* and the
hoch greeted him from the throats of the welcoming men. He
moved heavily through the surging tide of dogs underfoot,
booting them amiably out of his way—a big man with a
noticeable limp, uncut red hair and beard dulled and grayed to
rust, wild where it had once been delicately oiled and curled.
His scarlet tunic was well made but worn as the others.

He assumed his chair, took the drinking glass in a scarred
hand and held it over his right shoulder without a word.
Immediately a ragged woman stepped forward from the wall,
filling the glass with mead. He held the glass out to his
followers; as there was no priest or monk to give the blessing,
Wulfnoth spoke it himself.

"The benediction of God on this board!"

"Amen!"

"Let there be no sword drawn in anger, no word spoken in
unprovable boast."

"Aye!"

"And may the devil stay south of Solway with his Norman friends!"

"*Amen!*"

He spread his arms toward the feast. "May it well become you."

They fell to; serving girls scurried, carvers hacked at the mutton, trenchers were filled, and the skald's harp plunked clumsily behind the warm, sweaty babble—and one strident young voice rose over the noise.

"Wulfnoth! We've taken prize!"

Tall and rawboned in his oxhide jerkin, Beorn Gundar, youngest of the companions, swaggered before the table, placing a bow and full quiver on the board. While his thane inspected the find, Beorn Gundar added, "And three good horses, shod and saddled."

Wulfnoth grunted, mouth full of mutton, his hands caressing the beautiful workmanship of the bow. No scabby crofter made this, the yew perfectly cut, seasoned and oiled, the hemp string tough as gut and well rubbed with glue. He passed it to the man on his right and drew an arrow from the quiver.

"Look close," Beorn Gundar urged reverently. "There's a crafting to warm your heart."

Wulfnoth whistled, long and low. The arrow was a prize of the fletcher's art from the painstakingly straightened ash shaft to the needle-pointed head, gray feathers trimmed precisely and set in grooves straight as a new sword edge.

"Horses, too?"

"Aye," the boy grinned, flashing long yellow teeth. "And the riders: three grown, one boy."

The thane stuffed more meat and swigged from his glass. "What do they look like? Ransom or boat-bait?"

"Well," Beorn shuffled with some uncertainty, plagued by a vague scruple, "they be not Scot, but home folk. From Tees."

Tees was Norman; they could only be fugitives, and yet as Beorn Gundar herded them before him, Wulfnoth knew this was no ordinary lot of runaway serfs.

"A proud bunch," the red-haired servingwoman remarked. "Megan set them out a bowl by the dogs. They'd not touch it."

Up and down the hall, the chatter subsided gradually as Wulfnoth's men looked up, chewed and drank more slowly, taking the measure of this new lot. The women, by God, were handsome.

Wulfnoth belched absently, spearing his meat and chewing unhurriedly, absorbed in what fate and his riders had snared. The corn-haired boy brought a tender smile which he quickly willed away. He noted the rich material of the grimy little tunic. The child yearned toward the steaming trenchers with a hunger he could no longer disguise. The defiant little terrier of a man next to him in a torn ring-shirt: somewhere this one had been a soldier; his stance lacked the mark of servitude. *He's not afraid,* Wulfnoth affirmed. *It's not in his eyes.* The blonde woman—probably the boy's mother, there was a resemblance. And the other—from the first, he'd been drawn back to her. Tall as a fair-sized man, the gray streaking back from her temples, the woman was a presence he could feel. And Wulfnoth found he was trying to stare her down.

"Why didn't you eat?" he addressed her. "The bowl was set for you, good as we feed the dogs."

"Your bowl's as dirty as your stinking floor."

He caught and relished the Northumbrian burr. "Clodagh!"

At his sign, the servingwoman cut meat from his own trencher and placed it on a thick slab of coarse bread.

Wulfnoth waved the child close. "Come here, boy." The child only moved closer to his mother. Wulfnoth held out the food. "Eat."

Only at his mother's approval did the child scurry forward, lifted over the board by Clodagh.

"What's your name, Dirty Face?" she tousled his hair.

It sounded like *dairty feyass* to Godric. His blue eyes widened with amazement. "You can't talk proper," he told her. "How be it you smell so bad?"

Wulfnoth and the men around him exploded with thunderous laughter, spraying the table with half-chewed bits of the feast. The thane slapped Clodagh on her thin rump.

"By God," he boomed, "that's an Englishman. Come eat, boy."

To the amusement that spread around the north table, Clodagh paddled Godric lightly on his backside and set him in Wulfnoth's lap. "Well now," she sniffed at him, "you be no perfume box either."

"You," Wulfnoth pointed at the male captive. "Whose man are you?"

"None now."

"That's Norman iron you're wearing."

The little man spat noisily at his feet. "Was."

Wulfnoth took his measure. The man was old enough to have been well into his prime before Hastings. "You served an English lord?"

"Archer and fletcher in the Tees fyrd," Peter said proudly. "Huntsman and swineherd to the thane of Brandeshal and to his son's wife there."

Brandeshal. The name was familiar. He held up the arrow. "You made these?"

"He did," Hulda broke in stiffly. "And the archer like the arrows: the best north of Humber."

The thane's glance merely flicked over her in passing. He found his attention returning again and again to the dark woman, tall and still before him.

"We'll see. Beorn, your bow."

The young *gesith* strung his bow with the rapid ease of habit and took the quiver Clodagh handed him. An excited murmur ran around the tables as the men shifted about or stood up to see the contest. Beyond the skald, there wasn't much to liven the hall of a winter night. Wulfnoth pointed with his knife to the four round shields that lined the wall at the far end of the hall, not a great distance away but only half seen in the poor light.

"The four," he called. "The center of the boss."

Beorn Gundar nocked, sighted carefully and loosed. A few hands pounded on the board.

"The clout! Not a hair off!"

The missiles sped one after another to a rising tattoo of praise. *"Hoch!* Four in the clout, Wulfnoth!"

The thane nodded to Peter. "Now, match that and I might call you my man."

"Aye," said Peter laconically. He spoke gently to Godric who had ravaged the meat and the thick bread trencher as well. "Finished, lad?"

"Yes, Peter." The boy wiped his hands on dirt-shiny trousers.

"Then go to your mum. Don't forget your graces. You be not common folk. Say thanks."

Only when Godric had tendered his proper gratitude did Peter reach for the longbow, scarcely glancing at his hands as he strung it. He smiled at Beorn Gundar: not much more than a boy, he judged—blond, the hair parted midwise and braided. His cheeks were already burnished leather like his long muscled arms scarred from the battles that had won his high place.

"Peter Fletcherson," he introduced himself cordially. "You pull a fine bow, lad, but 'twas an easy shot. You down by the butts—take those shields off the wall."

Peter moved well back, much farther than Beorn, speaking casually. "Your stand is a wee bit tense. Stay easy or you'll shake when you sight."

Three of the four shields were down off the wall and stacked on a table. Before anyone could reach for the fourth, the arrow was nocked, the bow bent easily as a reed, and Peter's first shot lodged in the boss a mere inch from Beorn's.

"The clout!" reported the butts. "Fair shot, fletcher."

A few desultory thumps rattled the tables. Wulfnoth set his glass untasted on the board, trying to assess what he'd seen. His own sharp eyes could barely make out the shadowed target, yet the little bastard had barely paused to aim before he loosed. Wulfnoth hid the grin of excitement behind the glass again. The blond woman wasn't boasting.

"Hey, down in the butts," Peter nocked another shaft. "Pick up a shield and toss it high when the fancy takes you."

He's happy, Hulda thought with a rush of warmth. *I've not seen him like this since the day he brought the horses.*

"Another thing," Peter continued solicitously, as if to an apprentice. "You hold drawn too long before you loose, Beorn Gundar. You're only on it once. See it, feel it in your hands —ha! Rood!"

They had thrown the shield, thinking him off guard. They heard his oath, saw the fluid motion of arm and bow followed by the *tuck* of the striking arrow in the hardened leather of the boss before it clattered to the floor.

"The clout again. *Hoch,* fletcher!"

The hands beat louder on the table and ringleted arms beckoned for the spears and shields resting against the walls.

Beorn Gundar saw them and felt the hot blood run in his neck and ears. The gray little fletcher made him a fool, though it would do no good to challenge him out of mere anger. The older *gesiths* would say he was more boy than man for heating up because he was bettered in fair contest.

"For sure," Peter set another shaft, offhanded as a neighbor chatting by the fire, "a shield's not quick as a deer or a man. Your arm must be easy. Do you wobble about, there mightn't be a second chance. Throw!"

The third shield flew and was speared. "Holy Cross!"

"The clout again, by Sepulcher."

Now the hands beat themselves red against the board, joined by the deafening staccato of spears clashed against bucklers, and over it all rose the rich music of that voice that had reached into Wulfnoth's spirit from the first.

"*Hoch,* Peter!" Calla stretched out her hands to him in salute. "Hail the Death-Sender, Brand's pride. Hail the Woden-Son."

Wulfnoth breathed deep. There were women like Clodagh to fill his glass and his bed, but the dark one was a queen, a *hlafdian* fit to give the welcome in any hall. His memory nudged him again. Ulfson . . . Ulfson . . . yes. The raven shield at the head of Tees fyrd.

"Jesu!"

Once more Peter invoked the aid his arm hardly needed. His last arrow flew home, the spears and hands clattering before the shield hit the floor, and under the roar of the tables, he grinned at the vanquished boy.

"Don't feel shamed. My da set me to making them years before I could pull one. You grow to the feel of it." He winked. "Like a good woman."

Wulfnoth calculated rapidly. He ordered the women and child returned to the end of the hall—"with food in a clean dish, mind"—and Peter once more set before him. He dallied with the point of his knife against the trencher, conferred briefly with his assenting chief men. The archer was worth more to them than his slave price.

"Swear to be my man," he offered. "Put your skill to my service, and there'll be a place at the board and spear and shield. Keep your ring-shirt and the horse."

Peter hesitated. He peered down the hall to Hulda and Calla.

Always central to all he knew, they were grown so much closer now, dear as kin, the last marker stones from a world dead and gone. He needed no skald to tell him that world would never come again.

"And my folk?"

That was already decided. Duniskell couldn't be sanctuary for every runaway to cross the wall. It was not an easy decision but necessary. Wulfnoth carried very few delusions; he was a war chief so long as he cared for the needs of his men. They could choose another in his place. Slaves brought gold and gave them the illusion of place where there was one no longer. The two women would bring a good rate. The boy, if lucky, might be taken by sailors and raised to a life as free as any known. If not, that was not his worry.

And yet these four disturbed him: home folk with the home music to their tongues. The boy, that beautiful, corn-haired child; the big-boned mother whose eyes made him feel guilty; finally, the olive-skinned woman, the lure of her already reaching inside him. He wanted her. She brushed against a loneliness deeper than Clodagh could reach. After bed he might drink with this one, and when he'd drunk enough perhaps try to tell her how he felt when the skald sang of the lost things, when the meat and mead ran thin and the women whined their hunger, or in the cold, sour-mouthed morning when he saw the hall for what it was—not a new beginning but, for the forlorn lot of them, the last failing handhold on the last ledge before oblivion.

But it was the way of things. He wished to Christ Beorn Gundar had not found them.

"They'll be sold," he said flatly. "You're lucky. It might have been you, too."

Peter looked at his feet, a man with his own longings. For a while this night it had been the old times again, more than he'd ever had. He bathed in the admiration of English eyes in an English hall. They had beat spear against shield to salute him as heroes and lords were greeted. He could have this, could ride among men again, a *gesith*.

But like Godric Carpenter, he had placed his hands in de Neuville's and felt gelded for it. More than all this, Peter couldn't imagine standing there free while the three of them were chained and collared for sale. He unstrung the bow and dropped it on the board in front of the thane.

"Yonder's my folk. I go with them."

"Why, man?" Beorn Gundar saw only the stupidity of the choice. "Do you want to be a slave?"

"Boy," Peter said, "I've hand-sworn twice since I was baptized." He saw their bafflement closing behind something harder, knowing what would happen and accepting it. "And that was once too often."

The men around Wulfnoth fingered their cups and looked to the thane. Wulfnoth reached for the bow. He smoothed once more along the carefully oiled wood, then tossed it to Beorn Gundar. The young warrior held the gift awkwardly. Deeply, he knew he was not yet worth it. The shame surfaced as anger.

"Then sell him," he snapped.

Wulfnoth waved his knife. "Put him with the others."

II

No longer fighting for scraps, the hounds worried at bones around the fire pit, the women moved more slowly to fill the cups and horns and conversation lazed contentedly to the soft background of the harp. The old man in the greasy gown struck a chord and lifted his cracked but powerful voice over the noise of the tables.

"Who remembers the heroes?" he called over the stiff-fingered chords. "Who remembers Beowulf and the hall of Hrothgar?"

"Aye," they called. "Sing to us."

"Who remembers the men of old, the men of the Woden-blood? And where are those who still could weep for the passing of the gods and doomed Asgard?"

From the tables small coins showered around the old skald who loftily pretended not to notice, but bent his head over the harp as if his heart were too full for mean things. Crouched by Peter, Hulda elbowed his rib.

"Mark the old shithead," she muttered, "and his eyes out past his nose watching where the coin falls."

> "And who remembers the brothers,
> The first comers, Hengest and Horsa:
> The sons of Wihtgils, the son of Witta,

208

> The son of Wecta, the son of Woden,
> Who fought the Welsh king Vortigern—
> First bringers of the Saxon blood?"

"Tell us," the tables urged. "Tell us of Hengest!"

The old skald clawed at his strings and began the well-worn tale. When it was done and fitly reward with thumping applause against the board, he sang a lay on the virtues of good King Edward.

"Not only can't sing," Hulda seethed, "he's a bloody liar in the bargain."

The skald was no longer a shaper of magic. Laziness, drink and indifferent fortune had long since robbed his hands and voice of their real art, leaving only the cheap tricks and broad effects that commanded attention and concealed the lack of heart, but he was fortunate in an undemanding audience.

Mellow with drink, the door opened to memory, Wulfnoth found himself turning again and again to that fascinating dark head at the end of the hall. She accepted the skald's offering with calm pleasure as if he sang for her alone, but the other woman glowered contemptuously at the singer. She spat on the floor and rose. The dark woman uncoiled beside her in a graceful motion that hinted of supple muscles under the hide smock.

The harper's song came to an end. He cooled his dry throat with a generous gulp of beer and swept the harp strings with new vigor.

"Now," he called out. "Who will remember of Stamford Bridge?"

"By God, *I* do!"

Hulda pulled away from Calla and strode down the hall to confront the astonished singer. "Old man, you're like the ghosts you wheeze over—dead and gone. I remember Stamford. I sent my man," she pointed to Godric, "his father to fight with Harold."

Her eyes were cold, fixing Wulfnoth and his chief men. "God damn it, I've no silver pence to pay for flattery, but I'll give you men to sing of. Who remembers Ely and Hereward and the men who ate weeds before they'd surrender?"

"Woman!" came a deep voice from the south wall. "I remember. I was there."

The man rose, scarred and gaunt, not old but the youth pressed out of him forever.

"So you were," Hulda paused a little to study him. "I remember you. Can you recall Godric Carpenter who carried a raven shield? He was there, and myself and the boy there. A girl child, too," she added quietly. "She took sick and died when my milk failed."

"For sure," the warrior confirmed. "You were there. You were thinner then."

"Who wasn't?" Hulda's head tossed proudly. "We all had the fever, and I lost my child. We lived where crows would starve, but we held Ely against William." She rounded on Wulfnoth. "And you would call *us* slaves and sell us?" She broke off, vibrant with fury. The years flooded in on her: ground to dirt for a cause, ground again by foreigners and now by the pathetic remnant of her own kind. It was too much; in the next moment she might spring at the harper and break his dust-dry bones. "Old men, all of you. How many young like the archer there? Old wolves run out of their hunting ground, eating memories. You, harper! Sing of Brand Ulfson and the men who stayed!"

"Singer," the musical voice lifted without effort to fill the hall. "There are Saxons here. Do we sing of the *bear-sarks*."

Words to conjure with, and Calla shrewdly knew it. Proud of Hulda but older and wise, she gauged the men's reactions to what the young woman said. They were not untouched, not mere ragtag outlaws, though they'd fallen a long way from the glory they pretended. Hulda could get no more than uneasy shame from these men and their red-haired rock of a chief, and himself not unlike Brand in some ways, though the strong mouth hinted of more humor and less cruelty: a good mouth. You didn't batter the pride of such men. You blew on it gently as a flint spark, helping it to flame again. There were many forms of magic, some born in all women with the wit to use it.

"Thane Wulfnoth," she knelt respectfully before the dais. "Who remembers the old ways. Wulfnoth Ringshirt-giver, may I sing to your men?"

He felt himself begin to sweat. She invited him with her eyes, the soft-throated music was all for him. "What would you sing?"

"Of heroes, as the harper would himself."

He shrugged. "It will make no difference in the morning."
Wulfnoth wondered why he said that.

Calla placed her hands on the old skald's thin shoulders.
"Your fingers are stiff," she said, "but enough is there to show
the art that was. It is a long time."

"Aye." He held out the tarnished gold chain that swung from
his neck, the last remnant of elegance about him. "This chain I
had from Siward when he was earl, and others before that."

"In the old days," she caught and held his rheumy eyes, "the
skald was blind that he might forget this world and see inward.
Close your eyes, then." Her cool fingers passed over his
eyelids. "See and remember."

"It . . . is a long time," he murmured. "Some memories are
painful."

"Remember." The music fell softly on his ears, coaxing,
crooning. "Not all your best songs have been heard. Remember not with thoughts, but with your hands. Trust me," she
whispered. "Go with me. I'll keep you safe and bring you
back. Go with me now."

A great calm folded down around the harper. His breathing
became deep and regular, lost its wheeze. His fingers spidered
over the harp strings. The other sounds of the hall grew faint
behind the melody of her wish.

"Play for me . . . the music no hall has heard, not forgotten
though you thought it so . . . remember . . . when your
fingers were new with the art and the music came pure as water
from a clear spring. Remember . . ."

He experienced a moment of fear, of feeling himself out of
the hall, out of time. His eyes would not open. "No—I can't."

You can, the answer came from inside his head, lilting with
her melody. *The music that came for love, remember? That
flattered no lord, needed no gold.*

And then his fingers remembered.

A day half a lifetime past; a new harp and a warm wind, the
sun seemed to float for hours over the west, painting the fields
gold and red against the deepening blue. He had practiced all
day a song of heroes and battles. Sitting on a stone wall, the
song came strangely hollow and false, and yet his heart burst
with something he must sing. He saw the bondsmen driving the
slow cattle home, smelled the wheat, heard it whisper in the
wind. *I could hear the seed rustling in the pod, the heartbeat*

of the whole earth. And the music that came then was simple and profound as the land it sang of. The notes came without effort, a song to catch the ear of a farmer, not a warrior, and make him think *yes, this is what I hear myself*. But farmers didn't pay for songs and he had forgotten it.

Almost.

The old fingers curved over the strings. A single note throbbed in the air, seemingly not plucked but pressed out as a delicate afterthought to an inner creation; another, and still more, stretching out in a limpid arch of sound over the hall grown still around the harper—weaving, turning, returning like the earth it came from, like the promise of Barley-Maid, to its original theme. No great flashing chords, no runs or tricks of the hand, merely one graceful line of melody beyond sadness, defeat or even hope but filled with all of them. And over it, part of the music itself, Calla spoke to the listening men.

"I would sing of Stamford Bridge," she began. "And more than that, beyond that. I would sing of the *bear-sarks* who became more in the land than warriors.

"Of Brand Ulfson who marched to Stamford with Harold, the son of great Wessex. Wessex of the Lion banner," Calla recalled for them. "Who here has no memory of the Lions?"

There was a time, she said, when the *bear-sarks* fit the old songs, when they asked no more than sword and shield and their lord's enemy to fight; when home was the open sky and the deck of the longship, and wealth what they could carry away from the raid.

But men changed when their roots went five centuries into the same ground, not only at Brandeshal but anywhere men bore up sons and grandsons on the land that nursed their grandfathers. Why did they come to call the Norse shiftless pirates, who were so close in blood? Because under the old *bear-sark* battle cry was a deeper song of the earth that no Norman could ever drown out or even hear until his own guts went into the earth and fed it.

"Why, then," her arms stretched out to encompass them all, "why sing of dead heroes? Saxons, men of my blood, I tell you there is so much more."

They might have come with a sword in one hand, but the other sowed the seed, and while the proud Welsh kings looked backward into the past from their western mountains, and their sad minstrels promised an Arthur who would never come again, the Saxons loved the land and by this love were part of it, as a wife brought forth the face and soul of her husband in a child.

"The Saxon earth is yours," she whispered to them. "It will always be yours. Because it is you. Yourselves. Your true song."

Once more the simple theme rose on the air, slowed, returned to its keynote and ended, the last note limpid as the first. Calla was finished. She pressed her hand to the skald's and walked back to the end of the hall. And the harper looked about him with an old pride, understanding the silence, not caring that no coins were thrown. Some songs were their own reward.

The woman had created quiet magic. Wulfnoth roused himself, wrestled briefly with judgment and made up his mind. The blond woman was right. Some things a man couldn't sell.

Calla watched him as he bent to speak to the men on his left and right. They appeared not hard to convince, whatever his proposition. Beorn Gundar was called to the dais, addressed briefly, then Wulfnoth rose and left the hall, glancing at her as he passed. And Beorn Gundar, quite evidently relieved, came to Peter, holding out the bow and quiver.

"The thane says you're to have these back." His manner was distinctly warmer now, almost friendly. "And a place at table for your folk." He beckoned Calla. "Wulfnoth will speak with you in his bower."

Calla rose without a word. Hulda made to protest and Peter would have stopped her, but she waved them away, a glimmer of mischief in her reassuring smile.

"Peace, now. There be all kinds of magic." She followed Beorn Gundar.

"Make a fine archer, that boy," Peter caressed the oiled wood of the bow. "If he'll listen to me."

For the first time since they were herded into the hall, Hulda relaxed. "Peter, *gesith*," she growled. "There'll be no living with you now."

"*Och,* Hulda." And then Peter couldn't say anything else. He ducked his head over the bow to hide the ear-threatening grin of satisfaction. And little Godric squirmed in his mother's lap.

"Mum," he yawned, "can we go bed soon?"

"Soon," she promised. "And a bath for you in the morning."

"Don't need'n."

"Nor do pigs," she hugged him. "Come morning, by God, a wash."

Her eye roved distastefully over the grimy hall. Not as big or as well-built as hers before de Neuville burned it. Nor as clean. She hoped these Scottish sluts could wield a rag and bucket.

But it's home, I guess, and we're together. And Calla's right, she allowed in her unpoetic heart. *Whatever there was, we've brought it with us.*

She laced her fingers in Godric's tangled hair, smiling when he hiccuped drowsily, full of food.

"Go sleep."

In the small, unkempt bower, Calla enjoyed Wulfnoth's self-conscious movements as he pokered with undue care at the peat fire. She knew at least part of what he wanted, and while he couldn't take what she did not desire to give, he wasn't the plainest man north of the wall. There were worse ways to spend a night.

But Wulfnoth had something to say, she guessed. He passed her a cup of honey mead. She sipped it waiting for him to speak.

"I do remember Ulfson at Stamford." He eased himself into the one rude chair, sighing with dry nostalgia. "The old *bear-sarks*. He was one of the last. What were you to him?"

"We were hand-fast. I gave him a son. Four and twenty he is now."

"Well now," Wulfnoth shifted in the chair. He stroked his shaggy beard. He must look mangy to her. Come morning, he'd be trimming with the razor, if he could find one. "You bore him young then."

Calla recognized and accepted the compliment. "I was fifteen."

Not much younger than himself, but she'd worn better. He chuckled. "Summers were good then, weren't they?"

"And Tees good land to grow up on." The strong mead glowed through her. This was a good man—rough-edged, rough-minded, and perhaps with his own sad ghosts, but good throughout.

"Where's your son now?"

"On Tees yet."

"Bondsman?"

"Outlaw," she said proudly. "He killed the Norman that hanged his kin. And they be not able to catch him."

"Well," he grinned in spite of himself. "Well now . . ."

Damn, I'll be welling and nowing all night, and there she stands like she owns the place and knows damn well what I'm about.

"You're fortunate," he tried a different tack. "We've decided to let you stay, you and your folk. We prize the fletcher."

"For sure," she agreed tactfully. "The best in the north."

"What's your name?"

"Calla." She settled on the dirt floor near his chair, close enough for him to stretch out and touch her were he so minded. "Your garment's out at the elbow. When did someone last put a needle to it?"

"I had a wife." *Of sorts,* he amended tacitly. Easily taken, as easily left. He was younger then, in his pride. And not very wise. "She died."

She looked at him over the brim of her cup. "And the red-hair who serves you in the hall?"

"Clodagh is just Clodagh. I have no wife."

It was an old game, an old dance whose cadence had never left Calla. Because of it she had seen the trouble ahead for Gurth and Gerlaine and known yet that they were for each other like herself and Brand, whatever the end of it. And priests could lecture, lords punish, she herself warn, all to nothing. When this music played, the dancers would move in the dance.

Four years alone now; the hunger should be a memory, a mere glow. It was not. She felt as ready to start anew as the earth to whom she was Corn-Woman. He did remind her of Brand, though it wouldn't do to say it now. Men had their pride, and women should not be stupid.

"A man should have a wife," she agreed.

"I'm a soldier and a good Christian," he plunged into the core of it. "I don't think you'll find better."

Calla brushed back her hair. "Do you offer yourself to me, Thane Wulfnoth?"

He almost choked on his drink. "Offer?" he echoed, nonplussed. "Do *I* offer myself to *you?*" He gaped at her. "Now, hear me, woman—"

But the tiny gleam in her eye was infectious. She was smiling, then they were both laughing aloud at the truth of it.

"I swear," he suddenly felt marvelous, "I'll have to beat you three times a day."

"I doubt it, my lord. That sort of man would not have cut meat for a hungry child." Calla reached for his hand. "And do you take my promise to return, I'll bring you one who'd be a prize in any hall."

"You'd go?" he frowned. "It's dead winter."

"I'll go to Tees to find my son. He's scholar-taught at Paris to read and write. You can send proper letters under your sign and seal: Wulfnoth, Thane of Duniskell! Anywhere your men can ride. The scholars and priests will come, the men of learning with their books. Duniskell will be a hall to match Alfred's, and yourself a true lord again." He heard the deep pride in her voice. "I'll bring you my son, Gurth. Will you care for my folk till I come again?"

As she asked it, Calla rose and moved gracefully to the bed. She sat on the edge and began to remove the bronze clasp from her hair, shaking out the thickness of it over her shoulders.

Christ, he thought. *I feel like a scared boy with his first woman.*

"What promise can you give?"

She held out her hands to him. "I'll give it now. Come," she laughed with open pleasure. "It's a fair night for bargains."

III

—

With the middle of November, hard winter closed down on Tees.

No snow had fallen for five days. There was a slight thaw under fairly clear skies, but the weather-wise Saxons scanned the east and read the signs that were plain enough. A storm was building miles out over the North Sea. Perhaps it would pass them by; nevertheless, they looked to the chinking of their hut walls, conserved peat and brought into the huts those few sheep still left in the open. The storm would drive the snow before it like a billion cold knives, and no man or animal could stay alive very long without shelter.

At Montford the rhythm of life necessarily slowed. Hunting became harder work, the beach patrols a cruel ordeal ridden tortuously across the razor edge of the relentless sea wind. Additional searches swept Tees for signs of Bastard. Tracks were found that could not be traced to the steadings. Bastard was still on Tees and moving freely. A suspicious track never led very far alone through the snow before it mingled with others, sometimes their own, and became impossible to follow. Within the keep guards walked the walls now in addition to the tower watches, and Vaudan deserted his hut for the warmer closet that had belonged to Guy and Robin. Night fell at three in the afternoon and lightened only a little by nine in the morning.

Beyond the cold and the ubiquitous phantom of Gurth, a new rift appeared: the baron's children avoided him. They were correct and civil at table, did his bidding, but no longer spoke to him at all beyond necessity. Hugh became even more restless and preoccupied, and if her newly won grace brought Gerlaine peace, it did not show. Her familiar orders were despatched in monosyllables that invited not so much as a "save you" in return. She was growing into a chatelaine like her mother, though somewhere Élène's warmth had been lost.

Hugh's horse had developed a bad foreleg, surprising only in that it had not come earlier. The stallion was finely bred for fast cavalry, not the drudgery of endless patrols over a rocky beach. He gave Remy instructions to pamper him for a few days and was leaving the stable when Eustace entered, dressed in furs, followed by Aimeré.

"Why aren't you ready to ride?" Eustace snapped at him, pulling on his gauntlets.

"My horse is lame," Hugh answered shortly.

"It's past eleven," his father observed curtly. "Take another mount."

They stood apart in cold courtesy. Never much love lost between them, Aimeré reflected, but it hurt to look at them now.

"No word was sent me to ride," said Hugh.

"We hunt," Eustace turned away toward the saddle racks. "I will require you."

"I'll join you later. Your track will be easy to—"

"You'll join me now," the baron clipped. He stepped very close to his son. "Your sister is inexperienced. I can forgive her hatred of what she calls my cruelty, but don't you forget yourself, boy."

Hugh held his breath then let it out, steaming in the cold air. "My lord baron," he enunciated with icy formality. "I would have you recall that I was knighted—on the field, my lord—at the age of eighteen. I am no boy nor am I your vassal. I owe fealty to no man save William. And therefore," he tapped the gloves against his palm, "I will join you later, my lord."

He bowed with stiff *politesse* and stalked out into the crusted snow toward the bailey bridge. Vaudan was just putting away

the paraphernalia of the morning mass. It was a slow process.
Each article must be picked up and laid away with due
reverence, and the air in the church was almost as cold as that
outside; his fingers were stiff with it.

"Save you, Sir Hugh," he hacked through his pernicious
cold.

Hugh genuflected to the crucifix. "Père Vaudan, I need you
to write a letter for me."

From his writing stand pulled near the fire, Vaudan pondered the letter dictated to him. Pacing the dark chamber,
clipping out the sentences written and rewritten in his head for
days, there was not the slightest hint of ill-considered haste in
Hugh's message or his manner.

"Read it back to me, please."

The priest put down his stylus and ran nervous fingers
through his gray hair. "You have weighed this?" he asked
gravely.

"For eight years, Père Vaudan."

Still Vaudan hesitated. "You know what the baron will say."

"Clearly," said Hugh. "Read."

Raymond de Cayenne, Abbot of Sockburn
*From Hugh de Neuville, Knight: Greetings and my hope
for your prayer of blessing.*
  *It is my wish, after due consideration and a full
measure of worldly life wherein I have found neither
satisfaction nor fulfillment, to present myself to your
order in the hope of admission as a novice, there to serve
humbly the prescribed time till it pleases your wisdom to
admit me as a full brother. When my last duties to my
family have been discharged, I will present myself at the
gate of Sockburn. If I must wait, as is the custom, a day
or two or three, fasting the while, yet I will suffer it in all
humility of spirit until you find me worthy of entrance.*

                    *Written at Montford-on-Tees
                    The fifteenth day of November, 1073*

Vaudan laid the parchment aside and poured two cups of
wine, inviting Hugh to the small table.

"So this is what I could never understand in you, *hé?* All these years: this is why you did nothing with your rank?"

The young man fiddled at the cup but did not drink. "Father said, 'Come to England.' I didn't have the courage to refuse."

"And why now?"

"I have no more fear of him or what he stands for." He rose and began to pace again. "And no respect, either. When we've found Bastard, I'll go."

"And will you find him?"

"I found his hiding place," Hugh said confidently. "I proved him mortal when all of you screamed witchcraft."

"While he," Vaudan countered calmly, "was killing your brothers. Admirable logic. You have the failing of intellect, Hugh: its pride. Sit—no, come, sir—sit down. I want to speak to you."

He revolved the cup before his eyes, marshaling his thoughts. "Once a brother, what then?"

"With the goodness of the abbot, I will ask to take orders."

"A priest?" Vaudan drank and set the cup down. "No, Hugh. I do not think so."

The bluntness surprised Hugh. "Why not?"

Vaudan chose his words carefully. "Be a brother if you will. Learn your Latin, read, think, perhaps write. You will be of the same value as so many others nowadays who try to change things." His eyes seemed to recede into their wrinkles, remembering. "Or the others who sit copying in a cell, thinking they are close to God because they are removed from life. They are in love with an idea. I think you are one of these: in love with your notion of God. And I think," Vaudan emptied the cup with a warm little sigh of pleasure and refilled it, "that you would make a marvelous scholar to nip at the heels of the Church, but less of a priest than your father, God defend."

"I don't doubt the Church," said Hugh irritably. "I have merely doubted the wisdom of some of its men."

"As I said, drink your wine and listen."

Hugh shoved it away. "I don't want wine."

"I know," Vaudan smiled. "You never did. Your drunkenness suited your disposition like bad manners or whoring. They are not part of you. Hugh, my—" He broke off, leaning on the worn black elbows of his soutane, peering down into the cup.

"I would have said 'my son,' but that doesn't fit you, either. I can't imagine you as a son. Of anyone. You are alone."

Abruptly he reached for a taper. "It is too dark in here."

He lighted the candle from the log fire and set it on the table. "In all these years, I can count on one hand the times you have confessed a woman to me. That is odd: you are not effeminate."

"I've had women," Hugh shrugged. "They're a pleasure sometimes."

"Like a large dinner," Vaudan observed wryly, "rather heavy for your taste and not to be indulged too often. Like jealousy, spite, envy, greed—all the greasy, common things you have never confessed because you have probably never entertained them beyond a passing twinge. You are an ascetic, Hugh." The priest stretched across to him, eager to be understood. "And with my own hundred doubts a day, I could not come to you for absolution. I tell you only because you are deciding your life. Perhaps wrongly."

Hugh recoiled from the priest's urgency. His decision had taken courage. He didn't want to be told it was foolish. "You have never doubted, Vaudan. Who in hell are you to tell me I have no calling?"

"God was not sewn in my pocket," Vaudan met the challenge with calm irony. "I've lost and had to find my God a hundred times. I've lived with my own doubts and those of others, the men and women here who think God has left Tees. The Mass for the Dead," his head drooped on one elbow over his cup. "I can say it in my sleep; I *hear* it in my sleep now . . . *Agnus Dei, qui tollis peccata mundi, dona eis requiem.* I'm a man; how do you think I have *felt* as a man, saying those words over your mother whom I've known since we stole apples together? Or your brothers whom I baptized and scolded and loved? You think I don't doubt when I see the service of God to no avail here, the people frightened, your father dry-rotten inside himself? And me—poor clown—mumbling Latin, trying to comfort them, not knowing where or when that devil will come again to take another of you, always at the right time and place? He knows, Hugh! He *knows*, while I can only wonder, and I say *Where is God?*"

His voice climbed with the pent-up frustration. "Man or devil, the evil of this place *rots* us, and I watch it." He pushed himself away from the table with the force of what he felt. "Sometimes, I—"

Awkwardly, not to call attention to the emotion churning in him, the little priest made a show of poking at the fire. "Sometimes I go to bed with too much wine. I am that weak, Hugh. And when I wake up with a headache, there will be mass to say and confessions to hear, and . . . people."

He trailed off in a kind of hopeless weariness, staring at the pale light beyond the narrow shutter. "In the morning I am left with people to take care of. Perhaps that is all I'll ever know for sure of God."

He brought the letter from the stand with a stick of wax.

"You don't believe in Satan, Hugh. Don't deny it: you do not believe. Well," he sighed, "that is not to the point, which is that neither do you believe in *them:* Fitz, Audrée, Jehan, all of them. They're dirt to you." Vaudan poured more wine, settling into the point of his argument. "You block them out, I have seen it. Then be a bishop, cardinal, prince of the Church, be a martyr if that is attractive to you, and I suspect it is. But until you can feel for them—who are His sheep as well as you —you'll never be worth a damn as a priest."

Hugh drained his cup with a wry face. The stuff didn't taste good anymore. "I seek God, Vaudan. I need Him."

"And the devil take the hindmost?" Vaudan toyed with the sealing wax. Hugh noticed that his fingers shook slightly. Like Father, like all of them, Vaudan had aged on Tees. "Except that, as a priest, it is the hindmost who will concern you most. In the sacrament of confession, you become a pot full of other men's sins. You think they will come to you with scholarly questions like the nature of the Trinity—*hé?*"

The priest bowed his head over the wine, appearing to deliberate. When he looked up, the blue eyes were clear and direct. "We will speak hypothetically then. What would you say to a poor sow of a woman who confesses to you over and over that she lies with man after man because her husband cannot adequately perform his conjugal duties, that the men make her feel womanly? And what do you say when she comes back at last, knowing there will be no more men, no more anything, not with the marks on her that even her children will know?"

Vaudan gave his close attention to the wax, kneading it over

the candle flame. "Or to a strong, proud girl who fell in love
with a force and is dying inside because love has turned to
hatred. Or to a man," the little cleric looked up sadly, "who
comes to the confessional with all the weaknesses and
strengths of a man and talks of loneliness and loss and doubt
and pride; of blaming one very dear love for the loss of
another; of jealousies toward a daughter that drive him to acts
only God can understand or forgive. What would you say to
him, Sir Hugh?"

The knight stared down at the table. He had not expected
this force or depth out of Vaudan, battering at the bright core
of his dreams. The stylus offered to him was like a glove
dropped by an adversary. He turned the letter toward him and
lettered his name carefully at the bottom.

"There."

Vaudan heated the wax and daubed it over the edge of the
folded parchment. He took the seal ring from Hugh and
pressed it into the soft glob.

"It will be sent."

Late afternoon filtered gray through the shutter onto the floor
of Gerlaine's closet. Exhausted by her morning rounds over
the snow-piled bailey, she had thrown herself across the bed,
dragged the fur coverlet over her shoulders and sunk down into
a much-needed nap. It was not an indulgence. She slept poorly
of nights; nevertheless, she left the door ajar that Thérèse,
Clothilde or anyone else might wake her if need be.

She woke foggily, feeling that disorientation that follows
sleep out of the regular pattern. It couldn't be too late. The hall
beyond her closed door was murmurous with the sewing
women. Gerlaine turned on her back under the warm fur.

Who closed her door?

She opened her eyes again and saw the lighted taper on its
stand by her bed. She certainly hadn't set one, it was wasteful.
She turned her head toward the casement and then sat up.

Bête squatted by her low bed, huge arms resting on his
knees.

Gerlaine thought nothing of his being there. She might have
taken her bath in his presence with no more embarrassment
than when she bathed him. He rarely left her side now,
plodding after her on her rounds about the keep, and she'd got

in the habit of thinking her tasks aloud to him as she went. *We must visit Hugo, now. We must go to the cellar to see about the wine.* Bête was enough company for her. There wasn't much to say to the others. True, she could never be sure how much or little Bête understood, though in the last two months—since the night Gurth almost killed him—she was sure he'd improved.

"*Hé*, Bête," she yawned, brushing a hand over her face still numb with sleep. "Thank you for watching over me. Please bring a cloth."

Drowsy, it occurred to her that Bête might not understand her wish. But he rose, silent for all his bulk, wet the cloth from the bucket with which she did her toilet, and returned.

"Bête?" The small joy was tremendously amplified for her. "Do you know? Can you understand me?"

Her face was very close to his in the candlelight, searching the empty blue eyes for some contact. "Yes, God is healing you," she snuggled to his thick chest. "Maybe soon you will even speak to me. You can speak; I heard you once. Now," her finger went to his lips, "say after me: *Je suis Bête*. Try," she coaxed. "You are my only friend now. I want to talk to you. Please . . . *Je suis Bête*."

Again and again she formed the simple phrase, each time touching his lips. They began to move slightly; Bête's face worked with some incredible effort. Once he made the beginning of a sound and Gerlaine thought intelligence flickered briefly across the blankness. His hand reached out to touch her own lips.

"G—"

"Yes," she urged. "Yes."

His mouth moved again. "Ger—"

Then it was gone; abruptly, the game was over. Bête thrust himself away morosely, drawn in on his own dark center again. Gerlaine twinged with remorse. It was cruel of her to tax him so. It profaned God who would heal Bête in His own time or leave him silent as He disposed.

She sighed, stroking the tangled hair. She would work on it tonight. His hair was well-nigh lustrous after a brush.

"It is all right," she whispered. "It doesn't matter. *Je t'aime, ma Bête.*"

She kissed his stubbled cheek and rose, swabbing at her face and neck with the cloth. Her braids had loosened during the nap. She sat by the fire to plait them again before adjusting the black veil, her thoughts drifting free as long as they might before duty called her again to think, decide, command. Minutes passed; the women's voices pattered softly through the hall. A spoon banged against a pot below, and the wind whispered against the shutter, rattling it. Gerlaine almost forgot she was not alone, then she heard Bête move slightly by the bed.

"I—"

Her fingers stopped. She barely breathed.

Clear and deep, but struggling out of darkness, the voice labored to transform incoherence to words.

"Je . . . je t'aime."

"Oh, Bête!" She knelt by him. "I knew it, you *can*, you will. No, don't hide your face. Look at me, Bête. Look."

She saw then what the effort had cost him, tightening the muscles of his jaw, the tears streaking down the carved features giving the animal vacancy a lugubrious aspect.

"Say again, Bête."

He would not and she knew it. He turned away from her, retreating once more into his peculiar hiding place. It was enough though, more than enough. She would light extra candles and thank Mary specially for good Bête, and tell Père Vaudan that he might lend his weight to the prayers. And perhaps at vespers, instead of waiting for her at the church door, Bête might stand beside her at mass.

That would be good, she thought. One more place where she wouldn't have to walk alone.

IV

It was well past twelve when he finished with Vaudan. After a quick bite in the scullery and dressing for the hunt, it had gone two before Hugh was in the saddle.

His father's trail followed no perceptible logic. From the plateau south of the bridge, they turned east toward Eston Nab, fighting up the slippery hill. The horses must be half winded already. Broad skid marks showed where one had slipped and fallen on its side. They went on to the snow-buried earth house, then turned west again, retracing their own track for at least two miles, more like four to the struggling horses in this snow. Obviously Eustace meant to fan south Tees for signs of Gurth, but then the horses and men would be cold and spent and the daylight all but gone when they settled down to hunt.

Well short of the forest, the party swung south again, fanning out in a wide arc, then veered northwest again. Several miles east of the tree line, they intersected the footprints in the snow.

Working his toes against the cold, Hugh dismounted and bent to the tracks: two men, foraging out to this point from one of the holdings. Plowwright and his son, most like; they were the closest. A few shreds of cabbage leaf and other signs indicated one of the cunning snares at which their peasants were so adept. Hugh noticed the small paw prints leading to the trodden area. These were fainter, all but obliterated by the wind-driven dry snow. The two men had collected their game and returned by the same path, walking in their own tracks to save energy. Logical.

What was not logical—the hunting party followed them when it should have struck due west for the deeper woods and likely game.

Hugh urged the laboring horse faster, reckoning not more than an hour of daylight left. Clearly, Eustace had no interest in hunting, but was tracking the two men in the feverish hope that one of them might be Bastard. Small chance: Bastard was too cunning, the farmers too frightened to walk with him in broad daylight and leave a trail a blind idiot could follow.

The foot trail detoured again to another trap still baited and unsprung, stopped well clear of it and turned north again, Eustace and the others following doggedly.

"What in hell is he *doing?*"

The men would be worn out with cold before the hunt began while Eustace badgered after two harmless serfs. Hugh began to feel the unrelenting cold creep into him. Even with the long English tunic, heavy trousers and thick wrappings under his shoes, the chill worked steadily up his limbs. He worked his toes more rapidly in the stirrups, pushing faster in the wake of the party. The tracks were very fresh now, barely half an hour old as they neared the northern fringe of trees.

He sighted them at last, thirty or so yards into the trees. A small fire had been built; his father sat nearby on a log. Bound together across from him, Plowwright and his son sprawled in the snow. The fire was not large, yet the seven other men, Aimeré among them, showed no eagerness to crowd close around it or their lord. Though the sun was near the horizon, there seemed no general move to depart. Hugh stepped down and gave his reins to Bertin, greeting Aimeré who drifted disconsolately to meet him.

"Will you hunt, Sergeant?"

The man blew on his hands. "I don't know, sir."

Hugh lingered, not anxious to brook his father yet. Aimeré stamped his feet vigorously.

"What were you doing?" Hugh asked. "I followed your trail halfway to York and back."

"Aye," Aimeré's blue lips and chattering teeth punctuated

his misery. "And up and down and back across till I'm frozen through."

"And Plowwright?"

Aimeré was unable to conceal his disgust. "We found the tracks: two of them out after rabbits." Cold and fatigue scraped away his reserve. "Just the man and his son, out after a stinking rabbit. A *babe* could see what it was, but—we followed. The baron thought one might be Gurth."

The unspoken comment passed between them.

"It could have been," Hugh observed tactfully.

"The baron says they did meet him," Aimeré went on distastefully. "And they know where he is."

"Today?" Hugh frowned. "I saw the tracks; nothing but that rabbit crossed their trail."

Aimeré shook his head. "I don't know, sir. My men are cold. We want to go home, but—"

The other men seemed as low-spirited as Aimeré. One of them coiled the end of a rope used for trussing game into a complicated knot, his hands slowed by cold and reluctance. He gave it a final loop and then Hugh saw why the man didn't hurry.

"What in Christ's name—?"

"He's going to hang Plowwright," Aimeré told him. "And one a week, he says. Until they give him Bastard."

Wind swayed the tree tops, keening higher as the sun set, branches groaning in its wake. A horse whinnied, protesting cold and hunger while Aimeré struggled with his strained loyalty.

"They met no one, sir. Nothing. One can *see* . . ."

"All right, Aimeré." Hugh clapped him on the shoulder and walked to the log where his father sat contemplating the two peasants. They looked cold. Pitiful beside them was the half-frozen carcass of a rabbit. About Robin's age but much larger, the boy fought against brimming tears. Hugh sat down on the log, spreading his hands toward the meager fire. His father acknowledged him curtly.

"Messire knight."

"My lord."

Each sensed the tension in the other and coiled in preparation. Whatever was to be said could not be avoided another day.

Hugh looked at John Plowwright and his son, remembering them both in the fields in high summer. He was riding to hawk and heard them singing as they worked. As he rode by, Plowwright waved out of sheer good spirits. The boy once brought a cross carven out of bone for Vaudan to bless. Intricate work, the whole surface teeming with individual figures and designs worked in with awl and knife point. Fine, delicate work for such big hands. Must have taken him weeks.

Is Vaudan right? Could I hear your confession and really care?

"You're going to hang Plowwright?" he began at last. "Why?"

"Aimeré told you?"

"He did," Hugh nodded slightly. He let out his breath. "There was a time when I thought Gurth Bastard the biggest fool on the moor. But you, *mon père,* have made him appear a stumbling novice."

"I told you this morning to watch that tongue of yours," Eustace said levelly. "You think I will always stomach your insults because you are my son?"

"It is not insult," said Hugh with a rock-bottom stubbornness new to Eustace. "It is fact." He jerked his head at the bound farmer. "Look at Plowwright, just look at him: scared to death. I would be too, going to hang in five minutes and God knows why. And one a week until they give you Bastard? Or just for the vindictive pleasure of it? Christ," he finished disgustedly, "your own men don't know what to make of you."

Eustace rose, hovering over his son, looking for a hatred that he could fight openly. He found only revulsion. "I'm sick of you questioning what I do. Sick of your superior judgments, sick of you. You never did have any insides, Hugh. No pride, no—"

"What you mean," his son answered with quiet contempt, "is that I never had your ambition. You're the one needed to rise out of Neuville's barnyard, Baron."

"Yes!" Eustace hissed. "My father left me a name and a pride and damned little else. You think it was easy winning this place? I took you all out of that barnyard. I put you in front of the duke, made it possible for you to win your spurs. Guy or Robin would have been better; they wouldn't spit on it as you do. I don't know you, man. You had *everything.*"

"I had nothing," Hugh shot back. "I've had nothing long enough. I wrote a letter today to the Abbot of Sockburn."

Eustace stared blankly at him.

"When we've found Bastard, I'll go to be a brother."

"A broth—" The baron took a moment to assimilate the statement. "Are you serious?"

"Quite."

Hugh saw something flicker in his father's hard eyes, a tiny retreat behind the armor as the meaning sank in. "You are the last. Montford will go back to the Crown on my death. Out of the *family!*"

"I'm sorry for that."

"Is this to spite me?"

"No." Hugh rose to his feet. "I've always wanted it. When you took me to the duke's steward and said 'Here's my son. He'll ride with me'; when our horses almost went mad with the smell of blood at Hastings, when we could hardly get up that filthy hill for slipping in it; when I lay in my tent afterwards, listening to the Saxon women keening all night for their dead on the field, I wanted God."

He tried to keep his voice steady with all that could no longer be held back. "I'm not afraid of you anymore. Guy and Robin were closer to what you wanted. That doesn't matter now. But your treatment of Gerlaine—"

Eustace stiffened. "My daughter, boy."

"My *sister.* You've worked her like a servant; she bore it and loved you. You blamed her for Mother's death—"

Eustace stepped closer, white. The men couldn't help hearing, but they pretended not to. "Shut up, Hugh. I warn you."

"—and she's bled white inside for it. You shamed her in front of people whose loyalty and respect she must have. You . . . you," he began to tremble with it, "you've turned Mother's death into a vengeance that's killing us all like slow poison. Where do you *stop!*"

Their voices had sharpened and risen. The men watched openly now, awkward and concerned.

"You question my courage? Who fought Brand, Eustace? Who helped you take his lands for your own? And who took his wife down when our own hymn-screaming pigs crucified her like Mother?"

Strange—the pictured memory of it, horrible as it was, tripped that restless, dispassionate corner of his mind. *Cruci-fied,* the engine clicked into life apart from his anger. *Like Mother.*

"No insides?" Hugh quavered with mounting fury. "No stomach for war? You're damned right!" He whipped out his sword and rammed it into the ground with the massed force of his outraged soul. "There's the gift you hung on me like a penitent's chain, Baron. It and you disgust me!"

Eustace's hand whipped up and out, lashing the heavy gauntlet across Hugh's face. "That you were born first or at all," he clipped the words with icy precision, "is a matter of profound regret." He dropped the gauntlet at Hugh's feet. "You wish to make answer?"

"My lords," Aimeré stepped close to them, sibilant with urgency. "In front of the men. The English?"

"No fear," Hugh assured him. The blow stung doubly with the cold, but it had stopped his violent trembling. The taut muscles relaxed as he breathed deep. "The baron forgot himself. I will not."

They faced each other across the bitter chasm of years. *Damn him,* Eustace raged. *Why does he look so sad? Fight me. Touch me. Touch something, Hugh.*

"If Sir Hugh has no further objections," he said to Aimeré, "we will proceed. Bring the rope."

The noose was tossed over a tree limb, the slack end secured to a saddle. They hauled Plowwright to his feet and fitted the loop about his neck. Tied to a tree, the boy strained toward his father. Plowwright tried to stand straight, but the cold mixed with fear in his stomach. He shuddered violently.

"T-take care of your mum, boy."

The boy jerked at the ropes in a paroxysm of helpless rage. "Don't kill my da—"

He loves his father. Hugh envied him, not needing to understand the words. *He's got something I never had.*

He looked at the sword impaled in the ground. Without knowing clearly what he would do, Hugh stretched out his hand to it.

"Understand me or not," Eustace said to the struggling youth. "One week until you bring him in." He turned to Aimeré. "Ready?"

He's going to do it, Hugh realized, his fingers closing around the sword hilt.

"Pull him up!"

Smacked on the rump, the horse jumped forward three or four paces, restrained by the two men on its bridle. The boy screamed. Plowwright kicked frantically at the air, then the sword whistled through the rope, tumbling him to the ground. Hugh jerked the rope loose from his heaving throat.

"In the name of *God,* Father!"

They stood frozen in tableau, Eustace speechless with disbelief. Dissension, discontent, even desertion he might expect from Hugh, but not open mutiny. He tried in vain to discern a wavering of resolution in Hugh's crouch. The sword came up, pointing at him in accusation and challenge.

"Someone must stop you, man. Now."

Eustace threw aside his cloak and scabbard, drawing the sword.

"No!" Aimeré thrust himself between them, bewildered. "You are my lords; this is not needed. Baron, let the farmers go. They're not worth this."

But it had gone beyond turning back. They barely heard him.

"Get out of the way," said the baron.

"My lord!"

"Do as he says, Sergeant." Hugh handed over his cloak and belt.

Aimeré hung between them for a moment, then stepped back in resignation. "Then let the right prevail."

They circled slowly in the trodden snow, feeling at the ground with practiced feet for the slippery patch, the buried branch that might trip them up. Eustace had years on him for experience, Hugh knew. Without armor, any wound inflicted could be mortal, surely serious. Short of a deep wound, it would be hard to stop his father and equally difficult to escape harm himself.

The heavy sword spun like a toy in his father's callused palm: once, twice, each time checked at precisely the guard position. Hugh set his feet; the next spin might come flashing out in any one of several possible attacks. He was right. A blur too swift for the eye streaked forward in a vertical head chop. Hugh parried, his sword whipping in at Eustace's left shoulder. The blades met shrilly in the cold air, Eustace pressing in, Hugh giving ground, defending himself with a deftness his father coldly admired.

It would not be easy to take Hugh. Trick after trick, feint on thrust, Hugh's sword was there to guard, his movements pared to a masterful economy. He had not survived in the field out of sheer luck, and he might begin to take an edge on endurance. Already Eustace was breathing more rapidly than his son.

The blades poised, wavering and close, seeking a hole; then Eustace lunged in a straight thrust so sudden that Hugh's countering step backward was badly balanced, the parry flat against his gut. He countered in a backstroke, one smooth movement out of the steel-wristed parry, but his feet were badly set in the treacherous snow. As his weight swung forward behind the blow, he slipped—an instant only. The sound of Eustace's deflecting maneuver was light as a toy bell. His sword hissed in an arc to cut Hugh's left arm to the bone.

"Là!"

Aimeré sucked breath. It was over. The boy would be mangled for life.

Instead of the sickening sound of iron against flesh, he heard the *tang* of metal. Off-balance, Hugh had recovered swiftly enough to deflect the main force of the blow. He stepped back, crouching at guard, still in the fight. But his mouth was drawn tight, the lips colorless, and Aimeré saw the severed cloth of his sleeve.

The blow must have cut into muscle. He knew he was bleeding, perhaps badly. He was a fool to fight defensively. Now time was his father's ally.

So now we play a different game, mon père.

His sword flicked out like a snake's tongue, bare inches from Eustace's throat. His foot slid forward.

Hide and seek.

Again the blade darted out. Eustace sought to engage, but the sword simply was not there. Wherever he tried to meet Hugh's iron, it danced away.

And—so!

A wheel of light caught the last rays of the dying sun, changing direction in mid-whirl. Eustace, parrying overhead, felt the shallow sting lick across his shoulder. He backed. Hugh moved forward, his mouth set in a slight smile of concentration, sword circling in wide, rapid loops, evading the other blade. Suddenly he shot forward in a complex attack, the sword everywhere, battering in on his father. Eustace gave ground slowly, realizing just too late the deceptive rhythm of the strokes. It was a master's trick, the establishment of a false beat, a slower pattern before the sudden lightning move that would end it all.

"*Hé—là!*"

Hugh lunged, disengaging in a silver arc that flashed in again over Eustace's guard, slamming the flat of the blade cruelly across his cheekbone. Eustace seemed to hang suspended, then he dropped like a sack, stunned. When his vision cleared, he was lying in the snow with Hugh's sword pressed to his throat. Only their heavy breathing broke the silence.

Then Hugh stepped away, cut Plowwright loose and then his son. He scooped up the rabbit and heaved it at the bewildered boy.

"Go home, Englishman. *Va!* Go!"

Unable to comprehend any of it, John Plowwright knew only that he was saved. Like Hugh, he would never know why. The two Saxons scurried away out of the trees.

"Your arm, sir," Aimeré reached for him.

"Leave me alone," Hugh snarled. "Get away from me!" The words choked off as the killer intensity drained out of him. He raised the sword once more. "Let me be quit of this!"

Hugh swung the weapon broadside with all his strength against a tree trunk, snapping the blade. He dropped the broken hilt beside it. "Sergeant."

"Aye, sir."

"Look to my father." Hugh swayed against the tree trunk, dizzy, poking clumsily at his sleeve. There was not much blood.

But I'm cold. I didn't know it could be so cold.

Eustace staggered up unsteadily, thrusting away Aimeré's offered arm. He fixed on Hugh, saw the knight falter slightly and be steadied by one of the men.

"Take whatever's yours and get off my land," Eustace spat hoarsely, the bleeding bruise already swelling on his cheek. "You're dead to me."

Hugh put his foot in the stirrup, grasping awkwardly at the pommel with his good arm.

"You might as well be a monk," his father said. "Nothing of mine will ever come to you. I'd sell it to the Jews first!"

With difficulty, Hugh hauled himself into the saddle, reeled and then willed himself erect. He fumbled for the reins.

"You hear me!" Eustace threw at him. "Off!"

"God help you, Father."

V

Vespers was over but Gerlaine lingered in the church besieging patient Vaudan with news and questions and displaying her Bête like a trophy. Bête *spoke* to her, said words clear as she could, and in *Frank,* too. And did Père Vaudan mark how he stood beside her at mass, and were there special prayers to speed his recovery?

"I will give extra prayers for him," Vaudan promised, happy to see Gerlaine so animated. Too often now she looked older than her eighteen years, the firm mouth turned down at the corners in bitter parentheses.

"I'm sure God meant me to find him in that church. Still," Vaudan concluded, "I would have thought him born dim. Well!" He clapped the huge shoulders as Bête looked down at him impassively. *"Ma grande Bête. C'est bon.* There is hope. But the supper," he reminded Gerlaine. "Your people will be needing you."

"Yes, yes." She took Bête's hand, leading him like a tame bear. "I just wanted to tell you. God has not completely forgotten us."

"He has not forgotten at all."

He saw the smile harden on her mouth. "Do you believe that?"

She wanted an answer Vaudan could not give as readily as

236

before. When he did reply, he seemed vaguely troubled. "If I did not, I'd take off this cloth and work in the fields."

The church door swung open; the dim figure paused in silhouette, leaning against the arch of the doorway, then entered the nave. Gerlaine started toward him, saw him weave with fatigue.

"Hugh?"

He brushed past her and fell against the altar rail.

"You're hurt!" She gave a little cry. "Your arm is all blood."

"Leave it." His hands clasped together. He prayed silently over them, then fell back against the railing, his good arm around Gerlaine. Hugh was not badly hurt, she perceived, but drained by exhaustion and the cold.

"Come, be close to me. I did it, Vaudan. I broke that miserable sword across a tree. And Father has given me his blessing." He held up the bloody sleeve. "After his gentle fashion."

"You fought?" Gerlaine asked. "What happened?"

Hugh laughed weakly. "You should have seen, Père Vaudan: I actually cared. *Magnifique!*"

"So you have told him?"

"Indeed, a great deal."

"You're worn out and frozen through." Gerlaine fluttered over him. "What happened?"

He told her elliptically of Plowwright, the reasonless punishment. "I stopped him, God knows why. Perhaps I was just sick of it."

Vaudan pressed him for news. "Is the baron badly hurt?"

"Just . . . stopped. Maybe I knocked some sense into him." Hugh pulled Gerlaine close and kissed her nose. *"Ça va, jolie?* Vaudan, is there wine?"

"Just the Breton I use for communion. Miserable stuff."

"My throat is dry," Hugh said. "Please pour me some." He touched Gerlaine's cheek. "I must go tomorrow. Did Vaudan tell you of my letter to the abbot?"

"Yes." Her eyes clouded a little. "You should go."

He felt for the loneliness in the sighed words. They both sipped from the cup offered by Vaudan.

"Come away with me, Gerlaine. Bring your Bête and leave this miserable place."

"I can't."

"I won't let Father hold you here. I'll go to the king before Sockburn, all the way to Winchester if I have to."

"It's not him," Gerlaine said with a chill calm. "I don't want to go yet. Sooner or later, Bastard will come for me, and he must pass Bête. And Bête will kill him. After I've done with him," she finished.

She might have been giving orders to Bodo about rats in the cellar. "Now let me see your arm."

"Leave it," he tried to push her away.

"Hugh, let me see."

"No."

The word was hard as iron: "Bête!"

The big mute moved like a shadow and Hugh was pinned against the railing. He fancied the ghost of a gentle smile curved the thick lips. It was not worth disputing.

"You see," Gerlaine reached for his arm, "he understands enough. Now lie still."

She ripped open the sleeve and washed the wound with convenient holy water. Hugh's head tilted back; he let his eyes wander to escape the blankness of Bête so close to him. The crucifix lay across the corner of his vision.

Again, oddly, he remembered Algive. The engine worked in its box with something it could not accept, something not quite in balance.

Something missing . . .

"Pray for my lord!"

Aimeré stumbled out of the darkness near the open door, so drained with cold and fatigue he looked drunk. He flopped down beside Hugh; without invitation, he took a long drink of the blood-warming wine. "Père Vaudan, pray for us all. Jesus, may I see the last of this place soon!"

A cup was brought for him. "You're shaking," Vaudan said. "Where are your men? Where's the baron?"

"The men are here." Aimeré gulped at the cup, spilling in his haste. "The baron—I don't know." The sergeant's head wove back and forth in weary confusion. "We tried to help him, get him to come home. He pulled away from us. Held us off with his sword. Told us to get away, leave him. I swear," Aimeré begged their understanding, "I know that look in him. He would have killed us. Even me."

"Then," Vaudan looked at the son and daughter. "He is alone out there? Where Bastard can find him?"

"He rode off," said Aimeré weakly. "I think he wants Bastard to find him. To kill him or be killed or Christ knows what. Pray for him." The man's voice fretted on the edge of tears. "Pray for us all."

"You cannot leave him out there, Hugh." Vaudan was firm.

Gerlaine's head jerked up. "Why not?"

Vaudan stared at her. "You can ask that?"

"Better him than Hugh!"

"Sweet but debatable," said Hugh.

"Someone must go," Vaudan insisted. "That devil who has crept in even here past the guards—how hard would it be to take your father on the moor when he's weak and sick inside with things that neither of you will ever understand, *hé?*" The little priest bristled with conviction. "You must! You fail this, I'll damn you myself!"

"It's true, Sister. We have to go."

Aimeré lay against the railing beside Hugh, feeling himself drift the moment his eyes shut. "Go where?" he said with an effort. "Where can we start?"

Hugh dipped a finger into the wine and drew on the floorboards. "The keep, the forest, the holdings. Plowwright nearest. Father wouldn't go there, that boy would cut his throat if he closed his eyes. The next, Calla, Godric Carpenter . . . burned out. What comes after?"

Aimeré hovered over the makeshift map, then added a circle beyond the others. "Swegen and his wife. Would he go there?"

"We can start there."

Aimeré sighed; his head drooped. He raised it with an exertion of will. "How many men, sir?"

"Myself and two of your best."

"Yourself and me, sir," the sergeant corrected him. "That's a good man out there, the best damn soldier out of Normandy. And Fitz: he's good as salt when he's not—" Aimeré glanced quickly at Gerlaine. "—distracted."

"Eat and rest first." Gerlaine helped Hugh to his feet. "You'll be useless without it."

Hugh swayed, dizzy with fatigue. "Two hours, Aimeré. Tell Fitz."

When they were gone, Bête shambling after, Aimeré poured

more wine, tossed it off and made a face, "Damn Brittany vinegar. Père Vaudan, I wish confession. Now, if you will be kind enough."

Vaudan studied him: twenty years a soldier, the black hair beginning to thread here and there with gray. A strong, simple man, sure of his courage and aware of his limits.

"You are troubled?"

Aimeré looked into his cup. "No more than any man here, however that stands. I'm afraid. No matter what Sir Hugh says, that's a devil out there. A devil who only looks like a man. I don't want to meet him unshriven."

There was no clear purpose in Eustace's mind when he rode away from his men, only a heartsickness that had to be endured alone. His life was a running sore with Gurth Bastard at its rotten center. He wanted no more than to find and fling himself at the evil, destroy it or be consumed—now—tonight, before another sundown. Because of Gurth, life had blighted before it bloomed. The tough, ready boys were cold in the ground with Élène, her image gone sour and gnarled in his bleak daughter, the last hope spit back with Hugh's sword.

What infected you two? Gerlaine, you are so much like her when it was all new. Your body is like hers, hard and clean. I couldn't let him touch you.

The tired horse stumbled; instinctively, Eustace took up the reins. The horse was cold and spent as he was. He pulled her up and strained his eyes into the white twilight. His direction-less wandering had led him westward of the forest. The mount needed rest and grain and his own head throbbed. He could feel the bruise swelling under the break in the skin where Hugh had well-nigh clubbed the wits out of him.

He broke his sword like it was dirt; he's always been ashamed of it. A stranger out of Élène's body, neither hers nor mine. I could never touch him.

The horse faltered again and began to favor its left foreleg. Eustace stepped down and inspected the limb. It might be a sprain. Normandy horses were not surefooted in snow like this. He struck out toward the river, leading the horse by the bridle, shoulders hunched against the wind, trying to orient himself on the darkening moor. He was well past Plowwright's; he didn't want to see or think on them anyway. Swegen's would be the

closest croft. They'd be frightened but no matter. He only
wanted shelter for the mare and a bit of warmth.

The wind cut painfully at his bruised cheek as he peered to
recognize guiding landmarks. He recognized the Corn-
Woman's ruin half buried in the snow. Beyond that would be
Godric's place.

*Was the vengeance all for him, Bastard? Whatever you are,
man or demon, I never understood you either. You and Hugh,
you ask more than men should. God points to one and says
Make bread and till the ground; to Vaudan, He says Show
them the Way to Me. To myself He said Be a lord and take care
of them, keep order. Can I say to Him—No, I won't? I don't
feel like leading?*

Lords are lords. God forgive me, I am so sick of it all.

The mare coughed her misery.

"Old woman," Eustace eased her along. "We've about spun
our web, haven't we? Come on, not far now."

He was in actual pain from the cold when he struck weakly
against the rough boards of Swegen's door.

"Who's there?"

"Ouvrez! C'est le seigneur." Then he added, "De Neuville."

The door opened a crack and Swegen's arm thrust out with a
fat lamp. At once he pushed the door open, and Eustace caught
the fear in the peasant's eyes. *He thinks I'm going to punish
him again.* He started to push by the man, then something
deterred him. Their rigid custom of hearth-right for which
Godric died, that began their nightmare, came back to him.
Eustace waited for Swegen to wave him in. The two of them
led the limping mount into the shelter with Swegen's ox.

"Give him feed," the baron directed. "I will send more in the
morning."

He dropped down in front of the peat fire with a reassuring
nod to Gunhild who stood well back from the light and afraid
to come closer.

"It's all right." He rubbed his frozen hands over the fire. His
sense of smell tried hopelessly to ignore the stink of the hut. It
offended him, but through the barn odors one rich trace wafted
and courted his hunger: cooked stew in the pot over the fire,
delectable and hearty. He looked at the pot.

Swegen and Gunhild squatted across from him, watching

their lord, seeing for the first time the slightness of the body
that housed such infernal energy. Battered, cold and sick, the
drive gone out of him, he looked like a beaten fox gone to
ground, eyes distant and closing with fatigue.

"He's hurt," Swegen pointed. "His head."

Eustace signed Gunhild to fetch a bowl. She didn't move.
He found a bowl himself and dipped into the stew, seeing at
once why Gunhild hesitated. Beside the rabbit, turnip, cabbage
and boiled roots, the stew was thick with chunks of fresh
venison. A quick anger flared in Eustace: not three weeks gone
Swegen had been lashed for poaching, and now—

Oh, Christ, let it go. For once be blind and eat, fool.

He glanced up at them after several spoonfuls. They were
holding their breath. He tapped the spoon against the bowl.
"Swegen," he mumbled gruffly in bad English, "your wife
makes good rabbit stew."

He shouldn't take too much. They'd need every crumb they
could hoard before spring came. He allowed himself one
helping where three would not have filled him, emptied the
bowl and set it aside.

"Thank you."

He lay back on the dirt floor, one hand worrying at the
throbbing cheek. The fire's warmth released his exhaustion,
lulling him within moments to shallow sleep. He came up out
of a shadowy dream of fighting Hugh while Bastard watched
and laughed at both of them. Gunhild crouched over him,
dabbing at the wound.

"Lie down," she murmured. "Rest, man."

No woman had touched him since Élène. He submitted
gratefully. Hugh's blow broke more than his skin. It shattered
the tight knot inside where nothing else could reach. Detached,
he saw dispassionately the madness that had made him want to
hang Plowwright, saw it full-blown and how, step by step, he
had come to it.

The woman's hands were balm; like Élène soothing a
headache, or long ago when they lay together after love,
tracing slow patterns across each other's skin, full of the
unquenchable wonder of hands. He would take her fingers and
put them in his mouth—

"Élène . . ."

He snapped awake. Gunhild padded the damp cloth over his forehead.

"The man's sick," Gunhild said. "Like a fever."

Every movement an effort, Eustace raised himself on one elbow.

"Swegen, I must find Gurth. You hear? Gurth." Struggling with signs and fragments of a language he despised, Eustace worked desperately to make the Saxon understand. "In the spring we must plant. There will be no lord . . . no *hlaford* . . . to protect you. Danes may come. Help me . . . *helfen*, man. For all of us, Gurth must die."

The woman huddled by her husband. They spoke in soft, rapid gutturals.

"We don't know where Gurth is," Swegen evaded. "What can we tell him?"

But Gunhild's jaw set. "He's right."

"About what?"

"You heard enough. If the Danes come and there's no lord, what's left for us?"

Her husband looked away. "Gurth's a friend, 'Hild."

She hissed her impatience. "Brandeshal's dead as the thane. What have we to do with blood feuds? We've kept their secrets long enough. What else do we have but the planting?" She challenged him with it. "What else?"

Swegen's head dropped on his arms. "Yes."

Gunhild took a wooden spoon and began to etch in the dirt. "Not gone or frozen, there's only one place he could be."

She drew a large square with smaller squares about it, then pointed east. "Godric Carpenter."

"Yes," Eustace understood. "Godric's farm."

Within the largest square, Gunhild drew a smaller rectangle, then made a scooping motion with her hand, patted the floor and repeated the sign.

"Under," she said. "Under the floor."

A root cellar. For a farm like Carpenter's it must be easily large enough for a man to find comfortable shelter, even a fire at night.

In the middle of the rectangle, Gunhild cut a cross.

"Gurth."

VI

Even in exhausted sleep the engine would not stop.

Crucified, it whispered. *Like Mother.*

Someone touched his shoulder. Still asleep, his body spun in the bed. The hand closed about the dagger.

"Sir, it's Aimeré!"

Hugh blinked up at the dim form.

"We've overslept, sir. I thought you'd want to get started."

"Yes," Hugh shook the haze from his mind. "Yes . . . what hour?"

"Near ten," Aimeré lighted the candle from the fireplace and set it by Hugh's bed. "Everyone's abed, even *maîtresse*. I rousted Fitz. He'll meet us at the bridge."

"Thank you. I won't be long."

Hugh swung his legs over the edge of the bed, allowing himself a moment to come fully awake, massaging vigorously at his face. The engine stirred again. *Why?* The question nagged like a toothache as he splashed icy water over his face and hands.

It doesn't fit. Why?

A late start was unavoidable. Neither of them would have been much good without rest. Wrapped in thick, hooded cloaks, they led their horses to the bridge where Fitz was already mounted, a black mass huddled inside his cloak.

"Save you," Hugh yawned by way of greeting. Fitz raised a hand in salute, cradling his crossbow in the other.

"We'll make for Swegen's." Hugh ordered. "Rest the mounts if they need it and work out from there. If we see Bastard, don't wait the order from me. Kill him. Keep your bolts close to hand," he advised. "With a longbow he can get off three shots to your one. Hallo, tower!"

Out of the darkness above, the guard answered. "Sir Hugh? Aimeré?"

"Lower the bridge. We're going out."

A pale moon pied the moor, now clear, now covered by the broken clouds scudding rapidly before the sea wind.

"That's a dangerous sky," Aimeré said.

"Will it break tonight, you think?"

Aimeré studied the twisting clouds as the wind drove them westward. "Tomorrow sometime. No later."

They rode in silence awhile, Hugh and Aimeré roughly abreast, Fitz trailing half a dozen paces behind. The wind whispered about them, the only sound beside the steady crunch of hooves in the snow. Aimeré set a bolt, wound it cocked and held the bow aloft for the rider behind.

"Fitz! Load and be ready."

The rider held up the nocked bow.

Hugh began to feel the first of the insidious cold in his heavily wrapped toes. "I hope Father went to Swegen's."

"He did, sir. Or one of the others," Aimeré was confident. "He's too shrewd to let himself freeze."

Hugh wriggled his toes. "The question is, are we?"

The horses worked on; talk dwindled to monosyllables then died out as each man contended with the cold and the peculiar loneliness bred by the moor. They passed Plowwright's small steading and the ruin of Calla's hut, a dark smudge on the snow. Deep in the narrow world framed by Hugh's hood, his vision restricted to the horse's head and the ground before him, the engine growled again.

Why, it persisted. *It doesn't make sense.*

There was no reason for it, not even an emotional tie. Algive of Brandeshal was no relation, no blood to Gurth. Hugh recalled what Gerlaine had told him of the Deira Book, of "the moor witch and her bastard." Algive kept after Brand to put them aside, but he couldn't really leave them. He protected

Calla all his life and sent Gurth to Paris for an education any
scholar would envy. Would Algive welcome him in her hall,
the child of her rival, seeing him favored as much or more than
her own sons? Very likely she and Gurth met seldom if ever.
He even looks like Calla. He'd remind her every minute. How
close could they have been?

Not at all, said the engine.

To kill Élène, Gurth had his pick of place and time. Why
then should he make her death a painstaking copy of that meted
out to a woman he barely knew and could not possibly have
loved? As Vaudan pondered so desperately, it would be easy
for him—always knowing when and where to find the next one
alone. Mother . . . Robin . . . Guy, appearing as easily as he
vanished before them on the moor.

But he didn't really vanish, did he?

There was a place to go; they had discovered it. How he
found them so surely must have its answer as well. How?

He churned the question through all his proven assumptions,
added the factor of guards, the heavy odds against escaping
detection. How could Gurth know when to come, walk the
bailey and stay free as a ghost?

The engine groped at the question, worked it, turned it over
and gave the only possible answer.

He couldn't. Unless—

The thud of the bolt driving home through leather and flesh
jerked him awake before he heard Aimeré's shocked cry. Hugh
threw back his hood, whirling to see the sergeant fall forward
into the snow, one leg dangling from the stirrup. They were in
the open, no chance of an ambush. Hugh wheeled his horse. A
few paces behind, calm and intent, Fitz wound another bolt
ready.

"Fitz, what—?"

And then he saw what darkness and the heavy cloak had
disguised. The tall bulk of the rider, cleverly foreshortened
under the mantle's wide folds and rising now to formidable
height, was much too large to be Fitz.

*Unless I've been so clever, I couldn't see. We told him. We
pointed the way, signed their deaths every time.*

A wave of primordial hate burned through Hugh as the last
answer battered into his mind.

"You devil!" He kicked the horse into a running charge,

sword out and already spinning under the genius of his hand.
"You won't get my sister! You won't get her, damn you!"

The bolt took him full in the chest; the rider reined easily
aside as Hugh's horse plunged by. Then, with last instinct,
Hugh's hands tightened on the reins, knees transmitting his
will. The horse plowed to a stop, wheeling, and carried Hugh
forward once more as the pain rolled through him. The rider
had thrown aside his bow and drawn his sword. Hugh bent
over the horse's neck in his final charge, rasping out his
challenge.

"*Gardez!*"

In the last clear moment of his life, Hugh shouted aloud for
pure battle joy. He had found his answer.

He wanted Bastard tonight, alone and off guard, as Gurth
had taken them one by one. And with the evil of that hellish
mind blotted out, life might begin again.

He was changed: the fight with Hugh, the strangely poignant
hours in Swegen's hut, Gunhild's hands on him had taken
Eustace out of the prison of the moment and brought him
ultimately to the humanity long stifled under ambitious pride.
He was relaxed as after a deep, untroubled sleep—free of
tension, able to think of Hugh and Gerlaine without defensive
anger. There must be a softening from all of them, a reaching
out, otherwise they killed each other with no need of Gurth. He
would ask them—ask, not demand—to talk. They might take
supper in the bower where Élène had preserved the aura of
Neuville and home. They might talk as family again. But first
Gurth had to be cut from the healthy flesh of their lives.

He led the horse forward over the snow, listening to the
eternal whisper of the wind as it died away and then sprang up
again, snow ghosts dancing in circles as the current took them.
Only half an hour out of Swegen's hut and already the
loneliness of the moor seeped into him, palpable as cold.
Vaudan said he never felt lonely before coming here. It was
true. The moor made you feel small and alone. The thought
bemused him, but he did not pursue it. Carpenter's place
wasn't far. He'd best be ready.

The moon broke out of covering clouds into a patch of clear
sky, drenching the white moor with cold brightness. Eustace
halted, his hand clenching the bridle reins.

The tall figure waited directly in his path thirty yards ahead, leaning on the great sword, dead still except for the heavy fluttering of the hooded cloak. Behind him the horse waited.

"*Qui va là?*" Eustace called. "Hugh?"

The wind answered him. He knew it wasn't his son as he came closer, not that massive shape rearing above six foot. The omniscient Bastard had found him as usual, had come at last for the end. Eustace edged forward until a mere ten paces separated them. He felt marvelous, ready.

"Gurth Bastard?"

"*Brandson.*"

Eustace smiled with satisfaction. He undid the clasp of his mantle and let it drop into the snow. "We're well met, then," he answered quietly, without even the small thrill in his blood that usually came a moment before combat. The clear thing was here to be done, his world in focus again. He whipped the sword free and dropped the scabbard. "I've come for you, Bastard."

Still the silhouetted shape made no preparatory move to combat. "De Neuville—"

The deep voice constricted with passion. "You are the one I've wanted, the one I've waited for."

Eustace moved forward, learning the ground with his feet. The point of his sword rose toward the hooded throat. "Come on, then," he urged. "Why do you wait?" His sword flicked out. "Are women and boys all you can kill? Come on, Bastard."

Once more his sword darted out, close enough for a thrust if he had desired; the next instant the blade was all but torn from his grasp as the huge sword swept up with brutal force, knocking it aside. Eustace recoiled; *steady . . . steady. Not too close.* He had taken Hugh that night in the hall with a trick and those long legs. *Don't give him that edge.*

"You *pig!*"

The words ripped out on the cold air as the big man moved, lifting his sword in both hands and beginning to circle. The blades wavered closer like hostile dogs, touched lightly.

"You took everything," the clear voice shook. "Everything that was ours."

Abruptly the words broke off, rising suddenly in a quavering, intense wail that pierced Eustace beyond his courage like the howl of a maddened dog.

"Take him, Loki! He is yours!"

Screaming, the huge *bear-sark* threw himself at Eustace, flailing the sword like a sledge. Eustace fell back, unequal to the maniac strength, his skill and speed useless against the inhuman blows that shook him with each impact. Desperately he tried to use distance; closer and closer the wailing brute force lunged and swung, shortening strokes until the hilts clanged together and locked. Eustace's wrist was caught in an inhuman grip. The next instant he was lifted high in the air and slammed on his back, the breath knocked out of him as the big man dove at him, sword forgotten, clubbing with hammer fists. The first blow broke his neck, mercifully blotting out the end of it. Except for a spasmodic twitching of his limbs, he did not move again, but still the lunatic rage battered at the slight frame, ripping at cloth, then at flesh with knife and fingers, forcing apart the shattered ribs and tearing at the beating heart, flinging it with a shriek to the wind; until the screaming went hoarse in the rawed throat and subsided to a whimper and the arms struck pointlessly at the shapeless thing already turning cold.

VII

The storm edged inland, a gray smudge on the eastern horizon. Calla gauged it cannily, trying to estimate its speed.

"There. Aycliffe cross. The earth house is just beyond."

Leading the pack horse, Beorn Gundar sighed gratefully. For the last six days Calla had set such a pace that, had he not been too proud to show the weakness, he would have cried out a hundred times over to stop and rest. But now at Aycliffe even the Corn-Woman was haggard with exertion.

"I'll take an hour or two's rest and go on," Calla told him as they neared the well-concealed rock shelter. "Stay hidden. You're on Montford land now."

That wouldn't be hard. They'd dodged Normans for a week, aided by weather that would keep all but madmen by the fire. Let him off the horse and Beorn Gundar would sleep till Candlemas.

"When will you be back?"

"Four days," she judged. "You've food for that long."

"And then?"

"Then wait as you can," Calla said. "If we're alive, we'll come."

WILLIAM, BY THE GRACE OF GOD KING OF THE ENGLISH, DUKE OF NORMANDY AND BRITTANY.

MY SOVEREIGN LORD—

The bearer of these news will tell you of the ill fortune that has befallen our family in ordering this fief of Montford, received by my father from your hand, and how through hell or human agency, my father, mother, brothers, and other good men have died—

. . . Digging Fitz's body out of the grain bin, stretching him on the stable floor, the one familiar bruise on his broken neck.

—and of that Saxon house, now extinct, which in its bastard descendant is the source of this evil.

. . . Slow horses winding toward the gate, the awkward burdens jolting back and forth when they slipped in the snow. Aimeré and Hugh. The third they did not uncover in her presence.

Dear my lord, I ask your prayers. I do not fear death, for that will only release me to Christ for Whom I am, I hope, prepared. Yet it will be many weeks before these news reach you, in which time I shall have found and punished the author of these crimes or succumbed myself.

. . . Mattocks gnawing at the ground, the holes deepening slowly. Men working in shifts to make progress against the frozen earth, punctuating the bite of the blade with their exertion.

"*Maîtresse?*"

"Aye, Père Vaudan?"

"It is time."

"Lower them."

Exaudi orationem meam; ad te omnis caro veniet. Kyrie eleison, Christe eleison.

Lamb of God, who takes away the world's sins, grant them rest. Let eternal light shine on them, O Lord, with thy saints throughout eternity, for Thou art good.

"I wish there were flowers."

"What, *Maîtresse?*"

"Flowers. We have none to give them."

May the angels receive thee in paradise; at thy coming may
the martyrs receive thee.
Go home, Hugh. Bless you for being my brother.

—and since I am the sole surviving child, yet lacking two
years of my majority, I must ask your benevolence in
declaring myself king's ward and the fief of Montford
reverted to Crown land.

*Et cum Lazaro quondam paupere, aeternum habeas re-
quiem. Amen.*
"Lady Gerlaine?"
"What, Thérèse?"
"They are done. Please come inside. It is cold."
". . . yes."

Until I am relieved, I will hold Montford in your name
and if God grant me the time, sow the arable land,
minister the peoples and maintain defense of all as did the
baron before me—

*I'm sorry, Father. Not for what you did to me or I to you, but
so many things I can't even name.*
"Where was I, Vaudan?"
" 'the baron before me.' "

—in loyalty and obedience, both of which I now tender
my lord.

Written at Montford-on-Tees.
Gerlaine de Neuville

Copying the letters spelled out by Vaudan, she scrawled
precariously beneath her name: *Chatelaine of Montford*. She
pressed her father's seal ring into the wax and handed the letter
to Ralph.

"Two couriers to York as soon as possible."

"They must wait," Ralph cautioned. "The storm will break
soon."

"Yes, surely," she agreed, too tired at the moment to insist.
"When it's over."

She moved away from the trestle table which had served as a

writing desk to the chair on the dais, the black mourning, so much a part of her now, accentuating the slightness of her body. Bête slouched to his accustomed place at her knee. They waited her pleasure—Vaudan, Ralph, and further back a dutiful delegation of the funeral: Swegen and Gunhild, Plowwright and his family, a few others. Ralph had mentioned some petition; she called him close.

"What do they want?"

"They say they have barely enough to last the winter." Ralph waved them forward. "They ask that you exempt them from any relief payments on your father's death."

Gerlaine twisted her eyebrows with thin fingers. "Plowwright," she ordered. "Come here."

He approached hesitantly. She saw the livid rope burn still raw on his neck. "You understand Frank?"

"If you speak slow, lady."

"*Attendez-moi:* you'd be dead but for my brother. Now you ask for more?"

"We have nothing to give, lady," he struggled. "Perhaps in the spring or at harvest."

"Not in the spring, John Plowwright! Your lord is dead. You have duties as he did. Remember, all of you, that as much effort has gone out from this house to stand between you and undue punishment as in pursuit of it. We won't take what you cannot spare, yet—"

Gerlaine paused abruptly. Ear cocked to one side, she listened. "That's strange."

As quickly she swerved back to the point, rising to stand over them. "Yet it will be paid in boon work, which you can spare. My steward will call on you. I will be fair," she concluded decisively, "but so will you." She stepped down from the dais. "Ralph, send them away. No, wait."

She pointed at Swegen. "Was my father in your hut?"

She had to repeat the question several times, using such English as she knew, before they understood. To her irritation, they merely looked frightened. The more she pressed, the more they retreated. Yes, they admitted finally, the *hlaford* was to their holding and rested awhile and then left. That was all.

Not all by any means, but they'd pushed daring to the limits in telling Eustace of the root cellar. They feared vengeance, the more sharply since Calla loomed in their doorway, gaunt as the son she sought, and stalled two horses in their byre that would be hard to explain. They could not risk more. They hurried away after the others.

"Ralph," Gerlaine turned at her door, "the letter must go as soon as couriers can ride. Not every baron in Northumbria was loyal as Eustace. They hear we're lordless, they'll be on us like crows. Thérèse, I am tired. Bring me broth in my closet. Messires, I will be at hand if needed."

Gerlaine poured some of the broth for Bête in his corner by the fire, then sat while Thérèse unwound her veil. She had not plaited, Thérèse noticed, merely caught up the auburn mass in clasps. She removed them and shook out the thickness of it. *Maîtresse* had not given much attention to her hair for some days. It was full of snarls.

"Brush me, Thérèse."

She worked the brush through Gerlaine's hair. It was darker now for the long lack of sunlight.

"You are well, *Maîtresse?*"

"I suppose so," the girl sipped at her broth. "I feel tired all the time." She touched her cheek. "Give me my mirror."

She gave it her attention for a long time. The mirror showed tiny crow's-feet beneath tired eyes, the hard line of the mouth. She put the mirror down.

"One hears that a lined face is a sign of character." She tried to laugh, but it emerged tight and tremulous. "My God, Thérèse."

Her shoulders shook silently. Thérèse felt them heave under her soothing hands, then be gathered tightly and controlled by the girl's will. She suddenly raised her head, listening.

"There, you hear?"

Thérèse heard nothing. "It is very quiet."

"Yes," Gerlaine said finally. "That's it. The wind is gone."

She went to the casement, pushed open the shutter and listened again. "You can't hear a thing."

Just a low, distant whine barely above the threshold of audibility. The sky was closing in, leaden.

"Fetch my mantle."

The air had a peculiar smell as she stepped out onto the parapet and saw the guard at the battlements watching it come, already obscuring the estuary, a dark mass moving like

Doomsday in toward the land. Even as she stood there, the insistent whine had risen a pitch. A tongue of the coming wind licked about her, bringing the first hint of the snow—dry, half ice and hard as rye kernels. Gerlaine crossed quickly to the west battlement, seeing the tiny figures floundering through the snow—Swegen, Plowwright and the others. One ant-figure pointed east at the coming storm, and they bobbed on faster than before.

She bent far out to the few people moving in the bailey below: "You down there! It's coming. *Attend!*"

They gaped up at her.

"Light fires in the barn and stable and set a fire watch. Keep them going. The stock mustn't freeze. Shut every casement. Stuff them up with rags, blankets, whatever you've got."

She hurried back to the steps. With something to be done, she felt more herself. "Soldier, are there riders outside the wall?"

"No, lady. The steward said not with the storm coming."

Thank God for that. Gerlaine was already flying down the steps. *We don't need men out now. If I freeze, Gurth, so do you.*

The shrieking gale drove the snow horizontally before it. Passage across the bailey became a struggle. Thick trousers under her kirtle, draped in the hide smock fashioned after Calla's, face smeared with pork grease, Gerlaine fought from one place to another, seeing to the stock, the fire watch, the chinking of windows, herding women and children into the hall. Shifts must be organized to watch the peat fires in the barn and stable. With Ralph and Bête, Gerlaine trudged from cookshack to scullery and back, nagging at Hugo and Jehan, organizing a supper of sorts for everyone from the soldiers on watch to the frightened women huddled around Vaudan who swore they heard demon voices under the wind. At ten, with the snow drifting deep in the bailey and no weakening of the gale, she called in the suffering tower guards. Watch was pointless tonight; they could freeze solid in that boreal wind.

She collapsed across her bed at midnight, too tired to undress or even taste the joint of chicken which Thérèse, frayed as herself, insisted she eat. She lay propped against the headboard, chewing mechanically, washing the meat down with turnip gin. The liquor numbed through her. Her eyelids drooped and closed. If she would sleep, best blow out the candle. *In a minute,* she promised, already drifting. *One moment and I'll get up and blow it out.*

Something woke her. She jolted out of drugged sleep. The cup was still in her hand. The candle had guttered and gone out. The fire on the hearth was merely embers and the room cold. The wind still shrieked beyond her rag-stuffed casement, but under it now there was urgent shouting from many throats. Footsteps tattooed up the stairs to her door, then a hammering fist: *"Maîtresse, c'est Thérèse.* Fire! Fire in the stable!"

Gerlaine yanked open the heavy door, almost tripping over Bête.

"How did it start?"

"I don't know. The men were watching, then—*zut!*—all the hay in flames. Come, *maîtresse,"* she urged. "The men are out with buckets."

"The horses?"

Thérèse looked helpless. "Getting them out now, but the stable—they can do nothing. The wind is too strong."

Gerlaine took the stairs two at a time, plunging through servants, dragging them with her. "Everyone to the stable. Bring buckets."

As she ran down the keep steps, she could already see tongues of flame glinting through the timbers of the ancient stable. Men ran, horses screamed their terror as they were led blindfolded from the red-glowing entrance.

"Form a line!" Gerlaine shouted. "To the well. Buckets."

Wrathfully she came down on the first of the fire guard to cross her path. "How did this start? I swear I'll have you flayed!"

"No, *maîtresse."* The man was bewildered and terrified. "I was watching." He lied, frightened in his guilt. It was cold; he had drowsed by the peat fire but only for a moment. He thought he remembered the stable door creak behind him, thinking it was his relief. Then the hiss and crackle of the burning hay, the first panicked whinnying of the horses.

"The barn is going!"

Gerlaine ran from one place to the other, filling the line where there was a gap, passing the futile buckets to the impossible need. The gale wind sucked the flame in its wake, hurling galaxies of sparks into the darkness overhead. The bailey glowed with false day as they fought hopelessly to save the buildings, dragging out the bellowing cattle, Gerlaine herself leading sheep, struggling with whatever she could lift, whatever could be saved.

"The grain!" Her throat was raw with shouted orders and smoke. "Save the grain and seed."

A frenzy possessed her. With Thérèse, Audrée and a few men, she hauled at the vital sacks of feed, returning repeatedly to the burning barn until Ralph held her back.

"Let me go!"

"The roof is going. Stay back."

She twisted furiously. "Let me go, God damn you!"

The roof collapsed with a crackling rush and roar. They fell back before the fiery shower.

The barn and stable were gone. She wrenched her churning mind to decision. "Ralph, use my father's bower for the stock. The scullery too, if you have to. Anywhere you can squeeze them in." She rubbed a hand across the greasy soot on her cheeks. "You men! Keep those buckets coming, don't let it spread."

But the flame had crept across to the thatching of the steward's hut. The wind drove flame with demonic force, faster than the frantic buckets could stem. Gerlaine heaved sluices of icy water, hands raw in the wind, already freezing as she settled into a grim rhythm. Thérèse pulled at her suddenly; Gerlaine saw the doom already in the woman's eyes as she pointed.

"The hall!"

Oh, God, no, Gerlaine heaved the buckets mechanically. *We'll freeze.*

Père Vaudan hurried out of the darkness, a child squalling in his arms. Behind him she saw the dark figures scurrying from the keep.

"Where did it catch?" Gerlaine bawled at him. "Can we stop it?"

Vaudan was grim. "No," he said. "It is the cellar. The gin and wine sacks."

"That's impossible. They're below ground. They couldn't catch."

"They didn't," Vaudan said. "The fire had to be started."

There was no time for any thought now but survival.

"The church, Vaudan. It's windward, it can't catch. Tell the women and children. Come, Thérèse."

Gerlaine commandeered two men to work the bridge winch, then ran clumsily through the drifted snow toward the keep. Thick smoke poured from the timbers near ground level, but men and women still hurried back and forth, carrying food, bedding, whatever could be salvaged. A cloak-huddled stream of them filled the bailey bridge, the men bestowing women and infants, leading cattle and returning for more. Already the growing roar from the keep rumbled under the wind. Its bowels awash with flammable liquor, once the flame reached the scullery level and the hungry wind, the keep would burn like a soaked torch.

"Out!" Gerlaine herded them toward the scullery door, coughing with the smoke in her lungs. "There's no more to save. Get to the church."

Beneath her feet the warping floorboards were turning hot.

Thérèse hurried down from the hall with an armload of Gerlaine's clothes.

"Are you the last, Thérèse? Get to the church."

"La Bête," Thérèse jerked her head up the stairs. "He's up there. He won't come. None of us can make him."

Gerlaine mounted two of the stairs. Bête loomed above her. She had forgotten him completely. He must be terrified not knowing what to do, not trusting anyone but her in his fear.

"Bête, come."

He stared at her from the top of the stairs.

"Bête!"

Gerlaine heard the telltale rush under the floor. Seeking air, the flame below sent an exploratory shoot through the widening fissures in the scullery floor.

"He'll come if I coax. Go, Thérèse," she pushed her toward the entrance. "No fear, I'll bring him. To the church."

She started up the stairs, but he retreated. The beginnings of fear licked about Gerlaine's throat. The fire might seal them off if they didn't hurry. They'd have to jump from one of the casements. But she would not go without him.

"Damn, Bête—come!"

Gray worms of smoke sifted through the floorboards of the hall. Bête stood near one of the trestle tables. He allowed her to come closer now, apparently frightened or confused. There was only that odd sadness as his hands lifted to stroke her stained face and throat.

Light, swift footsteps bounded up the stairs. They mustn't come back for her. She could bring Bête—

"Gerlaine!"

She whirled at the sound of his voice. The smoke rising thicker behind him, Gurth stood at the head of the steps.

Her lips went back in a predatory snarl. "You."

He advanced cautiously. "She's mine, Bête."

The big mute pushed Gerlaine aside and started forward. Gurth drew his knife.

"Mine," he repeated. "It was a promise."

Gerlaine crouched to attack. "Bête!" She threw her girdle knife to him. "Kill!"

He caught it deftly and went on guard as Gurth edged toward him. "Get out of the way, Bête. Don't be a lunatic."

"Kill him!" The blood rage exploded in Gerlaine. She couldn't wait for Bête to do it. She ran to the hearth, caught up a heavy length of oak kindling and hurled herself, flailing, at Gurth, not caring what happened so long as they could finish him. He warded off the blow and thrust her aside, but the motion left him open as Bête's knife jabbed up, piercing deep into the muscle of his side, just under the ribs.

Gurth fell back holding his side as Gerlaine came screaming at him again with her club, but Bête caught her wrist and warned her silently away. Once more he bore down on Gurth, and Gerlaine saw how surely the once-crippled legs moved under him, cat-silent with controlled muscle. He jabbed and slashed upwards again. Gurth faded aside like a shadow, feinting at Bête's knife hand. As Bête recoiled, the feint snapped into a speed-blurred slash that creased shallowly across Bête's brow. Bête wiped desperately at the blood running into his eyes, as Gurth sprang at Gerlaine, tore the club from her hands and brought it down on Bête's head.

"Fool," he gasped. "Blind, stupid fool!"

Gurth was badly hurt. The club dropped from his hand as Bête slumped to his knees. Gerlaine dove for the dropped knife and came up at Gurth. Sigrid screamed in her, strode in her blood-spattered mail behind her eyes as she closed with Gurth, driving the knife into his shoulder.

He managed to pull it free and grabbed her wrist, trying to drag her toward the stairs, but she clawed and kicked at him.

"Gerlaine," he choked weakly, "listen to me—"

She went totally mad, clubbing at him with berserk power. Weakened, Gurth hardly tried to defend himself, but his grip loosened on her arm and Gerlaine put all her force into the shove that tumbled him heavily down the stairs into the smoke and flame of the burning scullery.

He would die. He was losing blood with every step. She picked up her knife and sheathed it. Bête would get him in the bailey or on the moor if he managed to get across the bridge. She and Bête, no one else. Gerlaine grinned tightly at the thought as she tugged at Bête.

"We'll kill him, Bête. You and me."

Dazed, he followed her hand down the stairs into the smoke. The scullery floor was a lake of flame. Gerlaine fought for one chestful of good air and pulled him forward.

"Now—run!"

Gurth snatched up the heavy fur cloak where he had dropped it near the entrance and lurched across the fire-lit bailey toward the bridge, mingling with the herd of people streaming toward the church. The knife wounds burned, but once across the bridge he broke into a stumbling run toward the south plateau, labored up the grade, swaying on his feet as he searched the shrieking darkness for his horse. There was a buzzing in his head loud as the gale. Twice the solid ground tipped up to meet him when it shouldn't before he grasped the bridle of the blanket-wrapped horse. He hung onto the pommel, hauled himself astride and turned west before the cutting wind.

Herding horses into the bower, Bertin was unprepared for the small fury that descended upon him masked with grease and soot, lit with more than the bailey fires.

"Saddle these last two!" Gerlaine ordered. "*Vite!*"

Vaudan was shepherding the last of the women and children toward the bridge as the two riders galloped across the bailey and reined up by him.

"*Maîtresse*, you ride?"

"You're right; the fires were set," Gerlaine croaked out of her smoke-rawed throat. "Bastard. We caught him this time. He won't get far."

Vaudan caught at her bridle. "You can't go out there tonight."

But she shouldered the horse into him, pushing him off his feet. "Take care of my people, Vaudan. See my letter reaches the king."

"You're mad, girl! Take men at least."

"There's no time," Gerlaine was already moving. "And this is mine."

Mine from the beginning, from the loving through the end. Mine alone.

"God with you, Père Vaudan."

She kneed the horse forward, Bête following. They wound around the human traffic, wheeling to find the tracks already drifting with snow.

"There!" She pointed to the staggering trail and dismounted, seeing the dark spots against the snow. *He can't travel fast bleeding like that. Go to ground, Gurth. It's over.*

She pushed the floundering horse through the snow. They gained the plateau, found the confusion of human tracks and hoofprints. The trail ran due west, fresher now, less drifted. They were closing. She read the track; the horse seemed to be barely managed, wandering left and right of its direction. Now and then she saw the dark stains near the hoofprints that showed what the ride was costing him. A trembling took her, a rage deep inside where Gurth had always been—in love, in hate, fermenting in her soul beyond confession or repentance. In the cold place where Sigrid walked in her red shirt to take her due. Her eyes burned; she was crying. It seemed strange to cry now. She wiped clumsily at the tears, but the sob could be held back no longer.

"Bastard!" The wind snatched at the cry, carrying it beyond her into the darkness as she whipped the horse faster. "Bastard, where are you?"

The gray divided into light and dark. He'd drifted again, crumpled over the big horse's neck. Painfully Gurth forced himself erect to see where he was. Calla's hut should be close —*no, I'm past it and didn't even know. Can't drift again. I'll freeze if I don't bleed to death.*

He recognized the first signs. No feeling at all now, where he'd been terribly cold before. Only a need to sleep. He snapped his head up. *Christ, I am freezing.*

He tried to move his legs, but they were dead weight. The

lightness took him again. Gurth fought it, but suddenly there was no up or down. He barely felt himself fall forward, hands grasping feebly at the horse's neck.

"Calla!"

Too far, she'll never hear.

And then that answer pursuing him down the wind—faint but coming on as his grip went limp and Gurth slid out of the saddle. He tried to stand, hanging onto the saddle, but it was too high, too far.

"Bastard, where are you?"

She was closer now, but it didn't matter. The gray was falling again. His legs wouldn't obey. He lost his weak grip on the saddle, fumbled to rise and then lay still.

The snow began to cover him.

She cried aloud to see the standing horse and the figure lying in the snow. She leaped from the saddle, knife already drawn, floundered to claw at his shoulder and heave him over on his back.

"It's me, Gurth! I'm here."

His head moved weakly. She saw the blood on the snow. Bête rode up and dismounted, standing like silent doom in back of her.

Gerlaine raised the knife. It did not come down. *Please,* she prayed to a faceless god, *please make me able to do it.*

"Gerlaine." He was trying to rise. "It's not—"

She screamed and dove flat at him, lying over him, their faces close together. She closed her eyes, both hands trembling on the knife as she pressed the point against his throat.

"—not *me*, Gerlaine."

Why did that coward hand wait? "God!" she wailed, "let me!"

But it was not God or Mary in her blood-rimmed vision. God had horns. God was in chains, the only deity she could think of now, the only one mad enough to rule in this mad world.

"Loki! Loki, make me able! I will give him to you. I will make sacrifice of him. Let me!"

"You're already promised to him," Bête said.

She froze at the new voice. Bête stood over her, looping a knot into a short length of rawhide.

She understood. She knew but her brain would not accept it

as Bête lifted her to him and she saw for the last time that strange sadness flicker in his eyes.

"Your turn, Gerlaine."

The knife was torn from her fingers. Gerlaine was spun about as Gurth tried to stagger to his feet. "Not her. Not Gerlaine. You promised."

Bête lashed out viciously, clubbing the weakened man into the snow. The cord tightened around Gerlaine's throat. She fought for one more breath.

"Bête . . ."

The cord strangled off the name and all of the world she knew. With the last consciousness, she heard the whisper at her ear:

"Brand, my love."

Calla found them, searching for Gurth, following the voices carried on the wind: the son and the girl already half buried by the driven snow, and Bête huddled on his knees between them, sobbing into his hands.

They were alive.

"Hoch, Brand Brandson."

He looked up to her; huge hands gripped convulsively at hers. "I can't, Calla. God damn her, I can't!"

"You need not." Calla lifted Gerlaine like a sick child. "It's over."

"It's not," he shuddered. "I'm lost, Calla. Bring me home."

"Where are you?"

"I don't know. Help me."

"Come," she urged. "Help your brother."

VIII

Light and shadow from the peat fire danced over the earthen walls of the root cellar. Gurth lay propped against the wall, his arm cushioning Gerlaine's bare head as Calla washed and bandaged him.

"She'll come round," Calla grunted. "Tough as oak." She nodded at the girl with some admiration. "Greased herself and made skins: turning into a proper Saxon."

It was enough, weak as he was, to touch the small, soot-streaked face. "That's a woman, Calla."

Above them, the storm still moaned, though the main force of the gale had blown itself out. In the furthest corner the other shape was like a bas-relief against the wall, head bowed over heavy arms.

Gurth bathed the girl's face lightly with a piece of rag. "She's waking."

Gerlaine stirred, hands clawing at her throat. Her breath rattled; the small breast heaved spasmodically.

"Gerlaine."

She opened her eyes to Gurth bending over her. She clawed at her girdle for the missing knife. She saw Corn-Woman and cringed away to the protection that had always been there.

"Bête!"

And remembered. There was no Bête. He was someone

else, someone never seen before. Stranger's eyes lifted at her voice, a stranger's face stared at her over an impassable gulf.

Gurth reached to her; she flattened like a trapped animal against the dirt wall. "Get away from me!"

But he was saying her name, whispering her name as he had that day a thousand years ago in the forest, before the scars on his back and all that followed. Saying her name as if he loved the sound of it.

"Gerlaine, no one will hurt you. It's over."

He followed the horrified line of her sight. "Yes, he killed them all. He thought he had to kill you, too. But he couldn't." Gurth looked at Brand with vast compassion. "He loves you."

"Loves me . . ." Her body vibrated with it silently, then the hysterical laughter emerged, a patter of dry, mirthless sounds. It was insane, that word. There was no love anywhere, no sanity, not even God. She would have screamed with it but Gurth dammed the flow with his hand over her mouth. Silenced, her eyes still blazed with the lunacy.

"Be still," he told her. "Listen and learn. It was his right, Gerlaine."

When she quieted, Gurth went on. "The *wergild:* de Mowbray was my duty, your father had his. Try—" He winced as pain shot through his side and shoulder. "Try to find a villain. There are none."

Still she was drawn by that other presence across the fire. "Who . . . who are you?"

She got no answer; so still he might have been dead.

"Can he hear me?"

"A kind of hearing," said Calla. "Hush now."

She crouched by the big man. Soft crooning sounds rolled from her throat. Time passed and the low fire threw less light. The two figures across the cellar became mere shadows. Gurth was quiet. Gerlaine allowed herself to look at him, to see Gurth, where for so long there had only been Bastard: dirty and too thin like herself. Her flayed mind picked up facts one at a time, too exhausted to connect anything.

"It wasn't you," she said dully.

"No."

They lay together against the wall, silent for a time.

"I've hated you," Gerlaine murmured. "And it was all him." His hand closed over hers. "I know."

"I prayed to Loki to kill you. We almost did. You're weak as a child."

"I'm bled clean," he said. "Calla has herbs. It won't fester." He lifted his head toward Bête. "He's the one we must save."

"Why? Who is he?"

"My salvation," Gurth grimaced with pain. "My enemy. He kept me away when I would have come for you. I thought the storm would cover me tonight. I was coming when I saw the fire."

The hardness began to fade; her face looked softer in the dim light. "You stayed for me?"

"Yes, I—" Gurth appeared to think on the answer. "I was tired of not having anything of my own."

"You're thin. You look older."

His finger traced the hard line of her mouth. "So do you."

She rested her head against the wall. "Who is he, Gurth?"

"My half brother Brand," he said. "The Loki-child of Brandeshal. We must be quiet now. Corn-Woman is with him. He's been lost for so long. We have to bring him home. Watch with me. You'll see. You'll know."

The magic could not be explained. To Gerlaine or any born Christian it was demon work, yet Calla had only the haziest idea of the Christ-Man of Jerusalem and even less of Satan. She knew the secrets of the earth and sky and how to heal, how to take one out of time. Gurth never knew how she did it, though Calla said once that all men hated the passing of time toward death. In some way they were always trying to stop the sand in the glass. When they submitted to her will and floated free on her soft-singing magic, it was because, in their secret hearts, they wanted to go back.

Four years Brand had crawled in a nightmare, unable to speak, without even the thoughts that could understand or form words. He only half awakened the night Gurth slew de Mowbray; from then on he could reason, calculate with just enough light to illuminate the single mission of his vengeance. It became his reason for living, the spine of his being. Finished, it still would not leave him. More than a fever of the brain, his soul still shrank back into the dark, bound like Loki, unable to escape.

Calla whispered to him, "Brand, can you hear me?"

Where are we?

"Inside you, beyond you, out of time. I will go with you."
It's dark.
"Remember."
Can't.
"There be snow on the ground. The Normans are coming."
No . . . please.
"The Normans, Brand. De Neuville is here."
De Neuville. William's ambitious little dog. Born in a stable and yearning for the hall. Any hall. Ours. Let me stay, Father.
The new voice rang through the cellar—resonant, timbred like Gurth's.
"Let me stay, Father. Send a servant. Let me fight."
"Where are we, Brand?"
Riding to your hut. Father sends an extra horse. You're to ride north with me. But the horse broke its leg in a hole.
"I know," Calla murmured over him. "There's only one horse."
Take it and ride, Calla. They'll never catch me. Father says God bless you.
"The gods ride with you, Brand."
He fell on his side, panting. "Soldiers!"
Not Aimeré's, not regulars but the scum of Normandy. They trot after me, taking their time. They're laughing. They don't know who I am. They think I'm a farmer, but it's all the same, they'll kill me. Can't run anymore.
His legs churned helplessly.
Trampling my legs. The ugly little man drawing his sword. I can see it coming. No—
A ghost of agony stabbed through him. He wailed his death cry, head buried futilely in his arms, then was still.
Barely breathing, Gerlaine clutched at the ivory cross on her breast. It was very still in the root cellar.
"Brand." Calla bent over him. She called many times, but he lay as if dead. "He's gone."
"Where?" Gerlaine whispered, frightened.
"Back into the dark," said Gurth. "Don't talk."
Time crawled by. The giant body began to shudder. He hugged himself tight in a fetal ball. Then the eyes opened and he rolled over on his stomach, heaving up onto his arms, dragging useless legs toward the peat fire. Shuddering as the hands wiped at his head and face. Slack-mouthed and vacant.

"Where are we now?"

Don't know.

Void, thoughtless, wordless, nameless. Chaos before the forming of a terrible new world. Strange people who uttered rapid, incomprehensible sounds. One face becomes familiar, less frightening.

Little Red.

An infant locked in the present, a series of unrelated pictures gliding past his eye without yesterday or tomorrow or even the words to frame them. He ate, slept, was warm. He tried to catch the sounds that fell on his ear.

Bête.

That was him, and there was another word to come and one to ride, and always Little Red was there with food or to wash him. The sounds began to leave their residue on the blank surface of his mind.

I—

Je—

I am called—

Je m'appelle . . . Bête.

More swiftly now the fragments pieced together as images. Little Red. The hall. Many people. Tall man in a red cloak.

"Father's mantle!"

He reared on his knees. "Don't hurt her, Gurth. Don't hurt her, I'll kill you!"

Gerlaine prayed silently, understanding some of it at last through the broken jumble of Frank and Saxon. *Holy Mary, he is my enemy. I must hate him for what he's done . . . for what has been done . . . what someone—help me, Mary.*

"NO!"

Again the cry tore out of him as she heard it on that mad night in the hall. She felt sick, remembering. Was it possible for Corn-Woman to so move him back and forward across time, dragging him through days like so many musty rooms? She was frozen next to Gurth, paralyzed with primitive fear of the witch's power, and yet Calla herself seemed to be striving against a power so vast and formless that to call it Satan was meaningless. Caught between fear and compassion, she huddled closer to Gurth.

Calla?

"Aye, Brand?"

It's as if my eyes were opening after sleep in a room still dark, and I know what I've been straining for. I feel time, much time passed. Faces, words, thoughts again. I remember. I am Brand Brandson.

"Are you ready to come home?"

No, I can't. Mother—

Close to his ear, Calla frowned, puzzled. "Mother?"

No—no, I'm in the hall; it's quiet. They're all asleep except the one called Hugh. I lie by the hearth and watch him walk back and forth, getting drunk. And I remember him and his father as they ranged their troops before Brandeshal, and Father coming to me with the horses and the order to ride.

"No." The shaggy head wagged stubbornly, denying some new image, erasing as it struggled to form. *"No!"*

An hour I just lie there, remembering what has been and what must be. My brother is chained in the blacksmith's, and they—och, Calla, it's funny.

"They don't know who I am."

His clear laugh, so much like Gurth's, rolled through the cellar.

"Je suis Bête."

It's easy to move without making noise. I swing over their heads on the rafters like an ape. I cross the bailey to the smithy. The guard knows me and says hello, what am I doing out so late? He looks away—

The sledge-hammer fist thudded into the dirt.

The smith is a strong man. I have to strangle him, and the anger takes me, thinking of the whip he used on Gurth. I can't make any noise, so I put the howling into my hands and leave very little of him.

Gurth slid across the floor to him, holding out his wrists. "Free me, Brand."

I work the chain and bolt back and forth. The hole widens and lets go of the iron.

The brothers knelt together in front of Calla, holding each other's wrists. They whispered urgently.

"Their lives are my wergild, Gurth. They owe me."

"Not Gerlaine. Promise it. Not the girl."

"She's part of it. She goes with the others."

"Gerlaine's cared for you. You owe *her*."

"You want that bitch when her father killed ours?"

"Her father!" Gurth gripped his hands. "Not her. That's my bargain, Brand. While she lives they can look for me. The day she dies they're going to know. Promise!"

At Calla's sign, Gurth let go of him and faded back to the wall. The man who had been Bête hunched by the fire, a slight smile curling his lips.

"You promised," Calla prompted over his shoulder, "but what then?"

But now I have work to do. I strain like a dog to understand Gerlaine and the others. She helps me, saying words over and over, and I begin to learn. These people talk in their throats and make funny sounds with r's, but I learn enough to know what's happening. And once I'm ready, I take them each in his turn.

He stared into the fire and beyond it into more shadows. "Calla, bring me home."

"When you want it."

Please, I can't get out. It holds me like a chain.

I've never had a woman.

Leofwine said that would come in time, but time stopped for me. The sand froze in the glass, and when it flows again, Gerlaine is there. She brushes my hair and kisses me, and the touch of her makes me hurt. She washes me and touches my body. Every day I tell myself she'll be next. Every night I say, tomorrow she goes to Loki. And tomorrow comes, and I . . . lie awake outside her door.

She takes the pleasure from vengeance!

There's Robin dead and me laughing with the ease of it, and she comes and says "Hold me." I want to tear her apart and scream I hate you . . . I hate you!

I love you.

She's better than all of them. They hurt her because of Gurth, but she sticks and walks alone with me, talking me out of loneliness, hoping I'll understand a little, and I want to speak. One day I have to.

I close the door to her closet and watch while she sleeps, bargaining with myself. Maybe Loki could forget. Maybe I can leave her. She wakes and smiles at me. There's a big knot in my chest and I'm crying, please, oh please, I've got to tell her now. Just this once I want to be a man with her, not a pet dog.

And I tell her.

*But then I'm sorry. Angry. What am I to her but her thing?
In her love, even in her hate, she turns to Gurth. Even when I
was a dog, I could hear the change in her voice when she spoke
to him or of him, see it in her eyes when she looked his way.
My clerkly brother. My da's bastard, and it's a knife in my guts
—please, Calla, bring me home. I'm ready. Why do you hold
me here?*

"You don't want to come, Brand. You're hiding."

"No." The huge hands knotted, drumming in the dirt. The
sightless eyes stared wildly around the root cellar, trying to
open and see, wake out of the fever dream four years long.

"Is it the girl?"

"No."

"Brand," she crouched by him, taking his face in her hands.
"You lie to me. You fight the magic. Whatever is hidden, you
must go where it is buried."

Afraid.

"I be with you," she laced her brown fingers in his. "Where
do we go?"

He shook his head.

She could not spare him now. "Where?"

"No."

"Is Brand's son a coward? Is he unworthy of the Loki-
sword?"

"We . . . we go . . ."

His eyes screwed tight, the last ounce of will prying at the
final locked door that held in spite of him against Corn-
Woman's magic.

To the church. I slip through the door.

I take the iron from Loki's chain, carry it to the forge.

Calla's expression changed. "Brand, where are we?"

*At the forge. I beat the iron and the sparks fly up toward the
cross—*

No. He winced, cringed away—*where she is working on her
silly altar cloth, I come behind her. She sees me, puzzled that
Gerlaine is not here, too.*

Où est ma fille?

*I let my tongue loll out in a stupid grin, like a dog too dumb
to scratch fleas. The sword has taken my brains. I'm harmless.
When she tells Gerlaine she is going to the church, why should
they worry if I hear? I'm like a chair, like a wall. A dead*

thing, but—there—when Hugh jokes with Robin about eating at night, and I know where to find him when it's time; there when he tells Gerlaine that Guy is alone in the stable; in the church when Aimeré chooses Fitz for the riding party, and I know when and where to find him and take his place. Always there. I hear everything.

And so I let Gerlaine bathe me and then, when she's busy with her women I use the fog to cross the bridge to the church.

"Walking . . . toward the cross." He knelt in front of Calla, his hands beating slowly but with rising fury against the dirt.

She turns back to her work. I look up at the cross—Calla, let go, please, I beg you.

"No, Brand."

Corn-Woman held him, relentless. "You be not in the church. You lie, Brand!"

No!

"Look at it, Brand. See it. I am with you, and I see no church."

I—

"Not—in—the—church!" Calla seized his wrists. "You be home. Home, where the Normans have burned everything but the cross. *See* it!"

With a shriek the last door tore open.

"MOTHER—"

Mother . . . Algive . . . nailed up there. I see her and know I'm mad. They took her down, but you could still see the mark of the spikes and the blood. And she is there. And she—

"—comes down off the cross, like the Christ-Man, with the wounds in her hands and stomach—"

—and helps me forge the sword, whispering in my ear while I hammer and hammer—

"Your turn, Élène."

The beating fists became a purposeful pantomime, ghost hammer battering down, ghost nail driving in.

"Hang there like she did, you bitch."

The cries filled the root cellar.

"Mother, come back. Come back . . ."

Gradually the hands stopped beating and lay limp on his knees. A deep even breath swelled his chest. His eyes opened. He gazed into the fire as if he really saw it now, brushing the hair from his eyes. By degrees he grew more aware of the others, of time and place. He clasped his hands around his knees, seeing the last picture in the peat fire.

"My birthday was late September. That year—'66 it was—I was fourteen and already tall as Leofwine, and King Harold came north gathering levies against his brother Tostig. The sky was deep blue and red in the west the evening he came to Brandeshal. Father held his horse, and after Leofwine knelt to him, Algive pushed me forward, shy as I was, and said, *This is my lord's namesake, fourteen today.* And the king put his hand on my head as I kneeled. A big man he was, already sad with the look of kings, and himself crowned less than a year. He gave me the kiss of peace and chose me to serve him at board that night, and I stood tall as I could behind his chair, filling his glass while he and Father talked of Normans and things I couldn't understand.

"It didn't matter. The torches were bright, my big brother Leofwine looked handsome in his robes and Mother sat like a queen with Maud and their women. The harper never played so well before, and of a sudden my chest got so full of the joy of it, I started to cry. And when the feasting was done, I went outside to Loki's altar, the music and the laughter drifting after me out of the hall, and it seemed—it seemed I could hear them all, all the *bear-sarks* from old Brand on down, singing with them, singing in the earth. The land, the hall and I were like one just then. When Leofwine found me, I was crying with the love of it, and I hugged him and wanted to shout, *Was there ever a place like Brandeshal, Brother? Was there ever a time like ours?*

"But it was foolish. I kept it inside, and we just stood there grinning at each other, and the air smelled of apples and autumn . . ."

IX

Brand left the root cellar before dawn. When first daylight washed the east, they heard his returning call. Calla, Gurth and Gerlaine climbed out, squinting against the whiteness.

Brand had brought the horses from Swegen's byre. He spoke little to them, tying a sack of provisions to his saddle. His movements were measured and purposeful.

"Where will you go, Brand?" Gurth asked him.

The placid blue eyes regarded him. "Why should I go anywhere?"

"More Normans will come. Ride north with us."

"I'll be here like my father was. We own this place."

Gurth might have answered with common sense but dismissed it forever. Brand was no madder than he, but an older way was part of him. When the Brands, the Herewards and the Godrics were no longer there to meet the Normans, something would be past, never to come again except in songs. Gurth put his arms around his brother.

"Goodbye, my brother."

"Take your women and go," Brand murmured gruffly against his cheek. "Best luck, Brother."

He led the horse to Calla and embraced her. "Freya be in your hand, Corn-Woman. Thank you for bringing me home."

"Madman. Thick as your da." She held him close then

straightened the cloak over his big shoulders. "Don't kill all the
Normans. Leave a few that the wee king be not lonely. You
should have been my own like Gurth."

"Sometimes I was."

"*Och*, that's past and gone. Only spring comes again, boy,
and that's enough. Farewell."

The big man twisted the reins around his hand, unsure for a
moment. Then he moved to Gerlaine. "You needn't wish me
luck, I'll understand. But you were kind. You took care of me,
and I loved you for that. Will you say goodbye, Gerlaine?"

She found when the moment came that she could neither
hate nor love nor say goodbye that easily. Try to find a villain,
Gurth said. He was two people, her Bête and a stranger, an
equal who asked no forgiveness.

"I'm sorry it was your family," he said. "I'm sorry it was
you. But you're new and ignorant in an old place. Go with
Gurth and learn from him. Try to understand some day."

"You can't fight any more. Go away from Montford. I'll
have to hunt you down."

Brand lifted her like a child in his arms. "If you can find
me." He kissed her smudged cheek and set her down with a last
hug, then mounted and turned the horse west. In a few minutes
the forest covered him.

"They'll be stirring at the keep," Gerlaine said. "You and
Calla should go."

"Not without you." Gurth shook his head. "You come with
me."

"No."

Gurth moved to her, urgent. "You belong to me, Gerlaine.
My God, haven't we earned each other?"

"Twice over, my love. But I have to go back."

"To what? To be a king's ward, tossed into the bargain when
he throws a bone to some vavasor?"

"I told you, Son," Calla chuckled. "Her back's straight and
nothing soft about her."

And so, at the end, they faced each other across the snow
and across a larger distance, and Gerlaine looked very much
like her father. "I told the king I'd hold this place until
relieved. God knows, there's little enough left, but there are
the people and I am their lord, and there is duty. Go to
Holywood."

"The hell I will." Gurth caught her in his arms. "Not without you."

"Gurth, how can you understand it so well in your brother and not in me? It will be months before Willian sends another lord, and what till then? What of Swegen and Gunhild and Plowwright and the others? They need a lord. Without a lord any armed band could sweep away what's left. They'd be Normans—aye, we have our own scum too, and I'd hang them just as quickly. I must stay."

"I could tie you on your horse and take you."

"They wouldn't like that." Gerlaine pointed east across the white moor where the tiny riders floundered along the faint remains of her track. Her arms went around Gurth's neck. "Yes, you're my husband. I chose it as well as you. That will never change."

"Hurry, Son," Calla mounted. "We'll not have much of a start on them."

"Go quickly." Gerlaine pulled his face down to hers. For both of them it was no less than that first day in the forest.

"What we started," Gurth marveled softly into her hair. "Lady, what we've started."

"More than you know. Hurry: if they catch you, you're just a runaway serf."

"Serf?" Gurth grinned suddenly with the truth of it. "You're more bound to the land than I ever was."

"Of course. I am lord. I'll buy what I can and steal what I have to. I'll patch the bailey and put up the hall, keep my folk alive through the winter and plant in the spring. You won't shake me off, Gurth. I'm here to stay. We Normans never gave anything back. Get used to that."

"And we English never gave anything up."

"It's still England, my love. Just better managed."

"Not anything ever," Gurth mounted, laughing and meaning it. "Not a right, not a dream. Not even you, wife. I'll find you."

Calla gazed around at the country that bred her. "All gone. All gone now." Her arm swept out to Gerlaine. "The gods send you luck, girl. Tell William he's won this far and he can choke on it. But let him not trust his luck north of the Wall."

Gurth called once more as they moved toward the forest. "I'll find you, Gerlaine."

She watched them ride, smiling a little to herself. *I'll find you, you stubborn English bastard. Spring and Scotland aren't so far, and I can hold what's mine.*

She walked the horse toward the searchers. In a few minutes they caught sight of her and pushed on faster through the drifted snow. With a rush of warmth, Gerlaine recognized Père Vaudan among them. Dear old Vaudan. She must never lose him.

Gerlaine turned in the saddle to see Gurth and Calla slip into the forest. As she rode on, she found her mind revolving out of habit on practical problems of *now*. She wondered how much of the bailey and keep were left. They'd have to cut rations and live in the church while building again. She'd be working from dawn to dusk; everything must be organized down to the last egg and grain of barley.

Dear husband, I can hold what's mine.

No, she wouldn't write to the king just yet. He'd find a working fief on Tees, but as to being a Crown ward, he could whistle for her.

More Bestsellers from Berkley
The books you've been hearing about and want to read

___ **THE BEVERLY HILLS DIET**   05299-0—$3.50
    Judy Mazel

___ **CHILDREN OF DUNE**   06173-6—$2.95
    Frank Herbert

___ **FAT IS A FEMINIST ISSUE**   05544-2—$2.95
    Susie Orbach

___ **DUNE**   05471-3—$2.95
    Frank Herbert

___ **DUNE MESSIAH**   06174-4—$2.95
    Frank Herbert

___ **THE FIRST DEADLY SIN**   05604-X—$3.75
    Lawrence Sanders

___ **THE TENTH COMMANDMENT**   06257-0—$3.95
    Lawrence Sanders

___ **PROMISES**   05502-7—$3.25
    Charlotte Vale Allen

___ **HOBGOBLIN**   05380-6—$3.50
    John Coyne

___ **THE SECOND DEADLY SIN**   05992-8—$3.75
    Lawrence Sanders

___ **THE SIXTH COMMANDMENT**   05943-X—$3.75
    Lawrence Sanders

Available at your local bookstore or return this form to:

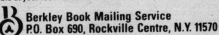

Berkley Book Mailing Service
P.O. Box 690, Rockville Centre, N.Y. 11570

Please send me the titles checked above. I enclose _____.
Include 75¢ for postage and handling if one book is ordered; 50¢ per book for two to five. If six or more are ordered, postage is free. California, Illinois, New York and Tennessee residents please add sales tax.

NAME _____

ADDRESS _____

CITY _____ **STATE/ZIP** _____

Allow six weeks for delivery.

85 D